THE SERPENT'S ROOT

AN UNCIVIL WAR 5

M. J. Logue

Rosemary Tree Press
TRURO, CORNWALL

Copyright © 2016 by M. J Logue.

All rights reserved. No part of this publication may be reproduced, distributed or transmitted in any form or by any means, including photocopying, recording, or other electronic or mechanical methods, without the prior written permission of the publisher, except in the case of brief quotations embodied in critical reviews and certain other noncommercial uses permitted by copyright law.

Publisher's Note: This is a work of fiction. Names, characters, places, and incidents are a product of the author's imagination. Locales and public names are sometimes used for atmospheric purposes. Any resemblance to actual people, living or dead, or to businesses, companies, events, institutions, or locales is completely coincidental.

The Serpent's Root/ M. J. Logue. -- 1st ed.

Dedication

To my boys, the big one and the little one, who put up with a great deal of metaphorical time-travel.

The Goodwives of the Apocalypse, without whom one Hollie Babbitt would never have drawn breath.

And distinctly not for Aubrey, the feline Philistine, without whose assistance this book would have been completed considerably sooner.

Rejoice not thou, whole Palestina, because the rod of him that smote thee is broken: for out of the serpent's root shall come forth a cockatrice, and his fruit shall be a fiery flying serpent.

—ISAIAH 14:29

M.J. LOGUE

AN UNCIVIL WAR

IN CHRONOLOGICAL ORDER

Red Horse (1642)

Command the Raven (1643)

The Smoke of Her Burning (1644)

Babylon's Downfall (1644)

A Wilderness of Sin (1645)

The Serpent's Root (1646)

FOREWORD

I started writing the Uncivil Wars series because I was very tired of that persistent myth that the King's supporters were all cultured, handsome, dashing gentlemen in feathery hats, and all Parliament's were sour-faced craggy old coves porting Bibles.

Both sides hired mercenary officers, at the beginning of the Civil Wars. Both sides fielded men - and women - of honour, fire, and principle. Both sides carried out appalling acts of cruelty against their opponents - and amazing acts of kindness.

It was, as the Parliamentarian commander William Waller wrote in a letter to his dear friend the Royalist commander Ralph Hopton, a war without an enemy, and there was no moral high ground.

To my noble friend Sir Ralph Hopton at Wells

Sir

The experience I have of your worth and the happiness I have enjoyed in your friendship are wounding considerations when I look at this present distance between us. Certainly my affection to you is so unchangeable that hostility itself cannot violate my friendship, but I must be true wherein the cause I serve. That great God, which is the searcher of my heart, knows with what a sad sense I go about this service, and with what a perfect hatred I detest this war without an enemy but I look upon it as an Opus Domini and that is enough to silence all passion in me. The God of peace in his good time will send us peace. In the meantime, we are upon the stage and must act those parts that are assigned to us in this tragedy. Let us do so in a way of honour and without personal animosities.

Whatever the outcome I will never willingly relinquish the title of
    Your most affectionate friend,
    William Waller

Rosie, Hapless, Luce, Cullis, Toogood, Venning - they're all fictional. You will not find their names in any dispatches from seventeenth century battlefields.

You will find men like them, though. On both sides of the field.

1. AS SURE AS MY PERSEVERANCE

Lostwithiel, Cornwall
1644

The river stones hurt his cheek and his ribs but he knew it was that or drown, lying with his nose and mouth just clear of the rushing water and the screams of fury of plain country men and women who wanted to kill him, ringing about his ears.

Kenelm Toogood did not move. Dared not move, in truth, even when the body of the girl who'd shared his mate's blankets last night drifted past him, her cap gone and her loose hair swirling like weed in the river Fowey.

There was a fist-sized bloody bruise on her cheek and her eyes and her mouth were open, drowned refuse brushing her white skin. Her head bumped against his hip, bobbing lewdly against him, and he heard laughter from the bridge again - shouts, and catcalls, and further missiles, thrown idly into the water. Their intent was to mock, not to hurt. He was dead, after all. What further hurt could they give him, other than shame as bitter as gall?

He was a Callington boy. He was born and brought up not twenty miles from this place. His father farmed there. His wife, his little girl -

Not any more, they didn't. His father was dead, their beasts looted and slaughtered to provision the Earl of Essex's army, or driven off. His wife dead of a fever, through the privations of being a rebel's woman, that none would give aid to for her having chosen a poor husband, and their daughter taken into fostering by her good Malignant family -

He had no more reason to love the Earl of Essex than any of these men and women on the bridge, and yet how could he love the King any better? For all the talk of protecting their independence, and keeping Cornwall free, all he could think was that if you'd believe that you'd believe anything. He was a Cornishman, bred in the bone. The King was an Englishman, like all the English, bent on stripping Cornwall of its independence and its pride. He remembered - his family remembered, at least: spoke of, quietly, with fear - the Prayer Book Rebellions, a hundred years ago. When the King - a different king, the same king, all the bloody same - had tried to force his version of the Word of God on the Cornish people. Had murdered good Cornish men in the name of imposing his will on the people, for wanting to be who they were. For not wanting to be English.

Put not your trust in princes. Well, seemed like there was a lot of men who wanted to run with the hare and hunt with the hounds, here.

He didn't trust the Parliament, neither, but at least the men who spoke for Cornwall in Parliament were men with Western blood in their veins, men who knew the land.

It was a wonder the river Fowey did not run salt with his tears, for the Earl of Essex had failed them, failed them all.

Beaten. Imprisoned. Abused, by his own countrymen, for following as his own heart dictated - for not bowing his neck and submitting to an English yoke. Spat on, and starved.

Traitors, he called them, those greasy, fat burghers of Lostwithiel. Selling their birthright for their weight in tin, which the English paid for.

Essex couldn't have organised a fair-day market stall with any competency. But then he'd saved his own skin, hadn't he? Fled in a fishing boat from Fowey - there was a joke in that, somewhere - leaving the rags of his battered troops to face the wrath of the people. Well, the great and the good of the King's men had condescended to give them free passage so far as Plymouth: aye, and then turned a blind eye as the men and women in Lostwithiel screamed abuse and stripped them of their weapons, their clothes. Their pride. Kenelm wasn't the only man to be taken from the bridge by a thrown stone. Or the only woman.

Aye, Essex's army had stolen. Looted, was what they said. And some had done it for pleasure. Most had done it for the emptiness of their bellies, and the griping in their guts. Steal what, from most of these folk? A handful of black barley? Some bluish skim-milk?

(Essex had failed them.)

He couldn't remember the whore's name, and that made him shamed, somehow. That she was dead, drowned in a bitter spring flood with her head dinted in by a flung rock, and he did not even know who she was, or who her people were.

(She was a Parliamentarian whore. No more.)

Loveday Toogood was dead, his bright chattering dark-eyed maid, silenced forever, and that he had not been there to hold her hand at the last. Had been in the castle on the hill yonder, with his men, fighting for what he thought was the right thing.

Little Chesten was taken from him, and given into the care of the Carews to raise. And she had been two when last he saw her, not yet speaking in real words, but only happy chirping, constant, like a little bird. (Would she speak in words to him now, or would she turn her face away from a father who had left her behind in darkness and want?)

The water was dragging at the girl's feet, whirling her sluggishly away. Out to sea.

The cold was dragging at him, too.

There was a tear in his shirt, and his arm was growing numb with chill. They had been kind enough to leave him his linen. Better than they had served some of his comrades - bruised, dirty bare arses, famine-scrawny thighs smeared with flung dirt and their own filth, where they had soiled themselves in the sickness of starvation and scant rations. Scuttling like beaten beetles back across the Tamar.

They thought he was dead, and probably, did the mob on the bridge not disperse soon, back to their homes and their ease, he would be.

He closed his eyes, and tried not to twitch as another body splashed into the water nearby - a live one, a very live one, his white legs and arms flailing as he fell, squalling like a calf. They were laughing at him, from the bridge, and the boy hit the water with a freezing splash.

And then, God bless him and keep him, he stood up, shaking his wet hair out of his eyes, stark bollock naked, all his ribs showing, dirty, unshaven, probably lousy.

He stood up, and he gave them the most courteous, flourishing bow a man could conceive.

They cheered him, then, whoever he was. Kenelm would have cheered him, too, save that his teeth were chattering too much for him to make a sound. He was going to be all right, that lad. He'd made them laugh, even in contempt, and they'd let him go. To Plymouth, to safety. Providing he didn't die of the cold, or a fever, or simple starvation, between now and then.

Captain Kenelm Toogood would not let go, not on this side of the grave.

He could wait. They would grow tired of their sport, and go home, and he could come out of the water, and not die.

But one day, he would come back.

2. OUR DISTANCE FROM ALL THESE GLORIES

Essex
January 1646

His wife thought, even now, that Hollie hadn't meant what he said about going West again with the Army of Parliament in spring, and that annoyed him, a little.

Het had no right to be angry. She didn't understand, but that was good. If she had understood even a little bit of what it meant to be a soldier and a senior officer, with duties and responsibilities to the men under his command – things that you could not set aside lightly, no matter how much your wife sweethearted you, or how hard the rain pelted down against the windows of a raw January day - it would have meant he was an even worse bargain as a husband than he suspected he might be at times.

The thing was, Hollie Babbitt had been fighting in one war or another since he was sixteen years old, and that was – that was twenty years in February, actually, though he wasn't sure of the precise date. Het had given him Candlemas as a convenient day to mind it by, but there was no one living who would ever tell him different, not now, not since his father had died at the end of last year's campaigning.

(Candlemas. It wanted but a week to Candlemas. He wouldn't be at home for the day his wife had appointed at his birthday. Wasn't sure where he'd be, actually, but he would not be here. He did not think that was helping her temper.)

He was a colonel, and he had the misfortune to command possibly the most ragged and insubordinate troops of cavalry in the New Model Army. That suited him well, being possibly the most ragged and insubordinate officer in the New Model, but it didn't suit Het, not at all. She reckoned he'd done enough. Someone else's job, now, to follow the King to the far West Country and make sure he stayed beat. Hollie's lads had beat His Majesty hollow at Naseby, last summer, and they'd followed him into Dorset and down into Somerset and now they were chasing him right down into the West Country, and maybe then it would all be over, God willing, and he could come home.

And that was what she wanted, she wanted her husband home: she wanted a man, not a collection of cack-handed letters and flying visits when he was close enough to snatch a few days from his duties. She wanted someone to sit down at the table with her and talk of the day's happenings, and what might be done about the culvert in the river meadow that was blocked with leaves again, and what marvels their daughters had done that day. As if he might not want the same, though. Did she think he didn't get lonely, far off in a distant strange town, surrounded by strange faces and strange voices – that he might not long for a little comfort of his own?

"Are you fit, Luce?" he said wearily, and did not look at his wife. "Best make a move."

And Luce Pettitt, who had been a very unwanted junior officer at the beginning of the war and three years later was a very dear friend, sniffed and nodded mutely, since he had no voice to argue or otherwise. Was quite amiable about it, as he was quite amiable about most things, but was presently streaming with a cold and consequently strangely quiet.

"If my nephew ends by dying from an inflammation of the lungs," Het said, and her voice was vibrating with fury, "I will hold you wholly responsible, Holofernes."

"'M all right, Auntie Het," Luce croaked. "Truly."

"You should be in bed," she said, and he smiled and ducked his head and shrugged a little, aiming for his customary appearance of smooth elegance. Actually, looking at the lad, Hollie was inclined to agree with his wife, because Luce looked bloody awful, and that was not like him at all – you rarely saw that young man in linen that was anything other than clean and uncrumpled, let alone flushed and feverish and wiping his nose surreptitiously on his shirt sleeve. Hollie raised an eyebrow at his friend – you sure you're all right? – but Luce just nodded, a little ruefully, as if he wasn't but it was going to have to not matter.

"It's raining," Het said furiously. Which, since Hollie had spent the last three days knee-deep in rotten black leaves clearing that benighted bloody culvert, was no surprise to him.

"He'll not melt, lass, he's not made of sugar."

"I would speak to you before you leave, husband. *Privately.*"

"Now you're in trouble," Luce said, meaning it in humour, to lighten the air in that rain-streaked parlour, and she turned her head and glared up at him.

"Oh yes, Lucifer, he is in trouble. I think it shiftless – *irresponsible* – shamefully so, husband. You should be – yes, you should be ashamed. You take these boys - Holofernes, they are boys, both of them, look at them, they are barely – they are so young, still! What else do you expect them to give up in your service?"

"Oh, now," Luce started to say, though whether protesting the injustice of Het's attack or being described as barely out of short-coats, and then he shut up because Het in a temper was a fearsome thing.

"Oh, now, indeed! You are twenty-two years old, Lucifer! I remember you being born! Twenty-two, and a widower – aye, and married less than six months, and to a woman that his family had not even met, let alone – Lucifer, you should still be at your books, you should not be old enough to bury a wife!"

Luce looked down, then, and his mouth trembled a little, because she was right, when all was said and done. He was twenty-two, and he should not have had to bury a woman he loved. But he had, and it was done. It could not be undone. Gray was dead, and buried at Bristol, and in all probability he would never see her grave again, nor mark it.

Another thing that Het would never understand, thank God. Hollie's own first wife had died after too short a time, and he had not set eyes on the place where she was buried in twenty years, more than twenty years. It did not mean he had forgot her, nor ever would. Het had never left Essex in all her life, and if she wished to visit her first husband's marker, she could go to the side of his grave and say all the prayers she would. Hollie said his in his head. But he still said them. (Despite what they said in the New Model, disapprovingly, about his Independent ways, he still talked to his God, in his head. Maybe with a bit more familiarity than most – but he still did it.)

The lad was young. He'd get over it. Which sounded harsh, and he'd never say as much to Luce, but even now, even after six months, you could see him starting to uncurl, when he thought people weren't looking. "She is in the bosom of Christ," Luce said, which was a very proper thing to say, and he very carefully did not look at Hollie as he said it because they had both known Gray and the chances of that fierce, sweary, disrespectful, violent young termagant in breeches enjoying sweet repose in the arms of Jesus were very slight indeed.

Het's mouth tightened. "Indeed," she said tartly. (She knew about the breeches. She didn't know about the sweariness. Hollie wasn't sure that his wife's tolerance went so far as having a niece by marriage who had not only dressed and fought as a man, but might as well have been born one, in all other ways than her body.) "And Thankful?"

"Are we going, then?" Lieutenant Thankful Russell said from his place by the fire, clearly not having paid the least attention to the rest of the conversation, and Het inhaled sharply.

"That young man has given almost everything in your service, husband, including his very life!"

"But has gained his soul," Russell said, and gave Het one of those melting looks up from under his eyelashes that Hollie wasn't supposed to know about.

Though he didn't mind that Russell fancied himself in love with Het. Russell was twenty-one, a year younger than Luce, and till he'd come here to be pieced back together after the battle at Naseby last summer he had never known affection, or kindness, in his life. Het had made a fuss of him when he was hurt, and patted him on the head a bit, and fed him and made sure he was decent, and he'd done what most normal healthy young men do when a well set-up lass feeds them, and gone like an undermined wall.

It was calf-love, it was no more than that, and it didn't trouble Hollie, for all Russell was a good-looking lad, from the right side. It was just good to know that the lad was yet an ordinary young man with red blood in his veins. The war had all but broken him, not once, but twice - but he was still hot to go back and pick up the fight again. There were times when Hollie suspected his austere lieutenant had more balls than brains, and this was one of them. Of the two, he'd have rather left Russell than Luce, for all Russell's ardent languishing and eyelash-fluttering. Luce had lost his wife, but he was pretty much intact, personally. Russell had lost his beauty, his faith, his hope, and near as damn-it his life. He could only be so lucky, so many times.

But, the lieutenant was scrambling to his feet, so far as any man can scramble in boots and a stiff oxhide buffcoat, and tucking his hair behind his ears, and he had that old look of intent eagerness about him again. Head up and eyes bright and quivering, very slightly, like a leashed sight-hound, and Hollie might be in trouble with his wife but the sight of Russell panting to be at his duty again was a thing to lift the heart.

Because six months ago Russell had been blind, shot in the head at Naseby, and they had not known whether he might even see again, let alone if he might be one day be eager to resume his old position. "More or less, Hapless," he said, and the unmarked corner of the lad's mouth lifted – that was a new thing, too, that was Het's doing, the smile – at his old troop nickname.

"His name is Thankful," she said, in a choked little voice, " - he is not your *dog*, Holofernes!"

And she pushed him. She actually put a hand to Hollie's chest and she pushed him, out of her way, and she fled, and he could hear her sobbing as she went thumping up the stairs.

"Oh, bloody hell," Luce said. "What did we say?"

"It's me, brat. Nothing to do with you."

There was a chirrup from the doorway, and he turned, and there was his little daughter, escaped from her nurse, all warm and bunchy as a little rose. "Mama?" Thomazine said warily. Her eyes widened a little. "Daddy, where you going? Zee go too?" She looked at her two hand-tame officers. "Zee go with Apple," she said firmly. "Coat on, please, Apple."

Which, of course, undid Russell, because the child couldn't say Hapless but she could call him Apple and she did, whenever she wanted to wind him round her fat little fingers, and then he fled. Not quite sobbing, but close.

Which set Thomazine to howling, because whatever it was that had upset her adored Apple must needs upset her too, for if that lad put his face in the fire she would copy him.

And then next thing the little one would start up yowling, and that he absolutely could not bear. At least Thomazine howled in words, for the better part, and he could understand the cause of her distress, but his little one, the new one, she was but a few months old and her distress broke his heart for he could neither comfort her nor reason with her, and so he picked Thomazine up bodily and put her into Luce's arms though she kicked and struggled mightily.

"*You*," he said over his shoulder, "deal with *him*!"

And then he went thumping up the stairs after his wife.

"Henrietta." He knew it. The little one was yelling fit to burst, and that made him feel all hot and miserable inside. "Henrietta, open this door!"

"Go away!" she shouted back. "Why don't you just go – go on, you need to be moving, don't you?"

"Henrietta, will you –"

Oh, the hell with it, he could stand here on the landing exchanging temperamental unpleasantries with her and all the servants in the house hanging round with their ears flapping, or he could just put his shoulder to the bloody thing and yell, "Don't you shut me out of my own god-damned chamber, Doraty!"

The door came open with a jerk, and the impertinent little trull who was maid to his wife stood glowering at him in a crack of all of three inches wide. "Mistress Het is trying to settle that baby, colonel, so begging your pardon but she says if you're going to go, just go. And do it quiet, will 'ee?"

"You stand aside, girl, or I swear to God I'll pick you up and put you out of the bloody window!"

Over her shoulder he could see Het on the bed, with her bodice unlaced, holding a scarlet-faced, kicking infant to her breast. "Het, that child don't want nursing any more than I do –"

"And since when have you been an expert on raising my children, sir? Since you were barely here for the first two years of your eldest's life!"

"They're mine too –" He didn't do anything intemperate. He just took a step towards the door, and looked long and thoughtfully at the maid.

"Don't 'ee look at me like that!" she squawked – he hadn't thought he'd been looking like anything, but evidently he had not the sort of features the Lord had intended for reassurance – and Het's head came up.

She was scarlet-faced and teary, too, and that hurt, and that made him even less inclined to deal gently with this silly wench who was stood between him and a lass in need of comforting. "Get out of my bloody way, Doraty!"

Had not meant that the little nursemaid should be afraid of him – not really afraid, not suddenly-pale afraid, but she was, she whirled and went scampering away and he wondered if everybody in the bloody house was set at odds today. If it was something in the wind, or a thing they'd eaten –

"Het – Het, love –"

"I see," Het said shakily. "*I see.*"

"Aye! Well! I'm not sure that you do, Henrietta." Because Hollie Babbitt could be stiff too, even with the woman he loved best of any in the wide world. "I am not sure you quite -"

She tightened her lips, and her eyes slid sideways to the open door, where you could still hear Thomazine yowling downstairs and

Russell hiccupping woefully back at her, as the pair of them consoled each other ineffectually and Luce coughed like a consumptive round and about the party. "You would take them back," she said, and looked back at Hollie. "You would take those two boys back to your - your bloody war, Holofernes, and that's swearing. Can you not let them be? Just for a little?"

"Het, do we have to have this -"

"Yes! Because you won't listen!"

"Can't listen, lass! Why should them two be let off, simply because you have a care for them? Why should not Venning go home to his Alice, or - or any one of a hundred lads in a hundred companies, who has a home to go to? Just because you happen to know those two -"

"Because they have suffered enough, husband. What more can your cause take from them? I spent almost half a year putting Thankful back together, after your battle at Naseby, sir. He was blind, for - almost a whole summer, while you were away, do you know that? Did *you* sit with him when he wept in the night, and see to it that his collar was straight in the daylight? Or did you not think that it mattered, Holofernes? That he might be made unhappy - *unhappier* - if he thought people would know he was broken, and pity him?"

She held the squalling child tighter, and sobbed as if her heart was breaking. "Just go, since you are so set on it! *Go!*"

And he could do no else.

And, if she was so set on her wilful stubbornness, nor would he do else.

3. BE YE NOT AMONGST WINE-BIBBERS

Well, his head hurt, and he felt scratchy and irritable – and, truly, if she had not been so bloody awkward about it, he would have stayed another day, for it was bloody miserable out, and Luce was snorting into a sodden handkerchief like an old warhorse, and Russell was as teasy as a snake.

They'd ridden as far as Brentwood, near to London town, and it had took them the greater part of the day, and he had wanted to get further even in the foul weather for at this rate it would take them the better part of a bloody fortnight to rejoin the company so far as Devon. And that had pissed him off as well, because the last time he had set foot in Brentwood had been Longest Night, four years ago.

And by supper-time, on Longest Night, four years ago, he had been sitting across the table from the woman he was going to marry one day, with his supper in front of him.

This night, he'd just smacked his head on a low beam in the White Hart inn, which was dark and crowded and smelt of wet wool and stale bodies, and he had Russell glowering like one of the less forgiving archangels at one elbow and Luce huffing and snorting wetly at the other, and people parted like the Red Sea before them in case either contagion or temper was catching.

It was not comforting, and Hollie felt *distinctly* hard done-to. "Do you have rooms?" Luce said indistinctly, and the innkeeper looked at these three orphans of the storm, shrugged, and would have turned away and dismissed them.

Russell dropped his hand on the hilt of his sword very deliberately, so it rattled a little in its scabbard - a blade that was well-used, then - and grinned his most damaged grin. By candlelight, Thankful Russell and his scarred cheek could look very menacing indeed. "I think you do," he said, in his careful, accentless voice.

"We are not short of coin," Hollie added. And grinned a menacing grin of his own. It had been a while and a while since he had been cut loose in the company of men, especially men of like minds. These two years past, he had been a staid married man, and a senior officer in the service of Parliament, and not a scruffy, unshaven, unpredictable rebel. Not tonight. If that was how she wanted it. "Well, Hapless. Are you with me?"

"Oh, *yes*," Russell said with a fierce joy, and Hollie nodded. Oh aye, that lad was off the leash this night as well.

He leaned his elbow on the table top. It was damp, outside. The old ache of a badly-set wrist niggled him. He flexed his fingers thoughtfully. "So. We'll be wanting supper, then. And rooms –"

"Always happy to share," Luce added quickly.

"Planning to keep us out of trouble, Luce? Aye. Well. What rooms you have. If he cops for a lass, he's on his own."

"I will do no such –" Luce sputtered indignantly, and Russell looked disapproving.

"Indeed, I will not share a room with a man about the business of fornication –"

Hollie nodded. "Quite agree. Bloody noisy business, fornication, and I imagine having us two keeping score will proper put the lad off his stroke. Well. Me and you will stop down here then, Hapless, if there's but the one room. We'll do the drinking, and our gallant lover here can do the fornicating. Fair division of labour, gentlemen?"

4. DESOLATION CAME UPON THEE SUDDENLY

Hollie thought, afterwards, it was all Lucey's fault. Possibly the weather, but more likely, Luce.

See, they'd left Essex in the rain, and they'd ridden down the country in the rain, averaging ten miles a day in the slippy, sucking mud if they were lucky, and then that spavined nag of Russell's that had been an unwanted cavalry screw and all he could manage when he'd been blind, poor sod - well, it had gone arse over tip in the filthy roads near Andover, and come up dead lame. (So had Russell, for that matter, but his natural state of being of late was mottled black and blue, and he seemed not to mind it.)

So he'd left Hapless and Luce in a benighted sodden ditch six miles outside Andover in the pissing rain, taking it turn and turn about with Luce's Leo, who was not impressed by either the weather or the buggering about. Hollie had ridden on alone to the town to try and find - well, two things really, a dry place to sleep, and a replacement for that misbegotten four-legged liability. And the latter had been the easiest, because Andover was a Malignant commissariat station and no bloody Roundheads were going to be daft enough to come limping into a Royalist occupied town with forged papers, and try and sell them a decrepit Parliamentarian cavalry remount. Surely.

One of Hollie's oldest strategies was to do the thing that nobody else would be stupid enough to do. Nine times out of ten, it worked. He thought he could have held out for a few more shillings for the hobbling brute, but beggars couldn't be choosers. His own gangly Blossom was hardly first-rate horseflesh, and the quartermaster he'd approached to buy Russell's limping jade offered him eleven shillings, with the harness thrown in. He suspected the bloody animal was like to end up in the pot, rather than in the horse-lines, so he took the silver and tried to look grateful. It was enough to find them food and lodging for the night, and a little bit over to go towards a replacement, and Hollie found them rooms - bloody cheap, squalid, bug-bite rooms, but dry - and he took his boots off and spread his wet cloak over the stool nearest the warm chimney-breast in the hope of drying it, and he lay on the bed and felt sorry for himself for a bit.

Cold, wet, lonely, and unhappy, and he gave an experimental little cough to see if he might be coming down with an inflammation of the lungs, but he wasn't. He settled himself with his back against the wall and pulled out the copy of Master Bridge's improving moral tract that he'd been working his way through every time he wanted to make himself feel even more miserable than what he already was, and listened to other people having a good time downstairs. Women laughing - *whores* laughing, he wasn't daft, and for one brief heartbeat of madness he considered whether he might himself go and spend a bit of his hard-earned back pay on the company of a woman who bloody *wanted* him there, even if it was only for the contents of his purse. To be with a lass who thought he was good company, and not a shame and a disappointment -

Aye. Well. He was away from- from White Notley. *"For thou hast trusted in thy wickedness: thou hast said, None seeth me. Thy wisdom and thy knowledge, it hath perverted thee; and thou hast said in thine heart, I am, and none else beside me,"* he said aloud, and pulled a wry face. He knew what happened next in the Book of Isaiah - should do, he knew the books of the Old Testament verse by verse, and the marks on his back from his father's hand to make sure the words stayed put. Evil was what happened next. Desolation came upon thee suddenly, which thou shalt know.

Well, bloody desolation had been coming on him for the last week, if he was honest - desolation, and more bloody chilblains, and a wrist that was aching near enough all the time, now.

Best cure for desolation and neglect, he reckoned, was a hot pie. Two hot pies.

Bollocks to it, they were three young - all right, not-old - well set-up lads, they needed their feeding, *three* hot pies, and roast meat, if he could get it.

Sausages, if he couldn't. His mouth watered at the prospect of a nice plump hot sausage, all speckled about with herbs and tingling with spice, with pepper and cloves, the country way -

He was going to end up lay here all night thinking of Het- of his wife's cooking, and the other two would starve did he not get up off his backside and see to it that they were provisioned. And he clapped his wet hat back on, and swathed himself in his cloak again, and prepared to do battle with the bakers and pie-shops of Andover town.

He marketed like a goodwife, and a bloody fond one at that, thinking on what his lads would like rather than what would be good for them - hot mutton pies, for those two would be half-frozen when they come in on a night like this, with nothing in their bellies since breakfast. A new loaf and a great wedge of cheese and some little cakes, that he sweethearted the baker's wife into wrapping in a napkin for it grew late and they'd not keep till the morning, surely.

He was not so daft that he didn't know he was fretting for their company, either. He feared for them, as it grew later and darker, and the rain carried on sluicing down. Could not bear his own company, in all honesty, for alone with the contents of his head he started to misdoubt what he might have said and done, that last afternoon in

White Notley. If he might have said, or done, a thing better, that they might not have parted so. That he might not see her again, if things did not go as he would hope, in the West. And that her last words to him might have been in anger, and he might never have a chance to hear them unsaid.

It was nearing curfew, by the time they came limping up the stairs. Russell was gone beyond speaking, but just sat down on his pallet with a thump and sat shaking, his teeth chattering with cold, till Hollie went downstairs and had a jug of ale warmed for them. Even then the lieutenant could barely unset his jaw to drink, but just sat nursing the hot mug against his scarred cheek. He was filthy, and bruised, and shivering, but he was all right.

Luce, poor bugger, was *not* all right. He was fevered, and Het had known it when they set off. Arguing that he did not want anything to eat, because his throat hurt when he swallowed, but he would be fine in the morning -

At which Hollie had loomed over him, narrow-eyed, and told him he would eat, and he would eat what was set in front of him, or they would hold him down and spoon it into his head like a babe, for a man who stopped eating in sickness was a man who faded and died faster than grass in a fire. (He didn't mention that last. But Hollie had seen enough fever to know that a man who couldn't face his meat was sick indeed.) And because he was an obliging brat, and possessed of a strong sense of self-preservation, he did as he was bid and poked his stew about in its bowl, giving the appearance of appetite. Which did not fool Hollie for an instant, but it was a polite little fiction. Enough went into his mouth that he would survive a few more hours, even if it was cold enough by the time he set his spoon down that the stew - which hadn't been that appetising hot - had congealed to a sort of lumpy grey jelly.

"May I now go to bed?" Luce said, sounding like a forlorn child.

No girls, this night. No drinking, then, from the other members of the party. And that was fine, because it was growing to be a thing that neither of them enjoyed, but something Russell did to keep Hollie company, and Hollie did not like to disappoint Russell, and neither of them wanted to be unmanly enough to admit that to be honest, they'd rather have an early night in a comfortable bed. (They wouldn't get one here. The blankets smelt of horse, and if the pallet didn't have fleas he'd count it a miracle, but at least the room had a whole roof on it.)

Luce looked like the one who needed the bed most of all, though, so Hollie waved a hand as if he didn't much mind, and the brat's eyes dropped with a fervent gratitude.

They were all living a lie, Hollie thought ruefully. All three of them pretending one to another that everything was fine and that they were all happy, eager to be back at the war, and in truth - what?

He didn't know what was waiting for them in the West Country, not now, not after a month away while the rest of the lads were at winter quarters.

He'd left his lads sick and on scant rations, in Drew Venning's competent Fenland care. Hollie had gone home with gratitude, for he had had a place to go to, and he'd told himself that Venning would do right by them, and that it was most important that he should see Luce and Russell cared for -

Did not know if that was true, or if he had run home from the endless, constant politicking, from the half-raw rations and the New Disease that had everyone with their guts turned to bloody water, from the flat, wet, grey endless winter landscape of Somerset.

From being tired, all the time. From death, and not knowing whose face would be missing from muster next.

His father, dead of the plague in Bristol - not with an understanding between them, for Hollie had never understood the old bastard's stiff Old Testament morality, and Lije had never understood Hollie's habit of never taking an order without question, even from God. But it had been a sympathy, then, the very first, faintest sympathy - of Hollie admiring the old bastard's unyielding adherence to his faith and his duty, though it cost him all. And for the first time in thirty-six years, of the old bastard approving of his boy.

Would've been nice if his father had had chance to say he was *sorry*, though. And now he never bloody would, and that was about all Hollie had ever wanted to hear from Lije.

Gray. Tell himself as much as he would that Gray would never have settled as a respectable Mistress Pettitt, and that her death was a brave soldier's death and what she would have wanted, he didn't believe it. What Gray would have wanted was *not to be dead.* To be still brawling and cursing and holding Luce's hand under the table when she was drunk enough that she thought nobody could tell, the daft little maid. All those bloody faces. They thought he didn't remember, or didn't care, because he didn't spend half his time ostentatiously poking God to mind their immortal souls, the way some of the other senior officers did. Praying and mopping and mowing all over the bloody place, as if they thought God had nowt better to do but listen to their mewlings. As if they were not part of a bigger thing than the care of this man or that one.

Ah, Christ, there were times when he sounded like bloody Russell, who'd been dragged up even more puritanical than Hollie had, and who was still prone under strain to turning zealous.

Russell, who was currently hunched under his wet cloak in a heap on the floor, with his teeth chattering audibly from this side of the garret. With a sigh, Hollie sat up, and dumped his own cloak over his shivering lieutenant. "Can do without *both* of you buggers catching your death of cold," he said.

5. A CHEERFUL HEART IS GOOD MEDICINE

Luce snored – very dignified little snores they were, no louder than the purring of a cat or the ticking of a clock, but he did, and it grated on Hollie's nerves something dreadful. And Russell talked in his sleep, whole bloody one-sided conversations that no matter how much you tried not to you always had half an ear to. Hollie tried to tell himself he didn't mind that so much, because the poor bugger spent his days being cold and austere and saying not a lot, but as soon as his head touched the pillow everything that he'd wanted to say for the last twelve hours came rattling out, all jumbled up.

But you couldn't call it quiet and restful, sharing rooms with them two. Downstairs half the Malignant population of Hampshire was whooping it up, noisily. The rain was still banging on the roof.

And Luce had stopped breathing.

Hollie sat up with a yelp of his own and shook the brat, and the lad came back to half-wakefulness, choking and thrashing frantically -

"*Lucey!*"

Coughing up great gobs of the thick phlegm that was blocking his lungs, wheezing, the breath whistling in his chest – Jesus Christ, how had Hollie not *known* how badly the lad was ailing?

And the poor lad was frightened, that was the worst of it. He was shivering with fright, his chest heaving, and his misty eyes were enormous and wild in his thin face as he fought for breath. Flinging himself about in the bed till the ropes creaked to try and find the right position that he could breathe easy, and it was almost a thing of panic now, like a horse with a twisted gut that must needs lie down and kick at its own belly to ease its pain. Hollie knelt at the side of the bed, trying to settle the lad back, piling his pillows so that he might sit upright and breathe.

There was a mocking little voice in the back of his head saying that he was acting most fatherly, for a man a hundred and more miles distant from his own babies, and he told it sternly to fuck off and die.

Russell sat up on his pallet, blinking stupidly at the pair of them. "What's amiss?" he mumbled, scrubbed his hands through his hair so it stood out most comically, and staggered to his feet dragging his blankets with him. "'S all right, Pettitt. Not much use," he added enigmatically, and dumped the blankets over Luce's body. Then he tied the loose hair out of his eyes and gave Hollie a lopsided grin. "Thom'zine. Seen her so. Sat up with her, too. Light?"

And he didn't know if Russell meant that it was almost dawn, or whether he intended that they should be able to see what they were doing, but Hollie sat on the floor with flint and steel and he wrestled to light a taper with hands that shook, for the sake of doing something usefully. And tried not to feel jealous that he had not been there, those nights when his little girl had been poorly in the night and needing him, and that marred, erratic Russell was more her father than he was.

Luce was just coughing now, miserably and painfully, taking great whooping breaths as his chest eased. Not so frightened, now that he had company, though it wasn't easy. Shivering still, under Russell's blankets and his own, but little thin shivers like a wet dog, and Hollie took the lad's hand in his own and squeezed it, trying to will some of his own warmth into his friend. "Be all right," Russell said, rearranging himself more comfortably against the chimney breast. "Not," he rubbed fiercely at his cheek till it eased, and went on more clearly,

"I am not going to sing to you, Pettitt. It would be neither to your consolation nor mine."

"He." Luce closed his eyes and panted, open-mouthed. "Used to sing to Zee. At home. When she was poorly."

"Bloody hell," Hollie said faintly, and Russell dropped his gaze in wry acknowledgement - he knew, then, what Hollie was thinking - and put his hand on Luce's foot through the blankets, absently, as if his mind was elsewhere.

"Het would say." And the scarred lieutenant looked up again, with a defiant spark in his eyes, as if Hollie might not care for the mention of his wife in another man's mouth. "Het would say, sage oil would ease his cough, and a mustard plaster to his chest."

"Bloody hell," Hollie said again. He couldn't help it. "Hapless, thee is more hand-tame to her than I am, and I'm married to the lass. Where the bloody hell am I supposed to get sage-oil from, then?"

"I imagine even Malignants have wives, sir," he said briskly. "Ask downstairs?"

"Not many wives. Down there," Luce wheezed, and he was still trying to be light-hearted even though his lungs sounded like someone was crumpling paper in his chest. There was something heartbreaking about that. "All *right,* Hollie. Not made of – glass."

No. No, he wasn't. He was made of flesh and blood, the poor little bastard, and frailer flesh and bone than they had suspected. He was sat up and bright-eyed but he was brighter-eyed than he should have been, and his hand, under Hollie's, was as hot and dry and fragile as a faggot of sticks on a bonfire. "Eh, lad," Hollie said gently, "there's no point us setting off in this bloody dirty weather, is there? We might as well stop a couple of days."

"Have we the coin?"

It was a reasonable question. The answer was no, of course. They had not the coin – they had sufficient for their immediate needs, but it wasn't enough, it was another hundred miles and maybe more till they rejoined Fairfax, and that was going to be a week's travel. If they were lucky. If Luce was fit. "Don't be bloody impertinent," he said coolly, "I'm a bloody colonel of horse, not an itinerant beggar."

Russell said nothing, but he looked at Luce, quite ostentatiously, and raised an eyebrow.

And that was also meant for no other reason than to make the brat laugh, which set him to coughing again, but at least he was smiling while he did it.

6. ...BUT A CRUSHED SPIRIT DRIES UP THE BONES

Luce went by fits and starts, for the next few days. One hour he would be sitting up by the fire downstairs, wheezing into a handkerchief and stinking of sage and mustard, like a joint ready for basting. Next he was flat on his back shivering under a pile of blankets and fighting for his breath again, while Hollie watched him helplessly and yelled at the serving-wenches for water and candles and blankets and a hundred other things that they neither wanted nor had coin for. Luce needed none of them, but it made Hollie feel better to do something, even if it was a useless thing.

The brat wasn't deathly ill. He was just wretched, and weak, and tearful when his feet were firmly set on the path to recovery, as though he had finally reached the end of the time when he could put a bright face on and be the same cheerful, uncomplicated boy he had always been. He lay with his face turned towards the wall and wanted to go home, for the most part. Was peevish and ungrateful, and would not wash, or comb his hair, or change his linen, but curled himself into a mute ball of resentment.

And it kept raining.

He needed decent feeding, and care, and – well, what the brat needed was loving, but you couldn't say so much to him. Luce was a lad who had always been made to give his affections careless and without thought, and now he knew how much it hurt. He was mending, and he didn't want to. He wanted to carry on feeling horrible, and being the most miserable man on God's earth. Oh aye, Hollie knew that feeling, and so did Russell. Both of them had done their time suffering, and they'd done it neither gracefully nor prettily. Affliction had not ennobled their spirits, nor brought them closer to God. (Job, with his patient travails, was a bloody fool, in Hollie's informed opinion.) If the brat had gone out of his way to find the two men who knew more about arsy self-pity than any other living, he'd couldn't have picked a better pair than Hollie and Russell, and that was no consolation either, for as Hollie knew all too well when a man is in that dark place he wants to believe himself the only man who has ever suffered so.

Luce needed to be back home in White Notley, tucked up in his bed with Het fussing and cooing over him, and that sensible wench from the next farm that he'd been keeping idle company with – sturdy, well set-up wench with good teeth and a lot of hair, though Hollie was damned if he could tell her one from another – her, anyway, trotting in and out telling him he was a brave soldier and feeding him little tempting savouries -

Babbitt, when thee takes to matchmaking thy junior officers, it is time for thee to resign thy commission and take up knitting.

They were almost out of money. Hollie did his poor best, and Russell was a fiercer bargainer than Het was, but even so. There was only so long you could make nothing, stretch. And he hardly liked to say as much, but they were quartered in a good Malignant town, and sooner or later, people were going to start asking questions.

Fairfax, for one, and Het, for another. (If she still cared.)

"You don't have to come, you know," he said awkwardly to the back of his friend's head. "You could go back. Essex, I mean. I – you could –"

The room went very still. Downstairs, one of the tavern wenches dropped something with a crash, and there was a flurry of abuse from the kitchen end. (It had broke, then.)

"I want to go home," Luce said dully, and turned his head on the pillow, though his eyes stayed closed. "I want to go home, Hollie."

"Aye, I thought –"

He was mending, and his hair was lank, sticking to his forehead with sticky sweat: bless the lad, there wouldn't be a girl in Hampshire who'd look at him twice, now, but he opened his eyes and looked up at Hollie.

"It's all right," he said, in that rusty, thready voice, strained with coughing. Closed his eyes again. "I'm sorry. I - she - I dreamed of her. Of Gray. It was nothing. The fever. I -" He trailed off, and under the blankets, his chest jerked, as if he might have sobbed. Only the once. "I almost believed it was real. That it - that she - that this was the dream, and she the reality. That I might wake and find myself at Bristol again, and be -. It was the fever. Nothing more."

"Just the fever. Aye. I know." And he wanted to do something reassuring, just a reaching out so that Luce might know that his lost girl might have faded like smoke, but that his friends were here, and real, and solid. But what comfort was that, when you had dreamed of a loss made whole again, and woke to find yourself in a lonely bed? Hollie put his hand on Luce's shoulder, and squeezed, gently. (The brat was a boy again, all skin and bone and tousled hair. That made Hollie's heart hurt, too, for the lad had no right to be so fragile.)

"Just the fever," Luce echoed. "Surely." And then he closed his eyes, and one single tear made its way from under his lashes, and slid down his face into his tangled hair. "It was a good dream, though. I wish -"

"No you don't," Hollie said, for that way lay madness.

"I miss her," he said, as if Hollie had not spoken, and his voice was as flat as ever, as if he were talking of a skipped meal, or a forgotten engagement. "All the time, I miss her. And I do not know how I might bear it."

And how could he answer that, without sounding as if Gray were a thing of no account? You get used to it? There will be other girls?

"Yes," he said, eventually, and hoped that was sufficient.

"She was not beautiful. I never counted her beautiful. But she was- alive, she was always so, so – she was never still, was she?" For the first time in weeks, another slow tear made its way from under his lashes, trickling into his hair, soaking the greasy pillow. "Hollie?"

"Aye?"

Luce covered his eyes with the back of his wrist. "How do you forget?" he said, in a tiny voice.

And all Hollie could say was, "You don't, Luce. You keep putting one foot in front of t'other. You don't forget. But you get used to it."

No consolation to think that after almost ten years there were still nights when he dreamed of Margriete, and still hurt to wake and find her gone. And that just for that first heartbeat, it hurt as much as it ever had. It did not get better.

"It will always hurt?" Luce said, and Hollie nodded, forgetting the lad had his eyes screwed tight shut.

"Like any scar, brat. It'll always hurt, if you're touched on it."

"Good," he said fiercely. "For – I c-cannot bear that she should not be here, Hollie, and yet I cannot bear to pretend she never was." And he sat up, quite forgetting that he was supposed to be on death's doorstep, with all his tangled dirty hair falling about his face, and he buried his face in his two hands and sobbed like a little boy, with no thought for his beauty or his dignity. "It hurts," he wailed, "it hurts, Hollie, it hurts!" Aye. Well. Luce had forgot his beauty and his dignity, but Hollie was reminded, suddenly, that he had a daughter. And that one day, as the sparks flew upwards, she would look to him to comfort her. It was thinking of Thomazine that he sat on the edge of the bed and put his arms round the brat, patting him gingerly on the shoulder as he wept.

"It'll all come good, Luce," he said, and closed his eyes and thought of Thomazine. "It'll all come good."

M.J. LOGUE

7 AS COALS ARE TO BURNING COALS

It took them less than a week, in the end, operating on pocket-lint and the sweetness of Hollie's temper.

Luce was on his feet, uncharacteristically pissed off - with *everything* - and uncharacteristically vocal about saying so. Russell had been provided with a decrepit brute at the end of its useful life that could only be persuaded out of a stagger with the aid of a stout stick, and he was pig-livid about it. And Hollie was tired, stiff, more or less perpetually hungry, and he couldn't take his eye off either of them for more than a minute lest Luce suffer a relapse or Russell an apoplexy -

And oh, God, without the prospect of a change of linen, and hot water, and being able to rid himself of a month's worth of itching bristles, he would have run stark mad.

It was near dark, and Luce was muttering darkly to himself, five yards behind, most of it incomprehensible but for the occasional explosive *"bloody"*. Tempting to tell him to shut up instead of loping along cursing and drawing the attention of every passing Malignant for thirty miles, but Hollie was pretty sure they'd passed their own perimeter pickets about a mile back. Not that he was suddenly going to start waving his hat over his head and asking to be escorted to Fairfax, lest he find himself escorted instead to Lord Hopton on the wrong side of the battle lines and having to answer some very awkward questions. But it felt like home turf. And Hollie had been around the block enough, himself, to know what home turf felt like, at war.

It had gone uncannily quiet, though, apart from Luce's eldritch mutterings. *Russell* was uncannily silent, but it was that sort of weather; the lad could not do else, in this damp, when his cheek seized. "Bed," Luce said firmly, and it was the first comprehensible statement he'd made since they'd left the hovel in Crediton, a day and a half since, where they'd managed to scrape together enough coin for a room.

Hollie turned in his saddle. He was knackered, but he was *never* too tired to bait Lucey Pettitt. "On your own, brat?" he said sweetly.

"Depends who'll have me, sir," Luce said, in that rather unnervingly gravelly voice that was all that remained of his illness.

He didn't mean it, of course. He was just saying it for saying's sake, and the old Luce would have said it thoughtfully and with intent, but he still said it, and Russell still sniffed with the same chaste disapproval as if it had still come from the old, cork-brained romantic brat, and it was almost like old times.

He could see camp-fires, now, here and there in the seeping mist. Proper warmed a man, that did, just the sight of those fires in the distance. Blossom raised his head wearily and whinnied into the darkness, greeting his old mates in the lines, and there was another neigh in response, almost in welcome, as if one of his mates had recognised his voice, for all he was only a horse -

"*Thomas,*" Russell breathed. It was a wise man who knew his own mount, and - as the decrepit knacker's-bait he'd been mounted on this last week stumbled again and nearly dropped the lieutenant over its head - a wise man who preferred the uncertain-tempered but reliable Doubting Thomas to a beast that had become uncharitably known as Dogmeat.

"State your business," a familiar voice said, and the sturdy, reassuring form of Captain Kenelm Toogood loomed up out of the dark. "Oh ha ha, very funny," Hollie said, with more cheerfulness than he'd felt in a month. "You know bloody well who it is. They don't grow many my size."

Toogood looked at him. Looked straight at him, without blinking. "Can't say as I know 'ee." And he never took his eyes off Hollie's face, not once, he just shifted his feet in the long grass and shifted his hand on the butt of his carbine so the pale, soggy moonlight that blew between the scudding clouds glinted on the barrel. The same breeze that shifted the clouds carried a whiff of saltpetre to Hollie's nostrils.

Lit match.

"You expecting trouble, Kenelm?" he said warily

"Expecting it? Ent *expecting* it. Sir. Been expecting *you* these three weeks and more. But you never come. Sir. Too busy at home, was you.... Sir?"

He heard the thump, and Dogmeat's relieved grunt as Russell dismounted, and the clink and swish as the scarred lieutenant stalked to Hollie's side.

(The snarling indrawn breath of a young man who was touchy on his honour at the best of times, and looking for an opportunity to haul off and belt someone at worst. But Toogood didn't know that.)

"Aye, I was, as it happens, captain. Brought the lieutenant back wi' me, ready to resume service, and -"

"Back in harness, are you? My *arse* are you, you god-damned fraud - aye, one of us when it suits you, when you want to play at soldiers, but I ent never seen you yet take an order from another like the rest of us has to!"

He wasn't expecting Toogood to suddenly lunge for him with the butt end of the carbine, and nor was Russell, but the scar-faced whelp had reflexes like a bloody cat and he pounced like one, as well. Kicked the legs right out from underneath Toogood and thank God, the blow that had been intended that Hollie might not sire further children caught him just on the bone of his hip, which hurt enough that he could not breathe, but when he went down gasping it was on top of the foul-tempered Cornish malcontent and giving as good as he got, and if that meant that Toogood had his carbine took off him and the butt end rammed into his unprotected belly, then that was just hard lines.

The Cornishman wrestled, and that was not good, for he kicked like a bloody baggage-mule, and he was as determined that Hollie should go down again as Hollie was determined he should not, and having Russell's weight in his back was slowing him down not at all. Despite the lieutenant's teeth sunk into his ear-lobe, and his arm about Toogood's throat so that the Cornishman's face was turning almost black in the moonlight, yet he would not go down. And there was a moment when Hollie was flat on his back, blinded by loose hair and being throttled by his own collar-band, with the blood thumping behind his eyes and fighting for every breath, and the next someone's knee caught him in the mouth so hard he felt his lip burst against his teeth, tasted blood, rolled free and piled back in wholly indiscriminately -

Russell fell against him, in a spatter of hot. (Might have been spittle. Might not.) On all fours, half-stunned and shaking his head, and then coming up again hissing like a pot boiling, and the thing with Russell was he got too mad to think and so it never crossed his mind that Toogood had a cocked carbine wavering at his midsection, so instead of belting Toogood Hollie belted Russell instead, elbow right in the pit of his belly, and the scarred lieutenant went down again whooping for breath, Toogood kicked him and he did not get up. That was the point where Hollie took the carbine off Toogood and assured him very calmly that did he not stop behaving like a prick Hollie would shove that carbine up his arse and pull the trigger.

Toogood didn't believe him, of course, and it was maybe that point when Hollie dumped the carbine and grabbed the Cornishman's jaw instead, shoving the man's head back till the bones creaked. Or maybe it was when Toogood had his fingers in Hollie's mouth and Hollie was biting down till he could taste someone bleeding, though if that was the Cornishman's own blood or Hollie's where Toogood's scrabbling fingernails tore at the inside of his cheek, he did not know.

Someone dug the toe of his boot into the fray, though, kicking the two of them apart like a pair of snarling dogs. "Captain Toogood, you will *cease* assaulting the colonel," Luce said crisply, and in case Toogood hadn't heard he kicked him a bit harder, for Hollie felt the man's body jerk atop him with the force of it. "Or I will put a pistol ball in your arse, sir!"

It was almost worth it, Hollie thought muzzily. It was almost worth being battered, throttled, and generally abused, just for the look of absolute indignation on Kenelm Toogood's face.

8. BREAD WHICH STRENGTHENETH MAN'S HEART

The dog lifted his head, barked sharply the once, and then put his head back on his paws having done his duty.

Drew Venning yawned. Barely dawn, and there was some wretch already wanting him. He could hear the clatter of hooves in the courtyard, a strident squeal from one of the horses, raised voices –

Raised voices.

Shit.

He sat up in bed, scrubbed both hands through his thick hair, made a mental note to keep his hat on and his coat buttoned to the collar the better to disguise tousled hair and a slept-in shirt. The sandy stubble, well, if it was Cromwell himself he'd have to put up with unshaven officers, it wasn't like Old Noll was that particular in his own grooming.

"Going to be a long day, bor," he said to his dog. He shoved his feet into his boots – Alice was going to have kittens when she saw the state of some of his stockings – and stood up, and Tinners got to his feet likewise, stretching and wagging his tail.

There was a heel of bread left from last night's supper, and something of a pie. He looked at Tinners. Tinners looked at him. "Come on, then, pup. Fair exchange is no robbery." He tossed the bread to Tinners, shoved the pie into his own mouth, and sloped off down the stairs with the dog at his heels.

He was an officer in the Army of Parliament, not a bloody housekeeper. And with Rosie Babbitt away, doing whatever nefarious deeds he was doing in Essex, it wasn't like anyone was going to give him grief for the state of his quarters. Bachelor quarters, at that, he thought gloomily, with his Alice at the far end of the country, and that lil' jasper of his growing up further every day –

"Shit," he said again, out loud this time, and the familiar, marred person of Lieutenant Hapless Russell gave him a coolly appraising glance from the parlour windowseat. "The temperacy of your language never fails to astonish me, Captain Venning," he said, without so much as a flicker of greeting.

And then, astonishingly, the cold and efficient Russell was on his feet, disregarding the saddlebag that slid out of his lap and hit the floor and scattered the contents: not sure what to do with himself, clearly, but wanting to do something human, which was a bloody first for Russell.

Venning put his hand out, expecting a formal handshake. Got, instead, two yards of distinctly travel-worn lieutenant, strongly redolent of horse and sweat, thumping him on the back somewhat awkwardly and peering at him as if he was some kind of divine miracle rather than a captain of horse who'd just been dragged untimely from his bed.

"Just got back," Russell muttered shyly, and Venning was still too shocked to speak, so he patted the scarred lieutenant's back in return and wondered what the hell they'd done to the lad in Essex. To have made him, well, almost ordinary. Scruffy as hell, ragged, but weren't they all, and that awful livid scar on his cheek stood out against the remains of a very healthy and ungentlemanlike outdoor tan. Not fat, he was built long and lean anyway, but all his bones didn't show through his skin any more. A lad who'd pass for normal, almost good-looking again, on a good day with a following wind – and he'd come back? To this? Out of *choice*?

On the other hand, Russell was sporting a black eye the colour and sheen of an over-ripe plum, and there was dried blood crusted all down his top lip. Possibly Essex had not been so kind to him, after all. Venning held the lieutenant at arm's length. "Hapless, bor, it's not that I ent glad to see you, but... not being funny, but... that bullet in the ear scrambled your wits, or suffen?"

"Not Hapless," he corrected. Smiling. Not a pretty sight – he smiled like Tinners, with most of his teeth showing on the one side and not the other – but it was a real, human smile, and that was new, too. "Not any more."

"You want us to start calling you, uh, *Thankful?*" Venning said warily. The lad might have been christened Thankful, but it wasn't a name that came easy to the tongue. Not with someone as, well, hapless as Hapless. That choice of nickname had not been coincidental.

"I am *not* calling him Thankful," Hollie Babbitt said from the doorway. "He's been Hapless for t'last three years, and Hapless he will remain."

"Het says," Russell began, and in two very abrupt strides the big redhead had crossed the room and was almost nose to nose with his lieutenant.

"Will you give over with the *Het says*! Christ! Bad enough I've spent the last week with you yammering down my ear, Het says this and Het says that – it's *me* that's married to her, Russell, I do know my wife's opinions!" He shook his head. "You are a soft lad at times. Hapless. Now bugger off to the kitchens, and see if you can't roust out summat close to breakfast." And then stopped, and grinned fiercely, looking even more ruffianly than ever. "Reckon as of about ten minutes ago you're back on duty, then, lad. No more mollycoddling. Fit as a bloody flea. You're not at home now, Russell, none of this idling about the place, go on!"

The scarred lieutenant's skewed grin widened. "Sir." And then he stopped in the doorway on his way out. "Apple. I *do* answer to Apple. In an informal capacity."

Hollie dropped into the chair by the window and eased his shoulders with a little murmur of sheer animal pleasure. "Ought not to sit down," he said, "I'll never get up. Been bumping across country since God-knows-when. You know what he is –" he jerked his head towards the door, "once he gets an idea in his daft head he has to do it now rightaway, and I've got bloody Lucey at my elbow quoting bloody Shakespeare at me. My arse is killing me. I am too old for this, Captain Venning. If it were done when it were done, 'twere better it were done quickly. The hell is that supposed to mean?"

"What?"

The old Babbitt was back, then. Definitely back. As arbitrary and casual as ever he was – and oh, bloody hell, Venning had missed the lollopin' gret mawkin, for all he did leave a trail of chaos in his wake. Even if he looked as badly done-to as Russell.

"Macbeth. So Lucey tells me. Place is still standing, I see?"

He shrugged. "Mostly. One or two bits o' mild villainy, but nawthen to report."

"Ward and Eliot?"

"The same. Incident involving a chicken and Captain Betterton's good shirt. The which has not been quite the same since, and what he is not best pleased about. Chickens," Venning mused gloomily, "they don't half shit a lot when they get fretful. D'reckon he won't get the stains out of it, nohow. Mind, our Alice, she do say, spreading smottered linen out under a full moon, that'll bring it up whiter 'n white –" he paused, and rubbed a hand across his bristly chin, "didn't put him in no better temper, though."

Hollie, who had been leaning his head against the back of the chair with an expression of idle contentment, sat upright, snorting. "Nowt changed in my absence, then!"

"Nawthen much.... where is our brat, anyway? He all right? You know, since –" Since Gray's death, he meant, and did not say. Hollie gave him a wry grin.

"Getting there. I left him unpacking his traps. His mother seems to be on a mission to provision the troop, so if Russell don't come good shortly, we might have to break into Lucey's boxes."

"But he's all right?"

"He wrote a quatrain last night," Hollie said meaningfully, and Drew nodded.

"Ah. Mending, then."

The old Thankful Russell would have had fresh bread and cheese and wedges of sizzling fat pork on the table by now. He'd have gone down into the kitchens and put the fear of God into the staff, and the maidservants would have been scuttling up in intimidated alacrity with breakfast. As it was, Luce was on his way down the stairs at much the same time as the new, mended Russell was ambling back up from the kitchens in his own sweet time, with a filched apple in one hand, in earnest and improving conversation with one of the maids. "Oh, well met, Thankful!"

"Hm?"

Luce leaned over the banisters and broke off a handful of bread. It was warm and fresh, if, distinctly, brown. "Starving," he said indistinctly. "I'm not used to going so long before breakfast."

The maid was looking from one to the other of them in some awe. They were both tall and fair and elegant, and you couldn't call either of them gorgeous, although one of them had been, and the other was oddly appealing. "Do leave the pattern on the plate,

Lucey," Russell said wryly. "If I'd known you were so under-nourished, I'd have asked them to roast you at least half an ox."

"Lieutenant Russell?"

"Yes, Cornet Pettitt?"

"Kiss my lily-white - bottom, Lieutenant Russell."

Russell blinked, opened his mouth to be affronted, and then broke out giggling instead.

"Will you two *grow up*," Hollie shouted from the parlour.

9. LITTLE BIRDS IN THEIR NESTS AGREE

Hollie's temper seemed to have improved, at any rate.
(Luce said, in a whisper, watching his commanding officer with his head down working his way industriously through his second plate of bread and cold bacon.)

"Mm," Russell said, and covered the bruised knuckles of his right hand with his relatively-unmarked left, and smiled to himself.

Luce sighed. It seemed that the scarred lieutenant had finally settled to his vocation. Russell must ever have a star to hitch his wagon to, and had Hollie ever wanted a hound of his own, it would seem that he now had one. And truly, Luce wondered if Russell cared more to be in the thick of the action than anyone had ever suspected, and although it gave the scarred lieutenant pleasure to set things in order, he took as much joy in a good brawl as any of them. "I imagine there will be hell to pay, and no pitch hot," Russell added thoughtfully. "When Sir Thomas finds out."

"Finds out what?" Venning said suspiciously.

"Oh, nothing of real import." (Russell was also a shockingly bad liar.)

"Lucey... *What* is Fairfax not going to find out?"

"It took us perhaps a little longer to return from Essex than otherwise it might," Luce said sweetly. "We took a somewhat circuitous route."

"You been off on the lash again, Hapless?"

"I? Not me."

Venning blinked, as the words percolated. "What – *him*?"

"Lil' bit," Hollie said cheerfully, looking up from his second breakfast. "It's all right, frog-fucker. All clean and sober now, aren't we, Hapless? Got it all out of our system."

Russell looked down at his bruised hand again, and his lips quivered. "Indeed, colonel. Some time around dawn this morning."

"Well the silly buggers shouldn't have challenged us! I mean, Christ... I'm two yards high and red as a fox, and there's no mistaking you, neither. Hell did they think we were? Stupid sods. Deserved all they got."

"What," he was at a loss for words, clearly, so he rubbed the dog's ears for a bit, "Rosie, what the hell have you two been up to? You been fighting again?"

"Well, really, captain, I should have thought that was perfectly self-evident. The colonel took exception to being challenged by our own troops, and expressed a reasonable amount of displeasure," Russell said primly.

"And Hapless piled in wi' me, because he's good like that," Hollie said. "When he's sober, he's not a bad lot."

"Thank you, sir."

"Oh aye, and then Luce said he was going to put a pistol ball in Toogood's arse if he didn't stop yammering –"

"Captain Toogood. Lucey, you said you were going to shoot Captain Toogood in the buttocks, if he didn't stop –"

"Yammering," Hollie said with satisfaction. "That boy was quacking like a frigging duck."

"You *had* just kicked him in the cods, sir."

"Just as well he's not as... *active* as our Lucey, then, isn't it?"

"He bloody ain't this morning, tell you that for free," Venning muttered, "poor lad's walking like he crapped hisself, Hollie! What'd 'ee do that for, to one of our own?"

"He was pissing me off," the redhead said simply. "He knew bloody well who I was, and he was trying to annoy me. And it worked."

"Hollie!"

"Oh, *he's* back, then, is he?"

It was a voice Luce knew, from the parlour doorway and he frowned for a minute, trying to place it.

"I might have known if there was rumour of a violent incident early this morning involving one of our sentries and a gentleman described only as 'that judas-haired bastard' – oh, it would have to be you, Babbitt."

They'd not set eyes on Charles D'Oyley in the better part of three years, not since Fairfax's first Yorkshire campaign. Hollie pushed his chair back and went to greet Fairfax's leathery orderly, grinning.

D'Oyley wasn't grinning. "It's not funny, colonel. Sir Thomas is spitting-mad."

"Oops," Russell said, not quite inaudibly, and D'Oyley glowered at him.

"I take it you find it amusing, lieutenant? Since you were implicated in the same insurrection, I should take the smile off your face, boy. I should not be surprised if the pair of you don't come out of this interview as plain troopers!"

"What interview?" Hollie said, suddenly wary.

"Your carpeting, gentlemen. Not so cocky now, are we? And I would recommend, assuming that you *do* wish to keep your commission, that the pair of you smarten yourselves up, because as officers you are both a disgrace to the Army!"

Very carefully, Luce crossed his legs under the table and gave the bridling Russell a sharp dig in the shin, and a meaningful look.

"Sorry, sir," Luce said meekly.

"Why are *you* sorry, cornet? So far as I know you were nowhere near that disgusting brawl!"

"Nowhere near at all," Hollie said, and Russell batted his eyelashes and added, "No, he was in bed, I believe –"

"On his own," Hollie added, and Luce gave a great sigh and said, "No I wasn't. I was with these two. I very much fear it was me that drew the pistol on Captain Toogood."

D'Oyley inhaled through his nose.

"Sweet Christ, Babbitt, you have been back less than a day and already you seem to have had a pernicious influence on what was previously a well-organised company. Well done. Well done, sir. We have no need of an enemy, with you back."

10. THE DAY OF THEIR CALAMITY IS NEAR

It was not a comfortable interview, although it was brief and to the point.

Fairfax on his mettle did not mince his words. Hollie knew better, and to deliberately lead two junior officers, at the beginning of their careers, astray was both shameful and reprehensible.

"I'll not have it, colonel," Fairfax said, perfectly amiably. "Sit."

"Well, aye, but what —"

"Sit!" the Commander-in-Chief of the Army roared at him, and Hollie was so surprised he sat, suddenly, on a chair that was not intended for two and a bit yards of startled officer. "*And* you two!"

"But there *is* nowhere —" Russell began primly, and Hollie had the suspicion that if Fairfax had been within belting distance he would have leaned across the table and given the scarred lieutenant a good one round the ear-hole just for the joy of it. As it was, he took a deep breath and went a little bit white about the mouth, and said, "Then sit on the floor, lieutenant. This is going to take some while, gentleman, and I would not see you — inconvenienced."

Luce sat tailor-wise on the floor with his back against the wall and his hands folded in his lap, looking like a somewhat bedraggled schoolboy. Russell said he preferred to stand, and managed to make it appear as a personal affront.

"Since you have seen fit to grace us with your presence," Fairfax said grimly, "may I be permitted to apprise you gentlemen of one or two developments?"

It wasn't so much that the war had shifted so much in the favour of either King or Parliament. Hollie had been in Essex, not on the moon. If he'd have had a sniff of things moving either way he would have been down like a shot, he wasn't neglectful of his duties –

"Shut up, Babbitt," Fairfax said icily, and he shut up.

The West Country, it seemed, was different.

Hollie rolled his eyes mentally, whilst retaining an appropriately respectful demeanour. Aye. Well. They were all different. The Low Countries had been different, ten years ago, when Hollie had been plying his trade there. Yorkshire had been different. (He looked surreptitiously at Luce, glumly picking at his fingernails while he thought no one was paying him attention. *Luce* was different. Luce was not so eager and shiny as once he might have been, not so keen that Parliament's cause was the cause of liberty. And that was little to do with Gray.)

"The West Country is different," Fairfax said, "because Cornwall is for the King. Almost to a man."

"I think that man may be presently at his breakfast," Luce said helpfully. "Captain Toogood is –"

"Pettitt," Fairfax said, "shut up." He looked at the three of them. "Since I am assured that if I kick one, all three of you limp, I will keep this particular debriefing short and to the point. At the beginning of this war my lord Hopton indicted Parliament before the grand jury of Cornwall as disturbers of the peace, and called out the *posse commitatus* to raise a militia for the King. Lest one of you gentlemen plead ignorance, I will speak plainer. The county of Cornwall was raised against Parliament three years back by Sir Ralph Hopton claiming that Parliament caused trouble. If you three go right ahead and prove his point, gentlemen, I am going to find me a good stout Cornish hedge and nail your ears to it. Do we understand each other?"

"That could prove difficult, sir," Russell said with a chilly smile. "I understand the term 'hedge' in Cornwall to refer to a stone bank – ow! Lucey, what d'you do that for?"

The Commander-in-Chief of the Army of Parliament looked at Luce with a glimmer of approval. "Thank you, cornet. The Earl of Essex endeavoured to carry the war into Cornwall two years back -"

"And he codsed it up. As Captain Toogood is keen to make the rest of the Army aware," Hollie pointed out. Fairfax did not smile, because Fairfax did not encourage scurrilous slander amongst his officers, but saying that Essex had made a lash-up of his Cornish campaign was common knowledge. And you didn't start that particular hare with Toogood and his lads unless you had a comfortable seat.

"I understand Captain Toogood to have felt somewhat – betrayed by my lord Essex's precipitate withdrawal to safety," Fairfax said, and his face was a carefully impassive mask. "He was amongst the troops left behind. You know that, I think? He had a hard time of it."

"I know that," Hollie said, feeling a slow burning flush at the back of his neck and fighting a desire to squirm in his seat.

"I think he lost a good – what, third? A quarter? Of his men, to disease and privation, on the retreat to Plymouth. A harsh campaign," Fairfax said musingly. "I do not imagine we will have an easy time of it, ourselves. By God's grace we may not be driven out of Cornwall by sticks and flung stones, as he was. Like so many stray dogs. I do not approve of my lord Essex's conduct, colonel – or rather that of his troops, I might say, for I have heard much of theft and abuse amongst our own men and that I will not countenance. You may also pass the message to Captain Toogood that if he were to read the book of Deuteronomy, it says, very clearly, *Vengeance is mine, saith the Lord. I will repay."* The emphasis was clear, and in case it was not clear enough, Fairfax folded his arms on his paperwork and leaned across the table, fixing Hollie with a hard, glittering black stare. "*The Lord* will repay. Not Kenelm Toogood. And not Hollie Babbitt. Are we absolutely clear on this head?"

"*For the day of their calamity is near, and the things that shall come upon them make haste,*" Russell finished, and Hollie glanced over his shoulder at the scarred lieutenant. Still upright, still as stiff and formal as ever, but with that wild glint in his stormy grey eyes that did not bode well for the good burghers of Cornwall. "You imply no quarter... sir?"

"I *imply* no such thing, lieutenant. The facts are as they are. Lord Goring is fled into France, taking his dissolute ways with him. My lord Hopton would have appointed Sir Richard Grenville as his major-general of foot, but it seems that Sir Richard will not recognise that authority. And is in custody on St Michael's Mount for his pains."

"Grenville arguing? Surely not," Hollie said wryly. "Didn't he fall out with Goring last year?"

"Everybody falls out with Goring," Luce added. "The man is an unprincipled bastard."

"Aye, but he's an unprincipled bastard in France, so he's not really our problem. Well, bloody Grenville's as bad, for knavery."

"Colonel Babbitt," Fairfax cut in. "Not a question I should choose to ask, but, ah, given Sir Richard's service in the Low Countries –"

"And the Swedish Army," Hollie said, with resignation. "Yes. Oh aye, I know that bastard. He's got eight years on me, but aye. I know him. And he knows me. He's not a nice piece o' work, that lad. He's got all the principle of a cut snake, and I'd trust him about as far. You know he's been in the Fleet prison for debt, then?"

"Colonel, you have a nose for gossip that would shame an old woman," Russell murmured.

"I have a nose for not getting my bloody head shot off, by a sneaking bastard as does not take kindly to young officers still wet behind their ears coming up on their tails," Hollie said, and left it at that. "Grenville's been in the Fleet for debt. Aye. I didn't tell you that to blacken his name, and you cut in 'fore I had a chance to finish, for the Fleet wouldn't hold him. He escaped. God knows how he did it, for *I* don't, but he broke out and came back to the Continent, and that was when I knew him." He paused, and dropped his chin into his hands, and sat drumming his fingers on his cheekbones. "Rheinfelden, or thereabouts, for Rackhay was still with me: both of us were commanding a troop, me and Rackhay, and that would make it – '33?"

"So he escaped imprisonment for debt." Fairfax looked disapproving, but not concerned. "And what of it?"

"He escaped his imprisonment," Hollie said dryly. "And you have that malign influence locked up on St Michael's Mount. Stout jail, then, is it?"

"It is an island," Fairfax said. "How much stouter would you wish, than entirely surrounded by water?"

"In that bugger's case, sir, I might wish it entirely surrounded by a ditch, a palisade, eight-foot thick stone walls and preferably an armed guard turn and turn about. I should as soon put my head into a serpent's nest as I should set foot in any county where that malevolent sod held any power."

"Why, Colonel Babbitt, I should almost believe you to be afraid of Sir Richard."

"He had me broke," Hollie said simply. "After my –" he took a deep breath. "After Margriete died. My first. My first wife. She died while I was laying siege to Nuremberg, a year before Grenville knew me."

"That was when you went a bit odd, wasn't it?" Luce said helpfully, and Fairfax's mouth twitched, but he said nothing.

"Aye. You might say. I was but twenty-five at the time, and I took it hard, losing her. And Grenville, not long out of his imprisonment, and wanting to make his mark in the world, thought it might be a thing of ease to have my command off me, to make him look the better."

"And -?" Fairfax prompted, with a look of sympathy.

"I punched him in the head," Hollie said, and was rewarded for his restraint by the sight of his own commanding officer blink in brief, startled amusement. "Couple of times. Maybe."

"And what did he do?"

"Got his sergeant at arms and a couple of mates to beat me up later, so he didn't get his hands dirty, and dropped me in it for being pissed on duty. Which, when you got a good zealous commander, is as good a way of any of getting rid of a lad who might threaten your position, for Sir Richard is not shy of the bottle himself when it's being passed round."

"I have not yet returned you to a plain trooper," Fairfax murmured slyly. "Have I?"

"Aye. Well. *He* did. And I'm not a man to bear a grudge – shut up, Lucifer, you're not a bloody pig, stop snorting – but, you know. He's shafted me once. He damn' near had me out on my arse for drunkenness and insubordination. If he finds out it's me, the chances are he's going to try and do it again."

"Well, I consider myself warned, then. Why should I pay any heed to a captive Malignant commander with a reputation for treachery?"

"It's not *you* I'm worried about," Hollie said.

11. THE MILLS OF GOD

It wasn't like nothing had happened in their absence, but it was not exactly that they'd been missed, either. The New Model Army was like that. It ground slow, but exceeding small, and once it would have mattered that he'd been out of the picture for just under a month, but it was all so neatly regimented and administrated that he counted for nothing.

So long as someone signed everything off, it was of no account. Could be Hollie, could be Drew Venning, could be Blossom the horse so long as there was a signature on the paperwork. Aye, the New Model was a well-oiled machine, and there was little place for a man who did not do things by rote, and as God willed it. It was a sobering reflection, for a man who'd quite fancied himself as indispensable, once. "Nobody bloody missed me, then," he said, and glowered meaningfully at Venning's dog, willing the beast to come within kicking range. Tinners disobligingly did not, but thumped his tail on the floor where he lay cheerfully sprawled in front of the kitchen fire, and returned to gnawing on his foul old bone. (It was a bloody annoying noise, too, and Hollie found himself growling at the dog.)

"Any mail?" he said, and Venning looked up at him, and stuck the needle in the stocking he was methodically butchering.

"Ah?"

"Correspondence," he said through gritted teeth. "You know, that what people write on sheets o' paper and give to someone to deliver? Writing, Captain Venning? That thing wi' the ink?"

"Ent no need to be sarcastic, bor. I happened to be thinking of suffen else."

"Your belly, probably," Hollie snarled, and sat down with a thump, and shoved everything off the table with his elbow. "Correspondence. Or. Not."

"I give it Russell. Or, I might say, Russell picked it up on his way through. Couldn't hardly keep him back from it, bless him, he's hot to get back to his duties, ent he? Bit of a rest and he's ramping at the bit to be in the thick of it, God love the lad –"

"Was there anything for me?"

He was not throttling the methodical Fenman, but it was taking some effort. Venning was nodding and smiling to himself, and grinning at his ravelled stocking as if he was receiving coded messages from its ragged toe. "Venning. Did I have any mail? Myself? Like – you know – to me? In a -" Sod it. He might as well get it said, because if he didn't one of them buggers was going to. "Personal capacity?"

"*You*, Rosie? No, not no more than warning orders, which Russell's got. Why – was 'ee expecting suffen?"

"Wondering if Het – if my wife might of written," he muttered, and felt the back of his neck get hot again.

"Het? Why'd she write? You only left her less'n a month back, bor, did 'ee have suffen urgent to tell her?"

"No," Hollie said, and they left it there.

12. SEEKING FOR WHOM HE MAY DEVOUR

He stopped for a moment outside the house to tip his head back against the wet stone and close his eyes with a shaky silent prayer, for it was not a thing he relished, and to be honest, Fairfax scared the hell out of him lately, for Black Tom was grown hard this winter. He'd always been stern, aye, but he'd had that core of kindness to him, before. And Hollie was not – would not –

It was his duty. He *had* to do it.

A pox on duty, Hollie thought sourly, and straightened up, and spat into the gutter. Hopton's men, the poor benighted sods, had occupied the little town of Torrington for nigh on a week now and he did not envy the job they had had of throwing up defensive earthworks for it had been pissing down for every day of that week and it must have been like trying to dig ditches in porridge. Hollie had done his mud-slinging, twenty years ago in the Low Countries. He did not choose to do it again. (Though he was tempted to send a messenger in to Hopton offering the services of Venning's Norfolk Fen-slodgers. They were rare men for ditches, that lot, and being web-footed almost to the last man they'd be up for the job.) What was it Lucey said, if it were done when it were being done, 'twere better it were done as soon as you could finish it – or something.

He had the unenviable task of telling three captains of horse, one sergeant at arms, one sarcastic lieutenant and a poet who wasn't even out of bed yet that they were going in tonight. In the dark. In the rain.

Coming down like the wrath of God on a little town who had been suffering the privations of five thousand or so ill-nourished and ill-disciplined Malignants for a week already. He doubted, somehow, that the town of Torrington was going to look on Thomas Fairfax as their saviour and deliverer. Better the Devil you know. And Fairfax in his current mood of intransigence...

He opened his eyes again, and shook himself, and looked up the muddy lane, where dawn was just beginning to crack in rags of bloody red cloud. "That's all I need," he said aloud, not quite quietly enough for the shabby figure slogging on foot through the mud not to hear, and Kenelm Toogood glowered at him.

"Talking to me... *sir*?"

Hollie did not want to go crashing into an innocent town full of innocent bloody civilians In the rain. In hock-deep mud where a horse could slip and break a leg as easy as kiss-my-hand, in the dark, on strange ground, on uncertain footing. Seemed like it was Fairfax's chosen method of storming a town, these days, and one of these days his luck was going to run out. (Sooner or later the Malignants were going to notice. Hang on, lads, it's raining, brace yourself for incoming.) "Funny you say that, Captain Toogood. I *was* talking to you. In the absence of any other intelligent life. I've got warning orders. So I suggest you go and round up the usual suspects and get your sorry arse into my quarters to take 'em. I've not got all day. Shift it."

And he was half hoping that the Cornishman was going to cut up about it, because Hollie did not relish the idea of hurting people who hadn't done owt to harm him, but by Christ it would have lightened his heart considerable to have an excuse to belt Toogood. *Anything* to wipe that perpetual sullen scowl off his face. It was bloody teasing, was what it was. It was an open invitation to smack him, and he did not let Hollie down this time, he stiffened and glowered and stuttered and he eventually squawked, "I ent your bloody dog! Get your bloody runner to do it!"

"Oh, I *do* apologise -" because he was hitting his stride now, he'd found the chink in Toogood's armour and if Hollie couldn't belt his subordinate he could wind him up till Toogood lost his rag. And then all bets were off, because they still had unfinished business from last time. "I didn't realise you was so keen on formal Army regulation....*captain*?"

"You think you're proper something, don't you -"

Hollie leaned forward till his eyes were on a level with the stocky captain's. "Aye. I do. I think I'm your fucking commanding officer. And whatever me and you might think of each other off duty, you do what you're told, or you will be off back to that fucking benighted barren waste you call a birthplace, on permanent unpaid leave. With my toe up your arse. D'you know what a dishonourable discharge is, Captain Toogood?"

Oh aye, he knew, all right. You could see him tremble at that, not because he was frightened, but because it leashed him, and Toogood hated being leashed, he hated it worse than the Devil. (And there were times when Hollie, who was not a superstitious man, wondered if there was a devil in Kenelm Toogood, and if a combination of the Earl of Essex's leaving him behind at Lostwithiel and what he saw as the treachery of his own countrymen, had put it there.) "Pettitt's in bed still," Hollie said, twisting the knife a little for the joy of it. "He had the last watch, last night. So you might have to wake him. Wish you joy of it. Might have to go looking for Captain Betterton, I think he took a patrol out this morning. "

"I'm not your errand boy, Colonel Babbitt." Growling for the sake of the growling, like a beaten cur still showing its defiance even when it was beaten.

"True enough. Lieutenant Russell is considerably more reliable. Reminds me - I reckon he's chasing Fairfax round the earthworks somewhere, trying to bend his ear about supplies. You might have to go looking for him as well. I'd not like to be without my lieutenant, now."

It was tempting to pat Toogood on the shoulder or something, just to get the message home, but he thought that might be going too far. "Off you go, Captain Toogood. That's an order, lad, in a military capacity. And I'm giving you a half hour to do it in. You understand that, or d'you want it in short words? I want you - Venning and Betterton - I want Luce, I want Cullis, and I want Russell. That's five, not including you." He held his hand up, fingers spread, for the malevolent pleasure of it. "Can you remember that, Captain Toogood, or d'you need me to write it down?"

13. NOT APPOINTED TO WRATH

"Tomorrow, at dawn," Hollie said, and as Betterton opened his mouth, "and yes, he knows it's raining."
Because Simon Betterton had been on the other side, he'd been one of the Earl of Newcastle's lads in Yorkshire, and he'd come over to Parliament after he found himself masterless suddenly last summer. And that meant he had little experience of Fairfax's partiality for inclement weather, and presumably thought - like a reasonable man - that you'd have to be off your bloody head to mount an attack on an armed town in the pissing rain in the cat's-light of dawn.

"Well, aye, but it's civilian, man," Betterton said, sounding bemused. "Rain's no trouble to me -"

"True enough, he's from Gateshead, he's bloody used to it," Venning said cheerfully.

"Storming it seems a bit harsh," Betterton said. He shrugged his shoulders and looked awkward. "Aye. I mean, I know what they are in there, but -"

"People?" Luce suggested, and then looked at his hands, because he wasn't often so critical in a public place, but Hollie nodded.

"That's right. People. Some of 'em are soldiers. And some of 'em are just people who have the accident to live in a town that got in the way of my lord Hopton thinking he can distract us from Exeter."

"What, with half the number of men we got?" Venning said, with a scornful laugh. "Aye. Right. In his dreams."

"I *said*," Hollie repeated, very distinctly, "there's people in there. So. That's some daft buggers who support His Majesty wholesale. I don't reckon you'll find so many of them. And that's some like me and you, who'd happen rather not be here, but who're stuck with it because they think the alternative's worse. And having met Captain Toogood, I'm not so sure they're wrong. And there's women and children in there, who have no choice but to be there, because Hopton's occupied the place and they can't get out. Like the rest of us, they're probably hungry, and they're *definitely* scared. Be gentle with 'em, so far as you can. They are not at fault."

There was a sound from the back of the room, and he looked up. "You mean to speak, Captain Toogood?"

The Cornishman's dark eyes were fierce, but quite unwavering. "Aye. I do. Burn 'em out."

Luce gasped, and Toogood looked at him contemptuously. "Soft on Malignants, cornet? Pen them in the town, and burn it. No quarter. All of them. They'd serve us the same, had they the choice."

"Bloody hell, Kenelm, that's a bit -" Venning began to say.

"No it's not, Venning. I'm telling you plain, though you won't hear it. Expect no loyalty from those bastards in there, and do not think for a second that because they are not fighting for the King they must fight for Parliament, because they won't. They will fight for who they think will come out of this the winner, and Devil take the hindermost. Don't you put your trust for a bloody minute in skirts and petticoats, Captain Venning, for I tell you in plain words the women fight worse than men in these parts, when their whelps are threatened. And if you don't know that yet you've had a god-damned easy war of it, boy, for the most vicious at Lostwithiel were the bitches, and I made a vow I'd never turn my back on another woman, were

I still in a soldier's coat. Cut all their bloody throats, and let God sort 'em out. I'd not waste the time."

It was the longest speech anyone had ever heard from Kenelm Toogood, and Hollie was not sure he had heard it from a feeling man's lips. "Captain," he said, "if you are still green enough that you think to show how brave you are in such - aye. Well. Don't waste your breath, boy. None of us are impressed."

And Toogood blinked. And Hollie would have been worried if there had been no feeling in those dark eyes, but there was.

There was rage, and bitter humiliation, and fear, and shame, and hate, all of it boiling together in a melting-pot of ungovernable passion. He meant it. And yet he didn't mean it, all in the one breath.

"You're fucking dangerous, Toogood," Hollie said, and he meant *that*.

Toogood nodded in acknowledgement. "I mean to be," he said flatly. And he got up and pushed past Hollie, and there was a little shocked intake of breath from the other officers, that nobody would have admitted to - a thing that was felt more than heard, because how could you do such a thing, an officer in his own right to treat his commander with such discourtesy -

And Hollie was very aware of his own dignity, such as it was, and he stiffened but he did not give in to his immediate instinct, which was to go after the Cornishman and belt some manners into him. "Well," he said, and grinned malevolently. "Take a peasant out of a ditch and give it a sash, and ...you got a peasant in a sash."

Russell gave his weird silent company-laugh at the back, and poor Betterton flinched. It wasn't that he didn't like Russell, as long as the scarred lieutenant was acting like any other man. It was just when Russell started getting odd, and laughing noiselessly at things that shouldn't have been funny, that Betterton started not wanting to stand next to him. And of course, Russell knew it, and acted up the worse. Hollie sighed. "Oh, stand down, the lot of you. Go and roust your lads out. I want 'em hot by dusk, d'you hear me? There's going to be no place for slackers, come tonight."

"Live fire?" Venning said.

"Not much bloody use to me dead, Andrew." He waited for the laughter. Such as it was. "Aye. Draw powder. And yes. Live. I want you up to three rounds a minute. It's possible. I seen it done."

"No bloody chance!" the freckled Fenlander scoffed. "Some of em, maybe, but -"

"All of 'em," Hollie said, and did not laugh. "By tonight."

"Presumably that will include your own?" Luce said with resignation, which cheered Hollie up no end.

"Certainly will, brat. Pull 'em in, there's a good lad. I'll come by in a bit and make sure you're all firing at the same thing."

"Oh, indeed? What do you suggest?"

"Captain Toogood," Russell said, and gave another silent snicker. Betterton made a hasty excuse and left, which amused Russell yet more -

"Pack that in, you marred bugger," Sergeant Cullis said grimly. "You got work to do."

Luce turned to Hollie as the door closed, and the brat looked as if he was expecting to laugh. "You mean it, about the -"

"Target practice? Aye. I do." Which wiped the smile off the brat's face. "We can't keep doing it, Luce. Sooner or later they're going to get wise to it, and they're going to have summat nasty waiting for us in there. Well, they might have it, but I'd like to have summat nasty of my own up my sleeve."

"Ye-es," Luce said primly, "Auntie Het has spoken of the state of your linen, before - oh. Sorry. That was meant to be funny."

"Try it again after she's written."

"She's not?"

"You know she's not."

"It's only been a month, Hollie. She might -"

"Aye. She might." He ran his hands through his hair, and it came loose from its bindings and fell in his eyes, and he did not choose to tie it back. "And then again, she might not. So. I'd prefer it you did not tittle-tattle to her, Luce, but I know you write home as often as you might, and I'm not so daft as I do not think your letters get passed around. I'll not tell you what you may write, but I'd ask you consider my pride, as well as hers." It wasn't the sort of thing he was good at admitting aloud, and he made a wry face. "You can tell her I talk of her often. And kindly. And that I've got a length of decent wool for the lasses' winter coats in my baggage."

"Have you? When did you -?"

"No. But by t'next time she sees me, I will have." There was a long pause. The rain pattered against the window, unending. In the street outside, shouting - amiable shouting, someone calling to his mate, or some company sergeant calling his lads to order.

"Are you going to let it go?" Luce said, and Hollie turned from looking out into the drenched greyness, where the mist hung unfathomable on the green-black hills, and put his elbow on the sill.

"Toogood," he said. Not a question. Luce nodded.

"It's not good for the men. To see him speak to you so."

"Be worse if they saw me put a well-deserved bullet in his ear, brat. I will let him go so far. No further."

"Why?"

"Because he was right." And Hollie grinned, without humour. "Looking forward to seeing his face when I tell him so, aall."

14. MAGDEBURG QUARTER

"I want a word with you."

Toogood looked up, and carried on with his breakfast. Very, very grudgingly Hollie had to admit that Kenelm Toogood had balls. Misplaced balls. But balls.

"If you're seeking an apology, you'll be waiting till hell freezes over. Sir. "

"Captain Toogood, I'll be as straight wi' you as you seem to think it your right to be wi' me."

It gave Hollie great pleasure to lean over the table and take the eating-knife out of the Cornishman's hand. "I'll begin wi' your manners. Which stink. Shut up. If you reckon being good at your job is a substitute for being civil, I've got twenty years of practice as says it isn't. And mind - on what I've seen of your military skills, I'd not trust you to run a fucking whelk stall. *Shut up*. You're sullen, vicious, unpredictable, and you're not that bloody good that you can get away with it."

Toogood gaped at him, his tanned face going white with a scarlet slash on each cheek, as if he'd been slapped. "Now you listen up, you slithery little turd. If you ever, ever show me up in front of my lads like that again, I will slit you from stones to gizzard and hang your worthless carcass over the fucking earthworks as a warning to the curious. What me and you think of each other in civilian life is none of anyone else's goddamn business." And almost without his conscious will, Hollie's knife-hand flew out so that Toogood's knife pressed against the angle of its owner's jaw, and a beaded ruby dimple grew there. "On duty, captain, you will say 'yes, Colonel' and 'no, Colonel' and repeat it like a nice little fucking popinjay. Now what you think in your own head is your own affair. But tell you what. Shall we practice a little bit? Say, yes, Colonel Babbitt, sir -"

"*No.* Colonel Babbitt. Sir."

"You - what?"

"You heard. I don't give a tinker's cuss what you think. On or off your goddamn duty. Don't you ever assume, Colonel Babbitt - don't you ever, ever assume I'm the same bought and paid for lickspittle sellsword as you are, cos I ain't. You don't own me. I don't owe you anything. I was directed to your company 'cause -"

"You were directed to my company 'cause no other bugger would take you, Captain Toogood," Hollie snapped back. "And you have made it your bloody business to make me regret it, every day of it."

"Not as much as I do - sir!" he yelped. "I raised a bloody troop in Cornwall to stick up for our cause against His Majesty - and remind me what cause you believe in, Colonel Babbitt? Oh aye, I raised me a troop three years back, and I stood with the Earl of Essex and he dropped me in the shit. I lost the better part o' my lads at Lostwithiel, and I'd have stuck with Essex to the death if he would have stood fast, but he fucking never. He got on his lil' fishing boat and he fucked off as fast as go could he, and he left the rest on us to die. Drowned, or starved, or beaten, or just to die of disease an' privation on the march up to Plymouth. By us own countryfolk, mind! So you will forgive me, Colonel Babbitt, if I don't have a deal o' sympathy for *your* fucking off likewise, soon as you thought it was quiet. Scat off home to the wife, spend your Christmas in peace and comfort, and you left the rest 'en us to squat in a ditch and die, just like he did. Where was you when we took Dartmouth castle? Powderham? At home, poking the missus. Sat on your arse with your feet on the fender. Leaving me and Drew Venning and Si Betterton to get us bloody heads shot off, and sit wi' lads as was puking stinking bile. Wi' no food, and no shot. So don't you be talking to me about duty, sir, 'cause you got less idea about duty than Venning's fucking *dog*, who at least has the grace to stay where he is directed! I thought you was better than that - sir - after Bristol, you had me on as you were one of us, not one o' they! You had me believing it, you gutless bastard, and you cut and run, back up along out o' harm's way, so soon as you could palm us off!"

"Now you listen -" Hollie began, and Toogood rounded on him again.

"No, *you* listen. How's your wife, Colonel Babbitt? She good, when you left her, was she?"

"My wife's none o' your business, Toogood!"

"Aye! Well! Tell you a lil' story, colonel. I raised a troop down here, and the half o' my family cut me for it, being good King's men. I had a wife, and a lil' girl, but I bloody ain't now, unless you call a plot in Callington churchyard sufficient. But you wouldn't know, course, you being a career soldier. You wouldn't know what it is to get word while you're a hundred miles away, that your girl's dead of a fever because none o' your fucking family would raise a hand to help her. No money. No man to put a roof over her head. And they said we were looting - wolves, they said in our church, they reckoned Essex come down like a wolf on the fold stripping the land of what he could devour. Aye. That'd be Parliament men, then, who wouldn't give bread to a starving maid and her baby? Don't reckon as it was, sir. Reckon it was good King's men and women, who reckoned a contemptible fucking rebel needed to be learnt a lesson. She begged, Colonel Babbitt. My Loveday sold everything she had to buy bread for her and our Chesten. And they wouldn't give her none, when she ran out of things to sell, for her man was a Parliament man, and when she ran out o' coin they let her die. Wi' me penned up in Lostwithiel, and could not lift a finger to save her. But you'd not know how that might feel, sir, would you? On a pound a day pay, wi' your nice house and your nice cosy lil' wife?"

Hollie thought of his younger self, shaking and puking with the flux outside the walls at Nuremberg, ten years ago. He didn't remember the words on the letter. He remembered the feel of it in his hands, stiff and a little frayed at the creases, as if it had been passed from hand to hand, following him around the war in Europe. He did remember - still remembered, in his nightmares of fire and siege - the way the words had looked, very black and very careful on that worn paper, and how they had burst like mortars into smears of ink. Under his tears? He did not know. He just remembered that he had sat and looked at black words that had made no sense, that shimmered and spread in his sight.

It had been Rackhay who told him in plain words, back then. Rackhay who had been kind - a thing he could be, when he put himself to it, when he had troubled to do it - had told Hollie in words that he understood that Margriete was dead, and all the light had gone out of the world. Aye. So. Hollie knew what loss was, and anger, and being cut adrift and not knowing who to hate first. He knew all that. He'd spent seven years letting it eat him from the inside. He knew what that felt like, too. "Then I'm sorry for your loss," he said stiffly.

"Why? Will words bring her back, or give my daughter back to me? Was men like you who lost them in the first place, colonel. Men without sufficient balls to stay where their duty bid them, no matter what it cost them -"

"I *said*, Toogood, I was sorry for your loss. And I am. Aye, and I made a bad call in going home. If I had it to do again, I should not have gone. But - all right, then, captain, what would you, then? That I should have abandoned Russell, who has served me a bloody sight better than you have - left him in Essex, with no place and no people of his own? Or Pettitt, who has had his own loss? Should I have left both of them, to manage as best they could, when they needed me?"

"*We* needed you," Toogood snarled.

No. No, they did not, and if he thought about it too much, that was a thing that would break Hollie's heart, for they did not. There was no place for people, in the New Model Army. There was only rank and role and regulation. Not like the good old days, he thought wryly. "Why?" he said, and he did truly want to know.

Toogood did not have an answer. Ah, Christ, the Cornishman made Hollie's head ache - all the time touchy and hot-tempered, always quick to blame, quick to affront. "I am sorry for your loss," he said, for the third time. And then - as if it would have made any difference - "I lost my wife, when I was not so much older than you are now. I was away. Fighting."

And he could not help it, just for that black split second he almost dropped his guard and he had to grip the edge of the door frame to stop himself punching the look off Toogood's face: the expression of a man who knows himself to be the hardest done-to in Christendom, always. "Aye, I do know what it's like. And you know what, Toogood? I *grew the fuck up*. I stopped blaming every other bastard for it. She died. It's hard. It's not my fault. I shouldn't have gone. Well, I did. It would have made fuck-all difference to you lot was I here or no. That is not how this army works, sir. If you're serving wi' me out of some perverted lust for vengeance, captain, I promise you, it will not happen."

The Cornishman stiffened again, his breath whistling through his teeth in fury.

"You think I come after you to tick you off for giving me cheek, captain, and in part, I did. Might point out that the King's General himself is presently locked up on St Michael's Mount for insubordination - so serving one plain captain of horse likewise will be no trouble at all, save that I doubt you have such influential friends as Sir Richard and your accommodation may not be so pleasantly serviced. You may cheek me as much as you see fit, captain, an you do your work as I command it. You will go in tonight and you will leash your god-damned rabble, sir, you will rein them in and you will do as you are bloody well told!"

Hollie was panting, himself. "Believe me, captain. You give that town Magdeburg quarter, and I will not only see you broke, I will see every man in your troop hanged. And Toogood - trust me on this. If you think the Earl of Essex served you ill, turn your sword against innocent civilians this night, and you will look back on Lostwithiel and wish they'd finished the job."

15. WAR AFTER THE FLESH

Dusk seemed to fall earlier, in the West Country, but then it had not been proper light all day, and the rain was coming sideways out of a leaden sky, blown by a bitter inimical wind off the moors. Hollie risked a glance up at the moor, hunched black as a shoulder over them. Luce hated it. He really, really hated this terrain, it was so unlike his own turf in soft Essex, but it was like coming home for North Country Hollie. Give Hollie a fierce fight on the wide-open, dangerous spread of the moor and he'd have been as happy as a pig. As it was -

As it was, they had the wind against them, and the horses were growing restless and edgy, wanting to turn their tails to the rain. Even the imperturbable Blossom was on edge, on tiptoe, his ears flickering anxiously at every sound - and God knows, with ten thousand men forming up around them, it was noisy enough, even without the eerie whine of a rising wind. He raised his hand. "Volunteering for advance guard, sir." Fairfax's dark face, even darker in the cat's-light, turned towards him, and Hollie saw his lips curve in a wry smile.

"Might have known, colonel. Hot to engage?"

He could hear muttering behind and around him, as some of the lads expressed disapproval at Colonel Babbitt's notorious eagerness to come to grips with the enemy. And that made him smile, a little, because it was nothing to do with an enemy and more to do with knowing the temper of his own men, keeping anxious horses at a churning halt in the bitter spring rain. "Oh aye," he said, with more cheer than he felt, and brought his hand down on Blossom's bony rump with a soggy slap. The brown horse sprang to attention, which make Fairfax's smile a little wider, and a little more real; Blossom amused most people, looking as if he had not yet grown into his legs, but he was a sweet beast, and willing. If not the brightest. Luce's Leo was as teasy as a snake, though, and the sooner they moved off the better before the big roan stallion lamed someone, kicking restlessly at his neighbours in the line. Hollie nodded at his cornet, and Luce brought the colours up, though the wet silk wrapped itself round the staff and would not flutter. "Follow him, he's the one with the stick," Hollie murmured to his friend, and Luce gave him a wry look out of the corner of his eye.

Aye, the brat had grown up, in the service of Parliament. Three years ago, he'd have been awkward and wrong-footed with his colours, and he'd have hated it that Hollie laughed at him for it. Now - well, now he loved his flag, but he didn't worship it. (He'd been known to belt ne'er-do-wells with the butt-end, too. Most disrespectful.) "Move off," Hollie said, and put his heels to Blossom. He'd ridden out in the rain before, with the splash of trotting hooves all around them, and the creak and jingle of wet leather. Slick, solid, chilled-wet shoulder moving under his hand, and the horse's breath coming in wet blubbery snorts. Leo dapple-grey with rain, and Cullis's white cob shining like a beacon. Russell's pied Doubting Thomas dancing, head tossing, bounding in his place in the line, and he shouted something reproving to his lieutenant about restraining that demented bloody animal.

"Aye - *and* the horse," Venning called, and there was a little ripple of laughter. And then they were gone, and the erratic jog of four company of horse on a wet track in the gathering darkness of a raw afternoon in filldyke February smoothed into a splattering hand-canter, as easy as a hound quartering on the trail. It was Toogood, in the end, who picked up the scent, coming wheeling back from a scouting party. "Company," he said, his teeth flashing white in the dusk. (And Hollie was supposed to be the one who was hot to engage. Ha.)

"Aye?"

"Coming out of the hills. See that 'en yonder?"

Troop of dragoons, coming out of Stevenstone Park. They were not expecting an advance guard of cavalry, especially fiery little bastards like Toogood who did not stop and think tactically but just rammed his spurs into his horse and pelted off with his company streaming after him like the hounds of hell. Which was contagious, and Hollie gave a wild whoop of his own and whacked the brown horse down the shoulder with the reins. Even Blossom managed not to fall over his own feet, but found a burst of uncharacteristic speed, and Hollie and Toogood came slewing into the middle of a scattering troop of His Majesty's dragoons shoulder to shoulder. Not, mercifully, entirely alone, and it was a remarkably quick engagement. Just about the only coherent thing he heard from the Royalist commander was "Oh, shit!" - which made Hollie giggle, and then Luce came thundering in out of the gloom, and there was a spark and flare as the brat's pistol cracked with deadly accuracy.

"Close order!" Hollie yelled, because dragoons were tricksy buggers, and wanted harrying rather than close engagement. "See the buggers off, boys!"

And then his own blade rang against a Malignant's, and he was urging Blossom forward with his knees while parrying three feet of expensive steel, cutting backhand at some elegant gentleman with an enviably luxuriant moustache. Blossom didn't like close work and the brown horse tended to balk at the chase: didn't have the same cat's instincts as some of the other cavalry mounts, to go in hard and push hard. Hollie found his back and his shoulders aching already, trying to drive his horse into doing a thing he was temperamentally unhappy about doing. Almost knee to knee with the bloody Malignant, and the pair of them chopping at each other like a pair of foresters at a tree, little short vicious cuts because they were almost tangled in each other's harness, so close that neither dared to be the first to disengage. So close he could feel the warmth of the other man's body like a banked fire, along the length of his thigh -

And then he heard Hapless Russell yell a very bad word indeed, sounding somewhat pained, and a pistol-ball went singing past his ear, and the Malignant went wheeling off with a squeal.

16. RECOMPENSE NO MAN EVIL FOR EVIL

"Were you trying to fight that lad, or cop off with him?" Cullis grumbled, bustling up in a spatter of mud. That squeal from Russell had been the sound of the lieutenant sustaining nothing more disabling than a bruising smack over the knuckles with the butt end of a musket, though his hand was swelling fast. He was swearing a lot, though, black-eyed and vibrating with a desire to kill something.

"Casualties?" Hollie said and Luce was smiling. No, not smiling, he was grinning from ear to ear, though even he'd taken a little nick to the point of his jaw. No worse than a lad might get shaving, but he was bleeding like a stuck pig -

"Not a bloody one, colonel," Luce said happily.

Even the dog was hale, though panting like a bellows.

"Not one," Toogood muttered sourly, leaving Hollie with the impression that the lack of Royalist injury was a source of grave dissatisfaction to him. "Give chase?"

Hollie shook his head. "Fall back. Cleared some space, at any rate. Back up the line and let Black Tom know there's dragoons loose about the spot. That way he can mind out for 'em."

But of all people it was not Fairfax he made his report to, but the Lieutenant-General of the Army himself. Hollie had not set eyes on Oliver Cromwell in two years, almost: not since he'd been a plain captain, and had refused a transfer to Old Noll's own Lovely Company, though it would have brought him closer to home. No, he'd refused a transfer to Cromwell's troops, and Drew Venning had forged the man's signature on a letter of safe passage when claiming that a most notorious and profane young reprobate was being released from lawful custody at his request, and he wasn't quite sure if that was all water under the bridge or not.

Venning looked sheepish. Russell, who had been that very reprobate, flung his head up and looked defiant, and very young, and terrified.

Cromwell said absolutely nothing, but he looked at the three of them - four of them, as Luce came barrelling down the track with his reins flapping and the colors wagging, elbows stuck out like a washerwoman on a mule. "Might ha' known," the Lieutenant-General said grimly. "Andrew Venning. I might have known you'd go to the bad, young man."

"I done no such -" the Fenman squawked, and then subsided into shuffling silence.

"That dog, an' all. Who d'you think you are, Prince Rupert? I'd not have that wretched mutt in my company, sir - egg-sucking, bed-widdling, pie-thieving lollopin' gret hound!"

"My dog ent never widdled on your bed!"

"Surely! Widdled on yours, when he was no more'n weeks old, and you took all the sheets off mine thinking I'd not know it was you! Tell 'ee where it was, too, it was at winter quarters at Warwick, after Kineton fight -"

"Ah. That be it," Venning muttered, and in the dark his freckles had all blurred into one blaze of shame.

"And I ent forgot you signed my name on papers to save some worthless rogue from swinging, boy. Without my knowledge or consent."

"That would be me, sir," Russell hissed, and Cromwell didn't bat an eyelid. His horse jerked and grunted, though, as if a spur had pricked its flanks.

"Ah? Steadied up marvellous, then, boy, by the Lord's grace. Well. Rosie Babbitt, as I live 'n breathe. Who'd have ever had 'ee marked down as a good influence?" His eye moved over Luce, consideringly. "Not all the time, then, maybe. What's this, Babbitt? An itinerant beggar?"

"My cornet, sir. Believe you've met Cornet Pettitt."

"Pettitt? You've come down in the world, boy! State of your linen! Have you suffered some reverse, sir? Some affliction?"

Luce rubbed awkwardly at his unshaven chin. "Um. No. An engagement -"

"Just come on a nest of Malignants at Stevenstone," Hollie said, and Cromwell nodded. "I heard. Walk awhile with me?"

He jerked his head to his own troops. "Stand down, gentlemen, take your ease. I'll take these boys as my company."

"I think we got away with it," Luce said without moving his lips.

Venning gave him a jaundiced look. "You reckon? Thass why we're slogging round the outposts wi' Noll, while they lads stop at their ease, then, will it?"

17. DARKNESS COMPREHENDETH IT NOT

No chance, they said. Not tonight, not this night, not in the dark, in the rain.

With Russell alternately sucking his bruised fingers and panting to kill something, and Luce quivering and grinning, and Venning's infernal bloody dog flinging his soggy stern about in an ecstasy of enthusiasm. "That's good," Venning said glumly, holding five bedraggled horses who all wanted to be facing in different directions. "'Cause if we heard suffen from yonder as meant they was stirring, we'd have to go in tonight, wouldn't we?"

"Like what?"

"Oh, like - mind what 'ee's doing wi' that shovel, nearly had my eye out, kind o' noises?"

"Very bloody funny," Russell said sourly.

"Reckon I'm being funny? Well, shut up and listen, then, know-all."

It was quiet. Still some fire and shouting, distant and spaced out, couple of miles off to the east where them bloody dragoons had gone scuttling back yowling they'd had their noses tweaked, and some good Parliament lads with primed muskets had gone to make sure they stayed tweaked. But nothing to indicate a gathering storm. Nothing more than a faint, distant creaking -

"Captain Venning, will you be still!" Russell snapped.

"He is being still," Luce said, quite reasonably. "He never moved a muscle."

Venning grinned smugly. "Thass right, bor. I never moved a muscle. T'ent me, creaking. Thass wood, that is. Bloody buggers in there trying to break out, you see if it ent. I d'reckon they must have heard me!"

18. KEEPING COVENANT

Cromwell looked at the three of them. "You come tear-assing over, disrupting my inspections, 'cause you heard suffen creaking?"

'Thass right, sir."

"Colonel Babbitt, d'you trust these lads?"

"Mostly," he said warily. There were no women involved, Russell was upright and sober, and there wasn't a swamp for miles. How much trouble could they have caused, truly?

The Lieutenant-General nodded. "That'll do for me, then. Good work, captain." Venning stared at him blankly. "I knew you'd turn out a decent soldier," he added, and grinned. "The Lord does occasionally guide me in the right direction, Captain Toogood. I ent as green as grass. Well done, lad. Lads - all three of you, a good job well done. Well, don't 'ee stand here gaping at me like a pack o' ninnies - you look likely, boy, take the Colonel's good horse and make some speed. Get back up the line, and let Thomas know we got company shortly!"

Hollie gave Luce a warning stare, and Luce gave him a nervous smile in return, and neither of them mentioned that the handsome roan stallion presently earning the Lieutenant-General's approval belonged to the most junior officer in the troop, and the draggled brown crow's-bait belonged to his superior. Cromwell's eye lit on Blossom and he shuddered. "My apologies, Rosie, leaving you wi' that - thing. Can you not have the beast shot, or suffen? Have some accident befall it on the field?"

Blossom decided to give the game away by shoving his nose into Hollie's pockets, as passionately as if they had been separated for months. And how could a man deny such loyalty, without feeling like Judas? "He is mine, sir. Picked him up at Selby. He looks like nothing on earth, but he's a good horse, when you get used to him -" Russell, neatly mounted on his own mismatched, foul-tempered brute, laughed his unnerving panting company-laugh, and Cromwell looked slowly round at him and then back at Hollie, eyebrows raised.

"You don't half pick 'em, boy, don't you?"

19. ALL THEY THAT TAKE THE SWORD

Hollie saw Venning off to the left, a bulky shadow on his big black horse in his blued-steel plate, saw Luce raise the colours to advance – sorry colours they looked too, wrapped draggled round the staff – and that didn't matter, it was just him and the brown horse, and the black rain coming in off the moors. The world banded by the bars of his lobster-pot helmet, and he put a hand up absently to push his helmet back a little, to see the better. His hand was shaking, and his mouth was suddenly dry as last night's ashes, but he knew that, too. The day he stopped feeling like this in the last few minutes before they went in, was the day he got his damn-fool head shot off. Fear was your friend, not your enemy, in battle. It kept your nerves taut and all your senses tingling, and that kept you safe, in a way that prayer and plate could not.

He saw the colours wag as Luce tried to wipe a rain-slippery glove on his thigh, and heard that young gentleman's muttered curse, and laughed to himself. Russell was trying to exhort anyone who'd listen that they were strong in the Lord, without sounding very convinced about it, and eventually Cullis's voice came out of the dark. "Consider us saved, Hapless, and put a stopper in it, eh? Because God does *not* mean you for a preacher."

And there was a laugh at that, and some wag started singing the ninety-fifth psalm, meaning the verse about coming before the Lord's presence with thankfulness making a joyful noise. ' *"A people that do err in their heart, and they have not known my ways: Unto whom I sware in my wrath that they should not enter into my rest."'*

Which stopped Hollie's breath in his throat, because it was - that was too coincidentally right to have been anything other than Providence. And Providence scared him witless. He looked up, feeling oddly sick. Met Toogood's fierce bright eyes, off to his right

Oh aye, that boy had done a lot of swearing in his wrath. "Close order, Captain Toogood," he said softly. "And on my command. None other."

And then they were in, hand to hand fighting behind a push of pike that wasn't sure what way it was going in the dark, with the sound of hooves and the screaming of hurt men and shouted orders echoing off the walls of sleepy little Torrington. Hollie had his sword in his hand, but he wasn't really making much use of it - it was all push of pike and clubbed muskets, close, vicious work, where you saw the faces of the men you fought as you fought them. (And would see them ever after, in your dreams, if you were a feeling man. They didn't mention that when they exhorted you to be strong in the Lord, either.) Blossom was afraid, backing and rearing - had never got used to this manner of fighting, remembering Selby, no doubt, when he had been hard-pressed and hurt and afraid - and someone behind him was cursing, and then suddenly they were in, breaking through the first of the shabby barricades. There was a big man on a big light-coloured horse pressing forward towards Hollie, a big man in a Royalist scarlet sash. The brown horse's hooves slipped and sparked on the wet cobbles as he shied off, terrified by the sudden impact of the pale horse's shoulder crashing against his own, and he stumbled to his knees. Which was as well, or the Royalist officer would have taken Hollie's head off like a child lopping the heads off thistles, for he was a big man and he had Prince Rupert's trick of using the horse's gallop to power the sweep of his blade. As it was,

Hollie was perfectly safe, briefly, with most of the breath knocked out of him, hanging down the horse's neck seeing stars. Blossom swerved again, and Hollie heaved himself upright and hauled the brown horse back round, bringing his sword up more by good luck than skill just in time to deflect the Royalist trooper's blade.

The man was quick. Quick and light on his feet, despite his size in that bulky oxhide coat, and the only light to see the deadly business was the occasional flare of musket fire, making everything glow amber and gold. Not a hot young man, but a old one, He was pushing the pale horse forward, and another whining musket-ball sparked overhead, glinting off breastplate and bridle and sword – Hollie threw himself half out of the saddle again as the man's blade lunged straight for him, and instead of skewering him like a bedbug the point of the sword went skating across his ribs, ringing on his breastplate. He yelped, more in surprise than in pain, and of all men it was Toogood who came clattering up out of the darkness with his pistol primed, and between them they gained a few inches of space, enough to be able to draw breath.

The fighting was bitter. There was a brief ease, round about dawn, when everyone was almost too exhausted after the battle had drawn off a little. And then it began again, the clash of steel and the shouting and screaming, and the crack and whine of musket fire. He was almost too tired to carry on. His eyes hurt, his shoulders hurt. He almost couldn't grip his sword. And still they came on, struggling through the streets –

He recognised the inimitable Doubting Thomas at his side, white with foam, his flanks heaving like a bellows, and still ramping at the bit to be given his head. Russell did not bother to salute. "Church," he panted, and both mount and man were trembling. "Venning - prisoners –"

Hollie nodded, couldn't speak even if he hadn't been too tired to think of words. Wanted to tell Russell to take himself and his spent horse to safety, before the pied brute was damaged beyond healing - opened his mouth and looked around, at Cullis and his tottering cob, at Luce's roan Leo black with blood and sweat, at Betterton with his arm bound up across his breastplate with a black-smottered rag. They all needed respite. None of them were going to get it.

Putting his heels to Blossom's soaked flanks, urging the horse into a limping trot. Round and back again. The church. Where the prisoners were being held, some two hundred of them. "He is." Russell swayed a little, looking as if he might faint, and Hollie looked at his scarred lieutenant for the first time, seeing the splash of blood across his buffcoat and his cheese-white face as if someone had thrown it there. "Captain Venning. Ish." Shaking his head furiously, because more than anything else Russell hated it when weariness slurred his words. "Is going to break the prisoners. Out. Church."

"Russell you're done. *Pull out.*"

"No!" Shaking his head again, lank pale hair falling in rags in his eyes. "Still. Needed."

Venning was going to try and break the prisoners out.

"Fairfax," Russell said, dipping his head at their general's distinctive white stallion. "Look to your weapons – be hot where he is. Breaking out. With hish - *his* - connivance." Hotting up again already, and the musket fire starting to concentrate on those few feet of cobbles where General Fairfax was. Whistling up Toogood, and Betterton - and Luce, always Luce at his shoulder - "Only big enough place in town with a lock on the front door," Toogood said over his shoulder, pushing his horse into the press. "The place is like an armoury!"

He didn't know, afterwards, what made Hollie think of it. If it was the noise, or the lack of noise, for surely it wasn't a sound he'd ever eard before – nor would ever hear again, the Lord be thanked. It seemed like the whole world stood still.

The place is like an armoury, Toogood had said. The only big enough place in the town with a lock on the door, Toogood had said.

In a town under occupation by five thousand King's men. Who had been there a week. Who would, presumably, be provisioned with powder. And shot.

Drew Venning's distinctive black horse, and Drew suddenly wheeling it, and the first dull light of dawn on his pistol as the big horse pulled to a weary halt in front of the church doors. A crying and a most piteous sound from inside the church, prisoners ill-used and hurt, and the scarlet light glinted on Drew's tear-streaked cheeks. "They are his men," Luce said, suddenly understanding, "I thought - he lost - some of the men inside, they must be Drew's?" And then his eyes widened, "Shit, no!"

As Drew Venning slipped under the noses of men and horses and raised his pistol to break the lock of Torrington church door."*General Fairfax, sir!*"

Black Tom turned his horse, questioning, his dark face lined and weary in the red light of dawn. Too red. Red like fire, like – Hollie stopped thinking, and kicked the brown horse from a standing start. Shouting, he didn't know what he was shouting, get away, get down, and he was five yards away, two yards away, the brown horse skidding on the cobbles, when the world shattered with a roar as Hopton's powder store in the church exploded. Blossom and Fairfax's white stallion went down in a flailing tangle of limbs, and for a minute, Hollie had no idea which way was up, buffeted and bruised under two terrified, screaming horses, and great chunks of masonry falling about his ears.

Deafened, and battered, and very, very frightened, he rolled himself slowly over onto all fours as the dust began to settle, because all the uproar was for the general's welfare, and none for one lowly, sore colonel of horse. (And his captain. Oh, dear God, if there was any justice in this world let that dear, hard-of-thinking freckled Fen-slodger be preserved by some miracle -) Luce was staring at him, across the rubble. Hollie shook his head, trying to clear the buzzing in his ears, and then took his helmet off, because he could hear little enough as it was, after the explosion. They were all staring at him. A hoof had caught him in the muscle of his thigh, and his leg was throbbing miserably. His nose was bleeding, he could taste it, and his right hand stung, suddenly, scraped raw. His left hand was fine. There was some use to that armoured bridle-gauntlet after all. Fairfax was on his feet. He looked sick and shaky, and he was bleeding from a gash in his cheek where a flying splinter of stone had nicked him, but he was whole, and alive.

What had been a place of God's worship was a pile of burning rubble, with what had been two hundred living men still inside it. Hollie barely made it to the mouth of the passage between the houses before he was very, very sick. He was standing with his forehead against the blessedly cool stone of the wall, trying not to cry, when something warm, and soft, touched the back of his neck. He was too sore and too wretched to even startle. He turned round, and the brown horse pushed his nose under Hollie's arm, wanting reassurance. A little scraped, a little singed, and very lame, but whole, and living, and suddenly very, very dear, and Hollie buried his face in the rough wet mane and wept his heart out, silently.

And then he straightened up, wiping his eyes on the sleeve of his stained and torn buff-coat, and put his arm over the brown horse's back, and the two of them limped back across the cobbles. Picking their way across shattered stone and burning wood, in the rain, towards their waiting comrades.

20. FIRE COME DOWN FROM HEAVEN

Luce thought of nothing, at first. After that first animal need to flee, to seek shelter, cover his ears, get away - all of that without any conscious will, just a blind need to not be in that choking hail of rubble - he was blinded and choking, and it was only Leo's panicked, frantic jerking on the bridle that returned him to the world.

For the roan horse was afraid, and hurt, and he had been given no choice in his presence here, and so Luce gave his mount as brief reassurance as he might, and then he gave the reins to - someone, to one of Toogood's lads, he thought, possibly - and he set to his business.

And at first he wanted to run away. He was used to the injuries of a battlefield, to shot and sword cuts, but - not this. Not bodies smashed like insects under great blocks of stone, dusty-faced men with blood running from their mouths where they were hurt inside beyond hope of mending, men burned like meat, or torn apart by flying splinters. He could do nothing. He was awkward, and inexperienced, and his stupid fingers scrabbled at hurts and made them worse -

And then Kenelm Toogood was at his shoulder, and a handful of his lads. The Cornishman was as filthy and streaked as a tinner himself, but he hefted blocks and heaved timber as if he had been a labourer, and not a captain.

Luce looked at what was left of what had once been a plain trooper, crushed on the stones under the roof-beam, and retched his guts up.

And then he crawled on his hands and knees across the shards and the splinters, drooling bile, with his eyes closed, and he sat with that shattered, bleeding ruin and he checked that the man was dead - though how could a man live, with such hurts to his head and his body? - because though he was sure and certain-sure that the poor soul was gone, yet he would not have left him had there been even a spark of life.

He crept, on all fours like a beast, from carcass to carcass, though his fingers grew numb and clumsy. He cried, and sometimes he knew the tears ran down his cheeks and sometimes he was only aware when the drops streaked the dust from his hands; thinking of the siege at Bristol, where he had set Toogood's arm after the Cornishman had been crushed under an undermined wall.

Not thinking of Toogood, not at all, though the Cornishman worked alongside him in grim silence to free those poor souls who could be freed. But thinking of Gray, and Bristol. Always.

There were few who might be mended, in the end. A dozen, two dozen, out of two hundred Christian souls, and those two dozen might never be fit for active service again, even if their wounds healed clean. The ones who had been crushed outright by stone and timber were fortunate.

And, of course, Drew Venning.

For the freckled Fenlander was whole. (And the news of that made Hollie Babbitt turn sharply on his heel and go for a brisk walk down the horse-lines. Everyone knew, and no one said, for the sake of the colonel's touchy pride, though Betterton offered him the use of a horrible bloodstained handkerchief.)

Luce did not know if he would remain whole. There had been too many men that he and Toogood and that glowering rabble of his had pulled clear that had been all but unmarked, but dead; or with blood pouring from ears and mouths, as if some great hand had burst something within them. Venning had been in the doorway when those eighty barrels of powder had burst, ignited by a haphazard spark from his pistol. The door had shielded him, for the better part. Trapped under an eight-inch thick door, with a handful of his own troop, under the great keystone of the church door and a few hundredweight of rubble. But intact.

They expected some godly remark from Cromwell, who had looked at his erstwhile captain where he lay bruised and battered and almost unrecognisable, with all his hair singed off on the one side and all the fingers on his left hand broken, the nails torn down to the quick. "Devil looks after his own, Captain Venning," Old Noll had said dryly. "Either that, bor, or 'ee has more lives than a stack o' cats."

21. A WAR WITHOUT AN ENEMY

"Captain Toogood. Sir. Reckon you need to come out, sir." The trooper looked awkward, and Toogood sighed and shrugged his coat on. "Action?"

"Bloody right, sir. Trying to keep it penned up, case it gets out, but - aye. Fight."

He picked up his sword as well and ran out into the rain without fastening his coat, bare-headed, his harness flapping loose. Pascoe ran alongside him, panting. "Sorry, sir, but I don't - reckon - Black Tom would be looking kindly on any - kicking up - from the lads. After yesterday."

"Neither would I," Toogood snarled, and splattered to a gasping halt in front of the picket. "What the hell maggot have you boys got in your brains? - oh, sweet Christ, why do you always have to do this on *my* watch?"

Russell was panting himself, but since it was taking two of them to hold him it looked uncomfortably as if the reason for the lieutenant's breathlessness was having been very recently punched in the guts. "What the hell is going on here?"

"Him. Creating. My land, but he was kicking up a dust!" Pascoe said primly. "Never heard such a fuss. I understand Colonel Babbitt's all right about it, but -" he rolled his eyes. "He'd have had half the Army down here wondering what was afoot, see?"

"You got a problem, Lieutenant Russell?"

"I should welcome half the Army down here. Want a word. Several words. I don' like the King. Tell him to his face, an' all."

"He's drunk," Pascoe said.

"Is he really? You surprise me," Toogood muttered.

"Bloody right I am. Got this unreasonable aversion to seeing a man's inner workings. They're called innards for a reason -" he gave a ghastly, bloody-mouthed grin. "Like 'em to stay in. 'Stead of on my hands." The scarred lieutenant closed his eyes, and inhaled sharply. "Too much blood. Altogether."

"You're a soldier, Russell. Pull yourself together."

"That's right. 'M a soldier. Soldier who doesn't like dead people. Partic- specially not when it's me that made 'em that way. Don't care what ever'body else thinks. Have to live with what's in my head. It has a trick of not going away, y'see. Ask Drew Venning. He knows. He don't sleep quiet, neither. Not now. Nor Rosie. Do you, Captain Toogood? Rest easy? "

"That's not a question I care to answer, lieutenant "

"'S a question I care to ask, though. Keep asking till I get a sensible answer." He breathed his odd mute laugh. "Have you ever read Master Walwyn, on the matter of our home-bred war? Or Master Lilburne? 'Who can live where he hath not the freedom of his mind, and exercise of his conscience?' That's Walwyn, on the matter of independency. I find I do not care for brother. Against brother. Nor care to be any man's tool in that fight."

"This is treasonous talk, lieutenant, and you'd do well to forget it, sober "

"We began treasonous talk when we took up arms with Parliament....captain. I am no man's creature."

"And nor am I!" Toogood snapped. "We fight for a common enemy!"

"No we don't, captain. This is a war without an enemy. I fight against the King. Not his people."

"They are *all* Malignants, sir! *All* an enemy!"

The lieutenant was drunk. It was a thing Toogood would do well to remember, or he might take offence at such subversive speech. He glared at Russell, who merely cocked an eyebrow. "Are they?" he said, thoughtfully. (He didn't sound drunk, though. He sounded like he might have been, very recently. But not now.) "So those soldiers you were heaving the timbers from. The men you gave your coat to, or prayed with. Enemy?"

Toogood set his jaw, and looked, very deliberately, at Russell's bloodied coat, and his shaking, dirty hands. (Thankful Russell is a disgrace to the Army. A failed adulterer, a lapsed Puritan, and a habitual drunkard when he is crossed. Remember that, before you rise to his bait.) "I could not tell," he said icily. "In the dark - amongst the smoke, and the confusion - I could not tell one from another. And in Christian charity, sir, I could not -"

"Exactly so," the lieutenant said, equally coldly. "You could not."

"They are the enemy, sir. You will do well to mind that. You turn gutless, lieutenant," Toogood snarled. "Pascoe, escort the lieutenant back to his quarters. I'll not have him preaching anarchy to the sentries."

"Guts," the lieutenant said, and lifted his bloody hands, "are the one thing I do not lack. I assure you, sir, I am surfeited with the internal workings of my fellow man. I know more about men's bowels than even Pettitt does. I have no desire to preach. Or to be preached at. I would like my bed. I would like not to dream. I imagine I may have one, but not both. Care to join me in another drink, Captain Toogood?"

22. SORROW WORKETH REPENTANCE

Casualties were light - so far as you could call Drew's losses of a quarter of his troop to be negligible. Drew himself, burned and bruised and strapped up and haunted. Simon Betterton, with a dirty gash in his forearm. Luce had not done the tidiest job on it, but by then his hands were numb and shaking anyway, and Betterton said he didn't mind none if it was a bit of a bodge job, so long as he didn't leak. Russell with an evil hangover, snarling over his accounts.

It was a couple of days' respite, that was all. A couple of days when it almost stopped raining, round about dusk on the second day, and the lad who brought dispatches had had an almost pleasant time of it, riding through an afternoon that was cool and damp, but with the promise of spring. Luce said the birds were beginning to peep, in the bare black trees, and certainly there was a bright eyed little robin who bounded in the walled garden of the house where they were quartered, and flicked his wings and his tail as if he were some child's spoiled favourite, in time of peace. Luce said the air was beginning to fill with rustles and chirrups, which seemed early to Hollie, but since he could hear bugger-all he could but take the brat's word for it.

It was only like having his head underwater, and Luce had peered into his ear and said he couldn't see anything. At which point Hapless Russell had snickered balefully and said he had always suspected as much, and Hollie threw a boot at his lieutenant's head. Luce did confess later that he had not known what he was looking for anyway, but that what he had seen seemed whole, and that probably, in time, Hollie's hearing would come back.

In the meantime he mostly folded his hands and looked attentive and took his lead from Luce, who, being a poet, had a habit of clear speech. Venning was stone deaf, too, after the blast, and the pair of them were cupping their ears and yelling at each other like a pair of old gatfers.

Fairfax had thanked Hollie - so far as he could tell - and he'd smiled wanly and nodded with very little idea of what he was being rewarded with, or threatened with. He didn't go a bundle on public displays of appreciation anyway, though he thought the telling of it might make Het laugh when next he set pen to - But there was still no letter in her firm, deliberate hand.

There was a fat little packet for Lucey, in his mother's hand, and a slip of a letter for Venning, which might cheer him up somewhat, but nothing for Hollie. Nothing. He might as well have ceased to exist. Him, Russell and Toogood, they were like the forgotten men. He was stiff, and deaf, and heartsick, and he felt a hundred years old and more, and yet what could he say? That he felt rootless and detached and lonely, with a wife and two daughters up the line and four troop of horse to his command? They'd laugh. Crying for the moon, Rosie, always wanting something tha cannot have, like a spoiled baby. Because thy wife cannot pet thee, being too busy with a new baby and a little one toddling, your nose is out of joint that you have a few scrapes and bruises and she is not there to hide your head in her petticoats? It wasn't that. It was that, in part. He wanted it to be simple, just he and she, and it could not, for both of them were part of a bigger thing: he did not yet know where their two worlds might cross, and where he might have a place in hers, nor she in his.

He was a fighting man sick of war. He smiled and said the proper words, but Torrington had turned his stomach, soured him for good and all against the business of breaking men's bodies. (Too many lads he knew in that church. Too many of Venning's fen-slodgers who would never see Norfolk again, or see it on an invalid's dole.) What was it Hapless called it, a war without an enemy? He did not mind - did not like, but could bear - to look in a man's eyes in battle, for it to be a game of skill, and chance. He thought he could probably bear it, to be killed so. Honestly. Not in some dreadful, unchancy accident. If he was a superstitious man - and he wasn't, of course he was not - he might have taken Torrington for a sign that the Lord was turning his face against them. But he was not, and so he laid a deal of the blame for stupid at Drew Venning's door.

And so did Venning, who was not credulous either, but only a very tired, all too human captain of horse who had given all his heart and most of his common sense in the service of Parliament. Hard to say, if Venning had been thinking straight, if he might have done something so wholly bloody stupid as to fire the lock off a powder magazine. The Fenman was notoriously hard of thinking at the best of times. Not daft, but - rigid. He thought in straight lines.

He touched Venning's shoulder, and the freckled captain looked up blankly and then shook his head, coming back to himself from whatever dark place he had been.

"Need to have a word, Drew," he said, and then, having a thought for what that word was going to be, and not caring to have it at battle-order volume in the middle of their quarters where any passing stranger might hear, who might not have a care for Captain Venning's pride, or his misery. "Care to have a walk? Horse lines?"

23. BE YE KIND TO ONE ANOTHER

Blossom was pleased to see them. Drew's big black Goliath was not, being singed and battered himself, and shuffled to the furthest extent of his picket and put his ears back, suspecting them of being about to inflict further indignity on him. "That was bloody stupid, Andrew," Hollie said flatly. He expected argument and justification. He got none.

"I know."

"What?"

"I know it was."

Goliath decided his master was harmless, after that initial suspicion, and put his whiskery chin in Venning's hand for fuss, and he stood rubbing the horse's black velvet muzzle and saying nothing. A state of affairs sufficiently unlike Captain Venning to be of concern.

"I been stupid for a while, bor," Drew said slowly. "I know it, too. Rosie, I need to talk to you."

"Now's as good a time as any," he said, and looked round. "I reckon there's not a soul around for miles. Just as well, wi' us two. Hey!"

Blossom had decided that if there was fussing to be had, he wanted his, too, and ambled forward, tangling his picket rope with Goliath's. The big black horse objected to this familiarity and there was a moment of chaos as two horses and two senior officers tried to resume order. It ended, as ever, with Hollie petting that brown bag of bones, and Blossom smugly reinforcing his place as possibly the shabbiest beast in the troop, but certainly the most indulged. "Get over, you lollopin' gret animal," Hollie said with mock severity.

"He can stop where he is." Venning scratched absently under his own horse's halter, and took a deep breath. "Rosie, I'm done. I ent coming no further West."

"Eh?" He surely had not heard that right. "But - Drew - here, you can't - we're all but finished up -"

"*I'm* all but finished up, bor. I know you lot reckon I'm daft a' best, but I ent so daft I'd put a spark to a powder store, if I were thinking straight. I been that bit duzzy since the autumn, Rosie, and it's time for me t'go home, I reckon, 'fore I does suffen worse than that."

He looked over Hollie's shoulder, up at the shrouded grey shoulder of the moor, and then smiled, and bent, and snapped his fingers to his brown and white shadow. A broad-shouldered, capable, sandy-haired countryman, with a grinning hound at his heel and a big solid horse at his back - but not a fighting cavalry commander. "I ent one to run on, 'ee knows that. Ent nobody can say I don't know my duty. Well, I done my bit, Rosie, 'ee can't ask me for no more than I give already, and t'ent like me to speak up and say so, but - here I be, and I go no further."

"But - " And then Hollie stopped, because the idea that he might remind Drew Venning of all people, of the meaning of loyalty, was shameful. "They reckon the King's finished. Just this last push."

"And then what, bor? We all shake hands an' go home? I don't reckon, and nor do you. Anyway, I heard ducks fart before -"

"You have *what*?"

"Them promises ent worth the paper they're written on." He gave a faint, shadowy smile. "Know that as well as I do, bor. Heard it all before, and me and you been around long enough to know when them up-along says it be all over by Christmas, they mean next Christmas.

Mebbe. Confident hope of a miracle, my lily-white ass. Me and you get the shitty end of the stick, Rosie, and it goes ill wi' me to hear you talking like one o' they, 'cause I know you better." The dog shoved his nose into Venning's hand again, tail beating against his boots like a drum beating the advance. "No fool like an old fool, sir, and 'ee might think I'm duzzy but I ent. Fool me once, shame on you. Fool me twice, shame on me. I ent coming. I'd ha' come West once for friendship's sakes, Rosie, and I would yet, but I got business to home, and that needs tending to first."

Hollie didn't think his friend knew that his expression had changed, almost imperceptibly. "Ah?"

"Got word from our Alice." And that explained much, for Drew Venning's Alice was a byword in the company for everything that was not Army - just like Hollie's Het, and every other trooper's girl; a little lighted window, a world in which every girl was sweet and faithful, and every bed was warm, and every table was full. Of all things, Drew loved his wife, his boy, and his home comforts.

The big freckled captain swallowed, audibly. "She been brought to bed of a lil' girl, bor. The lil' gal died, and our Alice been took badly. That letter that come? Some nice tabby up in Diss thought might be her place to tell me."

"Oh hell, Drew." Because that was the thing of nightmare for Hollie, the thing that he feared most of all in the world - more than his own death, more than the King's Army, the thought that one day he might one day get that letter from White Notley. He didn't know what he might do, if - "When you going?"

And to Hollie's discomfort, his friend covered his face with his hands, suddenly, and sobbed like a hurt child. "I don't know's I want to go, Rosie. I dunno what I'd say to her - dunno if gal'd want me there, even. Gret big clumsy lad like me, what use d'I be to her? But Rosie -" he looked up, blinking, "aye, I'm sorry. Ah, God, I'd be with her, I'd go tomorrow. But -" he puffed his cheeks out, and straightened up. "When *was* the last time you give me home leave?"

Which choked Hollie's commiseration like a ball of dust in his throat. He hadn't. Drew had never asked. He'd always been sure of Venning at his right hand, calmly and competently dealing with the shit in Hollie's absence, because Drew was as stolid and capable and unstoppable as a bull walking through a hedge. Without trying to be obvious about it, Hollie tried to count on his fingers. He'd seen Venning at Luce Pettitt's mother's, not this Christmas just gone, but two years before, with Alice. Drew had been at White Notley the spring they'd broke Russell out of custody, and Russell had been with the troop nigh on two years. Het had been near to birthing Thomazine, the last time Drew Venning had seen Diss. And Thomazine was two years, just. And if it had been two years since Venning had been at home -

The corner of Venning's mouth lifted, without much humour, and he nodded. "Aye, Rosie. That's right. Two years near enough to the day. Thass another reason I'd like to go home, and I dunno if the gal will have me." His fingers found the sweet spot under Tinners' jaw, and the dog grinned again, his tongue lolling in ecstasy. "Dunno what happened, d'ye see? Don't know if she was took against her will – could of happened, mebbe, we are at war, could've been the King's men, for all I know. Or Parliament's. We ent all on the side of angels, bor." He met Hollie's eyes, squarely. "Could be she got used to not having me around and she wanted for loving. Pretty girl, my Alice. Always was a pretty maid. And maybe we don't suit, no more. Maybe. Maybe I changed too much. Maybe I'm not much of a lad for laughing and japes like I was the once. Maybe. Maybe she'd rather I didn't come home, and she could start afresh. Maybe he sweethearted her, when she was sad, and it was just the once, for comfort."

He was looking at Hollie, but he wasn't seeing him. It wasn't like he was seeing far-off things, though. He was seeing the inside of his own head, and his own thoughts. "Could do with the comforting myself, bor. I done things, Rosie. I done things no decent lad should never have to do – and, aye, that's between me, my God, and my conscience, but how can I judge that gal, knowing what I done in my time?"

Not a lot Hollie could say to that. Hollie's hands were bloodier than most, if he cared to look too closely, and he did not, for the most part, because he was a career soldier. *Had been* a career soldier. Christ knows what he was now. Drew Venning was a gentleman by birth, well-born and nicely brought up, one of them eager passionate lads who had swung to Parliament's cause because they were well-connected enough to be stung by His Majesty's taxes, but not gentry enough to be personal friends. Poor bloody Venning had not come into this war to cause the death of two hundred prisoners in the house of God. Good lad to have on side one on one in a brawl, but Hollie did not think Venning could bear that he had – willing or not – caused the death of those men. It would eat at him, day and night, like a canker of the soul, unless he found his forgiveness.

"You want to go now?" Hollie said, elaborately casual. "Today?"

"Eh? Don't talk daft, how'd I – "

"You know how. I'd have Russell put you on the sick and hurt roll. Every other bugger is."

"Don't you *dare* tell Hapless Russell," Venning said, suddenly white with fury, and Hollie sat back in his seat and blinked in surprise. "I mean it, Rosie, don't you tell that judgmental bastard. He'd want to have her stoned or suffen, bloody woman taken in adultery, and I can do without having to put a bullet in his ear for wanton stupidity, an' all."

He did the lad a disservice, Hollie thought, but did not say. Wasn't a thing that was worth the arguing about. Russell had been taken in adultery himself, once. He wasn't likely to get zealous about it. "He's going to have to know summat," Hollie pointed out, "if you go off sick I'm thinking I might get him to act up. For a bit."

Two little spots of red burned on Venning's freckled cheekbones, and the dog stirred uncomfortably as if his master's hands had tightened on his ears. "Rather he didn't know nawthen, bor. I can't bear that smug godly bastard pitying me."

"You'd not have him take your lads?"

"I'd not have him in charge of my dog, Rosie. That lad ain't reliable, and well 'ee knows it. He'd act up like a good 'un for a week, and then he'd get bored and belt someone, and then where'd 'ee be? Lucey."

Lucey – amiable, gentle Lucey, in charge of a score of fierce Fen-slodgers? Aye, right. There'd be blood spilled, and it'd all be on the side of Parliament. That bird wouldn't fly. Venning ran a hand through his hair, and it all stood on end, making him look even more like an overgrown schoolboy than ever. "Can't go, then, can I? Was a kind thought, Rosie, and I'm grateful, but –"

"Toogood," Hollie said. "He'll take 'em. He's been under-strength since Yorkshire. Do him the world o' good."

"Oh, you are a bastard," Venning said admiringly. "That'll keep 'en out of trouble."

"Give the little bugger a bit of practise at minding his temper, too, 'cos them lads of yours will bite right back at him." He stood up. "Get gone, Andrew. Take you a wet week to get back up country, in this dirty weather. You all right for – you know?"

"Don't be daft, Rosie. You ain't got paid any more than I have." He looked so hopeful, though. With his lumpy darned linen and his worn boots and his ragged, shabby dignity, the poor sod, and Hollie wondered, with a cold stab of fear, just what Alice was going to think of what the Army of Parliament had made of her husband. And if maybe Het would make the same of him. And for the first time, maybe, if that had been why Het had been so keen to see him gone, him and his scruffy, hopeful; crew. He shook his head. No. Not Het.

"Get me traps packed, then," Drew said.

And Hollie wanted to say - he was sorry. Should have given Drew leave before now. Had put too much on those stolid, uncomplaining shoulders without asking. Should have thought. Should not have gone.

Wanted to say it, and did not, for the fear of what Drew might say in return; for the fear of opening a door that might not be closed again. The freckled Fenlander cocked his head on one side. "Want me to drop in on White Notley, bor? Take her a letter, just so she knows you're still in the land o' the living -"

Hollie thought of it. And then he shook his head. He could not ask so much, not of Drew, not after the words Het had had at their parting. "No. I'd not take you out of your way. Crack on, lad. Get on the road now, and you'll get a couple of hours' ride in before dusk."

24. AS FAR AS THE EAST IS FROM THE WEST

Torrington seemed to break them, the King's men disappearing quietly in the dust and the flames as if they had never been, and it was almost a gentle herding that sent Fairfax and his men down on into the West Country, like driving sheep to the fold on a winter's evening. It did a disservice to say they took Launceston, and the castle there. There was little in the way of a defence.

Lucey sat quiet and still and made sure he was facing in approximately the right direction to appear to be paying attention, whilst giving most of his consideration to the basket of bread rolls that someone had thoughtfully put in front of him. Too dark, in this draughty old-fashioned apartment upstairs in Launceston's main street, to see much more than a length up the frozen expanse of table, and the fire smoked abysmally, but he could at least do Fairfax the courtesy of looking as if he was listening.

Actually, he was keeping a very close eye on the rest of the rabble he was presently brigaded with. Black Tom Fairfax had a personal reputation of honour and temperacy. He was also either seriously misguided or supernaturally perceptive, because he surrounded himself with some very peculiar officers. Around this table, his peers ranged from the erratically godly to the - if you were being charitable - mercurial, and Luce, for his sins, was attached in some way to most of them.

It had not been the easiest of meetings. Launceston was a fair town, busy and bustling and intent on its business, though it was not at its best on a bleak February afternoon when the clouds were intent on touching the grass and everything was bare, black, and wet. Luce's diplomatic skills were stretched to their fullest, to exclaim over the house in Church Street's beauty, or the opulence of its furnishings. It was, indeed, a perfectly nice house. He had been quartered in the Bishop of Worcester's Palace. His uncle was the Earl of Essex. The house at Church Street was, as Hollie Babbitt rather uncharitably pointed out under disguise of his handkerchief, nowt a pound, in comparison.

Kenelm Toogood was an embarrassment, mute and glowering as far from anyone else at table as he could be seated. And if anyone was expecting Colonel Babbitt to be a formal and imposing personage of note, they were going to be sadly disappointed in the scruffy, dishevelled figure dabbing his nose to his cuff when he thought no one was looking, having exhausted three handkerchiefs in short order. Russell was saying nothing to anyone, but applying himself with his plate with as grim a relish as if the - slightly undercooked - mutton thereupon was the person of Sir Ralph Hopton himself, presently quartered at Stratton, twenty miles away. And poor Betterton, being from about as far north as it were possible to be without being a Muscovite, sat with his chair tucked up tight against the table and his eyes darting every which way in more or less total incomprehension, trying to make himself invisible.

This wasn't a council of war, it wasn't anywhere *near* being a council of war, it was at best a rather frigid social gathering of the new Commander-in-Chief of the Army of Parliament and a number of the Cornish Parliamentarian stalwarts. The pity of it was that even with wives and other assorted family impedimenta to bump up the numbers, they were still somewhat less than an impressive gathering, and there was a lot of rather hesitant smiling and a desperate scrabble to remember names. (Unless you were Hollie, who just honked like a Michaelmas goose whenever anyone spoke to him and pleaded an inflammation of the throat as his excuse for mute incivility.)

That good Parliamentarian gentleman Sir John Robartes, who owned the great house at nearby Lanhydrock where they were rather conspicuously not dining, was in Plymouth and notable by his absence. It was probably for the best. His wife, Lucy, was not well, they said: a poor, sweet, godly lady, but very pretty, and the sea air in Plymouth was likely much better for her, poor maid, than being at the mercy of the cold and the damp airs of a Cornish winter. Luce himself was presently very much at the mercy of one particularly well-preserved lady in her middle years who had her hand on his sleeve and her foot planted between his own two feet, and was alternately rubbing her toes up and down the back of his leg and telling him the intimate life stories of every family within forty miles since the Flood. Sometimes she did both together, which was deeply disconcerting. He rather suspected he was going to have to write it all down on his napkin, before the evening ended. Perfectly fascinating. All of it. Including the footwork.

So. Frail, pious, beautiful Lucy Robartes - "oh, some of the meditations she writes!" Tamsyn Launcells said ardently, "they're beautiful, and so thoughtful!" - quietly fading away in Plymouth while her husband got on with the business of ostentatiously keeping his nose out of the war. "Thinking of his family," Tamsyn said, and put her free hand to her bosom, though Luce wasn't sure if it was an invitation to partake or a indication of deep thought. Whichever it was, it made that scapegrace Toogood snort into his wine, and it crossed Luce's mind, possibly late, that Kenelm Toogood was a Callington boy; his home turf was not ten miles distant. By the ironic lift of his brows, Toogood knew Mistress Launcells very well indeed, not to mention the Robartes family.

But no help to be expected from the Robartes quarter, anyway. This meagre gathering was what there was - that, and the ten thousand men presently quartered in and around the town, halfway up a hill in the middle of a Cornish spring. Tam Launcells was a widow - or, you see, there would have been another company to hand, for it seemed that Master Launcells had been a good Parliament man, in his youth, and much as though she would have liked to have raised her own troop, it wasn't a thing that a respectable elderly matron ought to do - and she rolled a velvet-brown eye at Luce hopefully, expecting words of flattery in denial that she was neither elderly nor respectable,

"Now, Tam, you're confusing the boy," Toogood said across the table. "If you're trying to be an old woman, act like one. You know as well as I do Sir John Robartes had his fingers burnt with Essex -"

"Just as you did, Kenelm," she said tartly. Which did, indeed, imply a relationship of some standing.

"Just as I did. Aye, and if I'd been governor of Plymouth myself, I'd have made haste back there as fast as my sails could carry me when it all fell apart this side of the Tamar, and shut the door after me. Especially if it'd been me who'd encouraged Essex to come down here in the first place. I reckon if I'd been giving men that kind of advice, I'd keep my mouth shut thereafter, as well."

"That's a *terrible* thing to say about Sir John!"

"As you say," Toogood said dryly. "Thinking of his family."

"Ignore him," she said firmly to Luce. "You were never used to be a cynic, Kenelm."

"I was never used to be a rebel, either," Toogood said, and he sounded rather forlorn about it. Luce glanced up quickly, but not quickly enough to catch the Cornishman's sardonic salute. "Pitying me, now, cornet? Don't waste your time."

"Cadson is doing well," she said, changing the subject quickly. "And don't tell me you're not interested, Captain Toogood, because you are."

"T'ain't my bidness, maid," he mocked her, a faint, wry smile on his face, and it was possibly the first time Luce had seen Toogood sufficient at his ease to smile. At anyone.

"Surely! And no doubt John Trevaskis is none of your business, either?"

Which wiped even that faint smile from his face. "Correct, Tam. John Trevaskis is none of my business. Never was, apart from in your head. Now keep your long nose out of my affairs, mistress."

There was no way, of course, that Toogood could get up and storm away without causing offence, and so he must remain seated, white to the lips and furious, and bend all his attention on the stout gentleman to his right, his conversation ignoring Tam Launcells as ostentatiously as the washing of a ruffled cat. She turned back to Luce and smiled with gentle malice. "A troubled young man, our captain. He was not always quite so - complicated, you know." Her smile softened, grew reminiscent. "He was an easy boy to love, once."

"As you did?" he said sympathetically, and she looked at him, her mouth open in unflattering surprise.

"*Me*? And Kenelm Toogood? Young man, he is twenty years my junior, and his wife would have had me *horse-whipped* had I turned so much as an eyelash his way!"

25. A LILY AMONG THORNS

Russell was all too aware of his broken and not very clean fingernails, and of the fact that the girl next to him smelt of roses. For the last six weeks he had mostly smelt damp, black powder, and death. And now he could smell roses.

He folded his hands around his cutlery - looking, he suspected, like a clod who did not know what a fork was, but it was that or look like a gravedigger - and looked at his plate. She was wearing - he didn't know, something pale and crisp, with a perfect white collar pinned at the throat with a dark brooch. He wanted to look, and to shovel the whole of her into his memory, greedily - and at the same time, he didn't want her to know that he was doing it.

"The meat is a little undercooked," he said primly, instead, to Hollie Babbitt on his left, and seeing his commander's eye light thoughtfully on the napkin, added in a fierce undertone, "Don't you *dare* blow your nose on that thing!"

"Can use my sleeve, if you prefer?" Hollie said, and sniffed instead. Russell gritted his teeth, and wondered if it would be considered insubordination to stab his commander in the back of the hand with a fork.

On the other hand, he also knew when he was being baited, these days, and so he took a deep breath, which was no hardship, and contented himself with one hard look at the colonel.

It made him awkward. He knew of some of these people, by reputation, or by name. Decent, godly people, some of them, and people whom he would be honoured to know, and what did he have? Hollie blowing his nose on the linen, and Luce across the table inspecting the bosom of some sparkle-eyed baggage who was no better than -

Hollie who was ill, and unhappy, and would rather be in bed, and was adrift without reliable Drew Venning to anchor him. Luce who had been married and now was not, and was desperate to hold to the feeling of being loved, even if only for a moment. You saw things like that, if you were - alike, yourself. It made Russell feel very old, and very wise, and very forgiving. Still very lonely, but perhaps kinder than he had been, once.

"Hapless, are you getting this cold or summat?" Hollie said, in what he presumably suspected was a discreet whisper. His hearing was still not what it was. "You're huffing like an overladen baggage-mule."

"Thank you, sir," he said through gritted teeth. "I may assure you of my continued good health."

Something brushed his flank, as soft as a butterfly's wing, and he glanced down. It was the rose-girl's elbow. "Is he actually deaf?" she whispered, and he sat upright for a moment and said nothing and just looked at her.

"Well, then," she added, when he said nothing. "Is it both of you, then?"

And nobody, ever, in his life, had spoken to Thankful Russell so teasingly. "I," he began, and that wasn't how he wanted to begin, he did not want to talk of his miserable self to the rose-girl, "you -"

"Or daft, perhaps? An impediment in your speech? Or your understanding?" She was smiling. That was the part that stunned him. She was looking up into his marred face as if it did not matter, with her eyes all alight with merriment, and little dimples in her face that were so soft that they could have been put there by an angel's finger - "In plain words, sir, do you truly not talk, or are you simply too exalted for the present company?"

"I - I do," he said faintly, and dropped his knife.

"Aye. He talks, and some of it even makes sense," Hollie muttered darkly, and he and the rose-girl exchanged a look of amused toleration over him while he scrabbled for the cutlery. "You'll be John Trefusis's daughter, then? If he's the dark gentleman in the sober suit?"

"I am, sir. Mistress Amy Trefusis. Mama is Jane, but I fear she has the same cold as you do, so I am attending with papa in her place. And the young man talking to your friend with the little -" she wiggled a finger on her top lip to indicate poor Betterton's moustache - "the one who looks like a netted hare, poor sweet - that's my little brother. His name is Gaverigan, but really, we all call him Gavan. He's a pet."

Gavan Trefusis did not look like a pet, unless, possibly, a pet bull, or a mastiff. He was a large young gentleman with his sister's black curls, but built along somewhat more epic proportions than the pleasingly-plump Amy. "You watch yourself, Russell," Hollie said meaningfully. "That lad'd make two of you, and a bit left over. Bet he wrestles, as well, doesn't he, lass?"

She blinked, and twisted her mouth a little sideways. "Um. No? No, sir, he doesn't wrestle. I imagine he knows how to, though. All boys do, don't they? Before they are made gentlemen?"

"Oh, surely," Russell said firmly, and kicked Hollie under the table, before his commander could disclose that the last thing that had been wrestled in his presence had been a set of recalcitrant accounts.

It was an odd dinner, neither flesh nor fowl. The good Parliament families, the Trefusis family and the Corytons and the Eliots, and the rebel officers under Fairfax, all sniffing about each other's hinder parts like a table full of stray dogs, unsure as yet as to where the power would lie. A remarkably civil war, in which one might dine with a Parliamentarian captain today and call him your friend, and tomorrow in a military capacity - well. You might ask Toogood what would happen, when your friends and neighbours turned against you. And so Russell was careful, and mindful, and very, very abstemious.

Which was more than Hollie was, but then he was sick, and Amy Trefusis looked as if she wanted to laugh when the colonel's eye lit on the baked calf's-head for the fourth time. "Does nobody want that last bit of meat?" he said hopefully, and she bit her lip and pushed the dish up the table.

"Feed a cold, and starve a fever," she said, and would not look at Russell at all, for fear that either of them should laugh. And Hollie agreed, nodding approvingly that young lasses today had such good sense, and Luce across the table had given a great sigh of resignation and pushed the bread rolls skating across the great expanse of white linen. And there had been a little ripple of amusement, and a very little thaw, that even Parliament men who were not born and bred this side of the Tamar were creatures of flesh and blood, and appreciated good Cornwall feeding just as much as any other.

26. CASTLE TERRIBLE

Remarkably, it was not raining, and Hollie stepped out into the soft night and stared up at the violet sky, all freckled with stars above the steep black slope.

It was February, and yet the air was balmy, fresh and slightly cold and all alive with the scents of earth warming and things beginning to break through the frozen soil. And he wrapped his cloak tighter about himself, because it was not yet full spring, and they were up high, here in the castle on its old-fashioned mound, and the wind still blew chill.

He heard a step on the crumbling stone stairs and spun round with his hand to his sword. Not because he was afraid of attack, because the place was in such a bloody horrible state of repair that he wouldn't have troubled himself to repel one, but -

"Bloody unchancy place," Kenelm Toogood said, and aye, that was what it was. "They said you were up here."

"And so I am," Hollie said. "Came up for a breath of air." He laughed, feeling the last warmth of the spiced wine in his head, warm and slightly muzzy. "Bloody close in that apartment, if you ask me. I thank God Parliament has no more supporters in the West, or we'd not have fitted round the table."

Toogood looked at him blankly, and then his lean, shadowed face lit into a smile. The second tonight, as it happened. "Well, the Lord's blessings for small mercies, indeed. I'd like a word. If you're free. Sir. But not here."

"Good a place as any," Hollie said, but Toogood shook his head.

"Not here. Too many memories, sir. I don't care for Castle Terrible. Smells of blood to me, Colonel Babbitt. Got long memories in my family - long memories, and we bear a grudge."

"I'd noticed," Hollie said dryly. "Castle Terrible?"

"What else d'you call it, when thirty men are rounded up and brought here at gunpoint to be hanged, drawed and quartered? D'you ever hear of William Body, colonel? Aye. Well. Thought not. D'you know what his job was, here? He was sent by the King - hundred years ago, almost - to come down to Helston and vandalize the saints' resting-places there. Nice lad. Nice sort o' job, wouldn't you say? Cornwall being the land of the saints. He must ha' been busy. Two bright lads stoved his head in for him. This place? Vengeance. Thirty murders worth, in recompense for Master Body. Royal justice, that is. Funny thing, my family sort of took against kings a bit back then, and when this one starts telling me what I shall and shall not believe, I start getting a bit twitchy."

"I'll give you that one," Hollie said warily. The same thought crossed his mind, often, as the son of an illegal Dissenting lay preacher in the Army.

"Can see my house from here," the Cornishman went on, and for a minute Hollie thought he had changed the subject. "About ten miles due south, give or take. There's been Toogoods at Cadson since - ha! Since the Prayer Book. You might say rebellion's in the blood, sir. There's none there now. The bastards druv us out, with fire and sword. You know that. May we go down from this place?" He stopped again, and put a hand on the ruined parapet. "You look close, to the south, and there's a light. Could drive myself mad with that, colonel, if I had a mind to."

Hollie was delighted - perhaps not delighted, then, but a little startled - that Toogood was seeking to unburden himself in such a wise, given their previous relations. They picked their way down the spiralling stairs, out onto the grassy mound. It wasn't till they were a good half-mile away that the captain's taut breathing eased. Hollie propped his elbows on the damp, mossy stone of the churchyard wall, and stared up into the velvet black.

"Bugger of a thing, gossip," he said, when Toogood had finished apologising for his poor taste in in-laws. "So. Why d'you think I'd care, what that wench puts about in the way of old news? So your wife's people were Malignants. What of it?"

"You should. My wife's, and half my friends -"

"Should I? Wi' my reputation? Captain, believe you me, if Grenville has his way - and if he finds out it's me up here - a bit of stale tattle from when you was in short coats, is going to be nowt a pound." He laughed, because it was, after all, quite funny. "Let's just say when I knew Sir Richard last, I was not exactly the fine upstanding member of respectable society you see before you now."

"You must have been bad," Toogood said, before he could stop himself.

"Bloody horrible," Hollie agreed. "That godly lot in there wouldn't have owned me. Trust me, Captain Toogood. I can think of little more guaranteed to turn a decent party against a cause than knowing it's paying the wages of a degenerate sellsword who spent of the war in Europe drunk under a baggage wagon or under the skirts of a brothel-keeper, not to say slaughtering good Protestants in the pay of the Imperial Army." It was dark, but he could see Toogood's jaw drop slightly. "That's what Skellum Grenville'd have you believe. Aye, and I could say a few choice things about him, as well, but I won't. Plotting, deceiving bastard as he is. If we're in the mood to share confidences, captain, I was married to a lass who ran an inn. No more sinister than that. But it's not what Sir Richard put about, in the day, is it? A drunk and a whoremaster - he reckoned. He couldn't bear the competition - not the whoring, mind, I'd not care to comment on his proclivities - Christ, no, he was desperate for advancement and I had the advancement he wanted. So he took it off me. I would not turn my back on that man, Captain Toogood. I did once, and I spent the next three years as a plain trooper."

"A knife between the ribs?" Toogood said warily. (Not so old, then, as he liked to present. His eyes were as round as cartwheels, to hear these tales.)

Hollie snorted. "Him? Christ, no. Hanging's his kick. He'd have me throttled, if he could. That'd please him. No, captain, your petty misdemeanours pale into insignificance beside my - alleged - ones. Though, I give you it won't help. God help us all if they find out what Russell was like, in his daft days."

"Or that Cornet Pettitt was married to a man," the captain said primly, and Hollie laughed in spite of himself.

"He was no such - aye, well, I take your point entirely. There's none of us innocent."

Toogood took a deep breath. "No, no you don't understand. Aye, there was talk. Well, Loveday's family was - they are - they were - they're for the King."

"Lot of 'em about," Hollie said. "So?"

"Your mate Grenville - you know he had men posted this side of the Tamar with instructions to shoot any incomer as set foot over the county border?"

"Sounds about right. Building his little empires again, then? Any incomer as did not bow the knee to King Grenville?" He expected that to be met with a laugh.

"Aye," Toogood said, and was not smiling, "pretty much. He has - *he had* - visions of an independent Kernow. Keep the Duchy and the Stannaries, and hang the rest. Keep, mark you, that which benefits the rich, and the great. You can see why Loveday's folk would have had her marry higher than me. I'm neither rich nor great. Person of no significance, me. Well, she never said so much. Master Grenville and his like would ha' cut off their nose to spite their face, inviting His Majesty into bed wi' they. Well. I don't trust him, colonel. I've no more love for the English than Skellum has himself, but I'll not sell my birthright for a mess of pottage. Or tin, for that."

"I'm an Englishman myself," Hollie said, hoping he sounded casual about it..

"I know." Which was Hollie told. "I've no loyalty to you, either." He crossed to the parapet, leaned on it, so close that he touched Hollie's flank with his elbow. "The only loyalty I own is to this land. Which is not a thing you will understand. You - and your Cause, and your Parliament, can all go to hell, so long as I can come home to my hearth-place and live at peace. One day, colonel, you and your kind will be gone. God willing, and you can take the Grenvilles and the Kendalls and the rest of their Malignant brood to hell with you, an you leave me in peace to live as I see fit in my own place."

"Better the Devil you know?"

"The same. And I got me a long spoon, colonel."

And rather unexpectedly, Toogood grinned. "It's too bloody quiet, sir. I know Cornwall. And it's too bloody quiet."

27. DWELLING SAFELY IN THE WILDERNESS

"Quiet," Hollie said, and turned from looking down the slick cobbles of Church Street at a lowering raw February morning, and looked at Thomas Fairfax, cocking an eyebrow. "Don't you think?"

"I'm sure I don't know what you mean."

"I mean, it's funny that all of a sudden us lot turn up in Cornwall and there they are, gone. The garrison's melted away like the driven snow and there's not a Malignant for miles."

"That's not true, Holofernes. There was a little under a thousand Royalist horse still in good order -"

"And they're nowhere to be seen. Scared of the weather, you reckon? Think they might melt?"

"*You* are being insolent."

"I have got all the hairs stood up on the back of my neck and am expecting to be shot at any minute. Sir. They are up to summat. No - scratch that - he is up to summat."

"What - Sir Ralph Hopton? Oh, grow up, colonel! Stop seeing bogeymen under the beds!" Fairfax shook his head. "Or are you still starting at shadows? Torrington took the heart out of the King's men in the West. Hell itself could not have made a more hideous sulphur than it. All the Tamar crossings are in our hands, and it is more than clear to me that the hope of the Western horse breaking out to rejoin His Majesty is an increasingly forlorn one. What is it that you fear now?"

"Skellum Grenville," Toogood said grimly, stepping out of the shadows, and Fairfax grunted.

"Oh, marvellous. I see your ever-boundless optimism is as contagious as the pox, colonel. What ails you, then, Captain Toogood? Other than too close confinement with Job's comforter here? Gentlemen, I put it to you plain. There are no lurking bogeys. Sir Richard is safely on St Michael's Mount, and several miles out at sea, and he has been since January. Unless you suggest he might grow wings and fly. And then raise an Army of his own. Without access to funds, powder, shot, or horse. In the middle of an occupying force."

He smiled faintly. "The pair of you grow old-womanish. I have heard your warnings. Colonel Babbitt, I suggest you have more important matters to occupy yourself with. I might drop a word of caution into your ear for onward transmission, sir, on the matter of the behaviour of one unmarried gentleman of your household with a respectable lady of this parish? A little *too* forward, colonel. A word to the wise."

"Luce Pettitt was back in his quarters by midnight!" Hollie said, nettled, and Fairfax's lean face broke into an uncharitable smile.

"He was, and I know he was. Let us say, though, that there is a gentleman not too distant - no, not you, Toogood, I quit you of the accusation - who has an eye to the somewhat overripe charms of Mistress Launcells. Or rather, the late Master Launcells' goods and chattels, although I imagine that given the lady's tendency to display her goods like a fair-day market, his interest is not entirely mercenary."

Toogood made a horrible gurgling noise, and Hollie bit his lip not to make a similar. "Why, Sir Thomas, you grow unkind," he murmured, and Fairfax acknowledged it with a tilt of the head.

"Oddly, Holofernes, I am tired of ladies past their best setting their caps at my officers. I find it always ends in tears. I have a perfectly good wife of my own at home, and I should like to see my wench again this side of midsummer. So if Mistress Launcells could see her way to pulling her bodice up a few inches and keeping her hands to herself under the supper-table, and if your cornet could perhaps restrain himself from a flirtation that I suspect comes as naturally as breathing to that boy, I'd take it kindly. Or, colonel, if I may be plainer, Pettitt is likely to find himself keeping company with Sir Richard Grenville on the Mount, being the furthest place I can conceive from feminine companionship!"

"You are harsh, sir," Hollie said.

"I am *trying* to keep him out of trouble! It does not help the cause of peace if half of our allies are at each other's throats due to your cornet's inability to keep his breeches buttoned. Or what Colonel Bennet, who is a Godfearing man and does not approve of such lewd behaviour, thinks is his inability to do so, and felt it his duty to relate to me at some length this morning. I fear young Luce is not popular with our supporters in the West, Hollie. A little too handsome, and a little bit too popular. You may wish to pass that on to him, and suggest that he is - mindful - of that regard." He sighed, and pushed his hair out of his eyes. It was still raining, but even in that dim watery light through the thick green glass of the apartment in Church Street Thomas Fairfax was less Black Tom than Silver Tom. "No, gentlemen, you are perfectly correct in one regard. The war in the West will not be won or lost on the field, but around the table."

"Hope it's a better spread than last night's," Hollie muttered darkly. "That mutton were older than me -"

"And that, sir, is *exactly* the kind of remark I should rather you keep to yourself!"

Toogood opened his mouth to say something - unhelpful, probably - and Hollie looked at him and shook his head, just once. He knew a losing battle when he saw one. What he feared was that the war now was not on ground he was comfortable with. Like fighting in uncertain light, or in the rain, on shifting footing: an enemy you could not come to grips with, and who might attack from any direction, with any weapons. He had a suspicion that Toogood knew about as much about diplomacy as his horse did. Now was not a good time to stand their ground. Retreat, and regroup, and come about.

28. THE TABERNACLE OF ROBBERS

"He doesn't understand, either," Toogood said gloomily. The church seemed as good a place to intrigue as any. It echoed, for one thing, so there was no way anyone could creep around the freezing granite building without attracting any attention.

"Right, then," Hollie said, and flinched a little at how loud his voice was in that vaulted space. Ducked his head and looked at his hands, red with cold and a little chewed at the knuckles, hoping to look lost in godly reflection. "What does he not understand - and I'm guessing you mean Fairfax, not Lucey?"

"Bennet is at Hexworthy House, aye? Colonel Bennet, as he is now. I know him. Good family, know them well. Out at Lawhitton parish, off the Tavistock road. We'd have passed by his house on the way down." Toogood nodded to himself. "Robartes at Bodmin, you know that, though I'd not look to help from that quarter, not with Sir John in Plymouth keeping out o'trouble and the mistress failing. They say."

"Your point?"

"D'ee draw a line across this county, colonel, and all the good Parliament men are in the south east. This end. All good men in their way, if you take my meaning. But. Get down west - where the Prince is, stood off at Falmouth, where the Queen was, where Skellum Grenville is - I'd not trust to none of 'em, sir. They'm King's men, to the last. And them sat round the table last night, down Flushing and

Falmouth way - I'd not trust none of 'em. Now nobody can say, not for sure, this side of the county blows this way and this side blows that way, but I can say, the more I think on it, the more I'm with you. Like I said. Too quiet by half. That's not a thing I'd say lightly to you. Being an incomer, like you are."

He grinned, and picked at a splinter in the back of the pew in front of him. "That's by way of a joke, mind. Aye, we'll get so far as Bodmin, no trouble at all, and hunker down thinking it's all wine and roses. And then ten miles outside-a Bodmin, when you're deep in Rashleigh country, all bets are off."

"You make it sound like bloody bandit country," Hollie muttered.

"That's right, colonel. Bandits wi' gold and friends in high places. And they're the worst sort."

29. HIS CHILDREN WILL HAVE A PLACE OF REFUGE

There were men coming and going between Bodmin and Castle An-Dinas, twelve miles distant, at all times of the day and night, while Sir Ralph Hopton and his men were drawn off. Hopton was considering his next move. Fairfax was watching him, like a cat at a mousehole. It was a simple thing, then, for Toogood to take another man's horse and pick his way over the other direction. Towards Callington, and Calstock, and Harrobear.

He had thought of it - how could he *not* have thought of it, lying not thirty miles apart from his only child? But so far as he had considered it at all, he had thought only of riding in triumph at the head of his troop, into the peaceful garden at Harrobear.

Taking his men in martial order across the close-cropped turf where he'd once walked with Loveday, asking if she might one day come to care for him. Quartering his men - imposing his will - on a house that had never welcomed him, for all her people were only a little, a very little, younger branch of the Carews. The Toogoods at Cadson weren't wealthy, but they had been a coming family. Then. Respectable, and Kenelm the only boy, so that the manor and all the land and the rents it brought in - the holdings in the mines at Kit Hill - they would have been sufficient, to keep Loveday Carew in more comfort than she was customed to, in that old-fashioned granite manor. He had always meant to come to Harrobear again, and force them to own him, this time. Look him in the eye and tell him why they had cast her off to die, for giving her heart to a Parliament man.

(And then he would have put the manor to the torch, for once he had had his excuses, he had no further desire to hear anything from his erstwhile father-in-law. Other than, possibly, a begging for mercy. Which he would not receive, just as she had not)

Not really a plan, then, not a considered thing. But it was a thing of gossip that Kenelm Toogood was back in Launceston, though people did not seem to connect the ghost of a laughing, daredevil young husband with the lean, bitter veteran who leaned up against the wall in the shadows as one of Thomas Fairfax's own personal company, with his arms folded, and said nothing. They knew who he was, though they never spoke of the golden days before the war, not in his hearing. He did not think he could have borne it if they were kind, or sorry. Instead, they talked to him in Launceston as if he had been away for a week, on some petty errand that they need not even speak of.

As if it had not happened, as if the King's men were not melting away to their homes like so much cat-ice in the sun. (Grenville's men, then, for they were loyal to Skellum, and without him at their head, they did not seek to fight for an English cause.)

Pert lil' tacker, her be, they said. Bright as a button, and twice as pretty. Take after her mammy, she do. And so over a matter of hours that vague thought of taking Harrobear by fire and sword, became a much firmer, more realistic thing. Of saddling Babbitt's plain, reliable Blossom, who could be ridden on a pack-thread and was not so recognisable as his own rat-tailed Charles, in the light of a weeping dawn.

Of riding out west, towards Hopton, and of doubling patiently back on his own tracks, and plodding on back to Calstock, and the Devon border, and the little manor that crouched there in a fold of the hills, nuzzled against the moor like a piglet at a sow's flank. Of muffling himself in his cloak, and waiting, and waiting, for the beat of hooves on the track till little Chesten Toogood might ride out on a stout little pony, for fresh air and a little exercise, with none but a stout little groom for company - for these were her grandfather's lands, and what rogue would dare to offer her offence in her own family's back garden?

Babbitt's brown gelding was neither quick nor handy, but he was willing, and when Toogood set his spurs to the beast he picked up his pace quick enough, and came galloping in from the high trees like an eagle out of the sun.

The groom was dealt with easily. There was none to know that Kenelm Toogood turned squalmish at the last, nd did not cut his throat, but bound him hand and foot and slung him over his own horse's saddle, for the beast to wander as it would.

The fat little pony bolted, and he sat and watched with a feeling that was half mockery and half pride as his child wrestled with the little brute like a man, across the close-cropped turf and the boulders. She came off, though, in the end, a fall that must have bruised her, bum and dignity and all. He saluted the little wench in his head. (Her mother's spirit, to the life.)

And then he picked her up, spitting like a little vixen, an put her kerchief about her mouth so that she might not scream and draw attention to them both till he could get to a place of greater comfort and say the things that had choked in his throat these last three years, uninterrupted. He looked down at her, still muffled in his cloak, looking down into those slanted dark blue eyes that were so like the ones he saw in his own shaving-glass. She looked back at him without so much as a flicker of recognition.

"Time to go home, my bird," he said gruffly. And set Blossom's head back towards Bodmin.

30. CONCERNING THEM THAT REBEL

Sir Ralph Hopton stood off at Castle-an-Dinas, to consider what his next move might be. As if it were a giant, civilised, game of chess, in which ten thousand Parliament men and the rags of a defiant Royalist army, were no more than carved pieces on a great green and grey board, sea-wrapped.

So Luce thought, anyway, and had said so much to Russell, the once. And been looked at blankly for his pains, for Russell was a dear soul, and steadfast, but not much given to fancy. There were other fancies he could take, but up here on the edge of the moor, wrapped in rain and mist and loneliness, standing in command of a sentry picket on the edge of the world, you could imagine it.

There had been all sorts of goings-on today. Blossom had been taken out of the lines without his master's knowledge, and Hollie was livid about it, and stalking about the pickets looking for someone to punch. The sound of hoofbeats coming out of the mist made Luce's toes curl in his boots, because of all things what he did not need was some bloody Royalist marching in with a peace offering, or an unconditional surrender or something. What he was likely to get from Colonel Babbitt currently was a punch in the head.

But there was yet mercy in the world, because the advance party was none other than Kenelm Toogood, and he looked down from his horse and blinked and for once he did not look too intimidating, not at all. He looked, if anything, quite apologetic. Technically, it was not, in point of fact, his horse. The draggled brown gelding looked quite apologetic, too, but then Blossom often did.

"Captain Toogood," Luce said mildly, "that is - you are - that is Colonel Babbitt's horse, is it not?"

Kenelm nodded. "Aye. It is. And this is my daughter. Chesten - make your courtesy." He shook the little girl's shoulder, and she looked at Luce with great tragic wet eyes, as black as a little raven's. And then she spat at his feet.

"Damnable rebel," she croaked.

"Bloody hell," Luce said, and bit the inside of his cheek hard not to laugh. "Er - er, captain, um, that is the colonel's horse, and he has been looking for the beast for most of the day. And I - I - I thought your daughter was *dead*?"

A draggled little person, on a stolen horse. "How - how old is she, Toogood?"

"I am six years," she said.

"And malapert, I see," Hollie said out of the murk. "An explanation, Captain Toogood?"

"The horse is quiet, colonel -"

"I couldn't give a shit about the bloody horse!" he yelled, and Luce gave him a stern look.

"Language, sir. In front of the child."

"Lucey, I am going to -"

"Little ears," Luce said meaningly.

"Where is my grandpapa?" the little maid in the soldier's coat said, and her raven's eyes suddenly started to blink rapidly. "I want my grandpapa."

"Your mam's name was Loveday," Kenelm said in a very odd voice. "D'ee know who your daddy is, my maid?"

"I have no daddy," she said, stiff as a little schoolboy reciting a lesson. "He was a bad man, and a damnable rebel, and he went away and left me and mammy to fend for ourselves. Grandpapa said."

"What was his name?"

"*Enough,* Toogood. You're scaring the child," Hollie cut in, but it was too late, and the white-faced little girl had slipped abruptly down Blossom's flank and gone fleeing into the darkness. Toogood spurred the horse to pursue her, but thank God, Hollie's stupid, sweet brown horse was keener to bury his head in his master's coat, and only jerked his head up and rocked a little back onto his quarters.

"You stupid bastard!" Hollie yelped, "you could have ridden the little lass down!"

"Where's my daughter?" the Cornishman yelled back, "I can't leave her go so -"

"She's in a camp full of armed men, you dozy bugger, how much harm's like to come to the child, so long as we know to mind for her?"

"I'll give word," Luce said with resignation. He had no intention of doing any such thing, of course. He'd marked the child where she fled, his eye accustomed to seeking out small female Pettitts at family gatherings. It was an easy trick, once you knew the way of it. You just had to train your eye to look at waist height, instead of at the height of a man's head. And for where a picketed horse might spook, as a small, sobbing girl-child might run under his nose. He sighed, and tucked his hair behind his ears. "With your permission, sir?"

Hollie shot him one furious glare. "*Go.*"

She'd gone to ground in a pile of fodder. It was damp, at the base, and it must smell abominable, but the tail of her skirt protruded from the rotten hay. "Mistress," he said gently. "Mistress, um, Toogood?" - had they given her another name? was she truly Toogood's lost child, or had he mistaken a daughter he had not set eyes on in two years, for she must have been a baby-rounded little person when last he saw her, and this was a square, sturdy maiden. "Chesten? Is that a Cornish name?"

Silence from the hay, but Russell's pied horse, hobbled nearby, prodded his mismatched nose into the mound and blew with deep suspicion, and then jerked away as if it had bitten him.

"That's Thomas," Luce said, and settled himself on his haunches in the mud. He was wearing riding boots. The mud wouldn't kill him. "Thomas belongs to my friend. Do you want to meet him?" Still no answer, but the tail of the skirt slithered slowly into the mound, like a snake's tail into its hole. "Mistress Toogood," he said firmly. "Now look. Your father has asked that I mind you, while he is called away on regimental business." A pair of scuffed, muddy shoes appeared. One bearing a drabbled little rosette, and the other not -

oh, Kenelm, she has her own people, she has people who care for her, and you took her from them -

"That man," she said, in that muffled, hoarse little voice. "That man is not my *tassik*. He's a naughty bad man and he stole me away from Grandpapa. And my pony," she added thoughtfully.

"But you might have a new pony to ride," Luce said, with his fingers crossed.

"But I liked the one I had," she said reasonably, and slid all the way out, and scowled at Luce. "Grandpapa will come looking for me, you know. And he will kill you all. With his sword."

"Dear me. I do hope not."

"Grandpapa doesn't like rebels."

"I had received that impression," Luce said dryly. At least her tears had dried, though her nose had not.

THE SERPENT'S ROOT

And she was definitely a Toogood. She had her father's navy-blue eyes and wide, high cheekbones, and though it was hard to tell under her wilted little cap her shadowy hair grew springing away from a peak, exactly like his. She sat on her heels and stared at him. "Are you a damnable rebel?"

"I - um. Yes. Yes, mistress, I am a - a soldier for Parliament. Yes. And an officer. With your. Um. Daddy."

"Are you a gemplun?"

She had him there. "Am I a what?"

"Grandpapa says no rebels are gempluns," she said with satisfaction. "He says they are all rogues who should be hanged by the neck."

"Your grandfather is a remarkably bloodthirsty gentleman. Oh - am I a *gentleman*? I see!"

"Well, so. Are you?"

"I flatter myself so, mistress." He gave her a courteous and, he hoped, gentlemanly, bow from the waist. "Cornet Lucifer Pettitt, madam, at your service."

She folded her hands in her lap, on her creased and grubby apron, and looked at him levelly. "If you truly are a gemplun, how come you're a damnable rebel?"

Well, he was not a big brother for nothing. "Mistress Chesten, I am not a - that is a very bad word, and I think your grandpapa is a very naughty man to teach it to you. And if I hear you use it again, I will wash your mouth out with soap and water. Do you understand me, young lady?"

Her eyes had gone very round, but she nodded warily.

"I am not a rebel," he went on. "I am a decent - gentleman - in the service of Parliament. I happen to believe, very much, that His Majesty the King is not right. Not *fair*."

The child stared at him. "Fair?"

"No. Not fair. And that, young lady, is as far as I will trouble you with men's affairs - for you are but a child, and God grant you remain so for some time to come. Now. If your father was a naughty bad man, think you that I would call him my friend?"

Which was, perhaps, a little of an exaggeration. But the little girl nodded, and blinked. "No?" she hazarded.

"No. Exactly. I should not. And my commander should not allow a naughty bad man to be in our company. So. Captain Toogood must be a nice man, or else -"

She was unconvinced. "No he's not. He's a gipsy and he stole my mama away from Grandpapa. He said so. He said she was a nice little girl, just like me, until she met that naughty man."

"I think your Grandpapa says a deal of things he ought not to, in front of a little girl," Luce said firmly. "And they are not always *kind* things."

She looked at him, her father's direct confrontational gaze. (It reminded him of Gray, a little, on that determined little face. And that hurt. A little.) And then her eyelids flickered, and she wasn't Gray's fetch, or Kenelm Toogood's disputed daughter, but a little maid with her eyes black-sunk with tears and weariness, and her face pinched with cold. "Young lady," he said, "I think you ought to be abed. I cannot promise you sweetmeats, but I imagine that we might find something hot, at least. Do you like frumenty?"

31. THE JUDGEMENT OF SOLOMON

Well, talk about between the Devil and the deep blue sea. On the one side, Hollie had Thankful Russell, shifting from foot to foot with that dreadful wall-eyed look of terrifying innocence that meant he was deep-implicated in some villainy.

On the other, he had Thomas Fairfax, with steam coming out of his ears.

Hollie managed a faint smile. "I am popular, gentlemen, it seems. Is your business urgent, lieutenant?"

By the way Russell's gaze slid sideways, it was. Fairfax snorted. "It is not, colonel. Mine will not keep. Sir, I have just had Philip Carew in my quarters for nigh on an hour. It seems that one of your troopers has stolen his granddaughter!"

"Is it a love-match?" he hazarded, and Fairfax looked as if he was planning to hit Hollie with something.

"She is six years old, colonel."

"You sure it was one of my -"

"Mounted? In a Venise red coat, under his cloak? As sure as I may be, colonel. Do not play for time, Babbitt."

"Well, I'm bloody sure I haven't got any little maids squirrelled away in my troop, sir. She never turned out for muster this morning -"

"This is not a matter for levity, sir!"

And no, Philip Carew did not see it as a matter for levity, at all. His groom had been ill-handled, and it had only been by God's grace that the man's horse had returned to Harrobear straightaway to rejoin its fellows, and had not strayed onto the moors and been lost. He did not so much mind the groom, though.

"That child," he said grimly, "that innocent child, is all I have left of her blessed mother. That poor, sweet maiden - hurt, and frightened - I spit on the Army of Parliament, colonel, to think what kind of vile rebel would snatch a little maid away from her family to further their own evil ends! Well, if a hair on that child's head is harmed, sir, I swear before God -"

Carew - not, it seemed, a member of the important Carews, or Fairfax would have been making more of a fuss about it - he was a Malignant, then. Well, so. It couldn't be helped. He was an old man, though, and the marks of his tears and his distress were still clear on his face, for all he was trying to bluster and see the ne'er-do-well who'd stolen the child thrown into the bowels of Launceston Castle to await, at the least, hanging. Russell's twitchy cheek was ticking like a pendulum, though, and Hollie thanked God that the lieutenant hadn't left his quarters all morning, for he looked as guilty as sin. And he knew the lad was fond of children, and -

And Kenelm Toogood had ridden in with his daughter, not three hours back. Kenelm *Toogood*. Not Carew. It was a coincidence, no more.

Aye, right it was.

"She has no mother living?" he said carefully, and then looked at Russell, "We may be some time, lieutenant. I'll need to investigate this. Master Carew is making a serious allegation. If it's founded, flogging is *too good* for the villain."

"Shall I see to some refreshments?" the lieutenant said, and his eyes were suddenly bright with understanding. Hollie nodded, and jerked his head in dismissal.

"Well, so," Fairfax said grimly. "Do you know of this matter, then, colonel?"

"I fear not, sir." (He lied, and prayed God for a little understanding, here.) "I would hear more of the circumstances of the child's capture. What should one of my company want with your granddaughter, sir? You do not, I think, involve yourself deeply in the matter of the war, that a man might seek to use your family to ensure your compliance?"

"I have raised a troop for my King, sir, as any right-thinking man might! - Aye, and fought honourably for His Majesty, too, like gentlemen!"

"But not presently, then." Because Hollie could be malicious, too. Turn and turn about, Master Carew. He raised his eyes and looked at the old man. Shabby-genteel, a good name that went back centuries and not a pot to piss in, and still he'd raised a company to fight for the King. "Stood off with Hopton, or disbanded?" he poked, and Carew's face stiffened.

"Disbanded," he said, through shut teeth.

"You spoke of the child's mother -"

"I did, sir, though I'll thank you not to sully her name in your rebel's mouth!"

In the back of his head, Hollie heard the clash of steel on steel. A foeman worthy of his blade? Well, no, not really. The silly old fool was all sound and fury, and precious little wit. "The lady is in God's grace, then?" he said sweetly, and was rewarded by a flare of temper in Carew's face.

"The lady is dead, sir, and that is all you need to know!"

"And in such a manner as to turn you against rebels?"

"It is my duty, sir, to take up arms against insurrectionists and Dissenters who seek to foment rebellion! As it should be yours, too! There is a conspiracy of silence, sir, and I will know more of it!"

And that little heartbeat of a pause when you were perfectly balanced, with your sword in your hand and the weight of your horse's charge behind you, and the world stood still in its turning. Before you drove in under your enemy's guard. "Was the lady a rebel's wife, then, Master Carew?"

He had not truly struck Carew to the heart, though it looked as if he had, and Fairfax bridled and gasped. "Is this relevant, Colonel Babbitt?"

"Indeed, sir, I fear it may be." He tried to look meek. "Your daughter was wife to a rebel, then, sir, and died of it. I'm sorry for that. Does the child have a father living?"

"Not to me," Carew said grimly, and Hollie nodded.

"May I speak with you in confidence, Sir Thomas?"

"You insolent puppy!" the older man yelped, and Hollie got to his feet - all two yards of him, in his scruffy, worn, scarred, competent military capacity.

"I'd ask you to think on the judgment of Solomon, Master Carew. One living child. Split two ways. I promise you nothing, sir, but that I will make enquiries of my men. If I find that any of my company has stolen a child away from her rightful family may God have mercy on him, for I've two daughters of my own and I'd not protect any man who looked to come between *a father* and his beloved child." He paused. Smiled sweetly. "Oh. A grandfather. My apology."

"Babbitt, what the hell are you playing at?" Fairfax said, as the last of two doors' distance closed between them. That was swearing, coming from Thomas Fairfax.

"Toogood's taken his daughter back."

"But the child's name's Carew, not - " the same thought occurred to Fairfax as had occurred to Hollie. "*Ah.* It explains a deal, then."

"Ah. Indeed. It explains the silence, for Toogood tells me this end of the county's Parliament, with little love for the King's men - no love for Master Carew here, I suspect, and from what I've seen the captain was well thought-of hereabouts before the war. Well. I'd hear Captain Toogood's side first. *And* the child's. Before I start making any judgment calls. Carew's a Malignant, sir, but fair play to him, he's chosen his path and he's loyal to it."

"And your opinion of Toogood has changed, then?"

"Changed? No. He's too hot at hand, he's judgmental, I've known cut snakes wi' kinder tempers, and that bugger can bear a grudge like nobody else on God's earth. But from the way folk talk to him - aye, and of him, in passing, when they think I'm not listening - he has not always been so. And you know what, sir? If I'd have had my daughters took off me, I'd not promise you I wouldn't be the same."

32. FOOLISHNESS IS FOUND IN THE HEART OF A CHILD

Luce was sitting in the mud, cross-legged as a tailor, talking to a haystack. Toogood was managing to look mutinous and furious, both at the same time, and giving the impression of a man who was considering dismembering the stack a straw at a time and paddling someone's arse. "What the hell possessed you?" Hollie said, and the Cornishman didn't even need to consider an answer to that.

"How could I not?"

"You get out of there, mistress, or I will come in after you myself," Hollie said grimly, and prodded the stack with his boot. "I'll not have you spoiling my horses' fodder for wantonness. Out."

"No!"

He exchanged a look with Toogood, and for the first time, there was humanity in the Cornishman's dark blue gaze. Humanity, and resignation, and the look of an embarrassed father shamed in company. (God help him, Hollie knew that look. Thomazine could not always be relied on to behave properly, when you wanted it.) "Mistress Toogood, you're shaming your father. Now out."

"That's not my father!" she yelled, and Hollie grabbed one flailing foot and dragged her out. To Luce's disapproval, the haystack's detriment, and poor Doubting Thomas's consternation.

Aye, she was his double, bless the child. Not much to look at, though she had his eyes, and her hair grew a similar way, springing every which way about her square little face. No, it was the furious look of her, with her head up and her cheeks blazing and her grubby little fists clenched in the folds of a very reproachable apron, very stiff and very upright and like if you said one wrong word to her she would haul off and belt you. (He glanced at Toogood, who was absently rubbing a purple circle of teethmarks on the back of his hand. The little vixen had fangs, then.)

"Your grandfather wants you back," he said flatly. "Will you go, or no?"

Her eyes went to Toogood, and she scowled at him. "He stole me."

"You -"

"Shut up, Kenelm."

Her eyes widened a little. "My *tassik*'s name -"

"Lass, what was your mother's name?"

"Love," she stopped, and her chin quivered, "Loveday. Loveday Toogood, and grandpapa says 'twas because she was too good for this world, for -"

"Then this is your father. This is Captain Toogood, lass."

"Am I so changed?" he said sadly, and she stared at him again, and then nodded.

"You stole me," she said again, but uncertainly, this time. And then, "You *left* me, *tassik*. Why did you not come back for us? Grandpapa said you ran away and left us."

"Captain Toogood, sir, there is business requiring your attention at the- the -" Luce was a rotten liar, too. "Far end of the horse lines?" He glanced at Hollie and touched a finger to the corner of his eye. No, the Cornishman would not take it kindly, if he thought they pitied him, or knew that he wept, like a feeling man.

"He could not come back," Hollie said. "Your father is one of my officers, lass. He must do as I bid him, if he wills it or not."

"Speaking of doing as you are bid," Luce said, and picked a wisp of straw from her shoulder, "here comes Thankful with your bread and milk, and we promised him you would leave him no washing-up, did we not?"

So the austere Russell was on kitchen duty, and Luce was being used as a nursemaid. It was almost comical. It was also rather endearing, that the child put her grimy little hand into Luce's and marched at his side while Russell meekly carried bowl and spoon to a place of greater safety. Poor Toogood looked as if he had been stabbed to the heart, though.

"I haven't seen her," Hollie said conversationally.

The Cornishman stopped mid-stride. "What?"

"The little lass. I've not seen her, if he should ask. He wants her back, Toogood. And he's not wholly stupid. Be assured of that, the child is as much his grandchild as she is your daughter, but if there is a middle way, Sir Thomas will find it."

"How can he? A little girl in a soldier's camp, 'tis hardly fitting -"

"Should've thought of that before you stole her, Captain Toogood," he said primly. "But. I would consider Cornet Pettitt to be a fit and proper person to see to her letters, and Lieutenant Russell can see to her scripture. Her learning won't suffer, for a week. Though," he said thoughtfully, "it may go a bit cock-eyed, for I doubt if Luce will stick to reading and writing. She'll be writing poetry by the end of it. They'll be glad to give her back."

"What - what - what do you mean?"

"I mean, captain, that she's on a week's - leave, then. Aye, and I'll tell Carew she's here, safe - he's worried sick, give him that - and stand the consequence myself. But I'll not send her back. Not without hearing the rights of it. Send her back to a Malignant? Rather cut off my own feet. When this is all settled up - when the dust's all laid, and the place is peaceful - then she can go where she wills. I'd be a bloody poor excuse for a father myself if I were to send an innocent child into danger just because her grandsire's a power in the land. "

"You would do this? For me?"

"I *am* doing it, captain. The child has a father. She might not, after a time in his company, reckon much to the one she's got, but she has one, and she had best know him. Poor tool that he is." And then he stopped, and if it had been Venning, or Luce, or even Betterton, he'd have given him a playful cuff and tipped his hat into his eyes. But it was not, it was a stiff, wary Cornishman, who was a little red about the eyelids yet. "Fairfax would have us understand that the King's cause in the West is all but wrapped up. No doubt it is. Probably. I can't say as I mind having one or two weapons to my hand to make sure it stays that way."

33. PRIDE GOETH BEFORE DESTRUCTION

And so Tristan Toogood joined the muster roll, and was given a soldier's coat and a ration of his own.

"Tristan?" Fairfax said, and blinked in some confusion.

"Captain Toogood's younger brother," Russell said blandly, and you might have known it would be Hapless Russell who'd finagled a warm coat through official channels for the little maid, and got her provisioned properly. It would seem that young Tristan was in more perpetual trouble than his big brother, for other than his coat and his meals, almost all his pay was reclaimed in disciplinary stoppages. Insubordination –

"She had not learned her verses sufficient," –

Sloppy drill –

"Her handwriting is dreadful," Luce said, sounding horrified –

It seemed poor young Tristan Toogood was the worst reprobate in the company. Although *Chesten* was not too bad.

It was a bitter learning for all of them, those next few days. She wanted desperately to believe that the lean, intimidating Cornish captain was still the daddy she had adored two years ago, and he wanted to believe that this half-grown hoyden was still his baby. They were alike, and yet not alike, and he could not bear to have her out of his sight lest harm come to her, nor could she bear to let him go out of her sight lest he disappear again. But though they could not bear to be apart, nor did they know how to live under the same roof, and so like two strange dogs they snapped and fought till they had worked out who had the mastery.

Carew had known bloody well she was in Hollie's keeping. "You will keep my granddaughter a hostage?" he said disbelievingly.

"When I find her," Hollie said. "I will return her to your keeping. And aye. You may consider her a hostage to your continued good behaviour. Your impartiality, shall we say."

It seemed, though, that Carew had never cast his daughter off. In so many words. Loveday Toogood had cut herself off, rather than deny her husband. She had chosen her path, and she had kept her feet on it to the bitter end. Aye, she had gone hungry. She had not starved, though. She had died of a fever, and her daughter been given to the Carews, but where the hell else should she go? And Hollie wondered whose interests might have been served in turning Toogood's mind against his relations by marriage, for though neither party was full of warmth and fellow-feeling to the other, yet they could bear to stand in the same room for a space, now. ("Pride goeth before destruction," Hollie had said softly, and felt a little hollow inside. Though not sufficiently chastened to humble his own and ask for his wife's forgiveness. Not yet.)

Aye, well, Carew was an old man, and he was not accustomed to not having his own way, and he was hurt and bewildered that he could not simply snap his fingers and the child be given back to him. Mar another couple, Kenelm and his late wife, and he wondered what kind of lass might have loved a stubborn, proud, fierce lad with too much steel and fire in his backbone to give way, no matter what it cost him - love him enough to go to her death for him, for she had remained faithful, though it cost her her life. Nor could he imagine what kind of lad he must have been, then, to be so loved. ("Am I so changed, then?")

No wonder little Chesten needed her arse paddled. No wonder the little maid was wilful, and rude, and haughty. She had it from both sides of the family, it seemed, and grandpapa Carew doted on her, and would undo whatever discipline her parents had tried to instil into her. Spoiled-wilful, and proud as – well, not quite as proud as Lucifer, for Luce had her nose to her books as often as Hollie could spare him his duties, and Russell had her adding up figures like a little merchant within the day. And Hapless was not a tolerant tutor, so the child was sharp. What scared Hollie was what the poor little lass had been brought up thinking of – what was it she'd persisted in calling them, until Luce had threatened to wash her mouth out with saddle-soap – damnable rebels.

He'd never really met a civilian Malignant. Not in person, not socially, at least not without a troop of horse and thirty-six inches of Birmingham steel to back him up. And since he'd been knocking about with the likes of Luce, who believed in fairness, and Russell, who was even less realistic than Luce on the matter of equality, and that bugger Colonel Rainbow, up in Bristol last year, who was hot for the rights of the common soldier – well, Hollie had sort of fallen into the habit of thinking that Parliament had the right of it, that their cause was the just one.

This little lass had thought they were a pack of rebels and traitors, as unnatural as a talking dog, and she wasn't backwards in telling them so. She'd called Hollie a Crophead to his face, and he'd had to go out of the room not to laugh, because his hair was all but as long as hers. She'd been fair put on her backside when they said grace like normal men, and did not go at it till their meat was cold. They were not monsters, not the cold and zealous and joyless bastards some people portrayed them as. They were a ragged, weary company of lads who sent their pay home to their wives where they could, or diced it away where they couldn't, and made sure a little girl had honey for her bread. And she, poor maid, was neither a Papist nor a princess, nor an ogre, but only a little girl who missed her pony and her nurse, and so she sat in her oversized Venise-red soldier's coat by the chimney breast with her bowl of bread and milk in her lap and her mouth open, while the common soldiery of the Army of Parliament told her prodigious lies about marvels they had seen and great deeds they'd done. Nursemaided by a half-mad bachelor lieutenant, and tutored by a cork-brained romantic poet.

Philip Carew was going to go bloody *mental*, when they gave her back.

34. PUT NOT YOUR TRUST IN PRINCES

And so it carried on raining, and after a couple of days the Army carried on its relentless march westward, down roads that were hock-deep in sucking black mud. And Chesten Toogood went with them, mounted pillion on her father's rat-tailed bay Charles, in a stolen musketeer's hat that one of the lads had tried to pretty up for her with a handful of iridescent rook's feathers in the band, and her soldier's coat that hung to her knees.

Her broad, high-cheekboned face was not pretty, but it was serious, and wisps of her untidy hair blew in her eyes as she turned to look over the company. Luce raised the colours to her in salute, and she touched the brim of that awful hat in recognition. "Pity the boy as has her to wife," he said, out of the corner of his mouth. "A stubborn little wench."

Following the Prince of Wales down towards Truro – in the Queen's footsteps, from where she had fled to France with her newborn child. And it felt funny, and sort of exciting, and sort of – well, it just felt odd, because this was a point from which there was no turning back. You could not harry the King's son down into the West Country, and chase his wife from the shores of the country, and have Sir Ralph Hopton and the last loyal core of the King's followers mewed up on a windy hilltop thinking about how to surrender – you could not do all of those things, and then go back to how it was yesterday. Fairfax – and Noll Cromwell, and, God help him, himself – could not have that kind of authority, and then hand it all back, and it be all like it had been.

And that was frightening, and yet at the same time it was as wild and exhilarating as a flying charge at the gallop, because what could he not do? And Hollie did not know what would happen tomorrow, or next week, or next year. There was nothing in his past that might give him a lead, for this was new, uncharted, unmarked. He was a commander in an Army that had brought the King of England to heel. (And then what? that sardonic little voice in his head wanted to know. Fancy the job yourself, do you?)

Well. He did not know. He did not care. The tide was in, and he could hear the creak and shout of barges coming up the slow tidal river from Falmouth, and the smell of cut timber and salt mud. No coincidence that Fairfax had settled himself on the bridge at Tresillian – aye, and kicked out the local justice from his house, to have his officers about him. A nice enough little house, with a shaggy thatched roof and low windows set thick in the walls: a snug, comfortable, stout house, all cockeyed flags and winding staircases.

And low beams, where a man could bound through a doorway, and smack his head on a lintel. Luce had a perpetual bruise between his brows, being the sort of enthusiastic young man who was still able to leap blithely into rooms, and even Fairfax himself had acquired a wary habit of pausing on a threshold before ducking and entering. A tiny cell, cold and smelling of mice. just by the front door, where a miscreant might be held overnight. Russell had told Chesten Toogood that was to be her bedchamber, quite coolly, and she had believed him. Until he'd burst out with his odd silent giggle, and then she'd kicked him in the shin, and no one had said her nay on that one because he fully well deserved it, the perverse-humoured sod.

No, Hollie was not quite sure what he had expected of the end of this war, but he had not expected it to be like the beginning, like the first surrender at Reading. A room full of respectable, middle-aged gentlemen, a little worn, a little weary — a little knocked about — Luce at his back, smooth and elegant as ever, if a little bristly and a lot tired. Russell passing round the cakes. (Not Drew Venning, though. It had been Drew Venning at the very first, who had been dealing with the diplomacy for the Earl of Essex. Hollie looked at the dented pewter platter holding the fresh-baked little cakes, and thought of Drew on his way back to Diss, and his heart gave a little squeeze in his chest.)

"Not like you to turn down cakes," Russell said pertly. That lad was in his element, stalking about dealing with the officious, and Hollie managed a faint smile at the look of him. Making a festival occasion of it, then — so Hapless felt it, too.

He was wearing his decent black suit — a little badly-darned, and a little faded in places, so that the doublet was as many colours as a black cock's tail from wind and weather, and he was a little less willowy than he had been, once. Which made Hollie smile a bit wider, and glance at Luce. There were many things that Hollie Babbitt was, and was not. He was sufficiently capable though that he had taken two cat-skinny boys and made solid, decent, competent young men of them. That made him proud enough that he took one of the cakes after all, and settled himself more comfortably in his chair.

He expected Sir Ralph Hopton to look defeated, or defiant. He looked neither. He looked like a weary, sad, unremarkable man in his middle years who had lost a lot of weight in a very short space of time, and Hollie nudged Russell with his elbow and nodded at Hopton, pressing him to take more cake. He smiled, and shook his head.

In all likelihood, Hopton still would not have surrendered. But troubles, like spies, had not come on him singly: the garrison at Truro had made it very clear they'd had enough, and if Hopton wanted to carry on fighting he was doing it by himself. The King's soldiers were deserting in increasing numbers. If they'd been hoping for reinforcements from Ireland, they were going to be waiting a long time, for Bristol was in the hands of Parliament, and any back-up was going to have to come by Scotland. Which was assuming the Scots let 'em through.

More than that, though, Hopton was jus*t tired,* by the look of him.

Speaking truthfully and for himself, negotiations bored the arse off Hollie, and so he put his head against the rough stone wall and looked out of the window and listened with half an ear to the soothing flow of voices, to and fro, to and fro, as they thrashed out their terms. Fair ones, because Fairfax was a decent lad, and Hopton had been an honourable opponent. But not that decent, because the King was still roaming loose stirring it up in Oxford, and if they could put a lid on the West Country once and for all it'd make Hollie that much the happier.

It was March. That was all. March, and yet out of the window he could see the bare branches of the apple tree that grew by the busy quayside where they were unloading the barges, and they were beginning to glow with buds. A little bird – bright little feller, the white flashes on its wings flaring in the silvery light – was running in the black twigs, flirting its tail at the rivermen. Men still had to make a living, even at war. Birds still sang, and the river still flowed.

The bridge, a mile up from the village, was a thriving place, and grubby children ran in and out pf horses' legs, and women marketed, and busy working-men swore at the lot of them for getting in the way. (Idle working-men loafed about the quay, pretending to be waiting to unload the barges, and that was the same the country over, too.

And that made Hollie smile, as well, because no matter where he had been – had he been in the Low Countries, had he been in flat green Cheshire or on the swooping hills of Dorset, it made no neverminds. Men and women were, and ever would be, the same, and they would be the same a hundred years from now – a thousand years from now. Though he hoped to God by then they'd have sorted out the present disagreement going on between the bargeman who was presently dumping his timber on the cobbles, and the bugger that was trying to get out of paying for it. It had been going on for a quarter-hour already, and looked likely to keep going for a further hour more. There was a lass had joined in now, her voice high and sharp and irritable, and he guessed she was trying to get past the piles of lumber -)

Then he heard the door slam behind someone and Toogood's stentorian bellow of "*Kemmer with! ty gwallok*!" across the cobbles, and he gave a snort of laughter that was not quite quickly stifled enough to escape Fairfax's notice, and the frown Black Tom gave him would have frightened crows.

"I'll just see what's going on out there," he said, and scrambled to his feet, and went out into the spring air.

35. THE DESERT SHALL BLOSSOM

It seemed they were going to be settled at the Justice's house at Tresillian for the duration, or at least till Fairfax and Hopton had come to some sort of agreement, and so there was a small matter of the quartering of four troop of horse. (The Justice could fend for himself. Toogood had smiled at him as he left, and he left somewhat the quicker. Funny how Kenelm Toogood's slow, intent smile had that effect on people.)

The options were limited. Fairfax had chose the bridge at Tresillian well, for his own quarters: it was as far as the barges could come up the river, laden with wood and coal, and with Black Tom in residence those vital goods could go no further, unless he so chose. Which put an effective block on the mining industry, to be sure, and Fairfax was a great believer in squeezing men by the balls - with the greatest of courtesy. The problem with the bridge, though, was that though there were river meadows, they were not sufficient grazing for nigh on three hundred horses, not this early in the year. It was a logistical bloody nightmare.

Just as well they had their own personal logistical nightmare, then, and such thorny problems gave Russell a deal of pleasure. Even if it meant he had to ride out before the sun rose with Toogood, which was not quite so delightful. Russell was polite, charming, and looked like the wrath of God from the wrong side. Toogood looked perfectly presentable until he opened his mouth. Well, between the two of them, they probably made an efficient force for persuasion.

"So," Russell said, and cocked his head. "Where are we going to try first?"

"They're all bloody Malignants in these parts."

"Well, yes. That is why we're here, captain. To encourage them to see their error of their ways."

"You're off your bloody head, lieutenant."

"It may have been mentioned previous. However. Personal abuse will not see the horses quartered, sir."

Toogood turned in his saddle, and looked at Russell very thoughtfully. "You do it to wind people up, don't you? Talk like that?"

"Works like a charm, too."

"I know this country, boy."

"I trust so, sir, or we are like to ride in circles."

"That river's nigh bottomless, at the bend. Put a bullet in your ear and dump you in it, do you keep on baiting me, and none to be any the wiser. Nobody'd miss you, Russell."

Which would have hurt once, when it was true, but now he could look up from his hands on the reins and say, very sweetly, "Your daughter would, Captain Toogood." And watch the furious flush rise from the man's grubby collar, and his hands tighten on the bridle so that his horse threw its head up in some discomfort. And then to add, a little apologetically, "She is a bright child, and eager to learn. You must be proud of her."

The Cornishman stared at him for a moment as if trying to find the sting in the words. And then he said, almost shyly, "I am."

"Well, then, sir. Let us make her proud of both of us, and perform a miracle, and find quartering for four troop of horse."

It was easier said than done, of course. It was a sweet ride, down the river in the spring dawn, and then it started to rain, and for a while that was cool and refreshing, and then after that Russell started to lose his hard-won optimism, and skulked in moody silence at a fast walk. He found that trotting jarred his teeth and made his head ache, and he had the suspicion that Toogood knew it, too. And was keeping the fretful Charles to a walk alongside him, despite the fact that the rat-tailed bay horse wanted to run.

"D'ee know where we could stop," the Cornishman said conversationally. "Trefusis Manor. I reckon once we washed up the King's men in Truro, we'll be looking for grazing closer to home, no?"

"Where." He shut his eyes and tried to loosen his cold-cramped cheek, discreetly. "Where is it?"

"Oh, not so long to here. I reckon it's twelve miles or so from Tresillian – couple of hours, an we push on – so, you know, be there in time for a bit o' crib? If you don't mind a run for it?"

It was not an unconditional surrender. It was not even a cessation of hostilities. But he had the oddest feeling that Toogood was trying – wanted to be kind. And so he nodded mutely, though even that hurt him, and tangled his hand in Doubting Thomas's mane, and kicked the mismatched horse into a splattering canter.

Not a great manor, but a little one, like Fox Barton, and for one brief, miserable heartbeat he expected Hollie Babbitt's little bright-haired daughter to come bursting down the front steps yelling in joyous greeting, with her mother four steps behind looking happy and disapproving all at once. He dismounted, and Thomas pushed his pied head against the stiff leather of Russell's sleeve, as if he was trying to be sympathetic too, and the pair of them stood in filthy, disreputable mutual discomfort, while the rain that had been a gentle mist turned into a steady downpour. He could have cried, except that he had his eyes tight-shut, and little starbursts of light danced behind his eyelids.

"You look bleddy awful," Toogood said at his ear, and he laughed silently.

"Doubt I smell too great, either."

The Cornishman did laugh at that. Outright, as if it had been startled out of him. "Give you that," he said, "you don't." And without opening his eyes Russell heard Toogood take charge, and the sound of running footsteps across the yard, and the unfortunate groom who hadn't been quick enough off the mark got the rough side of the tongue from a young man who was, suddenly and quite abruptly, a gentleman to the manner born. "Brace up," Toogood said, and touched his elbow to Russell's. "Lady's at home." And he unclenched his fingers from Thomas's rein, and straightened his back. And did not die, or puke, or fall on his face, though he suspected for a horrible second he might do all three. "What ails him?" the groom said suspiciously, and Russell was sufficiently himself to turn his marred face full to the pearly light and say, "The hell do you think ails me?"

Which was, he thought, the point at which he had fainted. Having apparently been reassured that he was neither a plague carrier nor yet a fugitive from justice, the lady of the house had unbent sufficiently to allow him entry. And that, God help him, was when he opened his eyes, and found himself laid out like a corpse on a bier, with someone's ragged handkerchief – oh, dear God, let it not be one of Hollie Babbitt's rags – over his face, feeling like a well-used pull-through.

Not a deserter or a malingerer, but a young man who'd been set to his duties at just before dawn and had not been given a space to sit to his meat since, and who lacked food and sleep rather badly. *Hollie* would have known that. Fairfax, in his haste to settle negotiations with Hopton, had not. Or had not cared, so long as he could find a space for his cavalry to be quartered.

Toogood knew it, too. "Give the lad a minute, he'll come about," he said gruffly. "Meantimes, Mistress Trefusis, I imagine you know why I'm here."

"I can imagine, sir," she said crisply. "It is not with my husband's approval —"

"Aye, well, if it was with his approval, I doubt poor Russell'd be laid out on the floor like a mackerel, for we'd have come straight here, wouldn't we, and saved us a pack o' time? Well. There it is. You just got yourself a troop of cavalry, mistress, courtesy of Sir Thomas Fairfax."

Very carefully, Russell turned his head. This was probably the point at which he ought to intercede, for Toogood's courtesy was no courtesy at all —

"Don't you play that game with me, Kenelm Toogood," Mistress Trefusis said sharply. "You forget, sir, my cousins have land in St Kew. I know your family. I know your family very well, sir, and I knew you when you were a snotty-nosed whelp running round Launceston market-day crying for your mammy."

"You still got a troop of cavalry, mistress," he said, and folded his arms, by the creaking sound of it. "D'ee like it or no. I'm new come from Tresillian, where Sir Ralph Hopton's playing for time before he signs the surrender, but surrender he will, don't you worry. He can only play that game so long, mistress, he got men running through his fingers like sand and the most of 'em are coming over to the Parliament side. Might want to think about that, my lady. Just saying."

"Saying as you're too big to turn over my knee now, Kenelm?"

There was a rustle of stiff silk, and a smell of roses. "Oh dear," the voice that had haunted Russell's dreams since Launceston said, very clearly. "Mama, you're standing there talking to that gentleman, and no one's paying any attention to poor Thomas –"

Well, she'd remembered something about him, at least. "Thomas is my horse," he said apologetically, and the little rose-girl bent over and peered into his face, upside-down.

She was still lovely. Even upside down, she was still soft and pink and lovely. "Gracious," she said. "I believe you have spoken more, and more willingly, from my parlour floor than you did in the whole of the supper at Church Street, sir."

"I think I may have found my place in the world," Russell said, and struggled to sit upright with a happy sigh. "At your feet, mistress."

"Well, you're not much use to me down there," she said tartly, and put out a hand and pulled him to his feet.

36. NOT CONFORMED TO THIS WORLD

He did not think Toogood approved, and he was very sure that her mother ought not, that Amy Trefusis – "*Bien aimee,*" he said, close to her ear – was still holding his hand. He was also fairly sure that he ought not to be holding hers. He did not care. He smelt appalling, he had not shaved or shifted his linen in a week and a comb had not touched his hair in almost as long, and – he did not care, it was spring, and he was standing in the underwater light of a rainy spring day and he could smell the honey-sweet of snowdrops -

And Toogood was looking at him with an expression that was part amused and part despairing and altogether very, very sardonic. It was not quite that he rode back to Tresillian in a happy dream, because it was difficult to remain in a happy dream with Toogood grumbling at his elbow. Seemed that Captain Toogood was affronted that Mistress Trefusis – *Mistress Treffry,* as was, like the Treffrys up at St Kew were any better than gentleman-farmers, for all they had relatives in high places down here – had not treated him with proper respect.

(It also seemed that Captain Toogood might have been set all on edge by something else that had been said to him out of Russell's hearing, too. But as Hollie Babbitt was prone to pointing out, Russell was daft at times, but he wasn't stupid, so he wasn't poking that ant's-nest any more than he had to.) The tide was in, and the sun was setting, and he halted his horse to look over the great width of the

Fal river, all lit amber and rose-gold. It was still and quiet, only a few late-pulling barges still making the journey down to Falmouth, out to the deep sea. Over the black trees, a few last rooks tossed like flung rags before they settled to their roost. The air was turning crisp, and chill, and he took a deep breath of it, of the tang of salt, and the –

"Captain Toogood," he said, halting Thomas.

"Might as well be Kenelm, lad. Since I've been acting in the capacity of nursemaid to you for the day. Reckon I know you well enough. Tell me your name's not truly Hapless?"

"Thankful," he said, and pulled a wry face. "Good Puritan family. I know. Kenelm, then. I hardly know how to – um – what *is* at the end of this river?"

"The sea?" the Cornishman said, with a look on his face that implied he was talking to an idiot.

Rather than a man from Buckinghamshire, who'd never seen the sea at less than two miles' distance, and did not care to be condescended to. "Surely. And then?"

"Well, hell, I dunno, do I? Sea monsters and wild men, for all I know! Why? You seen some-"

He stood up in his stirrups, and pointed. "What, pray, do wild men want with cannon, then? For that is, surely, a barge laden with guns, but headed to the sea, where it can serve no use?"

Toogood edged his rat-tailed bay into the water at the edge of the river, the better to see. "The little bollocks," he breathed. "The bloody little bugger!"

"What? What harm can –"

"Tell 'ee what else is down there, boy! Pendennis fucking Castle's down there, and my lord Hopton's shipping the goddamn guns out-a Trurra into the castle by the back door!" He yanked Charles' head up, and sent the bay horse splashing up the bank. "Come on, then, boy, let's choke that bugger off, 'fore he gets ideas!"

37. MERCY REJOICETH AGAINST JUDGMENT

Hollie closed his eyes, and settled his back against the warm plaster at the back of the hearth, and sighed with contentment. No, Hopton hadn't signed it off yet. But he would. He was just playing for time, that was all, trying to squeeze every inch he could out of Fairfax. All about pride - aye, well, and a bit of a pissing contest, to show that he had chosen to surrender, not been defeated - but Hopton had agreed the important bit.

The King's Army in the West was to be disbanded. All over, gentlemen. Done. Before the spring grass, the King's Army would be no more than a few hundred civilians talking of what might have been, over a mug of ale in inns the length and breadth of the West. And that meant, Hollie guessed, that the New Model Army would be broken up likewise, and he'd see in the summer -

Well. He didn't know where he'd see in the summer. Maybe in Essex. Maybe not. He'd wondered, idly, if he could settle in another place - if she didn't want him to come back to White Notley - and yes, he thought now, he could. Maybe him and Russell set up housekeeping in a place and be odd bachelors together, for he doubted Luce would be on the shelf long. Though the brat seemed somewhat impartial with his favours, of late - but he'd settle. Well. Couldn't see anybody wanting to make free with him or Russell, to be honest, but if it came to it, they'd rub along well enough together, pair of testy old soldiers -

He was being daft. There would be a letter, soon. He didn't truly think she didn't want him home, he was just teasing himself. Gone for months without hearing from Margriete --when he'd been young and daft and not in the same place from month end to month end, and a letter might have followed him from one end of Europe to the other without catching up with him-

He shook his head. He was growing old-maidish, sat out here watching the tide rise and fall twice a day, with no purpose to him.

The ink would be dry on Hopton's signature shortly, and he could start thinking about what the future might hold, for a colonel of horse who was going to have to learn to be summat else pretty bloody quick.

First, though, he thought he might sit here in the faint setting spring sun, and listen to the river stirring to dusk, and consider whether Fairfax was in a sufficient good temper to mind if one of his senior officers sloped off and got very thoroughly pissed.

(God knows there was little else to do, now.)

Or at least he would do, if Toogood hadn't kicked him in the ankle.

"What's she done now?" he said, without opening his eyes.

"Tidn't her. It's *him*."

"Aye all right, what's Hapless done now?"

"I've not done nothing!" Russell yelped, with a most uncharacteristic disdain for grammatical correctness. "It's him!"

Hollie struggled upright and glared at the pair of them. "Who - is - *what*?"

"Guns," Russell said, which helped not at all.

"Down the river," Toogood said, and it occurred to Hollie that whatever he - whoever he was - had done, it wasn't a thing that these two had done to each other, because the pair of them were bright-eyed and panting like a brace of hound puppies on a scent.

"What?"

THE SERPENT'S ROOT

"Horses," Russell caught his breath, "Trefusis Manor. Ten miles down the river. Not happy, but -. Well, life's hard."

"*Some* of 'em are happy," Toogood said significantly, and whatever that was supposed to mean went home, for the lieutenant turned a rather alarming shade of rose and went all wriggly. "Riding back up the river, sir, after arranging quartering at Trefusis Manor. Russell stopped to catch his breath, and bugger me if there wasn't barges laden with guns -"

"What? - musket?"

"Artillery," Russell said. "Three barges. That I could see. Headed away from us."

But Hopton had agreed to disband the Army. He'd just done it. He'd *said* so -

"But what -"

"Selling 'em for scrap, how the bleddy hell d'I know what he's got in his head? Seriously, Rosie! Hopton's been around the block, he's playing us for time while he arms the garrison at Pendennis Castle, he ain't daft."

"But he's just bloody surrendered!"

"He might have. *They* ain't."

Fairfax didn't like it, either, but at least by then those two had caught their breath sufficient that it was a coherent story, and not a pair of sweaty, wheezing young gentleman falling over their words and interrupting each other.

At one and the same time as Sir Ralph Hopton had been considering the honourable terms of his surrender as the King's commander in the West, and agreeing to disband His Majesty's Army, and promising never to do it again, it seemed he had had the presence of mind to be shipping the cannons out of the back door in Truro, and sending them out to the garrison at Pendennis Castle.

The garrison at Truro had had enough. Some of them had deserted already - some gone over to Parliament, where they were at least promised feeding and pay...though Hollie was keeping his mouth shut on that one. Some had just gone home. No, it made sense that Hopton should be stripping the guns out of Truro, where they weren't willing, and putting them in the care of Sir John Arundel, the governor at Pendennis, who assuredly was. Willing, mind, but about a hundred and fifty years old, and by all accounts a dothery old fart and there'd already been an element of concern expressed about the old fool's capability to hold Pendennis, no matter if it was bristling with cannons and provisioned sufficient to withstand a twelvemonth.

It still felt funny to Hollie, mind, that Hopton had agreed to disband the Army, knowing he was doing no such bloody thing - must have had his fingers crossed or something when he was writing that bit – but Toogood had just laughed.

"He said the King's Army in the West," he said scornfully, "he never said *Cornwall*."

"What, and Cornwall's not part of England, is it not?" Hollie had said, equally scornfully.

"It is not."

And it seemed that for a deal of the Cornish Royalists, it had been promised that it was not. Blame Skellum Grenville for that one, then, for it seemed that three years ago that treacherous bastard had been negotiating with the Prince of Wales for the Duchy to be all but independent –

"Save for the important bits," Toogood said, and his mouth had taken on a wry twist. "The stannaries, and the money? And you wonder why half the gentry down here are in favour of the King. All in favour of the penny and the bun, more like." He shook his head. "No, you bet you that Hopton has the authority to disband the King's Army in the West. He ain't got squit authority in Cornwall, though, not if they don't want it."

And so it was not all done, after all, because there was a garrison some twenty miles up the line that didn't know when to give it up as a bad job, and if there was one thing Hollie hated it was stubborn garrisons, and sieges. But the relief of it was, that it was not his business. For Fairfax was not impressed with the defenders of Pendennis Castle, not one piece.

"They get one warning," he said coldly. "You remember Taunton, Holofernes. My patience is not inexhaustible. I will tolerate so much, and no more. I have better things to do than play king-of-the-castle with Sir John Arundel."

"So?" –"

"So one messenger. One opportunity to surrender. And after that, he is on his own, and may God have mercy on him if he decides to push me." And rather unexpectedly, he had closed his eyes, and pushed his chair back, and leaned his head back against the rough wall. "I have a wife and family of my own, Holofernes. I am as tired as any other man of chasing shadows about the West Country. Sometimes I feel as if I am talking to little Moll – wait a little further, have a little more patience, and tomorrow there will be sweetmeats, and it will all be done."

"Aye? I feel like I'm wading through honey, myself," Hollie muttered, and it startled a laugh out of Black Tom, who sat upright and looked ironic.

"What a waste of honey, colonel."

"Now you sound like you're talking to Moll."

He glanced out of the window at the thought of Moll Fairfax – what would she be now, a great girl of nine or ten, and not the little moppet who had perched on his saddle all the way through one dark night in Yorkshire, when he had ridden with her father, and half the Malignants in the North on their heels. A child's voice, on the quay, and a man's in reply, but it wasn't Toogood and his daughter, for they were not so comfortable with each other as that, yet.

They were mending, though, and like all hurts, the healing would take time. They were at that point where an unexpected tug on the stitching and all would unravel and to be done again. Not afraid of her father, now she knew who he was, under the unfamiliar buff-coat, now that he had let his hair grow back a little, and now that he smiled, betimes, and called her his bird again.

But when she bumped herself, or when she had done a thing she was proud of, she went to Luce, not Toogood. Luce who was kind, and patient when he taught the child her letters, and knew pretty words and courtesies. And that was a new thing, too, that Luce was not some distant golden storybook figure to a child, but a competent, careful, gentle man, who might be trusted to comfort a little one. Not a little one himself. Not any more.

No, Luce was competent and careful in all he did, bless the brat, but that wouldn't make Toogood feel any the better that his daughter went to someone else with her childish little hurts, though it might mend with time –

The which they did not have. One messenger. One chance.

He looked out of the window again, at the river. At Kenelm Toogood on the quayside, standing with his hands behind his back, looking up the river like a sentinel. Maybe it was Hollie refining too much. As he said. God knows he had little enough else to do with his time, now. Maybe Toogood had not gone out at the sound of that seagull-high voice, was not standing looking up towards the sea and imagining the feel of someone's little fingers thrust confidingly into his own.

For surely Hollie never did such a thing. Surely Hollie was not thinking of Thomazine, and pointing out in his head the things that she might care for – did she see the egret in the trees on the far side of the river, there, or the little fishes that swarmed in the water that rippled at the foot of the steps on the quay. He shut his eyes. Missing her, suddenly, so much it made his belly turn: his bright-haired daughter, who barely knew him, and his dark-haired baby who was kitten-new and who had not had a chance to know him, and his dear, solid, sensible wife, who would have stared around her at the Cornish river with wondering eyes. Who would have snatched at the fish fresh out of the sea, so far inland as they lived in Essex; they'd have been eating fish for a week, for a month, till the novelty of it wore off. Hollie had a wife. He might be off-hooks with her, but she was yet his wife, and she was yet in the world, and if not this day then tomorrow – next week – next month – he would go home to her.

(He thought of Drew Venning again, suddenly and sharply, and hoped the big Fenman was safe home by now. You could be away too long for things to be mended, and he hoped – hoped more than his hope of heaven – that of all the little tragedies of this war, Captain Venning's pretty wife would not be one of them.)

Hollie had a place to go, and two girls, and Het. And if she had changed her mind, if he was not the man she had married, then he had – God willing – a lifetime to bring her about, and to become the man she thought she knew.

Toogood had nothing.

He had a daughter, who scarce knew him, and was afraid of him. Toogood did not deserve such grace. He was a hot-tempered, abrupt man, fierce and unforgiving –

(*And we said unto my lord, We have a father, an old man, and a child of his old age, a little one; and his brother is dead, and he alone is left of his mother, and his father loveth him.*)

He sighed. Be supper, soon, and someone down in the kitchens was roasting something, and it smelt good, and Hollie was hungry.

(When was he not, as Het often pointed out to him, with some asperity. When she cared enough to notice.) Out on the river, the air was starting to turn chill, and he eased his shoulders and his back with a crackle like a volley of musket fire.

"Who do you mean should stay, then? If Arundel will turn intransigent?"

38. ENTERTAINING ANGELS UNAWARES

It was raining again, but oddly, he did not mind so much, this time round. Well, apart from the physical discomfort of smelling like an old cleaning-rag, and having boots that squelched unpleasantly and - he moved a foot, carefully - left clots of sticky black mud on the good polished boards of Trefusis Manor. Russell stuck his fingers in his mouth discreetly and tried to suck off the worst of the grime that had rubbed off from Doubting Thomas's reins. He had volunteered. He had to keep reminding himself of that, sitting cold and wet - why was he always destined to be cold and wet, in this place? - in the parlour, with a small token of a fire lit for the sake of appearance, awaiting the pleasure of the mistress of the house.

The master of the house was away. Usually when some dour retainer said that to him it meant go away, but Russell was here on the business of the Army of Parliament, and he wasn't going anywhere.

He probably should not be as happy about it as he was. He probably should be stern, and unyielding, and disappointed that he and the rest of Babbitt's company had not gone hotfoot back to relieve the siege at Exeter with Fairfax, instead of sitting around outside Pendennis Castle cleaning tack and whistling and waiting for Sir John Arundel's belly to remind him that sieges were all very well if you had provisions, and, as Hollie Babbitt would have it, a bloody damn-fool idea if you did not.

Rather reluctantly, he had a degree of admiration for Sir John Arundel - though he suspected the admiration might not last more than a week or two, if the silly old fool continued to hold out. Hollie had gone in with the original terms of surrender, he and a couple of other officers of sufficient seniority not to be a direct insult. He had deliberately not shaved that morning, and had looked like the biggest ruffian this side of the Tamar. He came back with a deal more respect for Arundel than he'd gone in with, and in considerably short order - although Russell doubted that the man's dismissal of the Parliamentarian envoys had been so abrupt as Hollie claimed it was. Well. Possibly not so abrupt. They had gone, and returned, in under an hour. It couldn't have taken him that long to consider it, then. Hollie reckoned it was under a minute. But whatever it was, it certainly gave the lie to the perception of Arundel as a timid, dothery old fool that had been so popular in the Parliamentarian lines.

Well, there it was. After a month of skulking around the west rolling his eyes like a colicky horse and biting people's heads off if anyone dared to mention his wife's name, the colonel had had the opportunity to start on the road home, and he'd decided instead that he was going to stay in Cornwall and watch a team of artillery knocking chunks off Pendennis Castle. There was simply no accounting for him. And Russell had been going to pass some comment, and then realised how close the inkpot was to his commander's right hand, and decided that discretion was the better part of valour.

Even the child, even little Chesten, had become a formal and documented part of the troop. With a little sleight of hand, and a change of gender, for a little girl could not live on fresh air and her father would not have had her a charge on the Army. It was comical, and somehow sad, to see her grandfather deflate like a punctured bladder faced with a quiverful of rebels who behaved like gentlemen, not beasts.

He had clearly expected his precious child to have been debauched, and instead she had been scrubbed till she sparkled, groomed like a pony, and schooled to a point of proper rigidity. Back her up with Toogood himself, silent and grim, and Luce, that elegant young gentleman, and Hollie Babbitt with his colonel's sash and gorget, and Philip Carew had buckled like wet leather. She had recited her Bible verses, and showed her fingernails for inspection, and her grandfather had done all but look in her ears and at her teeth to see that she had not been ill-treated, but the child was clean and well-fed and decently cared for and it showed.

The only thing that grandpapa Carew could object to was that the child prattled to her sire in Cornish. And he said - apparently - that was not the language of a lady, but of labourers and peasants. You could see him flinch when she called Toogood her *tassik* - he did not correct her, but his mouth twisted a little, as though she had cursed in company. (It was the language Toogood spoke to his own men, and the language he spoke to his child, and the language he swore in. Which made Russell wonder if it might also be the language he thought in and prayed in, and if that made him a peasant and a labourer, or just more of a Cornishman than an Englishman.)

Oddly, there were a number of things that the company had objected to about Carew's upbringing of the little maid. She'd been brought up as a proper little lady, as Trooper Ward had pointed out, with a scowl that didn't intend it as a compliment. Didn't know how to do nothing, much, but embroider - and precious little of that, for she couldn't sit to much for more than half an hour without wanting to be distracted, and craving attention. And if that was Master Carew's way of governing a child, that he'd have the little maid cosseted and soft-handed, for all the use she'd be as any more than a rich man's wife -

Well, they had all put an act on, for grandpapa Carew. And possibly grandpapa Carew had put an act on for them, a thought which had not previously occurred to Russell. And the end of it was that the child was in the respectable keeping of a lady out of the baggage train - which, nominally, she was, so far as Thomas Fairfax knew - and there she would remain, for her own safety. For Sir Ralph Hopton might have surrendered, and agreed to the disbandment of the Army in the West, but the castle at Pendennis was still staunch for the King, and there were still bands of unhappy soldiers who had been in the King's pay and now were roaming the county masterless and unpredictable, and who knew what they might do? No - the child remained in her father's care, and saw her grandfather at Harrobear when her father and her chaperone could be spared from their respective duties, and with that they must all rest content. (And some of the lines were softening from Toogood's lean face, and he smiled more often, and had been heard to laugh - and so he was content. And the child - the child was six, she had a short memory, and a sweet nature, and she wanted, very much, to have a father again. And she was content, for now.)

So, here they were, and here they were like to stay, and once again he had the pleasure of being in this place, and the humiliation of having to beg, cap-in-hand, for more favour. They must come to dread the sight of him, for every time he came to Trefusis it was to ask for their service again. He wanted to come - he wanted to be here, and if nothing else to look at the tips of her slippers, for he dared not lift his eyes any further lest she see the look in them and hate him for it - and yet he wanted to not always be here in his formal capacity, begging quarter -

"Lieutenant Russell! What a lovely surprise!"

And astonishingly, Amy sounded as if she meant it. And she sounded - pleased. This lovely girl sounded pleased to see him. She was smiling, which made her rose-pink cheeks even rosier and softer than ever, and Russell did something he hadn't tried in a long old while and he looked at her and smiled back.

"Papa's ridden over to see a man about a horse," she said apologetically, and he raised an eyebrow.

"Evidently all the rage in fashionable circles, mistress, because I'm here on the same business myself."

"You want to see papa about a horse?"

"Another thirty, to be accurate, and stabling for same. I am sorry, Mistress Trefusis. It seems every time I see you I am asking for something. You will end by dreading the sight of me."

She shook her head at him. "I doubt that, lieutenant. I am always happy to see you." Was it his imagination, or had she emphasised the "I" in that last sentence? "Will you stay to supper, and await my father? If he is very late, I'm sure we can spare a bed for the night - mama won't mind, she always says we stand in want of civilised company, out here miles from town."

Russell pulled the sleeves of his travel-stained buffcoat down to cover his very reproachable linen. "Civilised, mistress?" he said warily.

"Well, we can always pick your brains about the latest fashions in London, can't we?" Amy said wistfully. "Colonel Babbitt told papa you used to be the Earl of Essex's own secretary. I'm sure you must have lots of stories to tell."

And he was racking his brains, because a certain inscrutability of expression was about the only benefit to his scarred cheek, but he couldn't think of any stories that were sufficiently decent to relate to a gently-reared young lady and her mother. "I should not believe a word Colonel Babbitt says," he said eventually. "He likes his little joke."

"You weren't the Earl's secretary after all?"

"I was, my lady. Regrettably, my lord Essex leads a very quiet and blameless life, and there is little to relate of his affairs. Were you to speak to our cornet - Pettitt, the -" he swallowed, he still couldn't say it without gritting his teeth -"handsome young gentleman with the fair hair, he would probably be better informed than I, given that he is Essex's nephew."

And to his absolute astonishment, Amy waved a dismissive hand. "Oh, him. He's not handsome."

"He's - not?" Russell said faintly.

"Don't be silly, lieutenant. He's only a boy. I don't like little boys."

"Don't you be fooled, madam," he said, with feeling. "That lad would get where water wouldn't."

She clapped her hands, crowing with delight. "Why, lieutenant, you have an accent! But you're not a Cornishman, I can tell that - now what is it? Is that a London accent?"

"No, mistress, it's Buckinghamshire." She looked at him quite blankly and it occurred to him she'd never heard of Buckinghamshire. And why would she? Russell's family home in a fold of the Chilterns was a peaceful, unremarkable little manor, with neither fame nor fortune to commend it. "Four Ashes," he went on, and she continued to look at him with blank politeness. "It's near London." It wasn't, but he suspected Amy Trefusis had a mental map which stopped at Devon and had London as the only landmark in the rest of England.

"I hope my daughter is not bothering you, lieutenant?"

He looked up. Amy's mother was standing in the doorway, with the same expression of unfeigned pleasure in his company. You could not mistake their kinship: something in the expression, a bright alertness, like a little bird - a wren, or a robin, one of those sweet, soft, round little garden birds that entranced the spring with its song. "N-no, madam. Your daughter was -" and he took a deep breath, "*enchanting* me. A delightful young lady. You must be proud."

Amy gave him a look of sparkling mischief, and Jane Trefusis sighed. "At times, lieutenant. At times."

It was an afternoon of a civilisation he had almost forgotten, winding silks and eating cakes and talking of decent, respectable people - of wonders he had seen, in his travels, and families he did not know, and what the year's harvest might bring. It started to rain again, as dusk drew on, and Jane sighed and shook her head. A wicked April gale started to stir up the ashes in the hearth and the rain grew heavier. "I doubt he'll come now, not in this dirty weather. He and Pellew have known each other long enough there'll be a bed for him at Scorrier, and that's if they don't sit up half the night arguing politics."

"Pellew being -?"

"Matthew Pellew - a childhood friend, but a misguided one, I fear. He lives ten miles distant, but -"

"What mama is tactfully trying not to tell you," Amy interrupted, "is that Master Pellew is for the King."

"It - does not matter?" Russell queried, somewhat bemused.

"It does not matter," Frances agreed. "You will find, lieutenant, that English politics are not always Cornish politics."

Which was as much as Kenelm Toogood had said, if more cynically, and not a thing he did not already suspect. He was grateful, for the second time that day, for a cheek that was scarred into immobility, and didn't give away astonishment. "You will stay for supper, I hope?" she went on, and he smiled politely.

"Madam, I have been away from my duties for the better part of a day already, I -"

"You came over to talk to papa about finding room for another thirty horses," Amy said sweetly, "and he isn't here, so you have to stay, really, don't you? And, lieutenant, if you decide you prefer that little boy's conversation to mine, I shall never forgive you."

"Amy," Jane warned her, and Amy shook her dark curls till they bobbed on her shoulders.

"It's all right, mama. It was a joke the lieutenant and I were having earlier, that's all."

Well, he'd been complaining he wanted for civilised conversation, and these two might look like sweet demure ladies but by God they kept him on his toes. He was also delighted to report that he neither wanted nor was given any more than the one glass of evidently precious wine, which he sipped at politely and then left at his elbow untouched, preferring to keep his wits about him. Jane Trefusis had wide dark eyes and a soft Cornish burr to her voice, but her husband was the Member of Parliament for Truro and she had eyes and ears. They did not talk of the war. He very carefully did not, and they very carefully humoured him. Their talk was sweet, and ladylike, and all of his comfort, and what little he might know of society: just two ladies all agog to know how the wider world should wag, from their quiet country bywater.

He knew when his brains were being picked. (Two sweet, ill-informed ladies, who knew nothing of anything beyond Plymouth. Which was funny, because when they touched on the matter of taxation, Jane Trefusis had a mind like a steel trap, and she knew how many pennies made five - aye, and whose pocket they should be in, too.) But it was a good supper, and he sought his bed just before midnight feeling quite content with life. A warm, well-appointed bed, without Pettitt's amatory mumblings or Toogood's stinking boots -

And with Amy Trefusis perched comfortably on the end of it in her nightgown.

"Bloody hell!" Russell yelped, almost dropping his candle in shock, and then swore at uncharacteristic length as he spattered his hand with hot candle-grease.

She giggled. "Hush, Russell, you'll have half the house awake. I can't stay long."

"For which mercy the Lord be thanked, mistress! What the - madam, what do you think you're doing?"

"I came to bid you good night," she said sweetly.

"Well, I consider myself bidden!"

"Do you?" The rain had cleared, and the moon shone high and full through the leaded windows onto Amy's white face and white shoulders and dark, dark eyes. "I thought you liked me?"

He took a deep breath. "I do like you. Very much. Now -"

"Then we've got a little time to talk. Russell - what is your given name? I can't keep calling you Russell, as if I'm ordering you about."

"It's Thankful. I have a good Puritan family." In the pale moonlight, her mouth didn't even twitch, although her eyes danced. "Though Colonel Babbitt took to calling me Hapless, when I first joined his company, and it sort of stuck amongst my friends."

Which brought her up stiff and quivering with indignation. "I am not going to call you that! That is a horrible thing to say!"

"It could be worse." Trick for trick, colonel. "The colonel is known as Rosie. Affectionately, of course. Because of his hair."

"I'm *still* not calling you that. May I call you by your own name? If we are to be friends?"

It didn't sound odd, when she said it. And it seemed such a little thing, to be grateful to be yourself. "I am appropriately, ah, Thankful," he said gravely, and she blinked at him, and then giggled.

"Your bed will be getting cold."

"Make yourself free of it, mistress. I'm quite warm enough - being, as you see, still dressed." He gave her a look which he hoped was considerably sterner than he felt. Russell - *Thankful* - hadn't been alone with a woman in a room with a bed for the better part of three years, and he was very aware of that fact, especially when she slipped her poor little cold bare feet between his sheets and sat there with her hands linked round her knees, smiling up at him. "As you wish," she said. But as he stayed perched on the heavy oak chest under the windows and made no move to approach her, she began to look unsure of herself.

"Do you not want me?" she asked, in a small voice, and the corners of her mouth drooped in a forlorn curve.

He gave a bitter laugh. "I think better not, mistress. I think it would be both cruel and unfair to both of us." Like giving a dog a bone then snatching it away, he thought, but did not say.

"That's not an answer, Thankful."

"It's the only one you're going to get." He smiled to take the sting from his words, taking the ribbon from his hair and running his fingers through the thick barley-blonde mass - hiding his scarred cheek in the loose strands, as he always did. She swung her feet noiselessly onto the polished wood floorboards and stood up. Crossed the room, padding across the moonlit squares.

"You have a lovely smile," she said shyly, and he turned his head abruptly to face her.

Not even getting as far as stammering, because Amy had her cool white hand on his cheek, very, very gently. "That must have hurt."

And Russell touching his lips to her hand, equally gently, with his eyes closed because even now he was afraid to look at her and find pity, or disgust, in her eyes. "Thankful, you are beautiful. Will you not believe me?"

"No," he said firmly, and she laughed.

"Well, you are. You came by that wound honourably in the commission of your duty and I think it is no more and no less than a badge of courage."

She sounded so ridiculously pompous that he didn't even need to ask how she knew where he'd come by the injury. She must have asked Lucey, in Launceston. Obviously. (And that knowledge, that she had been sufficient interested - intrigued - by him even then, warmed him with a tiny guilty flame.)

"Would you - do you want to kiss me?" she said, with simple dignity, and he laughed, and she drew back a little.

"Yes," he admitted, "very much so, but -"

"But what?"

"I am a little out of practice."

The clock at the turn of the stairs whirred, beginning to chime the hour. Amy's dark eyes widened. "Quickly -"

And before he had time to protest, or do anything more than catch his breath, her mouth came down on his, quick and fierce and hard. And then she was gone.

But not quite. Because his mouth tingled, and his cheek tingled, and his sheets were still warm, and for the first time in almost three years, Russell's heart was a warm and beating thing, and not a piece of ice.

39. DELIVER MY DARLING FROM THE MOUTH OF THE DOG

He thought he'd lie awake all night, and he didn't. Asleep almost as soon as his head touched the pillow, and that was a thing he hadn't done since before - in a long time. He also thought he might not be able to face John Trefusis over breakfast, and he could, without a tremor. Hapless Russell might have gone stiff and formal and cold, but Thankful was something of a morning-person, and able to face bread and cold bacon without turning a hair, and whistle cheerfully in the doing of it.

He didn't even blush when Amy passed behind him with her mother on her way to the parlour, in a rustle of silk and scent of roses, and trailed a surreptitious finger between his shoulders. He sat bolt upright with a squeak, which caused his host to look at him slightly oddly, but he'd turned it into a cough and pretended he had a crumb caught in his throat, and sat there looking intelligent, shaking, and quite incapable of speech for the better part of a quarter hour afterwards.

The minor issue of finding space and fodder for an additional thirty horses seemed to pass off easily enough, although Russell was no expert in the matter of dairy farming and any conversation around cattle and the relocation thereof tended to pass over his head. The which he was happy to admit to - "My own home is sheep country," he said innocently. "Chalk, you see, sir, at Four Ashes."

"Ah? How d'you find it?"

The temptation to say turn left at the crossroads and keep going downhill till you come to the big gates was enormous, but this man was a valuable ally to the cause of Parliament. And as of about eight hours ago, he was also probably going to become Russell's father-in-law. "Very good for sheep," he said, hoping he sounded intelligent. "In truth, sir, I have always, um, left that side of the business to the family agent."

Trefusis' eyebrows twitched. "Indeed?"

"I'm the last of the Buckinghamshire Russells, sir." - for which the Lord be thanked, he thought, but decided it prudent not to mention. Trefusis seemed suitably impressed, anyway, and that was the important thing. It was agreed that Babbitt's thirty additional remounts would be installed in the river meadow, with stabling if required in the empty barns. "How fortuitous that this campaign begins in the spring," he said, dabbing his lips with a napkin and itching to be gone now that Amy had left the room.

"A mild one," Trefusis agreed. "Not like last year's. I have my suspicions that had my lord Essex had better weather, he might have enjoyed more success."

"Ah." Occasionally daft, but not stupid. And not being drawn into any criticism of his former employer: partly out of a sense of loyalty, but more particularly, because Essex might be presently out of favour and Fairfax in the ascendancy, but in this world turned upside down on a daily basis, there was no guarantee it would remain so. He loitered politely until he could in all decency return to his rightful duties.

And then set off, having relearnt the ability to whistle, and feeling kindly disposed towards the world in general. And, possibly, light-hearted.

He was whistling like a lark, and it was not raining. Thomas was in fine fettle, the mismatched horse kicking up his heels after a night's rest in a warm, dry stable. Russell had done what he had been tasked to do -

And then there was Amy.

(There would always, *ever*, be Amy.)

It was spring, and the new buds were beginning to shimmer copper and gold on the trees, and he took a deep, shaky breath of the first honest happiness he had enjoyed in - well. A while. Feeling as if the blood was fizzing and tingling all through his body, Russell looked up at the sun and gave a little wriggle of silent, lonely joy.

(He was not so mad as he would sit in the slushy track miles from civilised company giggling to himself. Not quite. Not yet.)

He could smell roses, and he sniffed at the shoulder of his otherwise-unlovely buffcoat, where the scent of her still clung. (Where she had clung, briefly, not an hour since, in a snatched and all too short embrace behind the porch door.) Her little lace-edged handkerchief was tucked into his sash. He could, if he so chose, have put his hand on it, and thought of her dear, sweet little nose buried in its snowy folds -

Except that he wasn't quite that far gone. He turned Doubting Thomas in a half-circle, though, and saluted the house, despite the fact that it was behind a stand of trees a mile distant and he was invisible. He just wanted to. And there was no one to see him behave so, and laugh at him, and so he did not care.

Doubting Thomas cared, though, at being encouraged to curvet and prance, and so they had a minor difference of opinion which ended in the mismatched horse's splashing in and out of the river, his hoofs slipping great chunks out of the banks. Sheer, joyous foolery.

It was such noisy, chaotic foolery, that at first he did not hear the sound of other hooves behind him.

It wasn't till Thomas's head came up and the big bay horse snorted, his ears pricking alertly, that Russell saw the first shadows flitting through the leaf-shadows.

And then the first shot sang over his head, whining like a gnat, and he yanked Thomas out of the river and onto solid ground and he rammed his spurs into the horse's wet flanks.

The mismatched horse fled like a rabbit, but he was coming from a standing start and they - he? they? - had the edge of speed on him, and Russell could hear the crash and beat of heavy bodies now in the trees, catching him up with a terrifying speed.

"What do you want?" he yelled over his shoulder, but they - he - did not answer, and nor had he expected any, not really, for this nightmare was a thing in which you did not receive neat answers, but only put your face into your horse's flying mane and kicked him and kicked him until the ground flew by beneath you in a blur, hoping to God he did not stumble on the rough boggy ground for it would break both their necks. Crashing through stiff reeds - sweet Lord. let there not be water-birds here, to fly up in Thomas's face and make him swerve, or shy - and there was more than one of them, he dared glance behind him, there were two mounted men coming on at a reckless pace, and then another, and another, and he wanted to weep, or to fight, or to do something. Anything other than this mad headlong gallop, like a man racing on his destruction. He could smell his own acrid fear-sweat, his and Thomas's and in an agony of helplessness he took the buckle-end of the reins and belted the bay horse with them. More speed. He needed to get -

Did not know where he needed to get, for all he could see was the river and the trees, all around for miles nothing but slow-moving brown ripples and yellow grass and black mud, and there was no safe haven here. Part of his brain was scuttering like a rat in a trap, wanting to turn for home, to head pell-mell for Tresillian - too far, still ten or so miles yet, Thomas would be foundered - or to race back to Trefusis and beg John Trefusis for shelter -

Another shot went wide of him, ploughing into the earth two yards clear of him with a spatter and a sudden stench of turned wet leaf-mould, and Thomas swerved wildly.

He did not know them, that was what made him so afraid: he did not know these men, did not recognise them, they were not men in armour or in soldiers' livery but a handful of mounted ruffians. He had nothing worth the robbing, he was a rather worn young officer with a standard-issue buffcoat and a standard-issue backsword and a well-used brace of pistols, third-hand. He could not even claim to own the coat on his back. He was a person of no importance, on a good, but conspicuous, horse. A gelding. They could not want the horse for breeding-stock -

Because Russell was babbling all these things, as loud as he might, in the hope that they might only stop chasing him. They were silent behind him, and that was worse than ever, only the sound of hoofbeats and Thomas's breath heaving and blubbering in his nostrils. There were no shouts. Nothing but that eerie, purposeful pursuit, chasing him like a pack of hounds on the scent –

And another shot, and this time Thomas staggered under him, a sharp sudden coppery smell of blood and Russell shouted something – God knows what, a sound that the poor beast could not make, a great yelp of anguish as the big bay horse staggered and then by some miracle caught his feet again. A bleeding furrow through the muscle of his shoulder, but he was still on his feet, still reeling onwards. Surely some –

He dared look over his shoulder again. There was a horse's head almost at Thomas's tail, foam flecking from its muzzle, and there was no more he could do. He sent a silent prayer heavenwards, and apologised to his good horse in almost the same breath.

And then he wrenched Thomas's head round so that the big bay went slewing sideways, his backside slamming into the strange horse's chest. The other horse reared up with a panicked squeal, slithering in the riverbank mud, its hind legs scrabbling for a desperate purchase on the crumbling bank. Its rider was off-balance, but he was not unseated. It was enough that Russell could draw his sword and slash wildly at the man's face, driving Thomas straight for him.

He did not think he would ever forget the man's shriek as thirty-six inches of plain Birmingham steel took him full across the bridge of his nose, nor the moment of sheer, gut-churning panic as both horses tangled together on the riverbank, and the blinded man slid screaming beneath their hooves. Desperately, desperately afraid, and at the same time a sudden fierce joy lifted him, because he would not die in this place. Would bloody not. If he had to take every last man of them down with him –

Thomas squealed in pain again, and Russell twisted in his saddle, flinging himself to the side to escape a savage cut from the oncoming rider – and then there was a third, and a fourth on him, and suddenly there was nothing in the world but the clash of steel on steel, and the smell of river mud and horse-sweat, and the burn of his own sweat in his eyes.

This was not a battle Russell knew how to fight.

He met the fierce dark eyes of a man who looked as desperate as he felt. But whatever the man felt, he knew his work, and his sword slammed across Russell's forearm with a bruising force even through the finger-thick leather of his buffcoat. The length of his arm went tingling-numb. It would not stay that way, he knew that, and that frightened him – scared him worse than the prospect of a blade through the guts, actually, because that would hurt and then it would be done. This - when he glanced down out of the tail of his eye he could see the blood starting to soak through the parted cut edges of the leather, and he did not know what lay underneath it, save that his fingers would not answer him any more.

And that meant he was useless. Because he could either control his labouring horse, or he could defend himself, but he could not do both. And Thomas was all but done. A one-handed man on a spent horse – oh, Christ, why could someone not choose this moment to bring a barge down the river. A barge full of anything, the King himself could sail down the river for aught he cared so long as someone would only help him, and he wanted to shout for help, but nothing came out of his mouth but a feeble cat's mew.

"*Syns dha glapp!*" he heard – which meant nothing to him, but did not sound kindly - "*Meregyon!*"

No, he didn't know what the words meant, but he knew the look of cursing, and he swore back at the heathen Cornish bastard – in plain English - with all the breath that was in him, and spat in his eye for good measure. And someone went to fire at him again – a misfire, dear God, he was blessed – and Thomas's feet slipped on the bank, his quarters dropping with an unsettling lurch as his back legs plunged into the shallow water of the river –

And the lunge that would have skewered Russell like a bedbug on a pin went skating across his flank instead as the bay horse splashed on the loose stones, churning wildly in and out of the deeper water. *"Toll-din!"*

The *deeper water,* Russell. Use your wits.

He dragged Thomas's poor foam-flecked head round, away from the riverbank – rest soon, my brave heart: one way or another – and then he hammered his spurs home into his horse's flanks. Thomas hesitated, but only for a heartbeat. Yes. Well. Only a fool or a madman would ask an innocent beast to launch himself out into a churning brown channel of moving water.

Only an equally mad or foolish beast would have done it. But Thomas did it, he heaved his hind legs under him and flew out into the river like a clumsy dark bird, hitting the river twelve feet away belly-deep in a great wall of dirty water.

Another shot, and this one struck home, but by now they were swimming strongly out into the tidal flow of the river, and although he felt it, it felt no worse than a sharp poke with a fingertip in the muscle of his thigh. Thomas was sinking lower in the water, still striking out against the tide, and Russell did not know how much more the big horse could take him.

He did not know how much further he could take himself, for that matter, for though he was being carried, he was suddenly weary almost past bearing, and he let the current drag him from the saddle.

They were still shouting from the riverbank, and one of them urged his horse into the water, but not so far out. He could hear splashing, and cursing, and another shot – two shots – spattering water over his head. He didn't mind, though. The water was cold, and the tide was pulling against him, the sodden leather of his coat pulling his limbs into weights.

It hurt a little, now, to keep swimming, and so he did not.

He felt Thomas surge past him, buoyed up by the loss of the deadweight in his saddle. And that was all right, because the big horse would make it to safety, and in his head, Russell smiled. Rolling in the current now like a piece of wood, and soon he would drift into the current, and be washed out to sea.

He was only sorry that Hollie Babbitt would not know what had happened. Might think he had deserted, at the last, and that made him sad, because Hollie had trusted him.

But it did not matter. Not really. And he closed his eyes tighter, and let the current take him.

40. DELIVERED OUT OF THEIR DISTRESSES

It was coming on for midnight, and the cobbles were slick with the fine mist swirling in up from the sea, and Hollie was longing for his bed and at the same time he was starting to be seized with a horrible dread that something had happened to Russell. Missing for two days, and Russell unpredictable of temper at best, and a most distinctively-featured member of the troop.

Not that there was anything he could do by still sitting up in the back room with Luce, with conversation lagging, except - if the worst news came, he could be there. He owed the lieutenant that much. Possibly the most honourable man he'd ever met, and possibly, on his stiffer days, the least likeable. He thought he was doing an effective job of hiding his concern until Luce stifled a yawn and said, "I imagine we'll be up for the night, then, if we're to wait up till we hear word of Russell?"

"If we're going to stop up all night waiting for that waste of a good skin, I suggest we get a bottle of wine and get some bugger to put a brick in his bed. Bloody cold out there, if he's been out all this time." And Hollie had given one of his unconvincingly casual shrugs, as if he were not too troubled by it after all. "Probably turn up in the morning with a hangover."

"Who will?"

Hollie looked up as the door banged closed. "*You* will, you marred bugger." As white as skimmed milk, hatless, with a great ragged tear in the sleeve of his buffcoat that was seeping dark, and his hair plastered like weed down his back, and limping horribly. "Russell," said Hollie, "where the fuck have you been for two days?"

"Under a b-bridge," Russell said dreamily, or as dreamily as he could manage through his chattering teeth, "in Mylor."

"You. What?"

"Bridge. In M. Mm-mylor.. Up to the arm-pits in water."

"Russell, are you a fucking *troll* or something?"

"Come and sit down, Hapless," Luce said quickly. "Here by the fire."

"Thank.*Full*."

There was a soft scraping sound, and then an equally soft metallic ringing. Hollie Babbitt had drawn his sword. It looked ever so casual, though the metallic tick of his wedding ring tapping on the blade sounded increasingly menacing. "Lieutenant Russell," he said, with icy formality, "have you been drinking today, sir?"

Luce thought Russell shook his head, but that might just have been the shivering. "Some. Bugger," he said eventually, to the enlightenment of no one. "Raising a. Troop."

"What?" Hollie said blankly.

"Somew-what lighter in s-strength now."

"What?"

"Russell shut up and take that damnable wet coat off," Luce said irritably. "You will catch your death, if you haven't already."

Hollie sat with his well-worn munitions-quality backsword in his lap, still drumming his fingers on the flat of it. "A troop? You're serious?"

"Chased me. Up the river. From nigh on Penryn. Knew who I was, too."

"From Penryn? What the hell were you -"

"Had to take to the. Water." He gave a dazed smile. "This morning. Like a – fox. Lost the scent? Been under the bridge at Mylor since high tide."

"You'll not get a word of sense out of him while he's like this," Luce snapped, "and I'll not let you. Coat off, Russell, and come and sit by the - bloody hell-fires, Hapless, what -!"

Under the sodden buffcoat, Russell's forearm was laid open to the bone. Not bleeding, though the dark stains on shirt and oxhide gave mute testimony to the depth of the wound. "Cold," he said, and flexed his fingers obligingly to Luce, "doesn't hurt."

"It bloody will," Hollie said, and left the room abruptly. Was back very shortly with a great black bundle which he dumped across Russell's shoulders. "First thing, Hapless, you get bloodstains on that and the wife will murder me, all right? And second, if you're putting me on about that troop, I will have you fucking cashiered."

"Give me that," Luce said crossly, and grabbed Russell's wrist.

"All right, it *does* hurt," the lieutenant muttered, turning even whiter.

"I'm not surprised. Hollie, can you call for a bit of light over here?"

"Oh, yes, sir," Luce's commanding officer muttered sarcastically, and stalked out again, bellowing across the house for candles. People didn't refuse Babbitt. He returned with an incongruously elaborate candlestick, and dumped it on the table. "What're you going to do?"

"I'm going to stitch it, Hollie, obviously. Don't be any stupider than you have to be. Mind out of the way - oh. Colonel. You don't still happen to carry that perpetual flask of appalling brandy, do you?"

"Not for me," Russell said stiffly.

"I'm going to clean it out, Russell. God alone knows what was in that water."

And while he sat shivering under Het's fur-ined cassock coat, wincing as Luce stuck a blunt needle through his flesh, Hapless explained it all. Glossing over the finer details of where John Trefusis' cows were going to spend their spring, but having paid closer attention than he would have liked to the number and adequacy of a number of armed men who should not have been in a county that had just officially disbanded the Army.

It being now well past midnight, Hollie was being obtuse. Toogood, staggering down the stairs at the noise and smacking his head on the low lintel, was not.

"Say that again."

"Attacked," – the lad was starving, as well as chilled, and the servants were awake. A huge-eyed boy from the kitchens set a wedge of pigeon pie in front of the scarred lieutenant, and he tore into it like a man who'd never seen food before. Hollie watched with a degree of satisfaction as the pie was reduced to rubble, and then jerked his head to the kitchen boy. "Keep it coming," he said quietly. "And I'll not see a thing, if you happen to take a bit for yourself. If you get me. Perks of the job."

For ale was a quick enough thing to heat up, and easy to get the lad to fetch a couple of eggs up from the kitchen to beat in with the tip of your knife, and then to bring it up to heat with the poker red-hot out of the fire. Rough, but warm, and Hapless was beginning to look almost like a man, and not a thing out of the tomb. "They attacked me," he said indignantly, and sniffed. "The sods set on me, for no reason, and tried to bloody well kill me!"

"I reckon that's enough ale," Luce said meaningly, and gave Hollie a very reproving look.

"And I'm not bloody drunk, either! I was about my perfectly legitimate business and half a dozen well-armed, well planned, well set-up bloody ruffians tried to bloody well kill me!"

"Robbers?" Luce hazarded. "I mean, really, we are in Cornwall, and it is quite, you know –"

"Watch it," Toogood muttered. "We ent big on highwaymen here, boy. Would you know 'em again, Hapless?"

"My name is *Thankful*." The air of affront was hampered by his having to pause to wipe his nose on his sleeve. "Of course I bloody would. I killed one of 'em, didn't I? I have eyes in my head, and there were - I would guess, around half a dozen well-armed men, on fairly sub-standard mounts." He grimaced. "Including my Thomas, now, the bastards." He wrapped his hands around his ale-mug again, and Luce opened his mouth to remonstrate. "I am keeping my hands warm, Lucifer, so mind your bloody business. Some bugger is raising a militia, colonel."

"I never did rate that bloody horse," Hollie said. "Russell, they can't be -"

"They bloody are!" Russell yelled, and then sat back in his chair with a yelp as Luce thumped a wad of linen on his wound, hard enough to hurt. "Fine. They're not. You quarter our horses out there, sir, and you are going to find in very short order that that gentleman who isn't raising a militia but is possibly helping 'em out when they're busy, is going to be three troop of horse plus remounts to the good. Which, as our estimable comrade Captain Venning would say, 'll do us a bit o' no good, though may improve his prospects quite dramatically. I appreciate that it's late, colonel, and that you and Cornet Pettitt may be somewhat hard of thinking at this hour due to your concern over my well-being. However, I am not drunk, I am not blind, if I eat another morsel I will burst, colonel, so stop it, and I am telling you what I saw with my own eyes. Someone had taken the time and the trouble to see those men properly equipped, and for the Lord alone knows what reason of their own they would rather I had not come back from Trefusis Manor. Trust me on this, colonel, they were well-armed, they knew what they were about, and they meant that I should not come home. It was only by the Lord's grace that I was preserved." He paused. Considered. "That, and an ability to hold my breath."

"How'd you come by that, in Buckinghamshire?" – because Hollie did, actually, want to know. When the lieutenant started to flush a lovely shade of warm rose, he thought he might have worked it out. "Ah. All right. Enough said. By, Russell, you're a dark horse!"

"What?" Of all people, it was Luce who didn't get it, and Russell gave him one stricken glance.

"I'll tell you when you're older, cornet," Toogood said, in a voice that shook with laughter. And then, in a more serious voice, "were they in soldier's coats, Russell? The leftovers from a company fell on hard times, maybe?"

He shook his head. "No. No – worn, but good. But I know one of them. I know his name, Captain Toogood, because when they thought I was dead his comrade called to him. He called him – he said his name was – Tolden?"

"That's not a name I –" Toogood suddenly stopped dead. "Toll-din?"

"You know him?"

"It's the Cornish for arsehole," the captain said, and his lips were twitching. "Local boys, then, Hapless?" And he put his hand out and very awkwardly, and with a certain uncomfortable fondness, he patted the lieutenant's shoulder. "Well done."

"Aye. Well done," Hollie said grimly, "though not such good news, lad. But no fault to you for that. But Russell! Why d'you not just double back, and go back to Trefusis? They'd have given you aid, surely?"

"I – uh –" he looked at his hand, and flexed it gingerly. "Neat work, Pettitt. I thank you."

"Out with it, Hapless."

"I am rapidly concluding, sir, that as Captain Toogood points out, there are a number of men in these parts who run with the hare and hunt with the hounds. In a manner of speaking."

"You mean Trefusis?"

His eyes flew to Hollie's face, very wide and rather scared. "I - well, I think I should need to be closer acquainted with the family before I made that judgement, colonel."

"You're right," Hollie said abruptly. "It is late, and this is too bloody complicated for me, all these Tre-s and Pol-s and Pen-s. Simple boy from Lancashire, me. Wi' no bloody relatives, thank God."

"On the contrary, sir," Luce said, with a faint smile. "Don't forget you're my uncle by marriage."

"I'm going to bed, before I'm tempted to throttle one or both of you buggers." He stopped on the threshold. "Hapless, you goddamned prodigal - *thing*. I expect to find you in bed tomorrow, and I don't expect you to leave it. And you pull them stitches out, and me and you are going to have words. We're going to talk about this in the morning."

Russell pulled the heavy fur-lined collar about his throat and glanced at Luce. "There are times, Lucifer, when I almost suspect the colonel of harbouring some fondness for me."

"There are times, Russell, when I almost suspect you of having a sense of humour. Come on. There's a hot brick in your bed and if you come down with some kind of low fever despite everything we've done - well, he will have you cashiered."

Russell said nothing, for a moment. Carried on staring into the dying fire, the rosy embers lending a kind shadow to the livid scar on his cheek. His hair had dried in wisps, gently framing his austere features. "Hap- " Luce stopped himself. "*Thankful.* You look - I don't know - different?" Softer. Almost dazed, somehow. The notoriously frigid lieutenant looked like a man who'd just woken from a long nightmare to find himself safe in his own bed. But - Luce the poet was notorious for seeing things that weren't there, wasn't he?

A log split on the fire with a report like a musket shot, and Russell looked up, his good hand absently touching the ridges of scarring. Fingertips moving over his cheek as if he were reliving another's kinder touch. "She says I'm beautiful, Lucifer. Me. She says I'm beautiful."

41. WRATH IS CRUEL

Not for the first time, Luce wished he didn't share his quarters with Hollie, who not only snored appallingly, but could be disconcertingly perceptive when the mood was on him. And who wasn't asleep. "Well, well," the big redhead said from the shadows. "D'you reckon her husband didn't like it, then? That what all that was about? Though it seems a little harsh -"

Was it his place to say? "I'm sure I don't know, sir."

"Brat, when you start getting respectful off-duty, I know you're putting me on. His Highness looks like a dying duck in a thunderstorm." There was a creak as of someone on a rickety bed propping himself up on one elbow. "I'm not that daft. Half a dozen likely lads get to chasing him off the premises, and he looks at me like a netted rabbit every time I mention the Trefusis family. Someone doesn't want a bit o' rebel blood in the family, do they? Though I reckon there's better ways of getting rid of unwanted suitors than drowning the poor buggers. Well, Luce, every time Russell gets himself into that kind o' trouble, I can't help thinking Churchay la famme."

"Eh?" French by way of Lancashire. It was almost comprehensible, at times. "Oh - yes. Possibly."

"She better not be married, Lucey. I'm not going through all that again. I haven't forgiven that bugger for the last time."

"You don't take it seriously, then? About the militia?" The look of amused disbelief on Hollie's face was answer enough.

"Brat, he's trying to get under Amy Trefusis's petticoats. Isn't he? He is hardly likely to turn up here and say her father caught him with his hand in the honeypot, and ran him off at gunpoint. Though I lay you a pound to a penny that's what happened. I know my lieutenant, Luce. He's been smirking one-sided for about a week. And I had noticed he's always the first to put his hand up to trot off there, though it's a good couple hours' ride out of anybody's way. I'm not wholly daft, Luce. The only thing that bothers me, knowing our Hapless and his form for the older lady - is it Amy, or is it her mother?"

And he wasn't going to shut up till he found out, was he? "I don't know who she is, I'm afraid. She may be eminently eligible, you know. She may be one of the maids, for all I know. All I know is that she apparently described him as, um - beautiful."

Another creak. Luce wasn't sure if his friend had sat up in disbelief or fainted in shock. "Bloody hell, Luce, I didn't know he'd took to haunting the blind school."

"That was unkind, sir."

A long silence, and then a sigh. "Aye. Well. I'm not feeling all warm and fluffy at the moment, brat. Not his fault. It's just a weird thought... how long we known Russell? Four years? And I never had him marked down as - well. Thought me and Russell was going to end up setting up bachelor housekeeping, at this rate."

"I don't - sir - um, Hollie, you are married? With daughters?"

"Am I?" He sounded as bleak as the cold moonlight. "You want to remind her of that?"

"Oh, hell-fires. Oh bloody hell, Hollie. Oh I am sorry."

"'S all right. I can see her point. She's not only married to Fairfax's bloody shadow, she's married to a shadow that's not even bloody there. What bloody use am I, as a husband? No wonder she doesn't want to know me."

"How - how is she managing, then?"

Hollie laughed bitterly. "How would I know, Luce? She's not telling me. Oh, it doesn't matter, lad. Just sort of rubs salt into the wound, the thought of bloody Hapless Russell on the arm. Christ, brat, you'd think I was the only man in the world had ever been off-hooks with his wife, the way I talk at times. Just put a pillow on my head or summat, will you?" He took a deep breath. "Not like you've been exactly blooming like the rose, either. You all right?"

Luce was glad it was dark. "Um. Yes. Yes, I'm - I'm fine, I - " he swallowed, hard. "I think I'll stay up for a while. I find I'm not tired."

42. SOWN IN DISHONOUR

But Russell was adamant on it, and in the light of day, looking at the great slash in the sleeve of his buffcoat, and the badly-stitched and bloody hole in his arm, it seemed - unlikely, then, that even the most outraged of fathers might have taken such action.

They could not stay at Tresillian, of course.

Not if God-knows-who was raising a militia between here and the garrison at Pendennis, a fact which increasingly outraged Hollie, the more he thought about it. That you could sign a surrender and before the ink was even dry some bugger would be breaking the terms of the treaty – the hell kind of low, unprincipled turd would do such an appalling thing? Arming a troop – troops, even, God alone knew – of men, in direct contravention of a man's agreement to disband the Army in the West –

Well, it stank, was all.

"So Skellum Grenville's at the bottom of it," Toogood had said. "Because there's no other bastard so low as he would go behind Hopton's back to poke the whole sorry mess up again. Can't put that boy down, now."

"Don't be bloody stupid, he's on his way to France! The Prince didn't want the likes of us laying hands on that bugger - God knows what might have become of him. Or us, for that matter."

"Come off it, Rosie! That man's slicker'n a wet fart. Safe on St Michael's Mount and all of a sudden, so soon as the surrender's signed, the Prince of Wales thinks it might be dreadful if he fell into enemy hands? Why? What bloody difference does it makes to them whose hands he's in, if they've given an honourable agreement to disband the Army in the West?"

"Just answered your own question, captain. Skellum and the words honourable and agreement. He's not honourable, and he's not agreeable."

Whoever it was, if someone was raising troops, the perfectly well-reasoned idea of leaving the horses safely eating their heads off a couple of miles up the river, was a risky one. It had seemed so sensible when the county was surrendered, and any Malignants with any fight left in them were safely penned up in Pendennis Castle. Aye. Well. There it was. And that meant leaving Tresillian – and the kitchens, Hollie thought with a sigh, and the bend in the stairs where the low beam was that he'd just about got used to not cracking his head open on, and the fish that was that fresh it was still flapping. He'd grown used to Tresillian. He'd been quite looking forward to seeing that apple tree on the riverbank behind the house in bud – in fruit, even.

And now it was going to be bloody siege rations, and up to the arseholes in mud and testy troopers, and a smell of carrion and charring, and powder smoke hanging low and acrid over everything.

"Bollocks," he said aloud, and Toogood jerked upright, twisting his hat in his hands.

"Beg your pardon, sir?"

"Muttering to myself."

"Colonel Babbitt. Sir." The man seemed positively awkward about something, and Hollie thought to himself, not for the first time, that Kenelm Toogood was a funny lad. Had the look of a man who was throttling on a secret he was longing to tell you, and yet dared not. "I been thinking, sir. About – about Trefusis. About quarters. I – " he gave a great gulp of air, and his eyes bulged slightly, and Hollie thought that whatever it was he needed to say, he needed to say it quick, lest he had an apoplexy. "See. We could split the company, sir, and leave half the horses at Trefusis, with Captain Betterton, and me and you could quarter the rest at —" a little muscle twitched in his jaw, "Trevaskis."

The name was familiar. He cocked an eyebrow at the Cornishman. "Why?"

"Six miles up-river from Trefusis, that bit closer to Pendennis. I'd not leave Chesten in a soldier's camp besieging a castle, sir. And," Hollie wondered if the man knew his eyes had widened beseechingly, "I'd not give her back so soon. I'd keep her with me a little longer. She – she calls me her *tassik* again, you see. Her – daddy. And I'd not – I'd –"

"Aye," Hollie said gruffly, "I know."

Toogood nodded. "I used to know the people at Trevaskis. Before." Dropped his eyes, and then looked up with a challenge. "I told you of them – John, as stood my friend before the wars, and his sister that keeps house for him?"

The Malignants. Of course. "They would quarter us?"

"Possibly," he said, and gave a little laugh. "If I know Hannah, first she would discharge a musket over our heads and call us all manner of bad things, and then she would call me changed, and – aye. Well. You know how it is. There was never bad feeling 'tween me and John Trevaskis, sir, for all he is – was – a captain in the King's Army. And he may be back at home himself, now, and I can promise you he'd make us welcome, for he's an open-hearted lad. He'd not bear a grudge. Such petty things as this side and that side would make no difference to John, not now –"

"And you would go back there – for what?"

Toogood ran a hand through his hair, and smiled shakily. "I - I had not expected this. That - I have a place here. Sir. When I spoke to you before - it was words, no more than words, I was bitter at heart, and afraid, and - and I - since Torrington - "

Had forgiven, and been forgiven. Aye. It explained a lot. Toogood had gone away hurt and frightened and angry, like a child - and why should he not, for what had been done to him at Lostwithiel by his own was cruel, they said - but he had come back and all was as it had been, for the Cornishman. And there was only so long you could go on trying to stir up the embers of your wrath again, amongst people who had been your friends, and would be so again if you would let them. Hollie knew that feeling. He very deliberately did not smile, or make light of it, for he knew all too well how it felt to be in a place where you could be your own self, without flattery or dissembling. To go home and pick up a different life again, like putting on a clean suit of clothes, and to forget what you might have done before, in a time of madness.

Well, he had agreed to keep his company in Cornwall and lay siege to an impregnable castle, so that Kenelm Toogood could be a father again to a motherless child. Maybe, in some little way, that would do to weight God's balance in his favour a little, might temper all the evil he had done, in almost twenty years as a man of blood.

He nodded. "Well enough, then. I'll do what I can."

43. BETTER A DINNER OF HERBS

But it wasn't Toogood, in the end, that went out to Trevaskis. Toogood had taken a patrol down to the castle, and it was Hollie himself, at the head of his own company, in his full formal officer's attire, colours and all, on a blustery April afternoon.

He was expecting something less formal, somehow, than the little rosemary-grey manor house that nestled in a fold of trees set back from the road, with the stiff little knot-garden set so incongruously in front of it, and the little granite porch at the front where the lichens grew as gold as honey on the slate roof, and the mullioned windows glowed amber in the chill spring sunset. It was a tiny, perfect little house, and it looked as if he could have picked it up and put it in his pocket.

He was proud of his lads, that day. It wasn't often they put on a good show, but they formed up in a body that meant business and Russell brought his borrowed horse to the front rank at a spanking clip, halting it four-square in a spray of gravel. He dismounted neatly, strode to the front door, and beat a purposeful tattoo with the hilt of his sword.

It was all done for effect, of course. Hapless Russell thought altogether too highly of his weapons, not to mention his person, to make a habit of such a vulgar military display. On the other hand, he was well aware of the value of his marred face as a weapon in its own right. The door came open half-way, and a wary middle-aged male face appeared in the shadows. His eyes widened in shock at the sight of a rebel angel in a lobster-pot helmet on his doorstep.

"Is the master of the house to home?" Russell said, in his most carefully slurred voice.

"He is not!"

"When is he likely to return?"

The man - what would he be, a majordomo, a menial, some poor ageing bugger who wasn't fit enough or committed enough to bear arms and so stopped at home with the women - choked on something.

And a woman's figure appeared in the crack of the door behind him, a tall, stiffly-braced figure in neat, unfashionable homespun. "Captain Trevaskis is one of the defenders of Pendennis Castle, sir. His return is in the hands of God."

"And you are?" Russell said, managing to put a tiny hint of contempt into his accentless voice.

"I am the mistress of the house in his absence, sir. And who might you be?"

Scenting a brawl, Hollie dismounted, and didn't quite elbow his lieutenant out of the way, though he considered it. "Madam." He took his hat off and tried to look as little intimidating as possible - which was hard, when you had the better part of a hundred mounted cavalry troopers at your back, and the woman was looking as if she might consider braining you with a candlestick. "Mistress – uh – Trevaskis? You are Captain Trevaskis's – wife?"

She looked at him, and her eyes narrowed a litle. "Captain Trevaskis has no wife, sir, as you would know had you troubled to ask. I am Mistress Trevaskis, right enough. I am his sister."

"And you keep his house?"

"What might that be to you, sir?"

The brown horse shoved his whiskery nose into the collar of his buffcoat, snorting. It was all but impossible to look stern and imposing with a slobbery muzzle investigating the back of your head, so he put his arm up round Blossom's neck and tried to stop the fond beast from showing him up entirely. "Mistress Trevaskis, I must tell you that I mean to quarter my men here for the remainder of the siege, under the orders given me by the Commander-in-Chief of the Army of Parliament. We will offer you every courtesy, but –" She gasped, and her face went a greenish-white, and Hollie realised slightly too late that Hannah Trevaskis didn't need to use a candlestick, if she'd chosen to brain him. Hidden amongst the folds of her skirt was a stout oak walking-cane.

"Oh, bloody hell," he said, slightly too loudly. Dropped Blossom's reins, and bounded across the courtyard to grab her by the shoulders before she fell. "Mistress Trevaskis, will you –"

"Oh, Hollie, you *are* a bloody idiot betimes," Luce said, dropped to the courtyard cobbles and was at the wench's side in a heartbeat, rubbing at her wrists and chafing her temples. "Mistress, breathe easy –"

And then there was a maid, or a servant, or some such, flapping and squawking about them like a chicken, accusing Hollie of rape and murder, oppressing the innocent, doing awful things to poor Mistress Trevaskis –

Luce, glaring at her over his shoulder, loosening her collar, which elicited a shriek from the servant as if he were stripping the clothes from her bleeding body in the middle of the courtyard. All it needed to turn a perfectly civil, if precipitate, intent to quarter a troop of house on a little manor, into the sack of bloody Magdeburg was for Thankful Russell to stick his elegant nose in. Obviously there were other curious members of the household. Bloody useless servants they'd have been, if they'd seen their mistress assaulted by a pack of rebels and done nothing. They weren't armed with pitchforks, they didn't have horns and tails, they did not need Russell piling in with his sword drawn, twitching and quivering like the wrath of God all over the yard. Had Hollie not had his hands full trying to secure Hannah Trevaskis on an eighteen-inch wide stone plinth in the porch that would have given a marble saint a case of the emerods, he might have been inclined to belt Thankful Russell round the back of the head for his pains, never mind any of the household staff.

Eventually he had her limp as a little partridge against Luce's shoulder while that fearsomely efficient young gentleman checked her breath and her fluttering eyelids and the vein in her wrist, and he was able to go and give Russell the full-on bollocking that equally efficient young gentleman richly deserved. (Which, of course, being Russell, he argued.) Like summat out of a bloody romance, he thought darkly, what with the fierce maidservant giving him mouthy hell-on and the wan, fainting mistress –

The wan, fainting mistress came to her senses, jerked bolt upright, and gave Lucey Pettit a box on the ear and a mouthful of very censorious abuse, and then they had to pick Luce up off the floor and pat him down. While trying not to laugh. Poor lad, you had to think of his poor dignity, measuring his length face-down in a chilly Cornish stone porch whilst a great raking wench dressed him down in no uncertain terms about what a lecher he was, and a shocking degenerate.

Hollie folded his arms and leaned his back up against the porch door and eyed a patch of blue between the skating grey clouds and let her go on with herself for a while. Let her stream of invective exhaust itself before he said, in his most reasonable voice, "Mistress Trevaskis, I'd thank you not to abuse my troop surgeon further."

Her mouth hung open slightly. "He?"

"Me?" Luce echoed, looking bemused. "But hardly – me – I –"

Russell sniffed, and cut his eyes at the dust and cobwebs that adhered to Luce's coat sleeve from his resting-place on the stone flags.

"I reckon but little to the state of Malignant housekeeping," he said primly. "Colonel Babbitt, I should choose to be quartered in a midden, rather than under the same housetop as this brawling woman."

"Oh, how *dare* you!"

"How dare you lay hands on an officer in the commission of his duty, madam!"

"*He* laid hands on *me*!"

Before she belted Russell, well-deserved though such chastisement often was in the lieutenant's case, Hollie cut in. Very mildly, he thought. "As I explained, madam. Cornet Pettitt is my company surgeon."

"Him? He's barely old enough to shave!" the noisy maidservant piped up. "Don't 'ee believe a word 'en it, my maid! Nasty little rebels —"

"Quartered under your roof," Hollie added, innocently, "eating your food, taking your tenants' rents, singing psalms all hours of the day and night – indeed, mistress, those rebels can be the very Devil." He looked at her limpidly, and blinked. "You have to be careful with rebels, madam. They can turn."

"Are you threatening me, sir?" she said, and of all things you had to admire that lass, sitting all a-sprawl in her own porch with her cap askew and her collar untied, with a tone of voice that was colder than those granite slabs in her porch.

It was a question he gave about a second's thought to. And then he grinned at her, because he couldn't help it. "I'd flatter myself if I said I was, lass. No. Here we be, and here we stay. And you can either put up wi' us, and we will behave as much grace as may be - or you may resist, in which case here we be anyway, and it won't be any more comfortable for you than it is for us."

Luce carefully got to his feet, and picked a fat grey strand of cobweb from his sleeve, and gave a stiff little bow. "Luce- Lucifer Pettitt, madam, as is cornet to Colonel Babbitt's personal company."

The maid snorted. "Oh, fine manners!" – not quite inaudibly.

"*Someone* in the present company has to have some," Hollie said sweetly. "Colonel Hollie Babbitt, madam. I won't say that I'm at your service, because I'm not. I'm very much not. This is Lieutenant Russell, who is – mostly – under my command. Sometimes he isn't."

Russell showed all his teeth on one side, and ducked his head in acknowledgement. He was actually being perfectly civil. He just happened to look like the wrath of God. And he knew it.

"Be so good as to form your – that's not what I meant – order your – Russell, what *do* I mean?"

"I think directions to form the household up will be sufficient," the scarred lieutenant said, with malevolent relish. "We are, after all, under martial rule, in this house. As of now."

43. BLESSED IS HE THAT ENDURETH TEMPTATION

April slipped slowly into May, and the defenders of Pendennis seemed as indefatigable as the sea, for surely they seemed as well provisioned and equipped as they had done when the gates had first slammed shut, ten weeks ago.

Arundel hadn't been lying. He did, actually, have no intention of giving in to a howling pack of rebel scum. (Which was all right, because the rebel scum had no intention of going away, either. It was growing to be a point of honour.)

She *stared* at him, that was the worst of it. All the time, when she thought he wasn't looking, or when he was about his business, he'd look up and find her odd fierce dark eyes fixed on him, as if she didn't quite know what he was. As if he was some kind of interesting, but strange, mythical beast.

She was an odd wench herself, mind. She haunted Luce, greedily drinking in his lessons with little Chesten, but there was something unsettling about her attentions. At first Hollie had liked to believe that she'd just wanted for civilisation and education, but she didn't. It was almost as if she were waiting for the mask to slip, all the time. Waiting for - what? He didn't know, because she wasn't telling. She just watched, and waited.

The thing that really unsettled him, was that she watched his *hands*. Never his face. Hollie had never been more aware in his life that he bit his nails, and his cuffs were a little frayed, and the little finger on his right hand stuck out at a funny angle. He'd have spent more of his time at Trefusis but he couldn't have borne the company there either, with Russell looking at him expecting him to palm the spoons or start picking his teeth with his knife at table any minute.

Ten weeks of being expected on all sides to lapse into the worst of incivility, and he was about fit to cut loose and do it. So he lurked at the siege headquarters at Arwenack House, which was a draughty and godforsaken pile in what passed for a town in Falmouth in the jumble of fisherman's shacks and rotting boats, and everyone assumed that Colonel Babbitt was a passionate and zealous soldier hot for the assault on the castle, rather than a landsman bored out of his wits. (Aye, and hoping that one of these days, maybe, soon, there might be a letter for him, from home. And that if there was not, that no one else would know.)

He found himself wondering, increasingly, what Hannah Trevaskis thought when she looked at his hands. What she felt, while all around her homes were returning back to peace, and her house was full of strange armed men who came and went at all hours of the day and night. If she saw it as a judgment on her for her brother's politics, or if it was a moment of excitement in the life of a woman stuck out in an outpost of nowhere.

And then one afternoon, with the buds on the trees in a green haze and the first cuckoo of the year beginning to see-saw his song on the hill, he thought - the hell with it. It had been a long day, and a hard one, for all the promise of summer. He was almost - almost - despairing, that the castle would ever fall. He was sick of the smell of siege, even if it was overlaid with salt and the smell of rotting seaweed. He'd been riding to and fro all day, and no more to show for it than a sore arse and a headache: there were half a dozen lads that were sick with a thing that he hoped to God was a chill, or a bad pie, and that he feared was the flux, instead. He'd lost - Betterton had lost, it amounted to the same - one of his troopers to a chance shot from the walls and he hated that, he hated that a man had lost his life by malevolent fortune. It was growing dusk, and though it was almost summer it was cold, with a niggly breeze off the sea, and he had been sweating all day and now he was shivering and he stank of burned wood and death, and Hannah Trevaskis was staring at him with those great owl's eyes and he hated that, too.

"Can I assist you, madam?" he said, and she shook her head with a faint smile.

"Not unless you leave my house, colonel, and leave me in peace."

"Best tell your brother that, Mistress Trevaskis. It's his call, not mine."

She dropped her eyes modestly, but he'd known Russell for long enough to know that look: I am not thinking what you think I should be thinking. "Why?" she said.

"Why's it your brother's call?"

She shook her head. "Why did you turn against your King? You are an educated man - I've watched you. All your troop are - decent, and civil, and respectable -"

He was glad of the deepening violet shadows, because they concealed his expression of disbelief. That lot, respectable?

"Why, then, do you fight for so dishonourable a cause?"

He was tempted to do what he'd done to Het, those five years back; when he'd been standing in the churchyard at White Notley, the day their banns had been read for the last time. When he'd quoted the Book of Judith, concerning them that rebel, and she hadn't quite known if he was zealous or merely humorous, then. And the memory of that long-ago spring day pricked him like a spur, and suddenly he was not minded to be kind to this woman who was not his wife. "Force of habit," he said curtly.

And then he was sorry, because her face crumpled, like a hurt little girl's - like Chesten or Thomazine, like a child who is not yet used to being hurt at the whim of an irritable adult – and she straightened her back and looked at him indignantly.

"I'm sorry, lass," he said, and meant it.

"I am not your lass!"

"No. True enough. I have two lasses at home, aye, and a wife, and I ought to know better. There was no excuse for me to be short with you, mistress, and I'm sorry for it."

She said nothing for a long moment, and then her brows drew together, just a little. "Thank you," she said, sounding surprised.

"For what?"

"Being sorry."

He wondered who it was, that had hurt her by not being sorry. Or if perhaps he just refined too much on a chance remark, because he grew worse than a greensick maid for putting too much emphasis on these words or that. Starting at shadows again. He gave her a faint smile in return – aye, he refined too much on these things, but he would not have the sister of a man who was presently defending a castle against him, think that she enjoyed too much of his confidence – and she smiled back, shyly.

And it was stupid, how much that heartened him: that this plain, watchful wench, who was the sister of an enemy and whose good opinions should have mattered to an officer of the Army of Parliament slightly less than the good opinions of his horse, should not be looking at him as if he was some kind of dangerously unpredictable wild beast. He glanced up out of the windows again, at the rooks flapping home to roost. "I think it might be cold, tonight. Once the sun goes down, it's still chill. Don't you think?"

"It is yet early in the year," she said, and he could have sworn she was laughing at him. "Once the summer comes..."

"I hope we'll be long gone by then."

She said nothing. She said nothing either way, which he thought was odd. And then, "I think you would enjoy a Cornish summer. I do – I hope you will see the first swallows."

As if he were some chance-met acquaintance, and not an enemy invading her house, and it suddenly seemed so important to the lass that they were civil to each other. Her hands were clenched together in her lap, the knuckles straining white against the skin. "Aye," he said, trying to sound gentle, "that would be nice. It's a lovely house."

And very carefully, he led the conversation away from those treacherous waters, and onto the sensible matters that Het liked him to talk of, in company, that no one's feelings would be hurt or offended: the price of bread, and the repair of fences, and the amount of rain they were having. It was a good thing, to see her fingers relax, and her eyes take on a less fixed glare. He did not like to think of anyone frightened by his presence. Well, no. That wasn't true. There were a few people. People who hadn't done anything to him, then. He was not such an ogre that a poor lass should be afraid that he'd suddenly spring across the table and bite her – dear God, his own wife did not treat him with such timid deference –

And that was the start of it. It was nothing that you could measure, nothing scandalous, just that he had ceased to be a faceless rebel commander and become Colonel Babbitt, and she had ceased to be an anonymous Malignant sympathiser and become Mistress Trevaskis. Toogood ran errands for her, betimes, though he wouldn't set foot in the house, or pass the time of day with her; Cullis had her mare re-shod, when the horse cast a shoe in the lane one day. Nothing that you could frown on. Only that – Cornwall was a county at peace, no matter what Captain John Trevaskis and his men on the inside of Pendennis Castle might have to say about it, and they were not one side and another any more, but people together. Kenelm Toogood wrote tetchy letters to the besieging forces at Pendennis, giving her people free passage from Falmouth back up the river, that the house might remain provisioned, and the wheat be planted for the spring sowing without such a petty thing as a civil war getting in the way.

Hollie gave long and hard thought to it, in a week turn and turn about outside the castle being shot at and biting his nails bloody, and then he agreed that she might write to her brother, and that he would see to it that her letters were received.

She cried, when he said that, and he thought that tears did not come easy to that stiff-backed maid. Her mouth had jerked in a very unlovely manner, and her eyes and her nose had turned pink, and she had gone even stiffer than ever, and of all things he was not sorry he had said it, then. And he could read the damn' letter, it wasn't as if he was permitting her to pass on secrets. He told her he meant to read the bloody things, and she'd looked at him as if he'd run mad.

"Well, of course," she said, as if she could not conceive of anything else. But what would she tell him, after all? That the Colonel was anybody's for a plate of fresh bread and decent cheese? That his cornet was teaching a little maid of not quite seven how to write poetry, and that the lass was terrifyingly quick at it, with an agile wit that made her the darling of a company of – of what? Evil traitorous Roundheads?

That was the only bit he was interested to see, and not because he suspected any great plot, but because he wanted to know. And because it mattered, that at least one person in this place should not think of them as the enemy, but as lads just like their own. He stood with his hands behind his back, staring out of the window while she wrote the letter, and trying not to read over her shoulder. She was a painstaking writer, though not a clever one. He found himself watching her profile, sharp against the black of the trees on the hill, lined with candlelight. Found his own hands clenching with the effort she put into forming her letters, willing her slow pen into greater facility – wondering if she'd mind, if he suggested that she sat in with Luce and Chesten and their versifying, and then thinking she probably would, which was a shame, for he thought she might care for it.

"There!" she said proudly, blowing on her handiwork. "I am done."

It was not a long letter. It told of the spring sowing, and the number of lambs that had been born to the Trevaskis flocks, and the new shepherd, and carter's new mare. A clumsy, gossiping letter, hoping in the polite stilted phrases of the schoolroom that he was well, and reassuring him that she and the house were well. It did not mention Hollie by name, or acknowledge that the house was tenanted by anything other than the family.

It made his heart hurt, reading those careful, polite words. A loving letter from a plain country goodwife, brisk and newsy and competent. He smiled, and folded it, and put it in the satchel for Russell to take with the other dispatches, and tried to think no more of it.

M.J. LOGUE

44. LET LOVE BE WITHOUT DISSIMULATION

Russell was run a little ragged, but he did not mind. Did not mind that he slept where he found it, be that bolt upright with his back against the warm place in the kitchen where Hollie debriefed his officers, or in the stable, or in his own bed -

Or, on one marvellous, snatched, blissful moonlit twilight, a few hours in hers, though he had been on one side of the blankets and she on the other and it had all been perfectly decent, if a little informal. Admittedly he had fallen asleep in appallingly short order, and she had given him hell about it for a week afterwards. He had not cared. There was nothing in the world so joyous as to sleep in the arms of a woman who loved you, on a cold spring evening. Even if she was grimly intent on dalliance and he was intent on remaining asleep, no matter how much she had breathed in his ear.

No, he was busy, and he loved it. He was useful, and happy, and active; he had not time to do anything but run messages and account for munitions and provisions, and try and balance the books. (*Tristan* Toogood was still very much present and correct, and it was hard work maintaining the company records so that that fictional young gentleman's debits and credits retained a rough balance. What he would do with her pay when it came in, he did not know. Put it as a contribution towards her dowry, probably.)

He could not see an end to this, and guiltily, he did not care. It was as if Pendennis Castle had always stood, and that the sky would always be blue and cloudless, and that from time to time there would be a great rattling of shot that echoed about the cliffs and set the gull-haunted skies to shrieking - but no more than that. It was not real. He grew tanned, and Hollie laughed at him for it, for he had one gentlemanly white hand where the bridle-gauntlet protected him and one freckled brown one, and his nose was speckled like a custard and the ends of his hair were bleached white. This from Colonel Babbitt, who had retained a fierce sunburn for weeks now, and itched and peeled most ferociously. Luce had suggested that he was shedding his skin, and would emerge scaly and leathery, like a dragon, and Hollie had thrown a boot at his head and told him to go forth and multiply.

No, he wanted for sleep, and regular mealtimes, but he didn't miss them. There might be a day again when he had a bed of his own, and clean linen, but that was in a place that did not exist, yet, except in his head. He felt a little guilty that he didn't know who shared that place with him, and guiltier still that when he thought about it at all, the sensible, calm voice of the place was Het Babbitt's, and not Amy's. But Amy was a - she was a dear, sweet, romantic girl, and she was fond of him, and she desired him, and -

And the bloody woman would persist in sending him messages by a courier who could be ill-spared from his real duty, that he must needs attend her as a matter of urgency.

Which was flattering, but which vexed him, and with that most unloverly thought he shoved his feet back into his boots and wrestled himself back into his buffcoat, and prepared to do his duty.

45. LET NO MAN PUT ASUNDER

It wasn't cold, and Amy was sitting by the window, looking at a bowl of wallflowers and idly musing on the matter of changing her shoes for outdoor ones and going for a walk in the garden to see what other first flowers of the early summer might be appearing.

It wasn't warm, though, and there was a stiff breeze off the river, and the smell of mud and salt. But even that coolness was refreshing, after a long wet spring shut up in the house. (With her mother, who was very nice, but who had a habit of following her from room to room, chattering. Amy had a nasty suspicion it might be an inherited tendency, and that she was perhaps feeling a little crosspatch today, after the long confinement. Amy had the bad habit of chattering to herself, in her head. At least she talked of sensible things to herself, and not of the weather, and the Luswell girls' new gowns.) She stood up, and put another pine cone on a fire that she didn't want, for the pleasure of the scent of it, and sat down and picked up her embroidery.

She was in the middle of matching colours for John the Baptist's hair, when Coakley came in. "Lieutenant Russell, madam. He is asking for you specifically, mistress Amy, or I should have fetched your mother. Should I send Deborah to sit with you while you receive him?"

She clapped her hands with a giggle. "How delightful, though! How does he look, Coakley? I mean, he isn't - in distress, or hurt, or anything? He is just -?"

"Difficult to tell, with the lieutenant," Coakley said dryly. "But if pressed, I should say - not as languishing as you might desire, mistress."

"Then I think you ought to keep him waiting a little, then. If he is of a mind to be businesslike." She arranged her skirts around herself, twitching the folds becomingly. "I think he must be a *little* distracted, to want to see me unaccompanied. Don't you think?"

"I do not believe he is here in an entirely civilian capacity, mistress."

"Oh." She was disappointed. And then - "In plate?" she said hopefully, because the gallant lieutenant in his civilian capacity was, truly, a little formal, a little bit stiff, but in his military function was as glamorous and romantic a figure as any the King could field.

Honestly, Amy thought they could keep Prince Rupert of the Rhine, for all the girls raved about him. And Maurice. They all said how dashing he was, how handsome, how brave. For herself, she could conceive of little more romantic than one fair, brooding young gentleman in a tawny silk sash. Even if he was a little draggled, which was not like the lieutenant, and more than somewhat scented of hot horse and sweat, and needed to put a comb through his hair. Coakley had been kind enough to supply him with an apple while he was waiting, and he was applying himself to it with the same dark intensity with which he applied himself to everything, and Amy set a hand to her fluttering heart. "Yes, Thankful?" she said coyly. "Was there a - a thing of import, that you needed to see me about?"

He took another hefty bite of apple. "You asked me to come," he said, rather indistinctly. "Had a message?"

"Did I?"

He swallowed, and frowned at her. (This was not how it was supposed to go.) "I've -" another bite of apple -"been out on patrol all night, mistress, and 'm not in the mood to be toyed with. There was a note. You wanted me. I am here."

"I didn't say it needed to be urgent," she said. "Oh dear. I am sorry. Have I put you out very much?"

"What was it?"

"I just wanted to talk to you -" he looked up from the remains of his apple with an expression of very unloverlike irritation and she added quickly, "about horses, you see. I had a thought. I - You know Thomas is here, don't you?"

"What?"

"Your horse. Thomas. His name is Thomas, isn't it? He's quite distinctive. I thought you had said he had been stolen? Well, he must have escaped," she said sweetly, "because he turned up yesterday in the river meadow, looking as neat as ninepence and very pleased with himself. I asked the stable-boy to bring him in and give him an extra brushing. Because he's yours, you see. Do you want to go and see him?"

46. HIS RIGHT HAND DOTH EMBRACE ME

Doubting Thomas was neither a pretty nor a well-mannered beast, but he shoved his pied head into the breast of Russell's coat making horrible slobbery noises of pleasure at being reunited with his master. It brought a shamefully sentimental lump to Russell's throat. "Absurd creature," he said sternly. "If you are to be a good Roundhead mount, kindly have the good sense to remain with your fellows."

It was cupboard love, it was no more than the mismatched horse's desire for that half-eaten apple, of course. And that brought a second shamefully sentimental lump to his throat, for he was Apple himself, to Thomazine, was he not? And that minded him of his little tibber, and he must take the time to sit down and write a letter to White Notley, that they might know he was still whole, and well. He wondered if there might be a thing he could send to her, a toy, a ribbon, something so that Thomazine might have a keepsake of her friend to remember him by –

"Thankful," Amy said peevishly, "are you attending to me, or are you daydreaming?"

She looked so sweet and cross, and truly, a stable was not a fitting place for her, because she was standing with her hands shoved in her pockets looking all ruffled and out of place. He was possessed with a strong desire to kiss her, right on the end of her little pink button nose. He restrained himself with an effort and slapped Thomas's shoulder till the big horse shuffled over in his stall. "He has been well taken care of, I see."

"I'm sure," Amy said, quite unmollified. "My feet grow cold, Thankful."

"Ah?" The horse had been very well taken care of. And she had said that she'd asked the stable-boy to give him an extra brushing, but really, it didn't look as if Thomas had seen a field in a month, let alone been out sleeping rough with Malignant patrols in the highways and byways of West Cornwall. His coat was still shaggy, but not unkempt. Thomas had been stabled since his capture – aye, and decently fed, too, Russell was sure of it. "Stand over, you daft animal," he said, and dug his elbow into the beast's solid quarters.

Thomas swung his head and looked at his master reproachfully. "You are spoiled, sir," he said sternly. "Spoiled. Time you returned to your duties." The horse had always been greedy, but someone had been making much of him of late, for as Russell turned to leave the stall the beast followed him, his mismatched nose whuffling over hair and pockets. Someone had made a lapdog of Doubting Thomas, this last month.

"Must you return to yours too, so soon?" she said, in a forlorn little voice, and he wanted to tell her of his missed breakfast, and how his head ached with weariness and with the biting east wind off the sea, that made all his bones hurt and set the muscle in his cheek to jangling, and how he was wet and he smelt of sweaty horses and unwashed linen.

(Het would have set him down in front of as solid a breakfast as she could contrive at such notice, and then sent him to his bed. But Het was not here, and was not his. And Amy could not be blamed for not being Het Babbitt, but only her own sweet self.)

He took a deep breath. It was only an hour's ride back to Tresillian. He was a young man, though he didn't bloody feel it, this morning.

He could do without his breakfast – his belly growled at him, giving the lie to that particular idea – and he was relieved of his duty, for the morning. He didn't need to sleep. (With another night patrol tonight, Russell? In your dreams, sir.) "I might spare an hour," he said carefully, and there was such joy on her pretty little face that he added, "Or more. If you would have me stay longer?"

"Oh, Thankful, I would keep you here all day if I could," she said ardently, and it was almost as good as breakfast. "Did I show you the wallflowers, last time you were here?"

She had not, and he walked at her side, trying not to limp because riding-boots were not suited to long walks in muddy gardens and he had a blister on his heel. She chattered like a magpie. It was rather soothing. If he could have walked with his eyes shut he would have, but every now and again she would point at some anonymously green part of the landscape and expect his admiration. Not being a great chatterer himself, he found her self-reliant conversation immensely comfortable: she seemed to expect no reply, other than that he might look intelligent and give the impression of paying attention. It was, he thought, a much under-rated ability.

"You look tired," she said eventually, and he looked down at her with fervent relief. Finally, finally they might go inside, and stop looking for budding fruit that did not exist, and sit down somewhere – "Shall we sit in the arbour?" she said. And then she squeezed his hand. "It is not overlooked."

There were no blossoms, and the rose arch was scarce a place of romantic inspiration, almost entirely naked of anything but greenery and liberally scattered with fat, striped spiders. He made her aware of one particularly juicy weaver before she sat down, though he suspected it might be the last thing he would be able to point out with any coherency, if she did not come inside out of this vile wind shortly, for the ragged muscle in his cheek was going to lock altogether. He gritted his teeth, and let her play with his fingers. "Tickly, tickly, on your knee," she chanted happily, "if you laugh you don't love me –"

Well. If she must be in the mood for loving, he leaned his shoulder against her, and eased his aching back as best he could on the wet marble bench, and put his head on her shoulder. He'd just closed his eyes, and the warmth of her soft little person was easing the ache in his head, when she quite abruptly squeezed his hand very tight. He sat up, blinking, thinking there was an attack, his free hand going to his sword –

"Why, sir, you grow passionate!" she gasped.

"Amy –" he did not want to hurt her. "'M not very romantic. Today." And more than anything else, more than kissing and whispering and petting, he wanted to take his boots off and he wanted to lie down. On his own.

She looked stricken. "'S not you," he said, with difficulty. "It's me. I can't –" and he couldn't, either, he rubbed his scarred cheek and he said as clearly as he could, "cold. Can't say things."

Which, for whatever reason, brought starry tears to her eyes. "Oh, Thankful," she breathed, "you would like to speak, but you cannot?"

He nodded enthusiastically.

"That's the nicest thing anyone's ever said to me!" she said, and flung her arms round him. Which was nice, but completely incomprehensible, and so he just returned the embrace. And then, "But Thankful, dear, I don't mean to marry you, so you needn't worry."

"What?" That came out clear enough, jarred out of him by shock and indignation.

"Well, I do like you, sweeting. But I don't think you would make a very good husband. And I like living here, too. And I don't know anybody in – where did you say you were from? Bedfordshire? So I don't want to go and live there, and all my friends are here, and –"

"What?" he said again, thinking he must have misheard, because gently-born young women did not just talk of such things, did not –

"I like you very much, Thankful. But not as a husband. I do not think we should suit at all, as man and wife. And I think papa would be very remiss indeed, if he allowed me to marry a penniless young adventurer -"

"Well, is it not as well that you tested my marital competency before you agreed to marry me!" he said stiffly. And very clearly, which gave him some small satisfaction.

"Oh, don't be so silly! I have kissed you a few times -"

"A *lot* of times!"

"Nothing that I should be ashamed of, sir! I have never allowed you any more intimacy than I should allow one of my own cousins -"

"Do cousins make a habit of sharing beds, in Cornwall?" he snarled at her, and her mouth twitched.

"Perhaps a *little* more freedom than that, then. But really, dear. You refine too much on kissing. I have never had the intention of marrying you, Thankful."

"That is *Lieutenant Russell* to you, Mistress Trefusis!"

"Oh, don't be so silly. I am very fond of you. You are a big sweetheart – *Lieutenant Russell* – but you are *far too serious* for my tastes. I do like kissing you, though," she said thoughtfully. "But honestly. If you plan to court a woman – truly court her, and not just a few kisses in a garden – really, sir, you need to be lighter of touch. To be more – more flirtatious, more -"

"You would have me be less honest?"

"I would not have you at all! But yes! Honestly, Thankful!" She let go of his hand. "Well – *do* you love me?"

"Yes," he said crossly.

"*Liar.*"

He bridled. "Madam —"

"Amy."

"Amy, I have loved two women in my life. One is you, and the other was not free to love me in return."

She put her hand under his jaw, and turned his head so that he was looking her in the eye. "Truly, Thankful? You love me?" Her dark eyes were sparkling with mischief and humour and —

"Well, I suppose I do, sort of," he admitted. He thought she ought to be rather more impressed with that disclosure. It was not a thing he went about telling just anyone, after all. He tried to look romantic, and suspected he just looked irritable. Which he was. "Well, I imagine I *must* do -"

"Why?"

She wasn't supposed to say that, either. She was supposed to melt into his arms. Which he didn't want her to do. "Oh, for goodness' sake - ! Well, because you —" He trailed off lamely. "Because you, um, you like kissing me. And you're pretty. And you smell nice."

"That's not *love*, Thankful."

"It might be!"

"Is the other lady pretty?"

"I — she — well — " part of him wanted to be outraged. Part of him liked talking about Het Babbitt, and thinking about her. Part of him couldn't remember if she was pretty or not. "I'm not sure," he admitted. "I don't think pretty comes into it, much, with Het- um, with that lady."

"Exactly," she said firmly. "Thankful, you no more belong in Cornwall than I belong in - in the Indies. You are a very dear young man, and I am very fond of you, but one day you will ride away to your own place, and you will forget all about me. And that, sweeting, is as it should be, for I have every intention of forgetting all about you, so soon as you are over the Tamar. And I will miss you, and I will miss talking to you -"

"And kissing me," he said wryly, and she smiled, and nodded.

"And kissing you. I shall miss all of that, but not sufficient to want to throw myself away on a penniless young officer. I am not made for a worthy soldier's wife, my darling. I have every intent of finding myself some nice rich boy and settling down here in Cornwall and having a lovely brood of little fat dark-haired babies." Her hand was still on his cheek. It was warm, and soft, and it still felt nice, even if she didn't love him. "Until that time, dear, I am more than content in your company. But no more than that."

"Amy," he said shyly, because it was a thing that troubled him, still, "is that – is it permitted, that a man and a maid might be friends, and take joy in each other's company, without - ?"

She looked at him, and her mouth quivered a little. "Are you actually that daft that you need to ask?"

"Not sinful?"

Her fingertips moved, very gently, over the scars on his cheek. "There are people who might call it sinful, Thankful. For myself, I know little of such matters. *I* would call it sinful were you to come between another man and his wife, or were you to make false promise to a girl so that she lay with you. For two friends to take comfort in each other's company, and no more in it than that, is no sin, surely."

"Surely," he agreed, with a flicker of the sense of humour that she didn't think he had. "You would have me continue to comfort you, then?"

Her soft mouth curved up at the corners, rather wickedly, and the little dimple in her cheek deepened as if someone had pushed it in with a finger. "On the contrary, Thankful, dear. *I* will do the comforting today."

M.J. LOGUE

47. THE EAGER BRIDEGROOM

Luce thought Russell was comical when he was sore affronted, and he was distinctly affronted, though hiding it well.

He was suddenly spending a lot less time at Trefusis, although he denied that there was anything in that, and although when you saw him still in young Mistress Trefusis's company he still looked at her -

Well, actually, no. Luce had assumed, romantically, that the scarred lieutenant had looked at his girl with his heart in his eyes, and in point of fact, he did not. He looked at her like a dog looking at a bone, and although Luce had known dogs who longed for bones, he had not yet known a dog form a happy and lasting friendship with one.

They looked at *each other* like that, and yet he made a point of treating her with his old chilly courtesy, from as far away as he could conceive, and it evidently hurt her.

And so what could Luce do as a friend, but encourage Russell to sink more ale than was strictly good for his discretion, and extract the sorry tale from him?

It wasn't much of a story, in the end, except that Russell had thought he had found love, and instead had found lust, and was feeling hard done-to about it. Which made Luce - who had also had a little more ale than was strictly good for his discretion - feel all warm and paternal, and suggest that the lieutenant should be flattered by the discreet attentions of a pretty young woman, and enjoy it while it lasted.

"I do not enjoy being made to feel like a he-whore!" Russell said irritably, and then giggled, "- *is* there such a thing?"

"Dear God, I imagine so. There is no end to the perversions the Malignants can conceive -"

"Can't imagine Mistress Trevaskis availing herself of one. Can you? Being the only Malignant wench I know. Socially. I think. Here. Luce. D'you think - you know - Amy, do you think she is one?"

"What, a - a whore?"

"Dear God, no! Amy's a - a decent lass. Well. I mean, I've seen her in her shift, and that's not strick- strictly decent, but I didn't know I wasn't going to marry her, then. I thought she was in love with me, and she just fancied me." He snorted, a most unromantic noise. "Reckoned she was too good for me, the little madam. As if some bloody backwater belle can do better for herself than me. Holding out for a rich husband, she said. Ha! I got a few pennies -"

"In Buckinghamshire," Luce pointed out.

"Buckinghamshire money's as good as bloody Cornwall's! No, do you think she's a Malignant? *I'm* not sure. Never been sure about that family, y'see. I know he's a Member of Parliament, but - I don't think they think, King and Parliament. Not really. I don't think it matters, down here. I think it's like 'nother country all on its own. Got its own kings and queens and everything. And I think missy fancies herself as a little princess. And that -" he cocked an eyebrow, "*that* is why she wouldn't go to bed with me. Kissing me, aye, that's all right. But she's holding out her innocence for some bloody Cornish gentry. Can't blame the wench. Holding out for the highest bidder, poor girl, she got sod-all else to bargain with down here."

"Bloody hell, Russell," Luce said faintly.

"Oh yes. Bloody hell, Russell, indeed. That. That is what I thought. *Bloody hell, Russell.* I don't mind a bit of a kiss and a cuddle but I have got *some* scruples, Lucifer. We're not all fornicating with the chambermaids, sir."

"Once," Luce said firmly. "It was *once*. I do not make a habit of fornicating with the household staff." And then he had grinned, and poured another drink for them both. "Think a bit too highly of yourself for that, you do. Nothing short of your actual princess will do for you, young man."

"Put not your trust in princes," the lieutenant had said darkly, and then grinned, and raised his mug. "Well. Here's a health to Black Tom, and confusion to His Majesty. No - the hell with that - bollocks to His Majesty, and he can kiss my horse's scabby arse. "

And when Luce had finished spitting ale across the parlour, and was able to breathe for laughing, he said, "Thank you for that, Russell. It's almost like dining with the colonel."

But it had been nice, actually, and he thought Russell had enjoyed it, too. It was odd to think of him as an ordinary, indignant young swain touched on his vanity - Russell, of all people. (Not to mention possessed of a positively un-puritanical and Babbitt-like vocabulary, when he had more drink taken than was good for him. And that was new, too..)

So. A pleasant, uncomplicated evening, with two young bachelors ill-used by the fairer sex, even if it was under the walls of the castle with the sea two hundred feet below them and the smell of rotting siege refuse and spent powder hanging in the air. A funny place for a friendship to grow, but there it was. Russell had fallen into bed at dawn - the wrong bed, as it happened, and Luce had had to shift as best he could with the lieutenant spark out, muttering and giggling in his sleep, and Hollie sitting up in his blankets with a face that would crack a glass, encouraging them both to be elsewhere.

The lieutenant had reappeared at breakfast, bright-eyed and crumpled, and been about his employment as blithely as a lark. Luce had dragged himself with somewhat less enthusiasm from his makeshift bed in Leo's stall, and prepared for a long day of holding his aching head from splitting asunder before the perpetual sound of heavy gunfire, six miles distant.

Dawn had been stifling, red and raw as an open wound, without a breath of air to stir the trees. He had planned to take Chesten over to Harrobear, but not on such a day. Not fair to poor Leo, whose neck was already lathered with sweat before he was out of his stall an hour. Not fair to Luce, whose hair was plastered to his forehead and whose shirt clung to his back limply. Not fair to little Chesten, who would have to be laced into her stays, like a little hermit-crab into its shell, and dressed in layers of wool and linen, her poor little feet shoved into Sunday-best shoes, her collar neat and starched -

Oh, the poor little maid, no. He would turn her over to her father for the day and give her French leave -

Except that when he came back into the blessed coolness of the house, after unsaddling Leo and turning him loose under the trees, there was a deeply awkward-looking trooper standing in the hall waiting for him.

"Tis the liddle maid," he said, and smirked horribly. "I talked to the Colonel, but he d'say I need to see you, or her daddy -"

"What about her?"

"Well, sir, 'tis like this. See, she took a fancy to the Colonel's Blossom, ever such a good-natured beast he be, dear of him. Follow her about like a dog, he do, and her not even big enough to put a saddle on him, let alone a proper fitty saddle for a liddle maid -"

And Luce was hung over, but not sufficient that he did not comprehend that his little charge was a delinquent horse-thief who had been apprehended riding Hollie Babbitt's amenable nag - dear God, did everyone in the Army of Parliament need to take advantage of Blossom's simple nature? - astride, of all things. And when this poor trooper had remonstrated with her -

"She bit me," he said apologetically.

"Oh dear."

"Ah. So, well, I brought Blossom back up to the yard, poor soul, 'tis no weather for galloping. Sweating cobs, he was, proper in a muck-sweat. Liddle maid she said she would go and see her grand-pappy, and I knew you'd said she might not, so I said no, she wasn't to take that poor beast no further than the end of the field -"

And one thing had led to another, and it seemed that Chesten had convinced herself that gawky Blossom was the fleetest steed in the Army. He was not, and there was a limit even to his patience. She had turned him for the stone hedge, and not unreasonably, Hollie's brown gelding thought it was too hot to be bounding about West Cornwall. And he had put her quite neatly on her bum, and made his escape.

Luce silently applauded the brown horse. Chesten Toogood, it seemed, had been transported to a place of safety, and the door firmly latched behind her while a decision was made what should be done with such a disobedient little maid. She'd yelled, kicked the door, screamed, cried, banged, thumped -

"I never did see such a temper," the trooper said disapprovingly. "D'ee tell Captain Toogood that liddle maid needs her arse tanning, were she my daughter."

'Leave her to me," he said, and opened the door of the vacant still-room that was currently imprisoning her.

"Now young lady!" he said firmly, and that scarlet-faced, snotty, sweaty ball of fury rounded on him and roared "I will not!"

Luce was fond of children. He liked his sisters, and he liked his little charge. He was not being talked to like that, by some spoiled, disobedient little whelk out of the schoolroom, and all his fond ideals went suddenly swooping out of the window. He came down on Chesten Toogood like a wolf on the fold. "Don't you dare speak to me like that, mistress! You're not too big to go over my knee!"

"You wouldn't dare!" she yelled back at him, "My grandpapa says I am a lady born! You would not dare lay a hand on me!" By which time Luce, who was hot and furious and had a headache, had picked her up and dumped her over his knee most unceremoniously, and gave her well-padded bum one good smack with the flat of his hand.

He doubted, afterwards, if she'd noticed, through the layers of wool and linen. But the little wench was outraged. Her head went back, all the cords standing out in her neck in a way that was most disconcerting, and a long, furious animal howl came from her wide-open mouth. "Chesten!" he said firmly.

It wasn't as if he hadn't been warned, either. Toogood himself had worn a perfect oval set of purple prints for the better part of a fortnight, and Trooper Joyce this very morning had said that the little maid was a biter. He didn't know what he'd been thinking - afterwards. She sank her fangs into his wrist with a ferocity that was deeply unsettling, and he gave a howl of his own, and set to her discipline with a will. By the end of it his palm was smarting, he was out of breath, his shins were bruised, and her howls of outrage had turned to wails of heartrending misery. She hung over his knee, snivelling and sobbing, and he felt like a murderer.

48. HE OPENETH THEIR EAR TO DISCIPLINE

"I felt dreadful," Luce said woefully. " It was like - I felt as if I'd sent the poor child to her execution. Toogood was - oh, he was terrible, I should have been frightened. He came in with a willow switch and he said he would whip her poor little legs raw for her disobedience - oh, Hollie, she did cry, poor little maid, I don't think she had ever been beaten before! And twice in one day! Poor lamb, I fear her grandfather has spoiled her, and here she is fallen amongst decent men who are zealous to correct her - it must be a shock for her, after being so accustomed to having her will."

Hollie, who had seen the maid in question not half an hour since, smiled faintly. She had been wan and draggled and crumpled and tearstained, surely. Toogood had said that he was sending her to bed supperless, in addition to her other penances. Well, the Cornish captain had seemed ravenous at supper himself. He had taken two helpings of everything. Hollie had watched him go up the stairs with one of them.

It was the discipline that troubled Luce - and aye, Hollie could see that, it troubled him too, and he was a father himself. That little lass was wild, under a thin veneer of civilisation. Well, he'd dealt with wildness before, half his troop were rough, it was something that either broke or gentled.

It wasn't that. It was almost a calculated wildness; it was like someone had schooled the little wench in arrogance. No, Chesten Toogood had altogether too high an opinion of herself, that was what bothered Hollie. Not that someone had had to paddle her bum, because he very much doubted that gentle Luce would have given her anything to mind him by, and no matter how menacing her father had been Hollie suspected that what had reduced her to miserable tears was the revocation of her riding privileges, rather than that threatened whipping. She was not insolent. Precisely. But she -

Had too high an opinion of herself.

Luce just stared blankly at him. "She is a little girl," he said, and Hollie nodded.

"She is. She is a little girl. She's a little maid, from a piss-poor family with a good name. She's not pretty, she's not that well connected, they're not that rich. She don't half think she's summat, though, doesn't she?"

"Blame grandpapa," Luce said with a grimace. "As fast as I may put some manners into her, grandpapa will undo them. We being nothing but damnable rebels, you understand." And that was the thing of it. Hollie did not understand, and it got right under his skin. He'd been a mercenary officer of some standing in Europe. He still was an officer of some standing. Even looked it, on occasion, so it wasn't that she, and granddaddy Carew and his ilk, had seen Hollie in all his dirt before turning their noses up at him. He had known princes, he had known kings. He'd got pissed with one or two of them, in his younger days. Royalty cut no ice with him. He'd seen them with their breeches down. (Probably why he fought for this side, rather than that, then.)

"I should not have had to do that," the brat said again, forlornly. "What kind of upbringing has she had, that she defies her elders so - so wantonly? Little girls should mind their manners, to a grown man. A stranger, almost. Poor Kenelm must wonder what kind of people have had the keeping of her, these last two years."

It was stupid. It was Hollie, refining too much on nothing, like an old woman. Next he would take to spinning and matchmaking. It still bothered him, because he had been an officer of standing for twenty years, and that gave him a nose for trouble. And it wasn't just Chesten Toogood and the high-nosed Carews, it was a way some of them had of talking to him as if he was of no consequence.

Not of rudeness, not even of discourtesy. Just a habit of dismissing him, of speaking to him as if he were one of the staff. Maybe it was just his own touchy pride, then, that he wanted to have them bend the knee to him. (They had lost the bloody war, damn it. Did they not know that? Did they think Ralph Hopton had signed the surrender to disband the King's Army in another West Country, not this one?)

It wasn't just Chesten who thought she was above him. It was Hannah Trevaskis, a lass who kept a miniature manor that smelt of damp while her brother was still doggedly fighting a war he'd already lost, and talking to Hollie as if she was doing him a favour by passing the time of day with him.

It was John Arundel in the castle, taking something under a minute to give the emissaries from Fairfax his curt answer, dismissing them without more than the barest courtesy. Like tradesmen, or debt collectors. Philip Carew, who thought they had no honour, because they were rebels. (Because we are poor, must we be vicious?)

"Amy Trefusis," Luce said, and then looked awkward. "I probably shouldn't have told you that."

"What, that Russell's been keeping her bed warm? I knew. I'm not that stupid, brat."

"Well, no, true, he made no secret of it. You know it ended?"

"Aye, I did think he looked more rested, this last week or so. He all right about it?"

"Relieved, I think. I do not think it was a love-match. I think she, um, well, she -"

"Fancied him? Well, there's nowt so queer as folk, Luce. No accounting for tastes. It's not like she had to talk to him while she was bedding him - can't see our Russell as the most romantic of conversationalists."

"Oh, I think he was keener than she, actually, on the romantic end of the business. No, she - she advised him that although she was happy to retain his acquaintance as a - a - paramour, shall we say, that there was no, um, no future in their relationship."

The brat was blushing. Hollie stared at him for a moment, and then closed his mouth, and swallowed, hard. "Lucifer. You are telling me that John Trefusis's daughter told Hapless Russell that she didn't mind -"

"Dalliance," Luce said, and his cheeks looked so hot you could have toasted bread on them. "No further. I am sure of it. He was most indignant, that she considered him good enough for - dalliance - but not for anything more honourable."

He didn't know whether to laugh or cry. "Do I need to speak to him of this?"

"I imagine he would be mortified, sir! If he thought you knew -"

"If her bloody *father* knew!"

"Oh no - no, sir, not Russell, it had not - they had not - he wanted to marry her, he thought it was his duty to make her an offer, but it seems she - um - well. Um. *They* were not. In as many words. Though I think he wanted to - I mean, he is, you know. Hasn't. And I - you know Russell - after last time -"

Oh aye, he knew Russell. Knew that he had something of a high opinion of himself, and would not take it well at all, if some lass considered herself too high for his hand in marriage, if he had decided he was going to give it. "I think he's quite relieved," Luce said again, looking rather relieved himself.

"*I'm* relieved. I can do without his leaving any little blonde puritanical bastards behind from our stay in Cornwall. Christ knows we're unpopular enough already down here, without that."

And that was it, so soon as the words were out of his mouth, that was it. They were *not* unpopular. They were just - tolerated. It was as if the surrender had not taken place. It was as if the King's men - *and* women, Mistress Trefusis - in the West just did not accept that they were beaten. And that bothered Hollie. Because what did they know, that he did not?

Toogood's lads did not think themselves better than anyone else, so it was not a thing where he could point a finger and say "Cornishmen think," or "Cornishmen behave so"; Toogood's laocal likely lads were civil, wary, they kept themselves to themselves, but they considered themselves of the Army of Parliament. No, it was a western thing, it was very much the far west, , and it was the gentry that simply did not acknowledge Hollie's authority. Were polite enough, aye, but took absolutely no notice of him.

Toogood would say it was because he was an Englishman, no doubt, but then they took bugger-all notice of Toogood, either, and he was as proper-job as they came, so that bird didn't fly. It was stupid, and it was twitchy of him, that a little girl's doting grandfather had brought her up thinking she was a little princess, and a young lady had fancied a bit of rebel rough and then decided he wasn't as rough as she'd fancied. Arundel had been rude to them. So what? Could be as rude as he like, while they starved him out.

That was the other bugger of it. They weren't being starved out. There was well-provisioned to withstand, and then there was they must be getting help from somewhere - and maybe they were, but where? And how? They were cut off, even if they had food and water aplenty they were shut up on a headland in the middle of the bloody sea, the defenders would grow disheartened - and there was no sign of that, even. They were as bloody intransigent as ever. Rude, even.

There was one smart-arse - literally, a smart-arse - a young lad with bright carrot-red hair, who was cocksure enough to waggle his backside at them from the walls, and Hollie would have give much for a straight aim and a sure shot. (Be a bit embarrassing if that was Captain Trevaskis, wouldn't it, shot in the buttocks by a disenchanted cavalry colonel?)

"Rain again overnight, I shouldn't wonder," Luce said, sounding like some old countryman. "I imagine they're not short of water, at least, up at the castle."

"They're not short of bugger-all up at the castle," he said moodily. "I don't know where they're getting it from."

"Give a man a fish, and you feed him for a day. Teach him to fish, and he can feed a garrison for months."

"Can he," Hollie said grimly. "Can he, indeed. I'll put a bloody stop to that, then. See how many fish the bastards catch with a blockade up the arse."

48. SLAIN IN THE MIDST OF THE SEAS

There were worse ways to spend a summer evening than flat on your back on warm turf as close-cropped and soft as velvet, with the waves sighing beneath you and the moonlight gentle on the sea, and a waft of almond-scented gorse blossom on the breeze.

Admittedly, when the wind changed there was a waft of the smell of a castle that had been under siege for the better part of three months, and that was not so great. But – that was only every so often, and you could ignore it. At his elbow, Russell was muttering; warm and drowsy, with his belly full of ill-gotten rabbit stew, the lieutenant grew positively chatty.

Some of Si Betterton's lads had taken to haunting Trefusis Point in a wholly unprofessional capacity. There had been something of a flurry of activity, after Hollie had most humbly petitioned William Batten to pile it on, from the marine side. For a rabble of landsmen, a sea blockade was something of a novel spectacle – for about a week. "*Truelove, Defiance, Lucy* and *Ark*," Russell chanted sleepily. "You could make something of that, Luce, were you so minded?"

"You forgot the *Hind*. And the other ones."

"I shall *never* make a sailor."

There was a grunt, and an abrupt rustle from the bushes a hundred yards away, and Luce sat up abruptly with his hand flying to his weapons, but it turned out to be Trooper Warwick and his snares. It seemed that Trooper Warwick was something of a man for trapping, back home on the fells. His speciality had been wild birds, but as he pointed out, if it'd run, he'd snare it. He wasn't so daft as to strip the Trefusis warren. ("Coney meat ain't for the likes of us," he said indignantly, and various people had very patiently pointed out to him that he would, in fact, be provisioning the Army and so it was in fact his duty before God and his senior officers to crack on with it.)

That was not to say that it was not something of a perk of the job to take sentry duty with Trooper Warwick –

"*Constant Warwick,*" Luce said comfortably, and Russell grunted in agreement, because that was the name of one of Batten's other ships, floating about out there in the darkness, and the one they always forgot. With it being two words, and not especially militant. Wasn't especially militant that whoever was posted on Trefusis Point tended to end up fetching bread out, and there they'd sit comfortably in the dark, watching the tide going out and eating cold rabbit stew and bread. It was rather nice, though. Hollie himself joined them, when he was free, though they preferred it if the colonel was not personally present at such occasions. Nothing personal, just that he had a habit of absent-minded consumption, and by the time it came to seconds what you had was a smug senior officer, a bag of crumbs, and no more stew.

John Trefusis had apparently complained to Colonel Fortescue, that the cavalry company quartered on his premises were eating him out of house and home. Fortescue had - not unreasonably - been somewhat reluctant to call in a fellow colonel for explanation, although Hollie had gone in with an air of martyred innocence and claimed that their foraging had been merely an exercise in undermining the morale of the occupying troops in the castle, for they must be able to smell the good meat roasting and be made wretched by it, on their diet of rotten salt pork and scant limpets. (He was almost convincing, too, until you saw the tiny patches of brighter red on his coat where he'd been obliged to move his buttons a finger's width further out. Admiral Batten wouldn't touch rabbit with someone else's. Or rather, that zealous and godly man who didn't believe in pagan superstition wouldn't touch rabbit on the deck of a ship, and wouldn't be seen dead eating it, but if he happened to be on land at the time and none of his men happened to be watching him he might partake of a haunch or two in the interests of debunking the said pagan superstitions. Batten was one of the few sailors Luce had met who said he didn't believe in pagan superstition - and meant it. But then, he was a Priest-biter, straight down the line, and he didn't hold with much in the way of superstition.

Batten's main interest in life was blowing holes in Royalist ships, and sometimes firing on the castle for the sheer joy of making the buggers jump. Luce rather thought it depressed him, plying his trade up and down the Carrick Roads with no sign of action and a flat-calm sea under a warm summer sun. Didn't depress Luce, not one bit. He closed his eyes and wriggled his shoulders and felt the rabbit-cropped turf prickle through his shirt where the linen was worn thin, at the points where his buffcoat was heaviest, or his harness pressed. Had this shirt a long time. It was patched, and a little stained in places, and as soft as butter. It would, God willing, see him through the war. It was all over, and he was lying on a clifftop in the far west of Cornwall talking of rabbit stew, and idle, and rather disrespectful, conjecture on the size of Her Majesty the Queen's breasts - you got thirty healthy young men together, bored, on a clifftop, and sooner or later they fell to talking of this woman and that woman they had seen - and listening to the sea -

The horses were restless, though. He kept hearing the clink of a shod hoof on stone.

"Don't be daft, Lucifer, we didn't bring the horses," Russell said sleepily. "You said it would be too much trouble."

"Then what -"

"Shut up," the lieutenant said, "and bring more stew over this way. I find I've space for -"

Luce flipped himself upright, crouching in the darkness and wishing he'd had the forethought to bring a coat. Not cold, just sticking out like a sore thumb in a white shirt on a dark headland. After an initial squawk of protest from Russell the lieutenant followed him, and they scrambled through the gorse looking for the mysterious invisible horses -

And suddenly a great flare of rosy light leapt into the sky a hundred yards away, as the dry underbrush of the headland caught with a crackle. Where some bugger with steel and flint had been ticking away trying to catch a spark for the last - God knows what Luce said, for it was surely neither decent not godly, but he shouted something and he threw himself at the sudden leaping flames because of all things the last thing you wanted was a fire on a summer-dry clifftop, be like a bloody beacon. And five yards behind him Russell suddenly yelped as if something had bitten him, and yelled, "Stop that man!"

A body hit Luce. Did not bowl him over, for he was half-braced for it, but it took him off balance with most of the breath knocked out of him, and he could not see in the dark properly who or what it was that scrabbled wildly for purchase, only a confused gleam of firelight on eyes and bared teeth. Not a man he recognised. Only barely recognised him as a man, save that he was wiry-thin, and drenched to the skin, and kicked like a baggage-mule.

"Douse that fire!" he screamed, and the man lunged for him again, to try and stifle him, he thought -

Someone was on it. A great acrid cloud of sparks flying upwards as something hit the flames, and then another leap of fire as another branch of furze caught light elsewhere, and there was a confusion of shouting and boots drumming on the sun-hard ground. "Put the fucking fire out, boy!" - had to be Captain Betterton, for the voice was distinctive, and then the wet man butted Luce full in the face, bucking like a horse

Luce hit the ground on his back, which was a mercy, for it was only the ends of his loose hair and his shirt that pressed into the burning embers, and that was sufficient that he squalled and kicked and fought himself upright, and then the wet man was under him in a cloud of choking smoke - so wet, then, and he must have swum the river, but surely such a thing was not possible, surely a man should drown, if he sought to make the crossing from Pendennis to Trefusis Point by water -

"Look to the cliffs!" Luce yelled, through a mouthful of blood, and the wet man sought to choke him, his hands tearing at the collar of Luce's shirt, and all he could think of was to grab a handful of the scalding ashes and fling them in his assailant's eyes, which caused the man to scream and convulse - but not to let go, and there was a moment of buffeted, whirling confusion.

And then he bit the wet man, hard, in the soft part of his arm, and sank his teeth in like a terrier, and tore.

Oh yes, he tore, and flesh parted in his mouth under the rent salt-drenched linen, and his assailant screamed out again, and this time he was free - free to howl for help, for someone to come to his aid -

Luce would have gripped him, in spite of it all. He would have held fast, and he wrapped both his arms about the wet man, and hung on, but he could feel the ground shaking beneath them as the detail came swirling back in from quartering the cliff, and the wet man punched him, hard, in the thigh, and threw him aside.

He would still have given chase, but he could not seem to get his legs under him.

Betterton gave chase, that distinctive voice bellowing out echoing across the sea - someone was sufficient prepared to get a single shot off, and a great cloud of gulls went flinging up into the air from their roosts on the cliffs.

And then one very short, very sharp, scream, cut off. He had heard a dog sound like that, once, in Colchester, after a laden cart had run over its body. The rabbit stew suddenly rose burning in his throat.

He opened his eyes to find Thankful Russell standing over him, very white in the moonlight. He put his hand out to help Luce up. He was shaking, and his fingers were cold. "What," Luce began, and then he stopped, feeling very odd indeed - cold and wet and sick and hurting, with the sea swishing in his ears and the gulls dancing black in the corners of his moonlit vision. "What," he said again, and Russell gave him a wild looks out of the corner of his eye.

"He preferred," the scarred lieutenant said carefully. "Preferred. To jump. Than be taken."

And then Russell had to sit down, too, with a thump, and put his head between his knees. "The tide is out," he added indistinctly, and gagged. "Nothing but. Rocks."

Luce closed his eyes, and tried not to dwell on that animal scream. "God rest his soul, the poor man," he whispered.

"Lucifer. Are you hurt?"

He did not think so. Bruised, and the muscle in his thigh hurt -

"Then why is there a knife sticking out of your leg?" - Russell sounded quite aggrieved about it, too, as if Luce was purposely trying to mislead him, and he wanted to laugh, very much. But he did not seem to have the breath for it, and so he fainted, instead.

49. A LITTLE WINE, FOR THY STOMACH'S SAKE

It seemed that whilst Luce had been unconscious all hell had broken loose.

With the turn of the tide, as if drawn by that brief beacon, Batten had had his hands full. No grand epic sea-battle, this, but instead a constant drizzling attack of little boats, of shallops, of fishing-smacks, trying to run the blockade, and the admiral had had his bellyful of petty action by the time dawn broke.

"Sum total of the breach, three hogsheads of wine, come in on the tide," Hollie said with satisfaction. "Split three ways, gentlemen. One for the Admiral, one for Colonel Fortescue, and one for the invalid."

He raised his glass and squinted at the contents thoughtfully. "Though I will say, as is no expert on fine wines, but this stuff does have a distinct flavour of cordage about it."

"That's why it's purely medicinal," Russell said. "I smelt it. I suspect the barrel may have been broached on the rocks. Either that, sir, or they were transporting some poor unfortunate home for burial in the contents."

Hollie put the glass down sharply, and wrinkled his nose, and Russell laughed his silent laugh. "I may have been exaggerating that last."

"Bloody exaggerate *you*, Hapless, if you pull a stunt like that again. It's a funny thing, fate, isn't it? If you'd not been stretching the leather with Amy Trefusis –"

Hollie must have had this conversation a dozen times in the last day, and you could still see the lieutenant's hackles rise, every time. Which was, of course, precisely why Hollie did it, and it was unkind of Luce to want to laugh, but he still did.

"I was not doing anything of the kind!" Russell hissed, eyes blazing, and even though Luce felt like a piece of limp rag and every muscle in his poor battered body ached, he still snorted with laughter, from his comfortable place by the fire with his stitched-together leg propped on a stool in front of him.

"Oh, aye, all right, if you'd not been intimate with the lady, we'd not have been quartered here – in the interests of you not continuing to get your belly rubbed by that lass you weren't bedding – and then if you hadn't *stopped* being intimate with her, you'd not have been sat out on Trefusis Point all night with our Luce trying to keep out of her way. So, if you hadn't been –"

"Don't say it!" -

"Dear God, no, I don't think my ribs will bear it," Luce said weakly –

"Well," Hollie added sweetly, "isn't it a good thing, then, that you hadn't actually got on with the deed of darkness? Or you'd have still been in bed wi' her, and them bloody Malignants'd be shipping in about another month's worth of provisions while your back was turned."

For that was their best guess. That they grew desperate, now, as the midsummer days lengthened, and Batten got bored, out on the

Carrick Roads, and would not allow so much as a ship's rat passage, and the supplies that were not now being bolstered by contraband began to dwindle, and to rot. Water was not a problem, in the castle. They had a well. Arundel had built a windlass, to pump water for the defenders – aye, and to keep them busy, Hollie suspected, for he'd been under siege himself before now and boredom was the worst of it. Boredom would drive men to desperation quicker than sickness, in the best-provisioned of places. "Buggered up their little plan, then, hasn't it? Bloody hell, the best-laid plans and all that, cocked up by the inability of one benighted rebel officer to keep a girl –"

"I could hit you for that," Russell snarled, and Hollie raised his eyebrows.

"Could you, so?"

"I *could*," Russell repeated, and tossed his head, "save that we are only still here by the inability of *another* rebel officer to keep his girl –"

And Hollie punched him in the mouth, and walked out.

50. I AM MY BELOVED'S

"You asked for that," Luce said.

Russell touched his tongue to his bloody lip, and shrugged, and wrapped his arms round his knees, on the floor. (Even having been knocked sprawling, he still managed to look elegant.) "He is *pithing* me off," he lisped, and spat bloody froth into the fire. "Becauth – *because* he hurts, he must needs lay about him. Aye. I know that. I have every –" he stopped, and his swollen mouth twitched with a most unexpected humour, "*empathy*. He will bait me because I bite. Like a fool, I continue to bite. One day, I will turn round and bite him in the *arth*."

Took Luce a minute to work that one out, and then he laughed, because it was hard not to.

"Boredom," Russell said sternly, "plain and – plain." He gingerly touched the tip of his tongue to one of his front teeth. "I have got thus far with all my own teeth," he said darkly. "That man has a hit on him like the kick of a mule. I suspect he is a good quarter mule, for stubbornness. Bloody man. Yes. Well. He annoyed me. I am *bored*, Lucifer. I tried fornication, and it didn't suit me, and much more of this unbearable monotony and I shall turn to drink!" And then cocked his head, and added, with that rather endearing honesty of his, "Again."

"I can do without such excitement, myself," Luce said mildly, and the lieutenant looked at him, and then laughed.

"I should give much to be in your position."

"You would be most welcome to this wound, Russell. It hurts. A good deal."

"But honourably come by." From the right side, he was still a good-looking lad, when he looked down at his hands and his barley-pale hair fell over his face. "I am not anyone's hero, Luce. I never was, and I fear I never shall be. You were. You prevented –"

"An invasion by a fleet of casks of salt beef. It's not exactly epic."

"Had you not been there, we should still be outside the castle, wondering how come they never seem to get hungry, and we should have remained so until Judgment Day. Even he – " the unmarked corner of his mouth drooped, "even that ungovernable bastard of ours, is someone's bright star. And how I envy him."

Luce blinked at him. "What – you –"

"I do not mind that she never loved me. I mind that she only – that I might as well not have had a heart, or a mind. Wanted for my pretty face, God help me, and I should never have thought that would gall but oh, it does, Lucifer, it *does*. There is no girl living in this world, to whom I am of worth for being my own self."

"Yes there is, you silly sod," Luce said. "*Thomazine*."

He blinked, and opened his mouth, and then shook his head. "You are being absurd," he said stiffly. "Thomazine? She is a baby - what should she care if I - Thomazine would not remember me, if I never came home - she is a little child, she - that is no consolation, none at all, Lucifer!"

"None?" Luce prompted, with gentle malice.

The scarred lieutenant shrugged, and would not look up. "Well. A little. A very little."

51. DRAWN AWAY AND ENTICED

He felt bad about it, so soon as the fresh air had cleared his head a little, but he'd belted Hapless before - had him flogged and took his commission, before, and the lad hadn't borne a grudge.

He'd come about. Hollie wasn't worried. He tapped his fingers irritably on the arm of the seat under the window - a funny thing when you came to look for it, how there was a seat or a wall or a place to rest every few hundred strides, or a place to pull yourself upright. John Trevaskis had a care for his sister and her game leg, then, that was touching. He wondered if she minded, or if she would like to tell him to take his cosseting solicitude and stick it where the Lord's grace did not shine, sometimes.

He was - ah, Christ, he was any number of things, all mixed up in his head: he was afraid, because this was a siege and he was in it, and that made him sick-scared by reflex, the way a horse scenting fire will spook and shudder without knowing what it fears. He was alert and on his duty, because they'd stopped up one rat's-hole but that wasn't going to stop desperate men, and of all things he had a wary respect for John Arundel and his men. That a man had swum eleven miles of open water to send a signal out to sea for aid, filled him with awe - aye, and dread, Hollie not being the greatest admirer of the leaden ripple of the Carrick Roads. That he had chosen to jump to his death on the jagged black rocks he'd struggled up from, instead of fall into the hands of such as amiable Lucey Pettitt, and earnest, helpful Si Betterton - it made you wonder what the hell stories they told, about Parliament men. That they were ogres, or ate human flesh, or some bloody thing, by the look of it - and that made Hollie bloody furious, for he was a man like other men, and he hated the idea that any man might fear him for what he could not help.

Fear him because he was a great raking judas-haired lad with a big horse and a bad temper, aye, but not because he was a soldier for Parliament, or that he was a free-thinking man. And he hated that, too, at the same time as it frightened him. He did not know what was afoot, save that something was, and so fast as they choked off one Malignant plan they could come about and find another, and he did not know from what direction it might come from - like a man fighting in the dark, who can hear and sense himself surrounded by enemies, tensed for the next blow, but does not know where to expect it first. A lot of things stirring beneath the surface that he did not know of, and could not brace himself for. Not all of them were to do with the war, and that - made him feel oddly lonely again, out here on the edge of the world. As if he were a ghost or a shadow, watching the world but not able to touch it, or to be touched -

There was a thin mist blowing in off the sea, and if he stood up, he could look out across the slate-grey water as far as the looming black cliffs of the end of the world.

The waves, white-tipped, flipped and rolled.

They'd been crashing in, rubbing the rocks to sand, for a hundred years, and they would probably go on doing it for a hundred years after Hollie was dust, and that thought probably ought to make him feel better and he bloody didn't. He was just - cold, and wet, and angry all the time, though he didn't know who with, or what at.

He blew his hair out of his eyes, folding his arms on his chest and glowering at the thin, fizzy mist clouding the horizon.

"Bloody, fucking, arseholes," he said, out loud, and then said it again, for the grim pleasure of saying it. Not being polite, to anybody, because he didn't feel very fucking polite. He unfolded his arms and flexed his fingers, thinking about hitting something. Somebody. A tree. The wall.

(Not her fault. *His* fault. Married to Fairfax's fucking red hound, trailing at his heels past the end of the world.)

"I think you should come inside, colonel."

He looked over his shoulder, and then back out at the sea. He was being pig-ignorant, and Het would have - well, it didn't matter what Het would think, because she wasn't here. He was a disappointment to her. Didn't matter what he did, he let her down. The lass needed him in Essex, and he was in here-be-dragons country, pissing about staring at the sea.

Well, he grunted something in response, at least.

And then, hearing the tick, tick, tick on stone, he turned round, with a sigh.

"I'm sorry, mistress," he said, and then added, "I wasn't attending. Business."

Hannah Trevaskis stood on the path, leaning on her stick with the wind stirring her skirts. "Will you come inside, then?" she said again. "Instead of sitting out here in the dark?"

He shook his head, and would have gone back to staring at the black rocks.

"It's not good for your poor hand, this night air," she said, so softly that he almost didn't hear her.

"For my - why, what d'you know of my hand?"

"It pains you. I know."

He turned his wrist with its usual ratcheting click, and ducked his head, feeling suddenly rather shy. "Well - aye, it's not always good, in the damp, but - " He was not so changed, after all. Regroup, and come about, and counter-attack. "And what of your back, then, mistress? Stood out here in the damp, in like manner?"

It was a funny thing. She was a plain lass, Mistress Trevaskis, with her fierce dark eyebrows and her colourless skin, but when she smiled she was a different girl altogether. The lines of pain shifted from about her mouth, and her dark eyes went from sullen to sparkling, like sunlight on water, and he found himself smiling back at her, with the wind off the sea blowing his hair in his eyes and the waves beating out on the rocks like distant thunder.

"You sound like my brother," she said. "It's been paining me for forty years, near enough, and it's not killed me yet, so?"

"Stubborn wench, isn't thee?" he said. Still smiling, but with a faint admiration, now.

"I have little choice, colonel. Do I? I used to come here," she said softly. "When John and I were children, we would come out here."

"Oh aye?"

For the first time, he found himself listening for the sound of the sea, and not dreading it. It was a part of the house, and of her, and he would miss it when it was gone. It was a distance off, yet: far enough that it was a soft, sighing noise, like a girl's sleeping breathing. (Or a child's. Like Joyeux's, when she slept in her mother's arms, and all you could hear was that faint snuffle, and it was the only sound in the world.)

You could see it from here, a ways off on the horizon, slate-grey. Not friendly, he didn't think he'd ever find it friendly or comforting, but he was used to it, now, and it was part of her, like her cane, or her ridiculous matronly caps, and he would miss it when it was not there. It didn't make him shiver. He stood up, because that bench was made for someone about a foot shorter, and leaned his elbows on the mossy bough of the apple tree, and looked out across the fields to that gap between the cliffs where the water gleamed sullenly.

You'd hardly know there was a war on, here. It was a summer dusk, and there was a finch skipping in the branches of the orchard, its thin, sweet song piping.

The bench creaked as she shifted, and he glanced down at her, to see if she might need his arm. (It might be summer, but it was cold, when the sun started to drop, and there was a damp in the dusk that must have struck a chill into the hinder parts of a gently-born lady.)

She looked up at him, and it occurred to him that Hannah Trevaskis was pretty, in the right light, with good luck and a following wind. With a bit of colour in her cheeks, and a bit of animation. "Some of the girls in the village," she said shyly. "It's silliness. It was all foolishness, and idle superstition - vanity. We had - we used to have - a wish-tree. A - a cloutie. With wishing ribbons, to tie to it. You know? And I used to sit out here with John and - and - "

She reached up, and put her hand on the nearest bit of him she could reach, on his side, and he started a little at the feel of her. "It's over there. I think I must have wished away whatever dowry I might have had, over the years. Were you to take an axe to that tree, there is silver enough wedged in the bark to outfit a regiment, I would think."

"What did you wish for?" he said.

She cocked her head. "Oh, nothing out of the common run. I wanted -. I wanted to be straight. To have a lover. To have a family."

There were times when he wondered at what went on in a lass's head, truly he did. "Could thee not?" - without thinking. "Tha's not a *plain* lass. Thy face is not marred, and thee is sweet-natured enough, surely?"

"And my crooked back, colonel? Is that of no account, that I might not run, or ride, or walk with grace?"

He did her the courtesy of consideration, but -. "Well, it wouldn't have bothered *me*, lass. Could thee not still? If thee met a - a good man, a decent man, what would he need thee to be galloping about the countryside for? Thee has a tongue in thy head, and two good arms for loving. What else might a man want?"

"Do you know," she said, as if she had not heard him, "do you know, that when I was a child, I should have given my immortal soul to climb a tree with John? He used to sit in the branches where you stand now, while I sat here." She sighed, and lifted her head to look in the direction of the sea, with the wind stirring wisps of her hair about her face. "He told me everything he could see. He was always very kind, even when he was a boy. You would like John, I think. He is - is a good man. So from where you stand, you can see all the way down to the mouth of the river, and on a clear day, you can see the sails of ships out at sea. Would they be your ships, colonel, or ours?"

"Sail is a sail, to me. You'd have to ask my mate Tom Rainbow for that," he said wryly. "He was a sea-captain, before the war. He knows all about ships. All I know about 'em is they make me heave."

Her mouth twitched. "I think this is not a fitting conversation for a maiden lady and an enemy officer to be having, sir." And then her whole face lit, in that unexpectedly sweet smile. "Isn't it marvellous?"

And Hollie, enjoying a rare moment of ease, agreed. It *was* marvellous. "Give me your hands, lass," he said, and her eyes flew to his face, but she put her cold, thin little hands into his, and he picked her up, for she weighed little more than Thomazine, and he settled her on the lichen-covered branch of the gnarled old tree. "There you go. *There's* a strange bird, now. Don't thee be flying away, lass. Get me into a whole heap of trouble."

And there they stood, the two of them, Hollie leaning his folded arms companionably on the bough beside her, and Hannah Trevaskis kicking her feet like a child and talking to him of what she could see, all the way down to where the sea grew red as blood with sunset behind Pendennis Castle.

52. LIVING BY THE SWORD

He was a married man, and she was a crippled spinster, for all she was almost a pretty one, when she had colour in her cheeks, and there could be no harm in it that he wanted her to look on him with favour. It wasn't *that* sort of favour he courted. He just wanted her to change her mind, and look on him - aye, and his cause - kindly. He was tired of being *the enemy*. He was not the enemy. He was a weary, sore man in his early middle years doing what he thought was the right thing - which made him smile, in spite of it, because it made him sound worthier than Luce Pettitt.

Kenelm Toogood would not come to the house. Skirted all about it, but never set foot on Trevaskis land, and nor would he ask in so many words how she fared. Acted as her secretary, acted as all but her go-between, but wouldn't let her set eyes on him while he did it. He was worse than a greensick lad, and being Toogood, he would neither admit nor deny it, but went stiff and ill-tempered and broke things and disciplined men who didn't deserve it, and so it wasn't worth keep teasing him on it.

Nor did she mention him by name. Though she knew he was around and about - how could she not? Chesten was the spit of her father, in some ways, especially now she'd had some sense either spanked or lectured into her. No, the two of them very studiously did not acknowledge that either existed, which made Hollie wonder if perhaps Kenelm Toogood's friendship with John Trevaskis had been entirely the innocent childhood idyll that the Cornishman had claimed it to be.

It wasn't a thing you could come out and ask him, although Hollie thought that possibly he might have such a friendship with Mistress Trevaskis, now, that he could have asked her, and she might have told him. But he did not like. It seemed - he didn't like to talk of lovers with her, or of marriage, for it didn't quite seem decent. And it would have made him awkward to go behind Toogood's back, as if he were an old goodwife prying for long-dead gossip. More than that, *it did not matter.*

It was the beginning of a golden summer, that one. Russell looked like a field-hand, and had put on a good six inches across the shoulders, in addition to his freckles and his sun-bleached hair. Luce seemed to have grown into his height and he was two yards of solid, and bloody well-nourished, muscle, although he was presently languishing like a maid because he said he couldn't put his full weight on the hurt leg for another fortnight at least without tearing the stitches out. (Hollie wondered, idly, *how* light his duties were, and whether they still involved the personal attentions of Hannah Trevaskis's chambermaid.)

Batten was still firing on the castle and the fishing fleet by turns for the indeterminate joy of it, and Fortescue was tightening the screws on the defenders by the day. Hollie wandered in and out of the lines passing unhelpful comments, criticising the gun placements, and eating other people's breakfast. Nobody seemed to have noticed yet that he hadn't brought Blossom with him. He'd brought a daft, scatty fleabitten mare from Toogood's pack. Almost wholly bird-witted, flighty as hell, unpredictable, testy - she put him on his arse a good four times a day, she had no manners, and if you laid anything heavier than a sack on her overbred spine she came up dead lame.

Lucey got it - eventually. "In the spring, a young man's fancy?"

Hollie - bruised and dusty, but feeling smug as hell - grinned. "Lightly turns to thoughts of Trooper Pascoe's mare?"

"Dear God, sir, I trust they are not *that* hard up in there! But - oh, you clever sod."

Trooper Pascoe's flighty mare. A warm, languid summer, and a couple of hundred under-occupied horses kept penned up in a tight-shut space. A man of a perverse turn of mind might take that flighty mare for long, slow walks as close to the castle walls as he may. A stallion could scent a mare on heat from a good half-mile's distance. A stallion with little else to occupy his mind, given the presence of a mare in her season within a stone's throw, would be a right pain in the arse, in an enclosed space. A force for destruction in his own right, on a bad day -

Sir John Arundell, presumably, would have some finely-bred mount worthy of his status in life - and oh, Christ, Hollie hoped Arundell's mount was entire, because the possibility of chaos within the walls as a result was not only constructive, but actively delightful. And he knew there was at least one entire horse in there, because the poor sod was yelling in frustration every time Hollie and the witless mare passed within scenting-distance.

And that was fun, and - yes, he did it in sport, in part, because he was as bored and under-used as Arundel's theoretical stallion.

More than that, though, he did it because he was growing to recognise that brassy masculine scream.

And he was going to *know* when they shot that horse. When the defenders were that hard up that they turned to the horses.

First the oxen had gone, and that just stank, though it was blessedly quiet. Run out of fodder, with the sunburnt grass on Pendennis Head eaten to the bare earth. Oxen were big, clumsy brutes, with broad, slimy noses, and splayed, clumsy feet. Those shots within the walls didn't cause Hollie any loss of sleep.

And that meat would take a while to work through, so he left it a week - two weeks - the fleabitten mare was replaced with a stolid chestnut from the baggage train whose only sign of excitement was that she would periodically port her tail with an air of resignation. (It was summer; it was the season of rising sap, and new, growing things. There was usually no shortage of mares thinking about rising sap and growing things, over the summer. The poor baggage-mare gave the impression of being a beast who had had a deal of babies growing under her sprung ribs, over the years, and who saw it as an unpleasant but unavoidable duty.)

She heaved a great sigh, and turned her head to look at Hollie, who was reminded unnervingly of Balaam's ass, and cocked her bound-up tail.

There was an uncanny silence. There were the usual noises. Gulls, and waves, and voices, and the crack of shot, and the echoing thump of the heavy artillery at Gyllingvase.

Some horses. Some whinnying, because it didn't matter how long you had beasts under fire, they never really got used to it, and it still frightened them.

But not that eerie, ringing scream, and the matron of the baggage train shook her head with a blubbering snort. And did nothing more. She did not protest. She did not seek to draw the attention of that fascinating piece of masculine horseflesh, she did not lift her head and flare her nostrils, snuffing the scent of the stallion in the castle. Maybe the old mare wasn't such a shocking trollop as Pascoe's four-legged tart.

And maybe Arundel's stallion was dead.

He took her round again, as dusk was falling, when it was cooler and the air already heavy with the smell of the parched earth greedily sucking up dew.

"A night made for love," Luce said wickedly, and pressed a hand to his heart and pulled a mock-romantic face. "How could you come between two such star-crossed lovers, sir?"

"It was never going to last. Too great a difference between their estates," Russell added from where he was lying on the cold slate flags of the kitchen floor, in nothing but a shirt and ragged breeches.

(They had somehow fallen into keeping bachelor's hall, since things had gone awry with Amy Trefusis, and it was informal and squalid and Hollie's habit of mending harness in the kitchen was growing to be a bone of contention with the household staff, for he was not a tidy workman.)

Toogood, mind, had taken himself lock stock and barrel over to Trefusis Point, on the spurious pretence of saving Russell the indignity of facing his erstwhile paramour on a daily basis. To which Russell, who had not been at all discomfited about seeing a lady with whom he was still - he said - on the most cordial of terms, had simply looked amused, and suggested that if anyone was in the business of awkward spurned lovers, it was perhaps Captain Toogood.

- The Cornishman had gone by then, and so Russell had not earned himself his second smack in the mouth in a week.

And so Hollie had gone, out into the close midsummer dusk, bare-headed and with his shirt clinging to his back and his shoulders with sweat, riding that ageing Jezebel bareback on a rope halter.

Once in and out of the gun placements, her hoofs slipping on the crumbling earth of the trenches.

Twice.

A third time.

Whatever the equine equivalent of a shrug was, she was doing it. She was bothered by flies, but when she called half-heartedly to the defenders' mounts, her intended was no longer calling back.

She didn't care, the old darling.

Hollie did. Hollie cared very much.

A faint breath of breeze carried a whiff of carrion - of shit, and blood, and rotting meat.

Little water, but salt-water. Not enough salt to salt down carcasses, and not enough fresh water to wash in. The oxen had stopped groaning about a week ago, and now they were stinking. He made a note to ask Toogood, over on the point, what was washing up in the way of whole carcasses, for he doubted very much that the defenders - what would there be, a thousand? less, by now? - would last long, on nothing but meat.

"What the hell do you think you're playing at?"

True, he didn't think he was the picture of formal discipline, but he was pretty bloody distinctive, still, and he spun the mare to face the sentry and said flatly, "Colonel Fortescue, mate."

"And who d'you think you are, skulking round -"

"I think I outrank you, sunshine, so I think you better get your arse down to the colonel and tell him Rosie Babbitt's playing silly buggers in the gun placements again. Tell him I've got summat he needs to know. And do us a favour, while you're at it? You got any cheese left in your ration, I'd be glad of it - for I find I've gone right off meat, this night "

53. IN THE SIEGE AND STRAITNESS

Do you not consider it beneath your rank - skulking about the gun emplacements, on that -"

"Don't you call Delilah bad names," he said smugly.

Fortescue opened his mouth, and closed it. "Delilah. I see. Of course. What else would you call a beast using her feminine wiles to entice the enemy to destruction? Babylon, possibly - the Great Whore -"

"Babylon is Lady Derby, colonel. As you know well. And I should prefer not to be reminded of the siege at Lathom House. If you don't mind."

"Ah yes." Colonel Fortescue's lips twitched, for it was not often you could see Hollie Babbitt writhe like a worm on a hook. "Did she actually *have* three breasts, sir? I often meant to ask -"

"I did not look closely," Hollie muttered, the back of his neck burning, and Fortescue's eyebrows raised delicately.

"Surely? That is not what your cornet says? He says you were quite taken with the lady in question - or vice versa, at any rate - is that not true? He thought it rather endearing, as I recall?"

Hollie managed a feeble smile. He knew when he was being baited. "The defenders," he said, steering the conversation into safer waters, "- started on the horses. What's your siege-work background, colonel?" A small revenge, but his own. He waited, politely, and then smiled. "I see. Well. A man may live on meat, and nothing but meat. No bread, no grain, no cheese. No apples. Be no good for that scrumping young rascal Pettitt, then, would it? Done it myself, for a few weeks, when we were down to eating the horses in Germany. Oh God no, it won't kill 'em, a diet of flesh. I imagine there'll be some sore arses, when they surrender - sonewhat costive, a diet of nowt but flesh, and I imagine the most of that is three parts raw, for I'd guess they run scant on fuel, an' all. Hm. I don't envy 'em." He blinked innocently. "Won't be the diet that kills 'em. Be disease, colonel. What d'you think they're doing with the carcasses, in this heat?"

Fortescue looked a little sick. "I -"

"I understand there's quite the little pile growing up there. The gulls grow perfectly fearless, I believe. I had Lucey firing on 'em, for a while, last week. Hell of a good shot, my brat. Then I thought, I'm not giving them buggers a variety of their diet. Carry on wi' their raw oxen till they surfeit of it, for me. No, they're burying theirselves alive in carrion, colonel. Every raven - dog - every unclean beast in the West Country will be making its nest in Pendennis Castle, shortly." Hollie tore at a strip of ragged skin on his thumb, thoughtfully. "They reckon in the bad old days, in Germany, they used to sling in carcasses over the walls of a town at siege, to spread foul air and contagions. Poison the wells. Draw vermin. Saves us a job, doesn't it? And there is not a bloody thing they can do about it.*

"Except surrender," Fortescue said, and Hollie grinned at him mirthlessly.

"Best hope they get on with it, then. Or it's going to stink in there."

54. DYING AT THE HAND OF STRANGERS

It wasn't a job Hollie was fitted for, and so he took it as something of a holiday – something more of a holiday, then, trotting up and down between Trevaskis and Pendennis running messages while men who were singularly more fitted to target-shooting than he was watched the point.

In the end, he wasn't there anyway. He was sat in the parlour at Trevaskis, very upright and bored within an inch of his life while someone else's daughter said her prayers in front of him because Luce had said the child must make her devotions in front of one of the senior officers. Hollie, whose devotions were between him and his God, had thought it was a daft regulation. But Luce had sisters, and he knew about these things, so Hollie had to sit there and look stern while the little maid asked for God's blessing on all the soldiers, every bloody animal in the horse-lines, the house cat, and His Majesty the King.

(She wouldn't be shifted on that last. She said she felt sorry for him, and her grandpapa said – and that was usually the point that Hollie raised his eyebrows at her and looked down his nose in the way that normally worked on recalcitrant troopers.)

Her voice was droning on, a funny sing-song little murmur, and he was looking out of the window over her shoulder. Thinking not a lot, watching the sky turn violet, out behind the trees. Rags of cloud blowing up out of the west, and he wondered if there'd be a storm later, for it had been blistering now for the better part of a month and the little fruit on the apple trees withered for want of water –

In the cat's-light, on the far side of the parlour, in that high-backed chair that gave her some ease, Hannah Trevaskis was sitting with her mending in her lap, her hands stilled as she watched the two of them. And it was pretty how she'd come to take on Kenelm Toogood's unprepossessing little daughter as her own, to be guided and brought up with a fair hand, for all she was a rebel's child. Hollie admired that in the woman, though the more he thought about it the more he wondered if in truth the lass had had a thing going on with Kenelm, back in the day. For Mistress Trevaskis looked at that little girl with softness, and she took an interest in the child's lessons and her devotions that was touching to see, no matter what her father's convictions were.

There was a crack as a log split on the fire, and he leaned from his chair to stir the embers, and then realised there *was* no fire.

There was no lightning, either, and he jerked the window open and was over the sill in a heartbeat, with little Chesten after him, skirts kilted in a deeply unladylike fashion to scramble through the rosemary bushes –

A little cry from Hannah Trevaskis and ah, Christ, he forgot, with these thoughts of rebels and Malignants, that out there in the crackling dark was that woman's brother. Her face was white in the shadows, and she was struggling to get out of her chair so fast as she would like, and hating it. Hollie went back in the window and got her, too, for if he had to carry her across the bloody garden she deserved to see as much as he –

Little, in the end, save a meagre display of sparks on the point, and a lacklustre return of fire from Batten and his boys riding far out at sea on the ebbing tide. Could hear nothing, could see nothing.

Chesten put her cold hand into his, and he could feel her trembling against his leg, like a little dog. He squeezed her fingers, wanting to will a little warmth back into the poor maid, and she squeezed back with a frightening strength. "*Tassik*," she whimpered, just the once, and then he *felt* her stiffen her spine and set her shoulders, for she was a captain's daughter no matter what colour sash he wore. Her teeth were chattering with fear, and her face was as white as cheese in the dark, but she was bolt upright and stiff with pride, and she clung to his hand like a drowning man.

And then, on his other side, he felt Hannah Trevaskis lean into him, and she was trembling, too, and she turned her face up to his as if she might read there that it would all be all right. So frightened, the pair of them, and so bloody heartbreakingly proud about it – and those two lasses might be prevented from fighting by age and infirmity, but by God they could love. He put his free hand on Hannah Trevaskis' shoulder and squeezed, and the three of them pressed together in the sharp rosemary-scented dark, watching a pretty display of lights and sparkles that might be a man's life.

It was not long. A quarter-hour, perhaps less. And then the sky tore open with a sound like ripping linen, and a bitter, stinging rain fell like shot, and Hollie took the pair of them back scampering inside, the formal way, through the front door.

Tears were running down Mistress Trevaskis's cheeks, but she limped – *oh, Hollie, you bloody fool, you did not bring her cane, no wonder she is distressed* – limped to her seat by the fire, and then she fell into it in a puddle of drabbled wet skirts and put her head into her hands and sobbed as if she did not care any more who saw or heard.

Chesten looked at her with a very adult care, and then looked at Hollie. Who was accustomed to taking unspoken orders from the women of his household, and who obligingly fled, for he felt rather sick and shaky himself.

So, then. That was how it was. That was how it had always been, when you were safe, knowing that someone you loved was out there in the dark, under fire. That when they had gone away, they might not set eyes on you again from that moment to – to the end of the world, maybe. And there was nothing you could do, for you could not see them, could not help them, could do nothing but pray for them, maybe, or clench your hands into the folds of your clothes and bargain with God to let them ride home again –

And that was how he had left Het.

That must be how she lived, every day he was away, and sweet Jesus, how might she *bear* it?

He had not known, when she said – Christ, how would he know, he had always been in the thick of it before, not out here with the women and children sweeping up the dust of the war.

Always been *busy*. Always been a soldier, about the business of war, but now there was no war – almost no war, then, with the army disbanding about him, and what then?

Well, he was bloody busy now. He was rattling up the kitchen staff, fetching a late supper for Chesten, poor maid, for she was chilled right through, and a posset for Mistress Trevaskis, to settle her – Het'd be proud of him, he grew proper domestic.

He had not known.

And that made him feel hollow, that he had been so set on his own martial affairs that he had never even considered how it might be for his own girls, that fear might be a very real presence in their lives, *all the time* – fear, and helplessness, and an impotent agony of mind -

Could do with that bloody supper himself, never mind for the little lass, and so he glowered at the cook till he gave Hollie another apple pasty, and a very unchildish wedge of squab pie, and he didn't like posset, but he wouldn't turn his nose up at a mug of mulled ale or something similar.

"Take it myself," he said flatly, because he could do without a houseful of Malignant servants who thought he was AntiChrist at best, to walk in and find those two wenches howling all over the parlour. "The mistress is poorly – I want her bed warmed – aye, and the little lass's –"

"You need to talk to the housekeeper for-" the cook began, sticking his nose in the air, and Hollie rounded on him.

"No, mate, *you* need to talk to her. *I'm* telling *you*." He wasn't in the mood for playing silly buggers over staff hierarchy.

Well, he was going to have to get used to it soon, wasn't he?

He did not mind that Chesten asked if they could pray for her daddy – very shyly, as if he might think the worse of her. And he did not mind that Hannah Trevaskis wept silently all the way through their prayers, with her eyes closed and her nose running.

All the time the thought kept running through his head – Lucey. Russell. Toogood. Betterton. Out there in the dark, as the rain beat on the windows, and the thunder snarled over the sea. Wishing he was there with them, but then what bloody use was he, without a troop of horse behind him? Thinking he could hear hoofbeats, and then realising what he could hear was the wind in the trees, or the rain on the roof –

The little girl fell asleep eventually, curled cat-wise on the settle with her head on Hollie's knee and his hand on her back. She was warm, and her breathing was steady, and he looked at Hannah Trevaskis, daring her to pass a remark about the tenderness of rebels, as he put his own doublet over her. Poor maid, she'd cried herself into exhaustion. He couldn't leave her so, she'd wake with a crick in her neck, and so he slid himself out from underneath her and carried her to her bed. The housemaid who'd been acting as her nurse had been asleep, and she'd looked up blinking and afraid in her turn as Hollie brought her little charge through the door.

"She's all right," he said gruffly. "She just fell asleep downstairs."

So brief a thing, then, that it seemed that the staff who had been on the landward side of the house had not even heard the battle, hidden by the sound of the storm.

Hannah Trevaskis said nothing. She only looked up at him when he helped her out of her chair – and it wasn't a courtesy, it was a silent order, that she should go to her own bed and leave him in peace – looked up with her eyes huge and swollen and ringed about with sooty rings. "Thank you," she said, and her voice shook.

"For what?"

"Being here. Being kind."

He patted her hand on the newel-post, as he might pat Chesten's, to comfort her. "It was nowt. Tha's been a brave lass, this night. He will be proud of thee. I'll make sure to tell him that his sister is a stout wench, when he comes home. Soon."

And she dipped her head with a wan smile, and trailed limping up the stairs, and he watched her go and thought no further of her.

He thought of picking up his pen, though, and writing to his own brave lass. And then could not, for that meant sitting still, and taking out his thoughts and looking at them, turning them over, and he did not think he could bear to do nothing. Not tonight.

He could not sleep – did *she* feel so, waiting for news, after a battle? – and yet he could not settle to writing that letter that burned in his brain, and so he walked the parlour. Sat down.

Went out to the horses, and did not look at the spaces in the line where Leonidas, and Doubting Thomas, and Charles usually stood. Passed the time of day with the sentry, and fussed Blossom, and groomed the brown gelding till his arm ached though it made precisely no difference to Blossom's disreputable appearance. He said it was because Blossom didn't like thunder, and since it had stopped thundering some hours since, it was a lie. Not that his horse minded the attention, for you could fuss Blossom all day and that shameless brute would still shove his head under your arm and push you for treats and loving, but –

It was near dawn when they came home, and even that was an informal rag-tag.

Luce first, because his leg was paining him, and he had been of what service he could so they sent him back. In the first pink light of a much cooler morning, the brat looked tired, and scruffy, and worn, and had it not been for his being mounted on that great flashy roan brute Hollie might not even have recognised him.

As it was, he crawled out of the nest of straw in Blossom's stall where he'd closed his eyes for a minute, and put his hand on the roan stallion's shoulder.

"What news?"

Luce dismounted with a wince, and rubbed his thigh. "I'm still not up to a whole night putting weight on this leg," he grumbled. "Not a lot of news, sir. Much ado about nothing, I fear."

"We heard an exchange of fire?"

"You didn't," he said, with a wry smile. "You heard one silly bugger." He shook his head. "Not one of their brightest gentlemen, I suspect. We thought he was a seal, at first – could just see a head bobbing in the water offshore. Talk about desperate! So. Yes. We gave him the opportunity to surrender, but he – " his face clouded, and he shrugged. "He didn't."

"Just the one man?"

"I think he was ashamed," Luce said softly. "I think he chose to – not be taken, rather than it should be recorded that he had run."

"So what –"

"Oh, Admiral Batten understood there to have been somewhat more activity than in fact there had been. There was no invasion, sir, if that was what you understood. No, the – gentleman from the castle, shall we say – came ashore with a barrel, to which he had lashed himself. Not, I suspect, the strongest swimmer, the poor man. There was a brief – a very brief – exchange of fire on the beach, in which one of our own company was winged, and the gentleman was – well, I don't know what he was, but Toogood and his men are still down on the strand waiting for the tide to come in."

"The hell for?"

Luce raised his eyes, and looked Hollie full in the face. "To recover the body."

Hollie swallowed, hard, and almost did not like to ask - "And Russell?"

"Oh, Russell is giving Admiral Batten holy hell on, in his most diplomatic fashion, for Batten saw the exchange of fire on the beach and decided that his contribution to the proceedings ought to be to fire on both parties. Thankful is whole, intact, and pig-livid. He asked someone to row him out to the *Constant Warwick* to, um, pass on your displeasure. So, um, when Batten starts chewing your ear about it – which I have no doubt he will - could you imply that you were – I don't know, sort of on the premises somewhere, and deeply grateful for the Admiral's interventions, but – well, you know?"

And then the sun crept up over the back of the house, and touched all the windows to burning gold, and lightened Luce's three-day stubble to a gilt that was raffish rather than disreputable, and Hollie thought – the hell with it, and he hugged his brat till the lad squeaked with astonishment.

"Well – colonel, I mean, really – Hollie, what was *that* for?"

"I am glad to see you whole," he said primly, and Luce grinned – hadn't minded the hug, then – and said, "I am glad to *be* whole. All that, for one foolish deserter! I don't suppose you had change to bespeak any breakfast, did you? I find the sea air –"

"See what we can come up with," he said, and left his arm round Luce's shoulders, and steered him back towards the house.

Feeding Lucey Pettitt was a fool's errand, and so Hollie sat opposite him at the table and occasionally poked the cook and let the lad talk with his mouth full.

An hour or two later Russell turned up, still ruffled about being fired on by the Parliamentarian fleet – *and*, he said, not only did they fire on us, Batten had the temerity to say it was our own fault and that we should not have been there in the first place!

"Not apologetic, then?"

"Not in the least, the unregenerate swine! Next time I shall let the Malignants swarm up the cliffs like bloody rats, and be *damned* to Admiral Batten and his fleet! *He* can sort it out, himself!"

"No casualties?"

"Not when I left, but then on *that* showing I should not trust that man to shoot fish in a barrel," he sniffed.

"Russell, you are funny when you're mad. The bacon's just come off the skillet –"

"The bread is new-baked, too, sir," the kitchen maid said, with a shy glance under her lashes at the uncharacteristically-disreputable Luce that had Hollie stifling a grin. Even looking like he'd spent the night under a hedge, the brat was irresistible.

And then there was a clatter of hooves in the yard, and Toogood and his lads were back, and they looked shattered. Hollie got up from the kitchen table and piled a plate with bread and hot, crisp bacon.

"Kenelm?" He jerked his head. "You got a minute? Breakfast's made – "

The Cornishman sat, unasked, though he did not take food. Instead, he dropped his head into his hands and muttered something "Say that again?"

"I said." He looked up, and his face was suddenly sharp, hollow with grief and exhaustion. "You know who it was, don't you?"

"Who what was?"

"John Trevaskis."

"Oh, Christ."

They sat in silence for a few minutes, because Toogood could not speak and Hollie had nothing to say. "I owed him that much," the Cornish captain said wearily. "I would not have left him – I – ah, God, colonel, I would have given my life for his a hundred times over, if I'd known –"

"What happened?"

Luce had not known, then. Trevaskis had come over on the tide, right enough. The barrel? "No, he was not the best swimmer, though he could dog-paddle. He'd have wanted the help, d'you see – for floating, it was the kind of daft idea he'd come up with, to lash himself to an empty cask. He was a rare man for ideas, was my Jack –"

He blinked hard. "I wish to God I knew what had been going on in his head, mind. I'd have *helped* him."

"He was a Malignant," Hollie said – and he said it a-purpose, he knew it was neither kind nor helpful but it was a thing that needed to be said, for he fancied that Toogood needed to make his answer aloud. And that Hollie needed to hear it.

"It wouldn't have mattered," Toogood said, and then he put his head down on his folded arms and wept silent dreadful tears. *"He was not a Malignant,"* he choked, "he was my *friend."*

"Aye," Hollie said, and said no more than that.

55. NAKED INTO THIS WORLD

They did not know, and they would never know, why he had run. (*If* he had run.)

Toogood's eyes were wide and blank and shocked. Hollie dismissed him, and he nodded, and got up to go, and then wheeled back, unasked. "Will she want for anything? The mistress? She will be all right?"

"She has three troop of Parliamentary horse guarding her, Kenelm." Which is no consolation at all, he thought, and did not say, but instead fell to looking out at the trees, and the long dip of the fields that ran on and rolled out to the endless sea.

Wondered what it was that had driven John Trevaskis to such a madness. Desperation under siege, or fear for his sister, or sheer, simple bravado? He took a moment to put a comb through his hair, and to find a clean shirt. He owed him – her – that at least.

They pulled her brother from the sea, on the next tide. Toogood had told them where to look, where the waves might cast him up. His face was bruised, and a little discoloured, but he was still a man. The blue-black edges of the sound in his chest had been washed clean by the waves, and there was only a little sand caught in his hair, where the sea crept in and ruffled white ribbons through his tangled dark curls.

They would never know, why he had done such a bloody daft thing. If he had carried any secret messages, any gold, any clues, the sea had taken it. The sea had taken everything. Trevaskis was barefoot, bare-headed, his wet shirt sleeves blue-white on the rocks. He was unarmed. He had not even his sword harness. He could have said so much – he could have asked quarter, from Betterton's men, and been taken an honourable prisoner -

He had not.

"Naked we come into this world, and naked we go out of it," Russell said softly, at Hollie's elbow, and he turned and looked at the scarred lieutenant. Who looked back, quite levelly. "Will you tell her?"

She was sitting in the little chamber that overlooked the orchard, and he wondered if it was coincidence, that she looked down the hill to Pendennis. Could not see it, for the bend in the river, but her face was turned towards the sea, and the castle.

For the light, he guessed, for her head was bent over some bit of fancy-work, as it was often bent these days, and he stifled that flare of irritation that he often felt these days, that she could be put to no better occupation than pointless fancy-work. *She deserved better –*

Aye. Well. It was not fitting. He stood in the doorway for a minute and watched her, the clean white curve of the nape of her neck bent over the clean white square of the linen in its slate. She'd changed, since he had come. She had grown – almost young, he thought. There was a narrow edge of lace to her collar that she would have dismissed as foolishness, once, and a handful of roses in a glass at her elbow.

Having a houseful of lads had done her the world of good. She should have had a houseful of her own lads long since, not to be put to teasing Hapless Russell out of his periodic black-sullens, or getting the blood out of Si Betterton's little cornet's handkerchieves. She was in the world, now – *of* the world – in a way that she had not been, three months ago. She was alive. She was not suddenly beautiful, but she was a woman of worth in her own right, and not John Trevaskis's poor crippled sister.

By the window, a sudden flash of pink and gold, and he caught his breath in a sudden childish marvel at the tiny flash of the chaffinch's wings. (You did not often have a chance to look on skies, or birds, or flowers, with wonder, when you were a colonel of horse laying siege to a castle. Only a little space. Only here – he caught himself. That was not true.)

The pale sunlight caught on the line of her needle, and he wondered what it was that she was sewing so ardently. She looked up, and out of the window again, at the clouds that fled over the shoulder of the point, and the seabirds that tossed black. He wondered if she ever wanted to be out there, with the storm beneath her wings, and not in this warm closet, with the little fire that smelt of apple-wood and pine-cones, and the amber glow of polished wood and safety all around her.

"Mistress – Hannah?" he said, and clenched his fists at his sides like a little boy fearing to recite a badly-learned lesson.

"Colonel Hollie?" she said, and there was a teasing to her voice that might break his heart, if he thought about it: that she had grown almost happy, and he must needs send her back to the darkness. And she looked up at him, and smiled up into his eyes, and there was that in her face that made her good to look on – like a falcon, or a hunting-dog, that was straight and fierce and true, if not necessarily comfortable. "I am glad you are come, sir, for look – I have almost finished your handkerchief."

He stood behind her, and put his hand on the back of her chair, and looked at her work, and felt dreadful. "That is – kind, mis-Hannah. *Hannah.* Yes. Kind. I –" He put his hand on her shoulder, and he had never put a hand on another woman but his wife, in four years of marriage. Hannah Trevaskis's shoulder was stiff-set and unyielding, and he rubbed at it absently, like you might rub at a cramp in a muscle, to ease it. "Mistress Hannah, I – I am sorry. I – I hardly know how to say. I – I barely know how to say this, maid, I – I do not know what words – you have no idea, Hannah, you have no idea how hard this is to say, and yet say it I must, lass -"

She turned her head, very slowly. "There are no words necessary," she said, and she put her cool fingers over his, on her shoulder. Her fingers were cool, but her eyes were not. Her eyes were greedy, and Hollie, who had been a fighting man all his life and was not afraid of much, was suddenly very afraid indeed. "I very much fear there are, mistress," he said, and did not know how to dig his way out of this hole that he had not created, now, without causing her more pain than he must.

He could not do this.

Hollie Babbitt, a coward? Aye, where a woman was concerned, for he could not bear that he had caused this, even unwilling, and yet he could not undo it. Had not led her to hope, but hope she had, and would, against anything he had ever said or done. And so he fled, calling for Kenelm Toogood, who had stood her friend these many years, and who would know the right words.

56. THE VALLEY OF THE SHADOW OF DEATH

"How is she?" Hollie said as the door closed, and Toogood jumped about a foot into the air.

"How the hell d'you *think* she is, colonel? And can you give me a bit of warning when you're going to pop up, 'stead of lurking about in the dark like some kind of –"

"What'd you tell her?"

"Half," the Cornishman said sourly. "Tell her the rest some other time."

Which made sense.

Hollie could not guess what John Trevaskis must have looked like, alive, for he did not look like a living man, but like a marble carving, bloodless and cold on a tomb in the church on the hill, and a shiver went down him. He thought he would probably rather that Hannah Trevaskis had not seen him either, but it was not his business - he had deliberately made it not his business, and she looked at him as if he was stupid and brushed past to where her brother's body lay.

He did not care much to be standing in Trevaskis' own chamber to pay his respects, either - it was too intimate, too close, with all the signs of a living man who had ridden away but a few weeks since: a clean shirt, folded, on the press. A comb, with a few dark hairs trapped in the teeth. A discarded stocking, trailing long-tailed under the bed. Trevaskis's manservant was bustling like a white-faced hen, fussing and straightening. Toogood belonged there. It seemed to have been forgotten that those two had fought on opposite sides, as the Cornishman stood at the foot of the bed with his hat in his hands and looked at the thing wrapped in seeping wet wool cloth that had been his friend.

Hollie felt out of place here. He didn't know what Toogood had said to the woman, but he was grateful for it, for it scared him witless to be in the same place as her, looking at him out of the corner of her eye like a dog looking at a bone. Like a kicked dog looking at a bone, by which he guessed that whatever the Cornishman had said it had been characteristically sharp and to the point. If not, necessarily, kind.

He made his reverences to a brave and honourable and downright bloody stupid enemy, and he fled.

He had a shattered barrel to piece back together, for one thing.

It smelt of the sea. Smelt of brandy, too, and that troubled him, for it was not so old and weathered a cask, despite its travails in the Carrick Roads. He was no expert in spirits of wine, but he had been married for the better part of ten years to a woman who ran a tavern. He could tell the difference between a cask of ale and a cask of spirits.

Not so much as a couple of hogsheads of wine to comfort them, remember? Some bugger was shipping supplies in to Pendennis Castle. Had been. Batten had put a stop to that sort of thing. Yet this was a new cask, that John Trevaskis had lashed himself to. Aye, so? New, and emptied recently, then, to still smell of fresh liquor -

"Captain Toogood."

Probably not the most sensitive thing to broach, right now, but there were more important things at stake. He folded his hands on the dining table, in the midst of the broken staves, still bound about the middle with a rope that would have rubbed Trevaskis's wrist raw, had the blood still been flowing in his veins. "D'you mind if I ask you, sir, what you and John Trevaskis were to each other?"

The Cornishman's face went blank with shock. "What the hell d'you mean?"

"Exactly what I said. I'm ignorant, captain, I'm not stupid. I am not so daft that I don't wonder how a plain Callington boy might come to be hand in glove with a family sixty miles distant. How *do* you come to know the Trevaskis family, captain?"

He was expecting Toogood to bluster, or to grow aggressive. Instead that infuriating man just stared at him, and then his mouth started to twitch. "Aye," he said, and grinned an unexpectedly boyish and likeable grin, "might ha' known you'd catch to that, in the end. Let's just say John was a business associate of mine, shall we?"

Hollie did not grin back, because he'd known likeable rogues before, and they had a habit of dropping him in the shit. "We shall not. What nature of business are we talking about?"

Toogood leaned forward and put a hand on the barrel staves. "Oh, *that* kind o' business. The Toogoods have always been in the farming line o' work, you might say, colonel. Good sheep country, up by Callington. You might even say the wealth of the Toogoods is built on sacks of wool, like the bridge at Wadebridge."

"You might also say the good temper of the Babbitts is being pissed up against the wall by his officers. Don't jerk my chain, Toogood. This isn't wool country, this far down."

"Right enough. Remember Yorkshire, colonel? I believe Black Tom Fairfax took his first stand against the King on the matter of wool - and the taxation His Majesty was levying on the trade, putting them poor bastards in Yorkshire out of business? I believe poor old Colonel Lambert's family was near as nothing broke by it?"

"Aye, and what -"

"Well," Toogood said limpidly, "there's two ways of dealing with a problem like that, isn't there? Can either roll over and put our hands in our pockets and say yes, Your Majesty, here's your cut of our labour, d'ee want the coat off our backs while you;re about it? Not that I'd mind paying my wedge," he added hastily, "but I'd mind paying for that French whore's tame Papists to be kept at my expense. Mind paying for His Majesty's vanity - now, there, see, you got me started again. We could just put up and shut up, or we could arrange for what you might call a bit of independent free trade, d'you see?"

"You're a bloody *smuggler*?"

"No," Toogood said, and sounded quite offended about it. "No such thing. I'd be a poor show as a smuggler, twenty miles inland, wouldn't I? John was the seaman, not I. Might say as we had an - agreement. Wool out to Brittany - get a hell of a price for a good clip, in Europe - and goods inward, by return. No sense in coming home with an empty ship, now, is there?"

"Jesus Christ," Hollie said faintly. And he'd always assumed Toogood was one of the more upright members of the company. "I presume then that your past liaison with Mistress Trevaskis was intended to, ah, cement the business relationship?"

"*Hannah*? Dear God, no!" He laughed out loud at that. "No, colonel. Hannah has - she has a number of good points," and his face clouded a little, "no, when she was a little maid she had it in her head that I'd end up marrying her. She must have been all of, what, fourteen, fifteen? And John would have shot me if I'd laid a finger on her, even were she not a baby to me. That lass played hell with me when I told her I was marrying Loveday Carew and I had no intention of marrying her, the silly maid- she said I'd not set foot in this house again till she begged me to come back, and d'you know what, colonel? I've kept *my* side of the bargain, for I've not, not till now. I could have laughed out loud when she told me she thought *you* had an eye to her, for it was just like old times, bless the maid. If a lad speaks to her kindly she has it in her head that he's planning to run away with her. She's not the - I'd not call her worldly, d'you see? John always saw to it that she was looked after. Thinks she's yet a baby -"

And then he stopped himself, and his eyes flicked to the room upstairs, as if he had just remembered. *"Thought* she was yet a baby. Well. She must grow up apace, then, poor lass. She has ever been coddled, and now she has no one to do it for her."

Which was sad. But which was - "What, exactly, to do with this?"

Toogood stirred the staves of the stoved barrel with his fingers. "That's one of our barrels, I reckon. Poor sod."

"Brandywine," Hollie said, and sucked the end of his own finger thoughtfully. Not bad brandywine, either, considerably less rough than the stuff he had been wont to carry about his person.

"That's right," the Cornishman sounded impressed.

"Cider brandy. Comes by way o' the French coast -"

"French?"

"Well, aye, where else d'you think it comes in from? Fleece goes out, brandy comes back -"

"From *France?"*

"You keep saying that!"

"Where Skellum bloody *Grenville* is shacked up? And you've got a nest of bloody Malignants at Pendennis Castle that have been to-ing and fro-ing with the French since that son of a bitch went over? And it never crossed your bloody mind to *mention?"*

"Skellum Grenville's had his teeth pulled, colonel. He's no threat to nobody."

Hollie - who remembered, uncomfortably vividly, being beaten up in a back alley in Germany ten years ago by three of Grenville's hired bravos whilst that gentleman was supposed to be behaving himself in a proper capacity elsewhere - didn't believe that one for a bloody minute.

But then nor did he believe that Kenelm Toogood was a hard done-by independent free trader, now. And he wasn't going to take his eye off that bugger for a minute.

"Have you got summat in mind, captain?" he said coolly, and Toogood grinned, without very much humour.

"Them boys seem properly keen on their little bonfires off Trefusis Head, don't they? Shall we give 'em another, and see what washes in on the tide?"

57. AS AN ENSIGN ON AN HILL

First time he'd showed his face on the point, and he had most of Betterton's lads all eager to show him where that crackpot Malignant had dived to his doom a month ago.

One of the troopers – Brandon? Brendan? Great raking lad with an even bigger nose than Hollie and dire need of a haircut, anyway – sat in the gorse with his arms round his knees, grinning like a thing demented, and recounting the whole tale with a horrible relish.

"Ah," he said, shaking his shaggy head, "they say every bone in his poor body was broke when they brought him up. I should not be surprised if he *walks*, the poor creature."

"Not with every bone in his body broke, he won't," his mate muttered. "Give over showing off, mate. You're not impressing the colonel. I bet he heard worse."

Brandon rolled his eyes and moaned. "All I'm saying, is –"

"All *I'm* saying, Brandon, is shut up, eh?"

"It's a full moon, and unchancy things happen at the height of the moon!"

He had that right, at least. Hollie could conceive of little more unchancy than this cork-brained scheme. Even with Trooper Brandon dolefully pointing out the torn-up turf where that damned soul had thrown himself to his destruction – ah, and damned himself for all eternity, poor desperate bugger – and the jagged rocks beneath where they'd had to pull his body free at the turn of the tide –

"And then that other lad, not two weeks since. It comes in threes, you know," he said, and nodded. "Aye. Best watch yourself this night, sir. Always comes in threes."

Hollie peered obligingly over the clifftop at the tide, surging over the very black, very spiky rocks. "It's a long way down," he said.

"Ah, well, it's not the drop that kills you."

And that was pretty much all of Brandon's lugubrious company that he could stand, for much more of it and Hollie was going to take up knitting. He got up – carefully, for he wasn't sure he wanted to hear further tales of Trooper Brandon's friends and relations and who had met untimely ends by missing their footing in the cat's-light – and went over to where Toogood was squatting in the shadows.

The plan was a simple one. They would set the same fire on the point as previous, and see what happened.

Russell had blinked a little at that, and looked somewhat wary. "And this is a plan?" he said.

"Unless you have a better idea, Hapless?"

"Well, I –"

"*You're* not coming." Which had offended the lieutenant no end until Hollie had leaned across and tugged gently on the thick tail of sun-bleached hair that hung between his shoulders. "We got one beacon of light, young man. We don't need two. Or three, Lucifer, you're stood down likewise."

Luce, who was still pulling up short on his injured leg, had shifted his weight more comfortably and smiled. "Well, there are some benefits to being distinctively fair. And, ah, what of your own somewhat conspicuous colouring?"

"At night all cats are grey," he said enigmatically. And actually, he had meant that he would cut the bloody lot off, for it did not matter, and who would care? But in the end he found that he could not. He had put it off, and put it off, and he found himself sitting in front of a mirror with his ponytail in one hand and his eating-knife in the other, and he was going to bloody do it, too, saw it off at the nape of his neck so that he was not so conspicuously russet –

Had looked at his plain, bony, uncompromising reflection, and put the knife down with a sigh, for he could not do it. Maybe, in the months to come, it would not matter if he made himself as plain as a pikestaff. But not yet. It was a little too final, still, and - "She would not forgive me, if I come home looking like I'd been fired wi' godly zeal," he said aloud.

(And he'd look unnervingly like his dead father, which was a bloody frightening thought, though he suspected Het had harboured a sneaking fondness for the old bastard. Though he'd never suspected her of *that* kind of fondness.)

Luce looked at him with a certain wry affection. He didn't *say* anything, he just looked amused and rather sympathetic. "You'll be all right, Hollie."

"*You're* still not coming, either," he said gruffly. (He hated it when the brat read his mind.)

"Surely. Russell and I will set the beacon, though. There seems little point in *everyone* waiting around for it to take light – and since Hapless and I are too conspicuous to be of any use, apparently, we may as well occupy ourselves with setting fires. I think we may be trusted so far, sir."

"I did not say you weren't. I said as the pair of you, being both great long lanky streaks of blonde nowt, would stick out on a dark beach on a moonlit night like two sore thumbs."

"And doubtless you –"

"Will wear a hat," Hollie said smugly.

He did not need it for warmth, for sure, and he lay on his belly with the disreputable hat tipped over his eyes and watched the two of them struggle and swear over the matter of a pile of gorse catching alight. Not laughing, because he'd looked down the side of that cliff and it didn't make him smile at all, it made him feel hollow and sick inside, and that was without even seeing the most of it. Dusk bleached most of the colour out of the rocks, and it would be possible to see where he put his feet. With care. If he was distracted –

Well, he would not think about it.

(It was a long way down. And it wasn't the fall that killed you. It was the bit at the bottom.)

"You coming, colonel, or are you just going to lay there staring into the fire telling fortunes?"

"Fuck off, Captain Toogood." There was probably a clever and witty retort, but he could not think of it, so he wiped his sweating hands quickly on his breeches and scrambled to his feet.

Toogood looked at him and raised his eyebrows. "Don't have to come, you know."

"Never forgive myself if I didn't," he said blandly. For he did not trust Toogood, not entirely. A man who had been hot against Malignants until he came home, and then suddenly was taken back to their bosom as if he had never fought for Parliament? Aye, right. A little too easy, in Hollie's opinion. The Cornishman's feet were a little too secure under Hannah Trevaskis' table, slipping himself into her brother's place before the dead man's chair was even cold - "Batten knows we're coming. Does he?"

Russell, whose one task it had been to alert the admiral that there would be a little boat pulling out from the point, simply smiled enigmatically.

"*Does* he?"

"I thought it better not," the scarred lieutenant said, and Toogood swore.

"He's going to bloody fire on us, you fool!"

"I trust so, captain. It would be a sore dereliction in the Admiral's duty were he to see a boat full of Malignants coming on him and *not* fire on it."

"Full of bloody – *two* of us?"

"Three. You will need someone to handle the paddles, will you not?"

"*You're* not –"

"Oh no," he said sweetly. "*You* are, captain. You are the nearest we have to a sailor, sir. I barely know one end of a paddle from another. I simply thought it would add a degree of verisimilitude, were we to come under fire. Just as if we truly were spies."

And it was hard to tell with that marred, half-lovely face, but there was the veriest tremor about his mouth and Hollie thought you *know*, you little bugger. You're not sure of him any more than I am.

And that heartened him, oddly enough, for at least with Hapless at his shoulder there'd be no silly business. Not that he truly thought there would be, not really, but it was just a comfort to think that if this was all some elaborate game to have Hollie captured, or killed, or some bloody daft thing, Toogood wasn't going to get away with it.

Which would be no consolation at all, when he had to set foot in that pitifully meagre floating cockleshell that called itself transport, but there it was.

"Shall we?" the lieutenant said blithely, and looked down a two-hundred foot rocky drop with every sign of eager anticipation.

And they left Luce sitting cross-legged with his book in his lap, as if he were at home at his hearth and not on a midsummer eve on a clifftop, and started a slow and tortuous and careful descent.

58. THEIR BUSINESS IN DEEP WATERS

Nobody died, and that was about the best he could say for it. It probably took half an hour to pick their way down, and by then his knees were scraped, his hands were bleeding, he had a bruise the size of a twenty-four pound shot on his arse where he'd fallen on a rock, he was dripping with sweat, and his teeth were chattering with sheer, pitiful fear.

Every step of the way he'd expected to fall off and die. In the end it had been Toogood who'd stumbled and gone off the path, though he'd hit a bush about eighteen inches down. Had been weeping, when they pulled him back up, for very fright. He kept saying he was all right, he was fine, but they had to wait what seemed like an agonisingly long time for him to be able to get back on his feet for his legs were shaking too much to bear his weight.

"That happened to me, once," Russell said cheerfully, with his mad lopsided grin. "I was little. I fell down a an old well, at Four Ashes."

Toogood raised a white, tearstained face with a look of incredulity. "Did you, so. And what did you do?"

"Oh, I was there for most of the day. No one missed me. Broke my arm and pissed my breeches, though I'm not sure which teased my sister the worse."

The Cornishman giggled wildly. "Well, I've no bones broken, Russell. At least."

"I'm glad of it, for we left the company bonesetter up on the top, and God knows what he'd make of the descent," Hollie said.

Toogood heaved himself to his feet, and gave them a shaky smile. "My thanks," he muttered.

"For what?"

But he just shook his head, as if he were embarrassed, or did not have the right words, and halted off down the path again.

Possibly, the beach was the worst, for the tide was half-out by then, and they had to pick their way across slick salt-smelling seaweed and slippery rocks that turned under your feet, and then down into the shadows under the cliffs where the boat was stowed. *Hopefully* stowed. The lights of Batten's fleet were bobbing far out at sea.

"Not as far as it looks, I reckon, on the ebb-tide," Toogood said, and Hollie turned his head to look at the Cornishman, to see if there was some joke in his words.

There wasn't. He was just trying to be helpful.

"Turn and turn about with the oars, then?" He clapped Russell on the shoulder, and said, "Don't, in God's name, keep calling 'em paddles. We're plain fishermen, d'you see? Going out for us crab-pots, or some such. Be mindful."

It was pretty much as grim as Hollie had feared. He did not like the sea, he had never liked the sea, and now it was trying to kill him. No matter how much the other two reassured him that the water was flat-calm, and that he was not in any peril – this with an inch of stinking water swilling about in the bottom of the goddamned tub, and the waves that were flat-calm sloshing over the side while they rocked their stupid clumsy way across the bottomless deeps –

And it seemed that one minute Batten's ships were as far away as the moon, with their signal-lights rocking sweetly to and fro, and the next minute they were towering over the little boat like great jagged black cliffs that were going to smash them to pieces and they were all going to drown and be eaten by nameless monsters from the bottom of the ocean.

"Hollie," Russell said, in a very odd voice, "do you stop bumping about like a bee in a bottle, or I swear to God I'll put you over the side myself. Bloody have us over, and no mistaking!"

And it might have been funny; frigid Hapless talking proper broad country in his panic, except that Hollie was panicking too, for they were near enough to smell the tar and the rotting bilge-water of the big ships of the line, and to see the open gun-ports as the big ships swung on their anchors.

"Keep rowing," Toogood said in a low, urgent voice, "n'matter what, lads, keep rowing, for if they open fire they'll sink this lil' cockleshell."

And he bent to his oars like a good 'un, as if any of them could do any more than they had, these last few hours.

Hollie saw the musket barrel spark and flare on the lightening deck a heartbeat before the ball came skipping and whining over their heads, and he poked Russell to get down, widening his eyes at Toogood over the lieutenant's shoulder to mime urgency.

"Tide'll take us," the Cornishman panted, "heads down and stay down, lads, and hope to God they don't turn fire on the bloody boat!"

He did not dare look. He felt the little wooden shell jerk as musket balls skipped and thudded into its fragile body, and he could feel it shuddering like a hurt horse as the balls hit home. Hear voices over his head – shouting, cat-calling, laughing – mocking, as if they were shooting for sport, for what harm could a little boat, smaller even than a fishing boat do – what could they be, other than sport?

It was done in fun, to bait, and for what seemed like a hundred years Hollie lay with his head in Hapless Russell's lap and the lieutenant tangled about him while shot flew about them, and splinters cracked off the rocking boat, and men laughed at them.

Heard Toogood grunt, and felt the whole bloody frail vessel rear up in the water as the Cornishman fell against his oars –

"You all right?" he hissed, and there was no answer, and that frightened him, and then Toogood said through gritted teeth, "Bloody have t'be, won't I? Bleeding like a goddamn' pig, the sons of bitches. Have a chat with that Batten, see if I bloody don't, firing on bloody fishermen!"

"They do it to remind us that they are the masters," Russell said, and that cold voice of his was full of loathing. "We are supposed to be beaten men, gentlemen. Be mindful of that, and behave according."

It was an odd feeling, to have sympathy with your enemy. But Hollie did, right then, for if this was how you treated an honourable adversary -

But it wasn't. It was how you treated people who had no power over you, and who could not answer back, and so he set his teeth and promised silently that when he was back in his own place he would kick some serious arse with Admiral Batten. For what good it would do.

And he kept his head down, and the tide carried on pulling them out of shot, into the pale colourless light of a midsummer dawn.

59. SPEAKING IN TONGUES MORE THAN YE ALL

He thought afterwards that he would have nightmares about it ever after, that inexorable drifting out on a featureless nothing, with nothing before him and nothing around him, both Toogood and Russell drifting in and out of exhausted sleep. Toogood was whimpering in his sleep, for that idle, malicious shot had creased his forearm, and it must have hurt like hell every time salt water slopped into the shallow wound.

Christ, no, Hollie could not have slept, no matter that his back ached and his palms were raw and every muscle in his body felt like he'd been beaten with sticks. Not in this floating death-trap. It had been, what, six hours, and he wondered if they had been mistaken, would continue to drift, ineptly steered by the tiller lashed to Toogood's good arm, until they starved or drowned or were eaten by giant malevolent fish, like Jonah and the whale -

At first he thought his tired eyes were playing tricks on him, for there was a thing on the horizon, and it winked.

There was no land, not for bloody miles, and he was trying not to think about that, but it was a boat, and it had a light attached to it, and that was what was blinking to and fro, as the ship rocked. He wondered if he could row by himself, and decided he probably could not: not out of any infirmity, but because he was a bloody cack-handed liability and would likely lose the oars, or go round in circles, and that thought made him giggle out loud, and Toogood raised his head and looked at him blearily.

"We only been out a few hours, colonel, you can't be going mad yet."

"Hope not. Is that what we're looking for?" He pointed over the Cornishman's shoulder at the boat. "What is it?"

"Due south, six hours straight out of Falmouth - we're headed for France, but more 'n that, God alone knows. I'm not a real bloody sailor, am I? I been out with John enough to know how to handle one o' these, but no more than that. Fishing boat? Maybe?" And then he shrugged, and winced as the crust on his arm cracked. "And maybe not. That lad's out by himself, and that's wondrous strange, for they don't often go out singly. Anyways, we can stop off and ask him directions, no?"

"'Scuse me, good sir, could you direct us to the nearest Malignant plot," Russell murmured sleepily, and Toogood laughed and Hollie didn't, because that was, pretty much, the idea.

They hailed the boat. Oddly, the couple of likely lads they could see on the deck did not seem to find it unexpected that a little cockleshell of an open boat should be fifty miles or so out of Falmouth. Hollie was going to find that interesting, when he felt sufficiently in command of his queasy guts to look about him.

"Jan Trevaskis ent coming," Toogood said, over his head. "He's dead. Shot making the crossing a fortnight since. We buried him this Thursday gone. Pox on all fucking Cropheads."

"*Kows orthiv yn Kernewek,*" the answer came. Sounded curt, could have meant anything.

"*Prag? Kowetha,*" he said. "That one's mute - smart, but he ent said a word since Edgehill, poor bugger."

Someone - a someone whose hands were rough, and cold, but sure - leaned down and grabbed Hollie by the wrist, and hauled him over the side of the boat. (Which hurt, and took must of the skin off his ribs, but was much appreciated, and he lay on a pile of rope and what smelt like most of the deceased mackerel population of West Cornwall, and thanked God for his safe deliverance.)

"And that one don't speak a word of it," Toogood went on blandly. "He's a Plymouth boy. So, you speak to me direct, *me na vadna cowz a Sowznack*, but you'll get no sense out of these two boys unless you speak English. Strong backs, but no sense, eh?"

"*Piw os ta?*" another voice said, suspiciously.

"Wella Pascoe," Toogood said, "as is cousin to Jan Trevaskis. The blonde lad's Peder, and the big 'un's Thomas."

And they rattled off Cornish at each other for a while, peppered about with names Hollie recognised, until presumably the fishermen were satisfied that their castaways were who they claimed to be, and related to half the bloody Malignants in the West Country. He tried to look stupid, which was no hardship. They offered him beer, which was stale, warm, and fishy, having been kept below the deck of a working fishing boat for God knows how long, but which tasted like manna from heaven when nothing but salt water had touched your lips since the night previous.

"What we waiting for, then?"

"You," the first speaker said, amicably enough.

There was the sound of a stirring in the darkness below the deck, and a rough, greying, russet head appeared in the hatch. "Do you mean to pass the time in idle conversation till the tide turns again, Tamblyn, or will you hold your tongue and let the man tend to his business?"

60. HIS FRUIT SHALL BE A COCKATRICE

"Well?" Richard Grenville said curtly. "D'ye think we've all day? Hand it over, then!"

Russell, who was nearest, stared at him blankly. For some reason this seemed to inflame the King's erstwhile General, who stared back: the two of them eyed each other like strange dogs, until Grenville hauled off and slapped the scarred lieutenant back-handed across the mouth. "D'you dare, you great looby? Do you *dare*, so? Give it to me!"

"He's dumb," First Voice said quickly. "He don't talk. 'Tis not his fault, sir, he's not doing it for insolence, you can see -"

But Russell did talk, very much he did, and there was that mad glint in his eye as he lay sprawled across a coil of rope on the deck that indicated that much more of that kind of behaviour and he was going to say any number of things.

Hollie dared say *nothing*, because so soon as he opened his mouth he was going to be distinctive, so he looked at his feet instead and tried to look inconspicuous, but Toogood piped up.

"We've not got it, m'lord. I reckon as it went down with Jan Trevaskis, off the Point."

For a minute, Hollie thought Grenville was going to belt the Cornishman as well, and he wouldn't have been able to stop himself from responding in kind, then. But instead Grenville just stared from one to the other of them - not, thank God, at Hollie - while the colour faded out of his cheeks and was replaced by a mottled purple flush.

Not aged well, Hollie thought. Skellum Grenville had not aged well, *at all*. That purple flush was the result of wind, weather, and not a little loose living. Interesting.

He was still a bit too handy with the blows, mind. Still too hot at hand by half.

"And how, pray, do you suggest we proceed, without it?" he said silkily.

"Can get another one?" Toogood said. He was too bloody good at this, Hollie thought, that careful blandness, and that still surprised him. Grenville blinked, slowly, like a lizard.

"Think it's that easy, do you?"

"Don't see why not. Don't know till you ask, do you?"

"You're an impudent young bastard, aren't you?" he said, with grudging admiration, and Toogood smiled faintly.

"I am...sir."

He jerked his head. "Step into the cabin, Master – "

"Pascoe," Toogood said. "As is cousin to Jan Trevaskis. Had this conversation with these gentlemen already, mind. *Nyns yw unn tavas nevra lowr,* Master Grenville. *Kernewek, mar pleg.*"

Grenville's eyebrows jerked. *"Na Kernewegor,"* he said curtly. "We are all friends, Master Pascoe. *Onen hag oll,* as I believe you would say. Or would that be *Trooper* Pascoe, sir?"

"Not on this deck. I do no man's bidding but my own. After you, Master Grenville."

"You will bring your –" his eyes flicked up and down scruffy, draggled, unlovely Hollie, and silent, bloody Russell – "comrades?"

"I will. A quiet pair of boys – but attentive. Cheat me, sir, and it will be known."

"Do you not trust me, Master Pascoe?"

"I have supped with the Devil before, Sir Richard. Though I reckon I might have forgot to bring my spoon, this time."

First Voice laughed, and stopped abruptly when Grenville's eyes flicked to him – evidently Skellum's good humour was to be trusted so far, and no further. "Let us down to hell, then," he said, and withdrew below decks again.

Toogood recounted the story of Captain Trevaskis's death again, and in the light of a swinging lantern, Grenville's lean face was devilish indeed as he listened.

"Came ashore all but naked," he said. "Whatever he had with him, the sea took, God rest him. Aye, he lost the lot, Sir Richard, and we've all to do again."

Grenville swore. "And the garrison?" he said, "How do they fare? Can they hold out, for another month – two months, for aught I know, till we have the chance to replace them?"

"Short on water," Hollie mumbled, thinking it was about time he said *something*, "and down to eating the beasts. Doubt it."

"Batten's an efficient son of a bitch," Toogood added. "He fired on us coming off Trefusis, and we're sailing a bloody cockleshell. He has the Carrick Roads sewn up tighter than an Englishman's arsehole. Three hogsheads of wine come ashore intact since the siege began, and *they* went to comfort the fucking Cropheads. *Bàrth an Jów!*, those bastards have hell's own luck -"

"Taking my name in vain?" Grenville said mockingly. "Are you a coward, then? Do you hazard, Master Pascoe?" And he drew his pistol, and levelled it between Toogood's eyes. "I've no room for hen-hearted men, sir. *Cornwall* has no room for hen-hearted men. So. I'll ask you again. Do you hazard, sir?"

Toogood never blinked an eye. Hollie, though, drew his eating-knife quite unobtrusively from his belt and slipped it up his sleeve, and blinked at Grenville. "Hazard owt you like," he said limpidly, "an you tell me what the stakes are."

"I know you, sir, do I not?"

"Imagine so," he said. "I been around a while. Whatever it is, I'll do it – but I'm not in the business of second-guessing you. Can we stop pissing about, and just crack on wi'business?"

"Have you money?" Grenville said abruptly, and Toogood blinked, startled. (They were talking of money, then. That was worth knowing. Grenville had expected money.)

"What – me – not that I – not much, no, what –"

"So you brought no money, and Trevaskis took the notes to the grave. The hell do you *expect* me to pay an army with, Master Pascoe, fresh air? What is the point of your being here, sir, other than to *vex me*?" His voice was starting to shake, and Hollie remembered that note all too well, from Germany ten years ago. Last time he'd heard Skellum Grenville go off the deep end in like manner, he'd ended up with bruises round his throat that hadn't faded in the best part of a month. Aye, and that hadn't been the half of it –

"You leave him be," he said, and he knew it wasn't sensible, but the pistol barrel was still wavering at Toogood's face as if Grenville was yet undecided whether to give him a third eye. "D'you hear me? Let him alone! We come for *you* to tell *us* what to do – he's a bloody captain, and you're a general, it's your job to tell us –"

Well, he'd slapped everyone else, so it was overdue Hollie's turn, though his head rocked back with the force of the blow. "And you are a loose-mouthed fool," Grenville said icily. "I am no general. And I'll confess, I have not heard of *Captain* Pascoe."

Hollie sucked the blood off his split lip, where the heavy crest of the Grenville signet ring had burst his mouth. "If you don't want people to know who you are," he said, "I'd start by not wearing the family jewels. Pretty fucking expensive fisherman, mate."

"You are impertinent!"

"Aye. No doubt. I am sick of being sent to and fro at some other bugger's whim, and no man sufficient courteous to give me a plain explanation of what I'm doing. I might be a plain soldier, my lord, but I've not lived so long by just doing what I'm told. Aye, you know me. I was in Germany under you." He raised his eyebrows. "Me and you have fought before, Sir Richard."

- which had a degree of ambiguity that rather pleased him, actually.

It rather pleased Skellum, too, the stupid vain bastard, and he preened his little moustache and smirked at Toogood. "And they say I cannot command loyalty," he said smugly.

"Outside of Cornwall," Hollie added, unable to resist.

"Do you think I *care* what happens, outside of Cornwall? Dear God! The likes of you do not deserve freedom! Well – my congratulations, you nodcock, you have condemned your countrymen to a further month of tyranny!" He leaned across the cabin, and put his hands on Hollie's shoulders, and shook him. (Close enough for Hollie to smell the sourness of his breath, and to know he had had pickled something for his last meal, and had not been off this boat in some days. And close enough in Hollie's memory for all the hairs to stand up bristling at the memory of those long white fingers closed around his throat in brief intent, ten years ago -) "No money, and no notes of hand. You are useless. Worse than useless. You come here, mewling that *it's not your fault*, and *you lost them* – what have you done to correct your fault, you spineless, crawling vermin? What did the Carews say? The Vyvyans? Have you even *admitted* your omission to them? I'll warrant you have not, you cowardly filth!"

Hollie went scrabbling backwards out of Grenville's grasp, and the King's General in the West lunged after him –

- and was met by the point of Thankful Russell's eating knife, in the lieutenant's very steady hand. "If you lay a hand on him again," Russell said, "I will gut you like a herring. Sit. Down."

Grenville's jaw fell open in shock. "You speak!"

"A miracle," the lieutenant said dryly. "God smiles on our cause, indeed."

"These notes of hand. You would have us go to Richard Vyvyan, then – and the Carews, out at Antony," Toogood said, frowning, "and ask them to replace them? Is that what you would have me do?"

"Unless you suggest that I raise troops on the promise of fresh air, Captain Pascoe, I might indicate that is all you can do. Arundel cannot hold out forever, and the longer you drag your feet, you coward, the longer he must suffer. Had you had the sense to bring some gold, I might have been able to raise a few men on promises, but – ach!" He made a disgusted sound.

"Just enough to relieve the siege," Russell murmured.

Toogood gave him a startled look. "Enough to push the English out of Cornwall," he said. "Just like you always said we would – we always said we would. Right?"

Grenville said nothing. He simply looked at them, one at a time. "I do know you," he said, eventually. "I knew I did. You are a distinctive man – you have some outlandishly godly name, what was it? Abednego? Nehemiah?– *Holofernes*. Of course. You are perfectly correct. We did fight in Germany – is it still Trooper Babbitt, or have you regained your commission, since?"

Quite reflexively, Hollie's fingers flew to the collar of his shirt, and Grenville's mouth twitched. "You have not forgot your little discipline, then. No. Well. You are no more Cornish than this ship is, sir, and she is straight out of France. You have made a fool of me thus far, but no further."

He raised that pistol again.

He would have shot one of them – Hollie, probably, though they were never going to know, because that was the timely moment that the little fishing boat rocked like a shying horse on a rising tide, and the ball went wide in an acrid pissy smell of spent powder and a shower of sparks, and Hollie lunged for the ladder to the deck, and Kenelm Toogood belted the King's General in the West over the back with a chair.

It did neither the chair nor Skellum Grenville any good, and that was going to be funny, later on, seeing the look of almost comical dismay on his face as he went sprawling across the cabin. What was less funny was First Voice appearing in the square of daylight, peering into the murk with his mates behind him – ah, Christ, there were more than three, Hollie had thought there were no more than two or three of them, and as Grenville recovered his footing and his breath and started roaring orders to stop the Parliamentarian scum –

The tide was almost full turned now, and the little boat rocking and spinning on her anchor wanting to be gone, and there was very little else that Hollie could do, and he was sorry for it. He had liked First Voice. He did not like First Voice enough that he was going to allow the man a clear aim, and he had a sharp eating-knife tucked into his cuff: he swung his hand at the sailor's groin from the top of the ladder, before the poor bastard had had a chance to work out what was going on in the gloom below decks and sight accordingly. It would have been no more than a glancing, agonising blow, if the ship hadn't lurched again.

Hollie was *very* sorry for that.

He was bloody sorry for the fact that he was now standing on the deck of a little boat in a stiff wind with half the KIng's exiled Army - the less temperate ones - staring at him.

"Kill them all!" Grenville wheezed, from a horizontal position.

"Indeed. And God will sort the wheat from the chaff." Russell had armed himself with a boat-hook, hefting it gingerly as if it might suddenly rear up and bite him. He was grinning his frightening toothy grin, and his eyes were very bright. Not for the first time Hollie thought how much he'd grown to value that mad bastard, and how sorry he would be if any harm befell him.

"Hapless!" he called, and Russell flung his head up, and as soon as one of the sailors looked to see what Russell was looking at Toogood shot him.

And then one of the sailors shot Toogood, though by the sound of the cursing it wasn't life-threatening, but it was surely painful, and then it was just a rolling brawl of confusion in which Hollie pulled every tavern stunt in the book not to be tipped over the side. Someone tripped over a coil of rope, went sprawling smack into the side of the ship head-first with a noise like an overripe apple falling on cobbles. Did not get up.

Toogood, spraying blood in all directions, laying about him with his blade with an admirable lack of discrimination.

Russell wrestling with someone, the sharp end of his boathook wedged in the bloody meat of the man's arm, and taking the worst of it, though taking a pounding never seemed to trouble Hapless.

Probably the sensible thing to do would be to dive lightly over the side of the boat and swim to that floating death-trap they'd arrived in, and probably that would be the kind of cork-brained heroic thing that young Lucey would do, but Hollie was too old, too wise, and too shit-scared for that kind of bloody insanity, not to say presently having some Malignant sailor with all his teeth currently sunk into Hollie's leg, which hurt. He swore, and belted the man over the head with his pistol –

Jesus Christ, he could be stupid at times. *His pistol.*

Grenville was on his knees now, clawing at that makeshift noose with his fingers and croaking like a purple-faced raven, could these benighted bastards crewing his ship not even deal with three pathetic specimens of Crophead soldiery –

So Hollie shot him.

There was a lot of blood. Grenville was hurled backwards across that vexatious coil of rope, and there was blood, and confusion, and shouting, and in the confusion and the shouting someone touched Hollie's elbow. He spun round to face his assailant: sliced Hapless Russell across the ribs with his knife, though the lieutenant was so battered and bloody that he barely seemed to notice, let alone to care. Russell jerked his head towards the side of the boat. "Go," he said, and braced himself with his boathook. "I'll. Stay."

Not an offer Hollie needed giving twice. He went over the side.

Toogood went in after him, missed the pinnace, hit the water five yards away with a splash that obscured just about everything. The sailors fired on him. That was all right, he'd surfaced on the far side of the boat and was clinging to one of the oars like a drowned rat, crushed by the rocking waves against the side of Grenville's boat. There was blood coming out of his mouth, but his eyes were open, and he was swearing with the sort of ferocity that a dying man can't muster.

Hollie dragged him by the scruff of the neck into the pinnace. It all but heeled over, and there was a moment of sheer blinding panic while he hauled the limp and choking Cornishman into the bottom of the boat, but that was all right, because he was in. He was safe.

"Can't leave that duzzy lad so," Toogood gasped, with almost the last breath that was in him, and Hollie grinned, and thought about clapping him on the back, and then looked at the state of Toogood's torn flesh and reconsidered.

"Can you row?" he said, and the Cornishman closed his eyes and shuddered but he nodded. Couldn't, but would.

Hollie stood up in the rocking pinnace and commended his soul into God's hands. He was tall, and Grenville's boat was riding low in the water. Poor bloody Hapless. He'd always wanted to be a martyr, and here he was about to die a glorious death in the cause of liberty, and some bloody ne'er-do-well on his own side caught a boathook in the waist of his breeches and heaved him backwards off the side of the boat. Both ignominious and unexpected, poor sod, and he hit the water with a ferocious splash that had the little pinnace right over in the water.

And that was good, because what with the churning water and the upturned rowing-boat it was all but impossible for Grenville's men to see what they were firing on, and the worst that could happen was that the bottom of the pinnace was splintered, and that could be –

Could be not thought about, on a rising tide, and Hollie shut his eyes and tried not to breathe in water and clung like hell to the side of the boat.

62. SWORDS INTO PLOUGHSHARES

And that was it. It was done.

Batten tightened his blockade, and twiddled his thumbs, and Fortescue laid it on heavy and hard, and the whole of the Western Army of Parliament sat round Falmouth scratching their backsides and getting fat, or so it felt.

There was no more silly-buggery at Trefusis Point. Some of Fortescue's likelier lads paid a call to the Carew family at Antony - came home with some cockeyed story about a painting of Alexander Carew, that sometime Parliamentarian turned Malignant, being cut from its frame in the hall by his good Crophead brother. Some more of them popped down to the Vyvyans, at Trelowarren. Nothing formal. A word to the wise, you see. Nod being as good as a wink to a blind horse.

But no more supplies. No second Army, raised by a malevolent force and bought and paid for in promises of tin. Wind and weather would scour out the inside of Pendennis Castle, when the gates were left open.

Hollie could not quite stop himself from flinching, though, at the smell of it. Death, and rotting meat, and old blood, and shit, and unwashed bodies. The smell of a thousand men - and women, and children - who had been mewed up like rats in a trap for six months, falling sick, and dying of it -

And the faint smell of burned wet wood, from the ruins of Arwenack House, when the wind was in the wrong direction. (Thank God he'd been nowhere around when Arwenack House burned, though. If he'd been on the premises they'd have found some way of blaming that one on him. As it was, the Malignants were sniffy that the Roundheads had done it, and the Roundheads were putting it about that the Malignants had done it themselves just to annoy Colonel Fortescue.)

It was hot, even at this time of the afternoon, and the sun seemed to bounce off the sea and the wind-bleached stones of the castle, and he squinted a little in the glare.

Quiet, too, for all there were - there had been - a thousand people in the castle. There had been. There were not, now.

Blossom didn't like it, and Doubting Thomas was frothing and shying at his own shadow, long and black on the sun-scorched grass. It was funny how horses knew. Whether they could smell the fear and misery and the sickness that must have seeped into the walls of this place - or perhaps, that even though they had cleared so much as they could in great greasy choking clouds of bone-fires, that the smears of black soot and charred earth still smelt of carrion, to beasts. The men they had buried.

The women and children, too - those few pitifully small, wizened bundles of stiff flesh and bone swathed about in linen, in men's clean shirts and women's clean shifts, for a feeling man could not bear to put them into the cold earth uncomforted, so far from home. Hollie had lost his good shirt that way. Aye. Well. He would answer for it when he got home. He did not think he would tell Het that her handwork had gone into the Cornish clay around a little boy's body, for the child's own clothes were stiff with salt, where his mother had made a brave effort to keep them clean in what water she could bring up from the sea. She'd washed him, his poor little wasted limbs streaked with blood and shit where his guts had dissolved within him. And Hollie, who was a father, and who saw his own daughters' faces on every one of those hungry children, had handed over his spare shirt for that boy's burying-clothes without a second thought.

Ghosts walked here, and some of them lived and breathed.

Blossom shifted underneath him, the good horse, but he stayed steady, his big clumsy feet planted four-square. Although his neck was hot and wet under the rein, where Hollie patted it to reassure the beast.

(Thomas was being a skittering menace, and he was either going to put Russell on his arse, or the lieutenant was going to have to take him out of the line and every disparaging eye in the Western Association was going to be on them. But that wouldn't be the first time.)

Sir John Arundel's flesh hung pouchy on his bones, like a man who had lost a deal of weight in a very short space of time, but his eye was as fierce and bright as a kestrel's, and that was undimmed by either age or surrender.

Not Hollie's place, of course. It was nothing to do with him, if he thought Arundel was as proud as- no, not as proud as Lucifer, who was currently much occupied with binding up little hurts and being stern with people about how far they walked and what they ate. He could hear the brat, somewhere in the shadows of the guardhouse, pontificating to some poor bugger bedabbled with weeping sores about how he must take care to eat only strengthening foods. Red meat. Hollie could not quite stop himself from raising a sardonic eyebrow at that, though he knew Luce couldn't see him, for he doubted the poor bastard had seen much but red meat for the last two months, and that was, possibly, why the man's teeth were loose in his head and his flesh rotting on his bones.

Siege-rations did that to you. But Luce was not to know that, and he had - God be thanked - no real knowledge of what it was to be dirty and hungry all the time, and squatting in a ditch. It would have hurt the brat if he had known, and so Hollie was glad that he had no idea: that he thought this soldier would mend, and go home, and lead a happy, useful life. He would not. He would die here, the poor bastard. Even had he the money for the good, plain, strengthening fare that Luce was earnestly prescribing - even had he a place to go to, which Hollie doubted -

They would not all go home. And for that, he hated Arundel.

Some of them hated him, he knew that, he could feel the eyes of the ones who had the strength to hate resting on him - this is your doing. Though it wasn't. Gone beyond this man's doing and that man's doing, though Arundel could have ended it any day he chose, simply by agreeing to open the gates. Aye, and Fortescue likewise, he could have seen it finished simply by walking away, so they were each as much to blame as one another. Pride. Wilfulness. Honour.

It was done. The King's Army in the West was disbanded, and there would be no help coming from Richard Grenville, which was a crowning mercy, and the people could settle back to the business of living. Over and done.

Not finished by a long chalk, though. The dust that had been raised by this war would not settle in this many a day.

Arundel was looking his men over as if he was still proud of them, though, and he formed that rag-tag starveling rabble up as if they had been the King's own lifeguard, and not a halt, limping, sick rearguard.

It was in the terms of the surrender that the garrison had been given five hundred pounds, for their sundries and necessities. It

THE SERPENT'S ROOT

wasn't even going to touch the sides. Five hundred pounds would just about see them decently shod again, and in whole linen.

They formed up into an orderly body, those ragged, starved, dignified men, with their salt-bleached and wind-ragged colours at their head and their faded coats and their drums. A stutter - a rattle of drums, and Doubting Thomas went up onto his hind legs, dancing as if he'd never heard the order to advance before, and all those censorious eyes rested on them -

And then they started to march out, down the slippery flagstones, down the long bleached slope towards the gate. Rags wrapped round worn-through shoes slapped on the sun-baked stones, bare feet, worn boots, beating out a rhythm that stumbled and strengthened as men who had known nothing but the perimeter of a besieged castle this last five months hit a marching stride again.

A bloody halt lot, they were. But proud, and their heads were up as if they'd won the day, and were not marching out in all honour as defeated enemies. They had their drums and their colours and their muskets, the officers' weapons were well-kept - God knows he thought they had had little else to do, these long summer afternoons, but look to their weapons -

The women and children, bringing up the rear - babies hefted on hips, or little feet pattering, and that made him smile faintly, for they bounced, these Army brats. King's men or Parliament's men, it did not matter, for small children flourished like weeds wherever and whatever happened, if you let them. (And he heard Het's voice in his head, tart and loving, for the first time in months, as clear as if she were standing beside him - So long as you don't drop them on their heads too often, dear.) No, God willing, this little army would take root and thrive, somewhere.

They were marching out in silence and dignity, stately keeping pace to the rhythm of that unbreakable drum. One young lieutenant, trotting round the back of the camp followers like a sheepdog, trying to keep them all safely gathered together.

And his little dog tagging behind him.

"Malley!" he hissed, scarlet-faced with mortification, "To heel, madam!"

And she came trotting at his heels with her plumed tail aloft, grand as a little duchess despite the way she had three inches of chewed rope hanging from her collar, as if she had gnawed her way loose from her place of security and gone to join her person as was her right.

She was a dog of no account: other than her dignity, there was little of note about her. A taking little thing who, Hollie suspected, had chosen the life of a vagabond over the comfort of a lady's lap: he suspected she'd escaped being eaten alongside the rest of the garrison dogs because she was little more than a handful of silky black and amber fur and a pair of merry dark eyes. She was as ragged and unkempt and wind-bleached as the rest of them, but she clung to her man's shadow because she must keep faith or die.

Aye. Well. There was a lot of them like that, on both sides.

He watched them march out across the sun-bleached grass. The rattle of the drums echoed off the castle walls, out across the sea. Someone was whistling - a defiant, thin whistle, as if that someone was determined to show that they were not hurt, were not afraid, did not care.

Lot of them like that on both sides, too.

He wondered if that was how it would end. Not with a man's age-shaken signature on a paper, but with an old dog's unshakeable faith, and a baby crying as his mother marched away with him jolting at her shoulder. With Luce, still holding forth about good feeding and the importance of keeping wounds clean, to a Royalist soldier who was going to die anyway. With Kenelm Toogood still unfit for duty but chipper as a popinjay with his daughter at Trevaskis, while the mistress of the house grew stubborner and more independent by the day, given her head. (Hollie had asked, not quite daring to hear an answer, how a man's courtship might progress, if he and she were on different sides of a war. Toogood had looked at him as if he were quite mad and said they fought like cats in a sack.)

With a letter to home, that had not been so hard to write in the end. That did not mention blood or fire or death or this fight or that, but had talked of Toogood's courtship, and the receipt that Hannah Trevaskis's cook had by him for a new kind of cheesecake, and the many and various types of fresh fish to be found in Cornwall that a man might feast himself on.

There might be a reply, one day, and there might not. It did not matter.

The world might have turned upside down, but like an hourglass, it would settle again. On its head, maybe, but it would settle. Was settling.

He watched the last of the Pendennis garrison march out of sight, and then there was silence. A long, golden, bird-haunted silence, with nothing but the sound of the waves against the rocks, a long way away.

Seemed wrong to speak, somehow. It felt almost like being in the presence of God, just the last of the sun and the distant sound of the sea, as quiet as a baby's breathing in its cradle.

"Colonel," Russell said quietly, and flicked his eyes up and sideways, where Arundel's battered, shot-holed colours fluttered still atop the castle. "Take them down?"

It was not his call, of course. He should by rights tell Colonel Fortescue, who commanded here, and who would have them brought down and folded and put somewhere for safety, with all propriety and pomp.

Or he could leave them here, undefeated, for the wind and the rain and the sea to fade and tear.

He shook his head. "Let them be," he said. And then he edged Blossom sideways, close to the restless Doubting Thomas, who was still seeing ghosts. "I take it, Hapless, that you will be coming back to White Notley with me, when we are stood down from here?"

A small thing of joy, in all this loss, that the scarred lieutenant's dark eyes lit with a quiet happiness, as if Hollie had given him a precious thing that he still did not believe he could have. The daft bugger. "If you will still have me, colonel," he said softly.

"I'm not so sick of you yet. And Het would never forgive me if I didn't bring you back wi' me. My wife will not be happy till she has you safely married off, Lieutenant Russell. You can't hide from my good lady's matrimonial meddling, even in Cornwall."

Russell smiled shyly into his horse's mane. "I should not seek to hide from Mistress Babbitt, sir. I should not be so uncivil."

Hollie grinned at him. "You know what? You might as well get used to calling me Hollie. I reckon we will shortly be off-duty on a permanent basis."

And he glanced up at those brave, ragged colours, dark against a rose gold sky. "We're done."

AUTHOR'S NOTES

Luce, Hollie, Russell, Toogood and the rest of the rebel rabble are fictional.

Trefusis - the manor, and the place - are real places: Trevaskis is not, and nor was there a Captain John Trevaskis in the siege at Pendennis. Although there really was one of the defenders who was daft, or desperate, enough to swim from Pendennis to Trefusis, and it is possible. Don't, as they say, try this at home...

And as for Grenville's plan for Cornish independence? True.

Richard Grenville - and yes, he really was known as Skellum, although possibly not to his face - the King's General in the West, had been involved early in the civil war with talks with the Prince of Wales on the matter of independent rule for Cornwall.

It's assumed that these talks then came to nothing.

But what if they didn't?

It is a matter of record that in March 1646 Sir Ralph Hopton sat down to negotiate with Thomas Fairfax to disband the King's Army in the West. At the same time as these negotiations were taking place, the guns were being shipped out of Truro - where the garrison was close to mutiny, many of them threatening to go over to the Parliamentarian Army where at least they'd get paid - down to Pendennis Castle, eleven miles down the river on the Carrick Roads.

Pendennis and the castle at St Michael's Mount, off the coast at Penzance, were still held for the King until the summer of 1646.

Sir Richard was imprisoned by Hopton on St Michael's Mount, on grounds that he was a subversive element who (I quote one Colonel Babbitt) could take exception to the company in an empty room and he refused to accept the authority of anyone but himself in the West. Can't fault Hopton for that, the last thing an Army needs is a command stucture falling out amongst themselves... right?

So why St Michael's Mount? Why not Pendennis, or St Mawes? Why put a man who had previous form for escaping lawful custody, on an island held by a Royalist garrison who would have an inbuilt loyalty to Grenville, where there was nothing but the sea between him and absolute liberty? And then why, during the last negotiations at Tresillian, would the Prince of Wales decide that he didn't want Grenville to fall into the enemy's hands, and spirit him away to France from the Mount?

To which I can only wonder if he was never intended to stay in custody. If the fact of what we might describe in court these days as "previous bad character" was meant as smoke and mirrors: meant to blind the Parliamentarian command to the fact that although Grenville was - by all accounts - a deeply personally unsympathetic, bad-tempered, vengeful character who was exactly the sort of nasty piece of work who would break his parole and escape, he was also a fierce, efficient, successful soldier who commanded the loyalty of the Cornish militia and had fought as a mercenary in the Thirty Years' War. (He said. Actual evidence of this seems to be scant. Surely Richard Grenville wouldn't have exaggerated his experience, would he?) He also commanded the loyalty of a number of the gentry families of Cornwall, who would have been in a position to fund any enterprise to raise troops in Europe. He had the experience, the contacts, and probably the resources, to do it.

And although the seaport of Bristol was in the hands of Parliament, the ports of Penzance and Falmouth were both still in the King's hands. So if young Skellum had been successful in raising troops in Europe, the door would have been open for them.

Assuming that he'd ever had such a plan, he failed.

What intrigues me is that there's a modern assumption that Grenville's attempts to gain a semi-independent rule for Cornwall were based on altruistic motives: and I have yet to see evidence that Richard Grenville had an altruistic bone in his body. He switched sides at the beginning of the war, from King to Parliament and then back again. He married a woman for her money, hoping to clear his debts, and then made her life a waking hell when he discovered that she'd spent it all before she married. He was imprisoned for non-payment of his previous lot of debts, and broke out of jail and fled to Europe. A more cynical soul than myself might think that any operation led by Skellum Grenville to make Cornwall semi-independent of England, might be motivated by financial gain, and the sense of entitlement that seemed to characterise his dealings with his peers.

Do I think he could have made Cornwall all but independent of England? Yes. Absolutely. I think he had the passion, the experience, and no one could ever accuse him of not commanding the loyalty of his men. (Although there was a rumour that it was because they were more scared of him than they were of the enemy - he had, shall we say, something of a predilection for hanging.)

Do I think that having made the county independent, he could have kept it so? Not a hope. On previous showings, I suspect that he'd have made himself a military dictator in very short order, and then proceeded to antagonise and then punish any of the families who'd previously supported him, for not treating him with due deference.

And as for my lads?

Well, it's August 1646. And if Hollie thinks he's due his peaceful retirement in Essex for another two years yet, poor lad, he's got another think coming.

Printed in Great Britain
by Amazon